THE
SUMMER HOUSE

For a preview of upcoming books and information about the author, visit JamesPatterson.com or find him on Facebook, Twitter, or Instagram.

THE SUMMER HOUSE

JAMES PATTERSON AND BRENDAN DuBOIS

Little, Brown and Company
New York Boston London

Little, Brown and Company
Hachette Book Group
1290 Avenue of the Americas, New York, NY 10104
littlebrown.com

First Edition: June 2020

Little, Brown and Company is a division of Hachette Book Group, Inc. The Little, Brown name and logo are trademarks of Hachette Book Group, Inc.

The publisher is not responsible for websites (or their content) that are not owned by the publisher.

The Hachette Speakers Bureau provides a wide range of authors for speaking events. To find out more, go to hachettespeakersbureau.com or call (866) 376-6591.

ISBN 978-0-316-53955-5 (hc) / 978-0-316-53959-3 (large print)
LCCN 2019951773

10 9 8 7 6 5 4 3 2 1

LSC-C

Printed in the United States of America

This is for my family.
—B.D.

AUTHORS' NOTE

There is no Fourth Battalion in the Seventy-Fifth Ranger Regiment, and Sullivan County and its residents and towns are also fictional.

THE
SUMMER HOUSE

CHAPTER 1

INSIDE THIS DUMP of a home in rural Sullivan, Georgia, Lillian Zachary's rescue mission to save her younger sister and niece isn't going well. Only because of her parents' pleadings did she make the three-hour drive this warm evening from the safety of her Atlanta condo to liberate Gina and her daughter, Polly, from this place.

She nervously eyes the guns that are on open display, their promise of violence making her uneasy. A pump-action shotgun is leaning near the sole door leading outside, a hunting rifle is up against the wall on the other side of the old home, and two black semiautomatic pistols are on the cluttered kitchen counter, next to three sets of scales and plastic bags full of marijuana. Antique oak cabinets and porcelain-lined sinks and metal faucets are on the opposite side of the room.

Lillian is in a part of the home laughingly called a "living room," and there's nothing in here worth living for, save her sister and her sister's two-year-old girl. The place is foul, with empty beer cans, two-liter bottles of Mountain Dew, crumpled-up McDonald's bags, and crushed pizza cartons strewn across a wooden floor worn and gouged from a century of wear.

Built in the small plantation-plain style and named The

Summer House, the place was once the getaway destination of a rich Savannah family fleeing city smells and sounds generations before the invention of air-conditioning. Now, decades later, the rich family has fallen on hard times, and their grandly named Summer House is a decaying rental property fit only for this group of lowlifes.

Lillian wonders if the ghosts of the old Savannah family are horrified to see how decayed and worn their perfect summer escape home has become.

Lillian is perched on the armrest of a black vinyl couch kept together with scrap lumber and duct tape, and Gina is sitting next to her, shaking a footless rag doll in front of little Polly, who's on the carpeted floor before her mother, giggling.

Lillian says, "Gina, c'mon, can we get going?"

Her sister shakes her head. "No, not yet," she says. "Polly's laughing. I love it when Polly laughs. Don't you?"

Lillian isn't married, doesn't seem to have that maternal urge to bear children, but something about the bright-blue eyes and innocent face of the chubby little girl in a pink corduroy jumper stirs her. Her little niece, trapped here with her single mom, in a crappy house in a crappy part of the state.

At the other end of the room is another couch in front of a large-screen television—no doubt stolen, she thinks—and three other people who live here are playing some stupid shoot-'em-up fantasy video game where fire-breathing dragons and knights do battle armed with machine guns. She's already forgotten the names of the two lanky, long-haired boys and their woman friend. Shirley? Or Sally. Whatever. And Randy. Yeah. That's one of the losers' names.

The two guys gave her serious eye when earlier she knocked on the door, and she feels vulnerable and out of place with them and their guns. Even though they seem to be having fun on their couch, there's a simmering tension between them that's growing along with the insults they've been tossing at each other.

"Missed it, you fag!" Randy yells.

"Bite me!" the other young man shouts back.

Upstairs in the old home is the other occupant, Gina's on-again, off-again boyfriend, Stuart, who's lying in bed, not feeling well, bitching and moaning like the community college dropout and drug dealer he is.

Plus the father of little and innocent Polly.

"Gina," she says, looking away from the video game players. "Please."

"Just a sec, Lilly, just a sec, okay?"

Lillian rubs her hands across her tan slacks, looking again at the shotgun resting between the television and the door leading outside. All she wants to do is carry the two green plastic trash bags holding the entire possessions of Gina and her daughter through that door. In just a very few minutes she'll get Gina and Polly out of this shithole and back up to Atlanta and leave this crap off-ramp to a loser life behind.

If those increasingly angry young men let her, Gina, and Polly leave, that is. Randy said a while ago, "Hey, you plan on staying for a while, right? We're gonna party hard later on."

Her plump younger sister is wearing black yoga tights and an Atlanta Falcons sweatshirt, but even through her bad complexion, her eyes shine bright with joy and love for her baby girl. That light gives Lillian hope. Gina moved down to this little town with Stuart, promising Mom and Dad she would study dental hygiene at nearby Savannah Technical College, and not telling anyone until a week ago that she dropped out last year.

Tonight it's going to change, Lillian thinks. She has a great job as a purchasing agent for Delta, and she's confident she can get her younger sister a job even if the work is physical, like handling baggage. Gina is a stout, strong girl, and Lillian thinks that will be perfect for her, and much better pay than the night shift at the local Walmart.

Her little niece keeps on laughing and laughing.

There's a sound of a helicopter flying overhead, and Lillian vows to leave in just one minute. Yep, in sixty seconds she's going to tell Gina to get her ass in gear.

Lillian thinks she sees a shadow pass by one of the far windows.

As he moves through the typical Georgia pine forest to within twenty meters of the target house, he raises a fist, and the others with him halt. He wants to take one more good scan of the target area before the operation begins. A helicopter drones, heading to nearby Hunter Army Airfield. The woods remind him some of forests he operated in back in Kunar province in the 'stan, right up against the border to Pakistan. He likes the smell of trees at night. It reminds him of home, reminds him of previous missions that have gone well. Some meters off is a small lake with a shoreline overgrown with saplings and brush.

He slowly rotates his head from left to right, the night-vision goggles giving him a clear and green ghostly view of the surroundings. He can see that the two-story place used to be a fine small home with two front pillars and classy-looking, black-shuttered windows. Now the siding is peeling away, the pillars are cracked and stained, and one of the windows is covered with plastic.

Only one entry in and out between the two pillars, which will be challenging but not much of a problem.

Four vehicles in the yard. Two Chevy pickup trucks and a battered Sentra with a cracked windshield and trunk held closed with a frayed piece of rope. Previous surveillances of the area showed these same vehicles here, almost every night.

But tonight there's an additional vehicle. A light-blue Volvo sedan.

It doesn't fit, doesn't belong, hasn't been here before.

Which means there's at least one additional person—and perhaps up to four—in the target house.

He sighs.

Embrace the suck, move on.

Has he ever been on a mission that went exactly, 100 percent right?

Never.

So why start tonight?

He catches the attention of his squad mates, and they move into position, with him leading the way to the open wooden porch before the solitary door.

He flips up his night-vision goggles, blinks a few times. He can hear music and sound effects from some sort of video game being played inside.

No worries.

He pulls out his pistol, gets ready to go to work.

Lillian puts her hand on Gina's shoulder, is about to say, *I want to get on I-16 before the drunks start leaving the roadhouses,* when there's a sharp *bang!* and the door leading outside blows wide open into the small, old house.

The woman on the other couch screams, and the guy to her right—Gordy, is that his name?—stands up and says, "Hey, what the hell—"

A man in military-style clothing ducks in with a pistol in his hand, and Lillian stands, putting her arms up in the air, thinking, *Oh, damn it, it's a police raid. These morons have finally been caught dealing their dope.*

Funny how all cops nowadays feel like they have to dress up

like soldiers, like this one, with fatigues, black boots, belts and harness, a black ski mask over his head.

Gordy says, "Hey, guy, I know my rights—"

He stops talking when the man with the pistol points it at him—and with horror Lillian recognizes there's a suppressor on the end of the pistol, just like in the movies—and in two muffled reports, Gordy falls back onto the couch, his skull blown open in a blossom of brain and bone.

A spray of blood hits the face of Sally, who is now screaming louder, and the other guy on the couch scrambles over the side, toppling the couch. Lillian pushes Gina, screaming, "Run, run, run!"

Gina ducks down and picks up her girl, who's still giggling, and Lillian shoves her sister and niece away as she grabs a dirty couch pillow and throws it at the gunman.

"Gina!" she screams at her sister. "Run!"

Polly in her arms, Gina runs up the stairs, Lillian pounding the steps right behind her.

CHAPTER 2

THE MAIN PART of the old house is cleared within seconds by his squad, and as he goes past the bodies, picking up warm shell casings and carefully digging out spent bullets as he does so, one thought comes to him: how often Hollywood gets this part wrong.

They love showing a squad like his breaking into a residence, screaming *Go, go, go!* or *Down, down, down!* Truth is, you move quietly and with deliberation, clearing and securing everything before moving on.

He heads to the wide wooden stairway, the others following him. Stops at the foot of the stairs. Makes the necessary hand signals, and they go up, sticking to the left side to reduce the sounds of creaking steps.

Halfway up the stairs he pauses, hearing frantic movement overhead.

When they got to the top of the stairs, Gina slammed open the door to the left with her free hand, saying, "Stuart, Stuart, oh, God, Stuart..."

Lillian broke right, going to the other bedroom, sobbing, panting, not wanting to think of what just happened, who that man was, not wanting again to see in her mind the spray of blood from Gordy being shot in the head, and above all, not wanting to think of the man coming up the stairs after them.

She nearly stumbles over the piles of clothing, shoes, and more crumpled boxes and beer cans strewn across the floor. Two beds. One bureau. Trash bags with clothing. Open closet door.

Two windows. One with an air-conditioning unit that's not running.

The other leading out to safety.

Lillian gets to the window, yanks at the bottom.

It won't move.

"Please, please, please," she whispers.

She yanks again.

Nothing.

She senses the man with the gun is nearing the top of the stairs.

Lillian is too scared to turn around, dares not turn around.

Another tug.

A squeak.

It moves, just enough for her to shove her fingers in between the window and the sill.

"Please, please, please," she prays, whispering louder.

She gives the window a good hard shove, leveraging her weight, her shoulders and arms straining from the attempt.

The window grinds open.

Fresh air flows in.

Lillian bends over, ducks her way through, as she hears the other bedroom door slam shut.

He's nearly at the top of the stairs when he hears a window slide open, and then he gets to the landing.

Room to the left, room to the right.

The door is open to the right-side room. The other door is closed.

He looks back at his squad, gestures to the nearest two behind him, points to the left door, and they nod in acknowledgment.

He steps into the room on the right.

Empty.

Trashy, of course, but there's no one he can see.

The window is wide open.

He's focused on clearing this room, but he can't help but hear the door to the other room open, a woman scream, and a man call out, "Hey, hey, hey—" followed by the friendly *thump* of a pistol firing through a sound suppressor.

Then a sentence is uttered, and two more *thump*s wrap up the job.

He moves through the room, dodging piles of clothes and trash. An overhead light from the top of the stairs gives him good illumination.

The closet is empty.

Fine.

He goes to the window, leans over, peers out.

Lillian is biting her fist, trying hard not to breathe, not to sneeze, not to do a damn thing to get noticed. She's under one of the two unmade beds in this room, trembling, part of her ashamed that she's wet herself from fear.

There are slow and measured paces of someone walking through the room, and then going over to the open window.

She shuts her eyes, her mother's voice whispering to her from more than twenty-five years ago: *There's no such thing as the bogeyman,* she would say. *Just close your eyes and pray to Jesus, and everything will be all right.*

Oh, Mamma, oh, Jesus, please, please, please help me.

*   *   *

He leans out the window, lowering his night-vision goggles to take in the view. More trees, more scrub, and a collapsed small wooden building that looks like it was once an out-house.

Possible. This place is so old it would fit right in.

He looks closer to the side of the two-story summer house.

He's up about six or so meters. Hell of a drop.

And what's below here? Two rusty fifty-five-gallon oil drums, a roll of chicken-coop wire, and a pile of wooden shingles and scrap lumber.

All resting undisturbed.

He flips up the night-vision goggles, ducks back into the room, sees his squad mates have joined him. He holds a finger to his lips.

Moves across the room.

Lillian is still praying, still trembling, still biting into her fist when a strong hand slides under the bed and grabs her ankle, dragging her out.

She shrieks and rolls over and puts her hands up and says, "Please, please, please, no, no, no!"

Someone grabs her shoulders, holds her down. Another man—the one who just shot Gordy—drops to one knee and looks down at her. Lillian takes a deep breath, hoping it will calm her.

It doesn't.

The man has military-type viewing equipment on his fore-head, he's wearing military fatigues with some sort of harness and belts, and over one pocket where there should be a name tag is a strip of Velcro, meaning the name tag has been stripped off so he won't be identified. The ski mask from before is pulled up, revealing a friendly and relaxed face.

"Please," she whispers.

"Shhh," he replies. "Just a few questions. I promise I won't hurt you."

Lillian just nods. *Answer him,* she thinks. *Don't ask questions. Just answer.*

He says, "There was a man in the bedroom on the other side, with a woman and a child. Downstairs there was a woman and two other men. Is there anybody else here?"

"No," she says, her whole body shaking, the hands of the man holding her shoulders down firm and strong.

"Are you the owner of the Volvo?"

"Yes."

"Did you come down here alone?"

"Yes."

"Is anyone expecting you to return in the next few minutes?"

She doesn't process the question until it's too late, for she answers truthfully, automatically, and hopefully and says, "No."

The man stays quiet for a few long seconds and then lifts his head to nod to the man behind her. When he removes a hand from her shoulder and she feels the cold metal of a pistol barrel pressing against the side of her head, Lillian knows her mamma has always been wrong, that the bogeyman does exist.

CHAPTER 3

AFTER MY "WORKOUT" for the day, I'm resting on my bed at my condo rental just outside the Marine Corps base in Quantico, Virginia, reading *Glory Road,* the second book in Bruce Catton's trilogy about the Union's Army of the Potomac. I'm enjoying the book and hating Quantico, because it's still not home, and it's definitely not New York City.

My ringing iPhone quickly pulls me away from the year 1862, and my hand knocks the damn thing from the nightstand to the floor. Bending over to pick it up, I gasp as my permanently damaged left leg screams at me to stop moving.

And I quickly think of those poor Civil War soldiers, both blue and gray, how a shot in the leg with a bone-shattering Minié ball meant near-certain amputation. Some days I'm envious of them, suffering short-term grievous hurt and then living on without a damaged leg constantly throbbing with burning-hot pain. I declined a chance to get my left limb amputated, and some days I wonder if I made the right decision.

I grab the phone off the floor, then slide my fingers across the screen to answer.

"Cook," I say, and a very familiar voice replies, "This is Phillips. What are you doing right now?"

"Besides talking to you, sir, I'm staring at my left leg and telling it to behave."

Which is true. My left leg is propped up on a pillow. I'm wearing dark-blue athletic shorts and a blue-and-white NYPD T-shirt. My right leg is slightly tanned, slightly hairy, and highly muscular. My left leg is a shriveled mess of scars, burn tissue, and puckered craters of flesh where metal tore through it last year when I was deployed in Afghanistan.

But my left foot looks okay. Thank goodness for heavy-duty Army boots, which protected my foot during the long minutes when my leg was trapped and burning.

Colonel Ross Phillips, who's probably a mile away from me in his office this bright Saturday afternoon, quickly gets to it. "We got a red ball case—a real screamer—down in Georgia."

"Hold on, sir," I say, and from my cluttered nightstand I pull free a small notepad and a pen from the Marine Federal Credit Union. I snap the pen into place and say, "Go ahead."

He coughs, clears his throat, and says, "Sullivan, Georgia. About fifty miles from Hunter Army Airfield, near Savannah. We have four Army personnel in civilian custody, arrested by the Sullivan County Sheriff's Department. Their duty station is Hunter."

"Four?" I ask.

"Four," he says.

"Names and unit?"

"I've got someone tracking that down."

"What are the charges?"

"Multiple homicides."

My pen stops writing. I scribble and scribble and no ink appears.

"How many?" I ask.

"Another thing we're tracking down," he says. "We should know in a few more minutes. What we do know is that it was a house holding a number of civilians and that they were all shot. Some historical place called The Summer House. How original, eh? Our four guys were arrested by the county sheriff about forty-eight hours later, in a nearby roadhouse."

"Who's CID head at Hunter?"

"Colonel Brenda Tringali, Third MP Group," he says. "But this case is no stolen Humvee from a motor pool. Mass killing of civilians by four Army personnel is one for you and your group. So far it hasn't hit the news media, but it will soon enough."

He coughs again. And again.

"Colonel...are you all right?"

"Shut up," he says. "I expect you and your crew there by tonight. The sheriff for that county is Emma Williams. Get to her, use your folks to find out what happened, where it happened, and why. Do your job. And get it done. This brewing shit storm is going to rile up a lot of people and groups. Lucky for the Army you and your crew are going to be out there, taking the heat and whatever crap gets flung around."

"Yes, sir," I say.

"Good," he says. "I'll contact you once I have more information."

My supervisor hangs up, and I throw the dead pen across the room, open the nightstand drawer—grimace again as my leg shouts at me—and find a new pen to scribble down a few more notes.

Then back to my iPhone. I need to reach out to the four members of my investigative unit, but there's one call I need to make—and now—even though I'm dreading it.

I tap on the contact number—the number that last year was my home number—and wait for the call to be picked up in Staten Island, about 250 miles away.

It's picked up after one ring, and the woman says, "What's wrong?"

I rub the side of my head. "Sorry to do this, but I can't come up tonight."

"What about tomorrow?" she asks. "You know how much Kelli is looking forward to seeing you."

"Tomorrow's not going to work, and Monday won't, either," I say, hating to say these words.

"Jeremiah."

"Yes."

She says, "Work again?"

"Yes."

"Germany?"

"No, that was last month. I'm leaving for Georgia later today. Is Kelli there?"

My ex-wife, Sandy, says, "No. But don't you worry. I'll tell her myself. How Dad is missing another volleyball tournament. And I'll even tell Kevin you're missing his Boy Scouts Court of Honor Monday night. Anything else I can do for you?"

Months ago these words were sharp blades that Sandy used so well, but now, after months of hearing them, the words have dulled some, though they still hurt.

"No, just tell them I'm sorry, that I'll do my best to make it up to them."

Sandy says, "Fine. And you got a call here from Gary O'Toole, wanting to know if you're going to Pete Monahan's retirement next month."

"Pete?" I ask. "Pete's pulling the pin?"

"That's what Gary told me," she says harshly, like I'm questioning her intelligence or her ability to listen carefully. "I guess Midtown South is planning a huge send-off. You should go."

"No," I say.

"You should go," she repeats, "and you should kiss and make up with the chief of d's... You know they were going to give you a nice desk job at One Police Plaza. I hear the offer is still out there, even if you've been a prick ever since you got hurt."

I say, "Sandy, thanks for telling the kids I won't make it. I'll try to talk to them later this week."

With that call out of the way, I send a text message to three members of my crew, giving them the raw basics. Rendezvous point and time to follow.

I pull up the contact of my fourth team member, but before I can call and speak to her directly, my iPhone chimes again. It's Colonel Phillips.

He says, "More information, all bad."

I get my new pen and pad and say, "Go ahead, sir."

"The four Army personnel . . . they're all Rangers. Assigned to the Fourth Ranger Battalion, stationed at Hunter Army Airfield."

"Shit," I say.

"Yeah," Phillips says. "These aren't four kids fresh out of Basic Training. Nope, these four are pros."

"Names?"

"Jefferson, Barnes, Tyler, and Ruiz. Four-man fire team, part of Second Platoon, Alpha Company. Jefferson is a staff sergeant, fire-team leader."

"Motive?"

"Your guess is as good as mine. And I got a count on the civilian deaths. Seven."

Seven, I think. *Seven civilians, gunned down by four Army Rangers. Jesus Christ on a crutch.*

I'm in a race now, to see who's going to get there first: my investigators and myself or CNN, Fox, MSNBC, and every journalist with a notepad, camera, or video equipment within a thousand-mile radius, ready to try to convict these men in thirty-second sound bites.

"Breakdown?"

He coughs once more. "Three men, three women. All shot at close range."

I stop taking notes.

"Wait," I say. "You said there were seven. And you said three men, three women. What's the correct number?"

His breathing quivers for a long, long second.

"Six adults were shot," he says. "And a two-year-old baby girl."

CHAPTER 4

AT SAM'S INN RESTAURANT on Potomac Avenue in Quantico, Virginia, Special Agent Connie York of the Army's Criminal Investigation Division glances at the dessert menu and quickly drops it on the table.

"Sorry, Pete," she says, trying to smile at her date, a pudgy gent who owns a landscaping business in nearby Southbridge. "I really don't have the appetite for dessert."

Which is a lie, because she's still hungry and loves sweets, and there's a chocolate fudge cake on the menu that's calling to her. But spending one more minute than necessary with Pete Laurion is going to be intolerable. Oh, not that he's a bad guy, but her condo neighbor Claire hooked her up with him, and since Claire took care of her leaky toilet while Connie was on a recent deployment to Germany, it was a favor she was happy to do.

But just this once.

Pete seems intimidated by the other customers in the restaurant, mostly off-duty Marine and Navy personnel, and his thick fingers end with nails that still have a ridge of dirt under them. His heavy blue eyes flick around the place, like he's expecting some officer to make him drop to the ground and do fifty push-ups. Yesterday Claire said, *Pete's a bit rough around the edges, hon, but he's got a good heart. And it'll be a nice change of pace from those gung-ho guys you always end up with.*

Which is true, for along with her ten years of service in the Army have come two failed marriages, both to fellow investigators in the Army's CID. While she feels she's good at solving crimes, Connie admits she so far hasn't puzzled out the secrets of a happy relationship.

Pete smiles with hope in his eyes. "I understand, you wanting to keep your figure and all that. Can I call you later?"

Her iPhone starts chiming, and with a sense of relief, she pulls it out of her purse and sees a familiar name. To Pete she says, "Oh, I don't think so. But thanks for the brunch."

With iPhone in one hand and purse in the other, she steps out onto a crowded deck, drops her purse onto the decking, and puts the phone up to one ear while plugging the other ear with a finger. "York," she answers.

"It's Cook," he says. "Call you at a bad time?"

"Actually, Major, it's a great time," she says. "I needed the break."

"I hear people and music in the background. A date?"

She shakes her head. "No, a dull brunch. What do we have?"

The tone of his voice instantly changes. "A red ball case, down in Georgia. Seven civilians killed in a house in the town and county of Sullivan. Four Rangers from Hunter Army Airfield have been arrested and are currently in the custody of the county sheriff."

"Oh, shit," she says.

"Get down to Georgia, soon as you can. I've called out Pierce, Huang, and Sanchez, but you'll be the first on the scene."

"Yes, sir," she says.

"And once you get there, arrange transport to Sullivan and get us accommodations with an extra room to use as a meeting area.

You're not going to talk to the county sheriff, the State Patrol, the Georgia Bureau of Investigation, or any news media."

"Yes, sir," she says again, biting off the words. "You want me to set up housekeeping, am I right?"

"Agent York," he says, his voice just as sharp, "that's right. And I'm trusting you, as my second-in-command, to do that job to the best of your abilities. Got it, York?"

"Yes, sir."

"Good," he says. "And among the civilian dead is a two-year-old girl. So enough with the pushback."

"Oh, boss," she says, "that's horrible."

"It's bound to get worse," he says. "See you in Georgia."

CHAPTER 5

IT TOOK LESS than four hours to fly via Delta from Dulles to Savannah and its small, fifteen-gate airport—grandly named Savannah/Hilton Head International—and I was fortunate to have an aisle seat to stretch my leg. The long, brick terminal is topped by a glass atrium. Using a cane and rolling my black carry-on luggage, I walk past a number of potted tropical trees in the few minutes it takes to get outside.

It's just past 5:00 p.m., with less than two hours of daylight left, and I'm planning to use as much of that time as possible. It's muggy warm—low eighties, it seems—and I spot among the coach buses and other vehicles trundling through the ground transportation area Special Agent Connie York standing next to a parked silver Ford Fusion, the rental vehicle of choice for government travelers.

She has on a simple black suit-jacket-and-slacks outfit, with a plain white buttoned blouse, and I have a quick, inappropriate observation that I've never seen her in a dress. That's the atavistic, chauvinist part of me, which thankfully is almost always over-ruled by the competent leadership part of me that recognizes her skills as a CID investigator.

Besides, I'm also plainly dressed in one of my two black

suits, and like her, I'm armed with a 9mm SIG Sauer P228 pistol.

Connie pops open the trunk, respectfully allowing me to pick up and toss in my luggage.

"How many history books do you have packed in there, boss?" she asks, slamming the lid shut.

"Just enough," I say. "Barely."

She steps to the driver's door, and as I enter the pleasant, clean, and cool passenger side of the car, I struggle for only a moment, fastening the seat belt without it tangling around my cane.

Connie accelerates from the concrete parking area into a flat landscape dotted with trees and mowed grass, and she says, "How was your flight?"

"On time."

"And how's your leg doing?"

"Still connected to my hip, still hurting like a son of bitch," I say. "What quarters did you get for us?"

We're out of the airport proper and on I-95, heading south, and Connie says, "The best the town of Sullivan has to offer. The Route 119 Motel and Coffee Shop. Less than an hour out. We have three rooms plus a room to use for work."

"Good job," I say. "What else do you know?"

She speeds up the Ford. "You told me to set up the unit's housekeeping. That's what I did."

"And I know you did more," I say. "Give."

The traffic on the interstate is moving fast and freely, and suddenly I'm back in my convoy roaring through the desert. Mouth dry, I scan for slow-moving trucks or cars, or clusters of men standing at the side of the road, looking for a particular man who holds a cell phone programmed to trigger a bomb.

I chew my tongue, try to get the saliva working. *Georgia,* I tell myself. *We're in Georgia. We're not in bandit country. We're in the*

Peach State, so relax already. We're not in Afghanistan. We're never going back to Afghanistan.

"The story's now made all the papers, from the *Atlanta Journal-Constitution* and the *Savannah Morning News* to the local *Sullivan County Times,* but no television coverage yet, though that will change," she says. "The initial reporting just has four Army personnel in custody, with no mention of their Ranger affiliation or the number of civilians murdered. But once the news gets out about who they are, who they killed, the headlines and coverage will go berserk."

A low bank of thunderclouds is off to the south. I see two flashes of lightning illuminate the gray-black of the clouds. Connie's thick blond hair, trimmed short, seems to be wilting after a day in the humid Georgia air.

"Where are the Rangers now?"

"They're being held in the town of Ralston, just south of Sullivan. The county sheriff arrested them late last night, at a roadhouse in that town, and took the four of them to the nearest jail."

"And the shootings took place Wednesday evening?"

"That's right," she says. "The local paper says a visitor came to the house Thursday morning, found it full of dead civilians."

"And less than forty-eight hours later they've made arrests for multiple homicides."

"Tells you the sheriff's department there is either very good, very lax, or very lucky. Or a combination thereof."

"What else?" I ask.

She says, "It's a typical small Southern town, boss. I showed the clerk my ID when I registered the group at the motel, and I'm sure everyone around here will know tonight that the Army's coming in."

"And when do we expect the rest of our crew?"

Connie looks at a watch encircling her tanned wrist with a thin gold band. I think I can make out delicate blond hairs there. "Captain Pierce will be here in about an hour. Dr. Huang and Agent Sanchez...they're both coming in from the West Coast, Huang from San Francisco, Sanchez from LA. Barring any flight delays, they should be in Savannah around midnight."

"All right," I say.

"You need me to pick any of them up?"

"No, we're going to need at least three sets of wheels for our work. I'm sure you told them where we're staying. What do you know about the county sheriff?"

"Emma Williams," she says. "Has been sheriff for a number of years. It's an elected position in Sullivan County, and most of the county is rural. Which means she and her deputies do the bulk of the law enforcement."

I take out my iPhone, work a few buttons and tabs, pull up a map, and say, "The Rangers live either at or near Hunter Army Airfield, south of Savannah. And they're arrested at a roadhouse nearly an hour's drive away. What, they don't have good drinking establishments near their post?"

"It's a puzzle," she says, and maneuvers us onto an exit ramp, and now we're on Interstate 16, heading west. The land is still flat and mostly covered with trees. Not too long to get rural from the grandly named international airport.

"Along with why they traveled to Sullivan to shoot up a houseful of civilians. Must be one hell of a motive."

"Or accident," she says. "Maybe they planned to hit a certain house and hit the wrong one."

"They're Rangers," I say. "They plan in their sleep. They don't hit the wrong house."

A few seconds pass and I feel an urge to ask her about the date I interrupted earlier with my phone call, but I decide to drop it. Connie's gone twice to the marital altar with fellow Army personnel and then to divorce court, and I get the feeling she's not interested in any particular male at the moment, including me.

I still have the iPhone in my hand, and after doing a bit of heavy and complicated research with the Great God Google, I find the number I'm looking for and dial it, then activate the speakerphone so Connie can listen in.

The phone rings once and is then picked up. "Sullivan County Dispatch. What's the nature of your emergency?"

A crisp, professional-sounding woman. I put the iPhone closer to my mouth and say, "This is Major Jeremiah Cook, US Army CID from Quantico, calling for Sheriff Williams."

The woman dispatcher says, "Please hold for a moment, Major Cook," and we're placed on a silent hold. No music, no sound of static, no chirpy voice thanking the caller for choosing Sullivan County for their law enforcement needs.

The dispatcher comes back on. "Major Cook? I have Sheriff Williams on the line."

A stronger, older woman's voice comes on and says, "Major? This is Sullivan County sheriff Williams. What can I do for you?"

I say, "Sheriff Williams, I'm from the US Army Criminal Investigation Division, out of Quantico. I've been tasked to lead the Army's inquiry into what occurred with these four Rangers."

"Well, you realize this crime took place in my county, on civilian property, correct?"

"Absolutely, Sheriff Williams," I say, "and I have no intention or desire to interfere with your investigation."

"Why am I talking to you and not someone from the MP unit over at Hunter?"

Connie looks my way, and it's not a hard look or skeptical. I think she's just paying attention, and I say, "Sheriff Williams, a matter of this magnitude, involving four Ranger servicemen and seven dead civilians, has gotten the attention of very senior Army personnel."

She says, "Well, that makes sense, I suppose. Where are you now?"

"On Interstate 16, heading to the city of Sullivan."

She chuckles. "Don't call the damn place a city. It'll just get the Chamber of Commerce all hopeful. Nope, we're a town, and a small one at that. Tell you what, how does thirty minutes sound? At my office in Sullivan?"

Now I look at Connie and she looks back at me, smiles, shrugs her shoulders. To the sheriff I say, "Ma'am, that's incredibly considerate and generous of you, meeting with us late on a Saturday."

"Not a problem, not at all," she says.

She hangs up and I disconnect the call, and Connie says, "Well, that's a nice change of pace. Civilian law enforcement offering instant cooperation."

I put the phone in my lap. "Don't get ahead of yourself, Connie. She agreed to meet with us. That doesn't equal cooperation."

Out by the horizon, lightning flashes, again and again.

CHAPTER 6

SPECIAL AGENT CONNIE YORK pulls the rented Ford sedan into an empty parking spot next to a Chevrolet sedan painted in the brown and white colors of the Sullivan County Sheriff's Department. Once they left the interstate and got onto a narrow state road, sporadically lined with pig or dairy farms, mobile homes, and one-story houses, a phrase from a Talking Heads song came to her: *And you may find yourself / Living in a shotgun shack.* The only bits of color were the campaign signs for races, from US Senate to county coroner.

She switches off the engine and looks across the lot to a small brick building containing three bays for the trucks belonging to the Sullivan Volunteer Fire Department. Two more buildings complete the cluster. A two-story, white-pillared brick one is topped with a pitched shingle roof and a clock tower, and wide concrete steps lead up to its double glass doors. Behind the taller building is a wide, freestanding, brick-and-concrete one-story surrounded by a high fence with razor wire curled along the top. Signs announce that these adjoining structures hold everything governmental for Sullivan County: the courthouse, the sheriff's department, and the jail. But there are no ramps.

She says, "Looks like the Americans with Disabilities Act hasn't gotten this far, sir."

In a level voice, Major Cook says, "Who's disabled?"

She feels her face warm as she removes the keys. "Sorry, sir. No offense."

"None taken," he says, undoing his seat belt and getting the door open. "I'll make it work. Come along. We don't want to keep the sheriff waiting."

Connie shoulders her leather bag and walks with her boss as he goes up the steps, leaning heavily on his plain metal cane. The humid air hits her like a soft blanket, nearly smothering her.

At the top of the stairs she looks across the street, to a small green park with benches and a statue of a Confederate soldier standing in frozen guard. There's a hardware store, a laundromat, a small restaurant, a barber, a women's hairstylist, and a few other one-story brick buildings, including a post office. A few residents sitting on park benches are staring at them.

She looks at her boss, grasping one railing with a strong hand, leaning on the cane, face red. His upper body is muscular, and his black hair is trimmed short, with a few flecks of white along the sides. Jeremiah Cook is thirty-five, and before his Humvee was struck by an IED in Afghanistan, she knew, he was a homicide detective in the NYPD and a member of the Army Reserves. Connie doesn't know the whole story, but she's heard the NYPD offered him a desk job, and he told them to go to hell, and despite his leg injury, he was able to transfer from the Reserves to regular Army. Oh, and along the way, he lost his wife, who divorced him.

Even with the painful struggle on his lean, honest face, Connie suddenly thinks that Mrs. Cook was a moron to divorce this man.

She goes to the double glass doors, opens one, and is surprised to see a woman there, waiting to meet them.

The woman is in her fifties, a bit stout but fit, wearing black sneakers, blue jeans, and a dark green polo shirt that has an embroidered department badge on the left side and "Sheriff Williams" in white script on the right side. On a wide leather belt is a holstered pistol, two spare magazines, and a set of handcuffs, along with a clipped-on gold sheriff's badge. She looks past Connie and says, "Is that Major Cook?"

"Yes, ma'am, it is," she says. "I'm Special Agent York, with his team."

The sheriff smiles, revealing deep dimples, and offers her hand. Her face is worn but attractive, and her thick black hair is cut short. "I'm sure you've figured out who I am," she says, and in a low voice adds, "What happened to the major? Was it the damn war? Which one?"

Connie says, "Afghanistan," and then the sheriff bustles past her to shake hands with Major Cook, and they all go down a dark and cool hallway.

The office is large, with tall windows overlooking a closely trimmed lawn and another parking area with two more cruisers, three pickup trucks, and a Ford SUV. Sheriff Williams sits behind her desk, which is large and covered with neatly organized file folders and a white legal pad.

Connie takes the left leather-upholstered chair while her boss takes the right. There's a small round conference table at the rear, next to a leather couch and coffee table, which is stacked high with police magazines. Connie reaches into her shoulder bag and takes out a yellow legal pad, thinking, *White versus yellow. We'll see who takes better notes.*

"Good trip, both of you?"

Cook says, "It was just fine."

The bookcase is filled, and so are the walls. Plaques and photos line every inch, and Connie recognizes the sheriff posing with important men and women, including two FBI directors, two presidents, a vice president, and three senators from Georgia.

A player, she thinks. *She loves her politics.*

The sheriff appears in all but one photo, and in three shots she's wearing an Army uniform, smiling and standing in front of a US flag, shaking hands with superior officers. *Either Army Reserves or Georgia National Guard,* Connie thinks.

The outlier photo is black-and-white, of a stern-looking man in a gray suit holding a homburg hat in his big hands and standing on the steps of what looks to be the US Capitol Building.

Cook says, "Again, my thanks for seeing us on such short notice."

The sheriff smiles, but her words don't match up. "Well, I hate to disappoint you, but that might be the only cooperation you get from me. Sure, the crimes were committed by four of your boys and they're stationed over at Hunter, but everything took place here, in Sullivan. Not on government property."

Connie waits to see how Cook plays it, and no surprise, it's going to be the apologetic and soft-spoken Army officer, grieved that fellow soldiers have been arrested for such a horrible crime.

"You're quite correct, Sheriff," Cook says. "And we're not here to obstruct or take over the investigation."

"Then why are you here, and all the way from Virginia?" the sheriff asks, pleasant steel still in her voice. "Twice I've had run-ins with your boys from Hunter Airfield, once for a DUI that ended in a jeep crash and the other for a brawl. Both times I worked with the Hunter MPs. How come you're here and they aren't?"

Cook tells the sheriff exactly what he had reminded Connie

of that morning. "It's our job," he says. "We have a team that consists of investigators, an Army JAG lawyer, and an Army psychiatrist. We want to get to the facts of the case as soon as possible so that justice is done."

"What kind of justice?"

"The kind that means if we—working with you—determine that there is clear evidence of their guilt, we'll make sure it gets to the right hands, either your office or your district attorney's."

The sheriff runs a finger alongside one of the manila folders. "I suppose that also means if you think these four are being railroaded or set up or somehow are innocent, you'll put that out as well."

"We will," Connie's boss says.

"Sounds like you're more interested in a cover-up than getting to the truth," she says.

Cook says, "Then perhaps I'm not making myself clear. My team is here to get to the truth, whatever it may be. And again, we respect your position and authority. We would just like to work here with your knowledge and cooperation."

The sheriff slowly nods. "All right, then. Nice to make everything clear and out in the open. What first?"

Cook says, "My apologies, but all we know is that you've arrested four soldiers from the Fourth Ranger Battalion, stationed at Hunter Army Airfield. Could you confirm their names and ranks for us?"

Sheriff Williams goes right to the top of the pile, passes a file folder over to Connie. "I had a duplicate made of their personnel information and their booking photos." She opens the top drawer of her desk and puts on a pair of reading glasses as Connie opens the folder and slides out four color booking photos with names and IDs printed below.

The sheriff leans over her own copy of the information and

says, "Here we go. Top to bottom. Staff Sergeant Caleb Jefferson, age twenty-eight. Corporal Curtis Barnes, age twenty-six. Specialist Vinny Tyler, age twenty-three. And Specialist Paulie Ruiz, age twenty-four. All belonging to...let's see, Second Platoon, Alpha Company, Fourth Battalion. The rest of the staff sergeant's squad are out on medical leave for various wounds and injuries." Williams looks up, taking off her reading glasses. "That's who they are. All residing either at or near the air base."

As the sheriff read off the names, Connie gave each photo a good hard stare. The senior NCO, Jefferson, is African American with a shaved head, small ears close to his skull, and a confident, staring look into the police camera. Corporal Barnes is white, Specialist Ruiz is Hispanic, and Specialist Tyler is also white. Ruiz is like Jefferson, staring into the camera with quiet confidence, black hair trimmed short. Corporal Barnes's hair is nearly white-blond, and his face is a blank slate. The last specialist, Tyler, has red hair—also trimmed short—and he's the only one who looks out of place, like he can't believe he's having his photo taken as part of a multiple-homicide investigation.

All four are lean, muscular, and wearing civilian shirts, from checked short-sleeves to polos.

"Tough-looking crowd," Williams says.

"That's their job," Cook says. "Tough and smart."

"What next?" Williams asks.

Connie expects the major to ask questions about the victims and is surprised when Cook goes in another direction.

"I'd like to take a look at the murder house," her boss says.

Sheriff Williams clasps her hands together on top of her desk and says, "Well, that's going to be our first disagreement."

"Excuse me?" Cook asks.

"The scene of the crime," she says. "It's sorta well-known around here. It's called The Summer House and is on its way to getting on the National Register of Historic Places...Lots of famous folks stayed there, including FDR when he was visiting Warm Springs."

The sheriff's face hardens. "And sorry, I'm not giving you or anyone else from the Army access."

CHAPTER 7

I'M GOING STARE to stare against this county's sheriff, and I realize I've just struck the first shoal of the investigation.

"Oh, I'm terribly sorry if I've crossed a line, Sheriff Williams," I say, trying to make my voice as quiet and reasonable as possible. "May I ask why you won't give us access?"

"Because," she says, "it's our department's policy only to allow sworn Georgia peace officers and forensics specialists access."

"I see," I say. My NYPD style of dealing with competing law enforcement agencies by raising my voice and pounding the desk won't work here. "Well, perhaps we should move on. The victims. Do you have an accounting of who they are?"

The sheriff goes to another file folder, and I have to admire her for her neatness.

"All right," she says, "and I warn you, it ain't going to be pretty."

"Warning taken," I say.

The first color photo comes to Connie and me. A man on his back on an old, wide-planked wooden floor, eyes open, forehead and nose torn away by bullet wounds. Lots of blood and exposed flesh and bone. Long brown hair. Upper part of a black T-shirt.

"Gordon Tilly," she says. "Age twenty-one. Student at Savannah Technical College, studying commercial truck driving."

The next photo is not as graphic. A young man sprawled out on an overturned couch, the couch covered with a dark gray blanket. The back of his head is a mess of hair, bone, and blood.

"Randall Gleason," she says. "Age nineteen. Not sure of his status."

Another flip. A woman this time. Black T-shirt as well. Eyes closed, mouth open, thick brown hair, neat round hole in her forehead. Resting on the same old battered wood floor.

"Sally Tisdale," the sheriff says. "Also nineteen. A student at the Athens Beautician School in Savannah."

The next photo shows a woman crumpled up against the base of a wall, the back of her skull a familiar mess.

"Gina Zachary, age twenty," she says. "Dropout from Savannah Technical College. Her body was on the second floor, in a bedroom."

The sheriff pauses, and realizing her hesitation, I say, "The next one is bad, I gather?"

Williams purses her lips. "The worst."

The photo comes over, there's a sudden intake of breath from Connie, and I stare and look away, remembering the first time I saw something similar, back on the job, and the only way I kept it together was to pretend I was looking at a doll someone had broken. And I also remember Duffy, a detective counting out the days and weeks before retiring, and him telling me, *Most of this new tech is good shit, helping us break cases, but I do hate color crime-scene pics. Black-and-white...you didn't get as sick to your stomach.*

Sheriff Williams nearly whispers. "A little girl, around two years of age...I...I just don't know."

We three sit there for a dark few seconds, and she says, "Last two."

Flip. Dead man in a rumpled bed, eyes and mouth open in surprise, another neat bullet hole, in his forehead. "Stuart Pike. Twenty-two. The dump was rented in his name. Also a dropout of Savannah Technical College."

Flip. I take a breath. Thank God, the last one.

An older woman, and I instantly see she doesn't fit. More mature, early thirties, a bit of makeup, the top of her blouse showing some taste and dollars, and the look on her face isn't that of surprise but of terror. The right side of her head is a gaping, bloody hole.

Sheriff Williams gathers up the photos. "Lillian Zachary. Thirty years old, resident of Atlanta and a Delta Air Lines employee."

Connie says, "Relative of Gina Zachary?"

"Gina was her younger sister," Williams says. "A Volvo parked in the yard was also registered to her."

The dead people go back into a file folder.

Williams's voice is somber. "Last homicide in this county... three, maybe four years ago? Millie Porter, she got tired of her boyfriend, Barry, tuning her up and so one night she cut him in half with a 12 gauge. That was a murder. These"—she taps the folder for emphasis—"were executions. And why? We don't know why. But we're sure it was done by your fellas."

I say, "Mind sharing what you've got so far?"

"Oh, we've got a lot," she says, "and our investigation is continuing, but the key part is a witness that places your Rangers at the murder scene, leaving in a pickup truck registered to Staff Sergeant Jefferson, right after there was gunfire."

Connie says, "And what else?"

Sheriff Williams glances at her watch. "What else is that I'm missing my favorite nephew's birthday party, and I think I've done enough for you folks tonight."

My words don't match what I'm feeling, but I say them anyway. "Sheriff Williams, you've been exceptionally kind and gracious. My deputy and I thank you."

Williams gives me a slight smile. "Glad I can help the Army. Me? I'm just a small-town sheriff in a small rural county. This... this is a horror show. And I mean to see it right to the end."

I gesture to the photos of her in military uniform. "The Reserves?"

She swivels and looks up at them as well. "Nope, Georgia National Guard. Ten proud years, in public affairs. Spent a lot of time deployed in Iraq."

"Same for me," I say. "I was a detective, second class, in New York, and in the Reserves, Criminal Investigation Division. Then this happened," and I spin my cane back and forth.

"Sorry," she says. "Mind me asking what happened?"

"Don't mind at all," I say. "After all, we've both been there, done that." I take a breath, hoping the good sheriff notices. "I was in a small convoy, heading out to a village as part of an investigation. I was the lead investigator. My Humvee got hit by an IED... typical story. Driver killed, gunner lost a leg, and I had a few broken bones, and I was trapped for a while as my left leg got roasted and toasted." I shrug. "Made it out alive, which is a plus. Came back home after a few months at Landstuhl in Germany and Walter Reed near DC, and then One Police Plaza wanted to put me behind a desk. Can't really blame them—I suck now at running—but the Army offered me a full-time role. That's why I'm here."

She smiles, a bit more warmth this time. "Good on you, Major Cook. I like your style."

I speak quickly. "One more thing, if I may, before you go to your birthday party. Any chance we can meet tomorrow morning for more of a debrief?"

"I don't see why not," she says. "Let's say...8:00 a.m. Just before church. Hey, you folks want to know the times and places for services on Sunday?"

Connie speaks up. "Thank you very much, Sheriff, but the owner of our motel passed along a church list to me when I registered."

I have a confident feeling that Connie is lying and say, "All right, ma'am, 8:00 a.m."

"See you back here."

And I toss in, "And perhaps you'll change your mind and allow us to visit the murder house?"

Her slight smile widens. "See you tomorrow, Major. At 8:00 a.m."

The shock from going out of cool air-conditioning into the hot, muggy outside air nearly takes my breath away, but Connie and I keep pace as we get back to the silver Ford Fusion.

"What a mess," she says.

"Biggest one I've ever seen," I say.

"What now, boss?"

"You show me the grand lodgings you've secured, and we wait for the rest of our team to arrive."

I'm standing by the passenger door, and Connie is standing opposite me. She eyes me and says, "Sir?"

She wants to talk, so I say, "Anything odd strike you about the good sheriff back there?"

She taps the roof of the rental. "Where should I begin?"

"Number one on the runway," I say. "Go."

Connie looks back at the municipal building. "She didn't ask for our IDs."

I nod, pleased. "That's right," I say. "Tell me more."

Connie says with confidence, "This is the biggest case she's ever had. Seven dead civilians, four elite Army Rangers charged, in her jurisdiction. And a man and woman appear, claiming to be Army investigators, and she doesn't ask for our identification?"

I say, "She knew we were coming, and she knew who we were. Good job, York."

"And there were a lot of look-at-me photos with prominent politicians," she adds. "But there was one photo that didn't fit. Did you see it?"

"The grumpy-looking old man standing on the steps of the Capitol?"

"That's the one," she says. "Wonder who he is and why his photo is in her office."

"Then find out," I say.

"I will," Connie says. "However you look at it, though, all those photos mean the sheriff is a player of some sort."

"That's right," I say, opening the car door. "Small-town sheriff my ass."

CHAPTER 8

CAPTAIN ALLEN PIERCE of the US Army JAG Corps opens the door to his room at the Route 119 Motel and Coffee Shop in Sullivan, Georgia, flips on the light, and takes in his temporary home. Two sagging single beds separated by a nightstand with a light. A low bureau against the right-hand wall, a television chained to the floor. The carpet stained and scarred with cigarette burns. An open bathroom with a small shower.

Several hours ago he was playing the fifteenth hole at the Nassau Country Club, on the outskirts of Glen Cove, odd man out in a foursome with Pop and two of his friends, all three Wall Street lawyers, all members of the Urban League, all summering at Oak Bluffs on Martha's Vineyard.

Pop was trying to grease the skids to ease the way forward for his lawyer son if he ever leaves the Army, and the incoming text from Major Cook meant Pierce didn't have to say no again to his father.

Pierce decides to take the far bed, thinking it'll be farther away from any noise in the parking lot, and dumps his go bag, then uses the bathroom to freshen up. He feels disoriented, like he did in the first few weeks after graduating from Columbia Law and going straight to Fort Benning, taking the direct-commission route from civilian to second lieutenant.

While at Fort Benning for his six weeks of initial training, he was in a huge complex, under constant supervision and in the company of other soldiers and trainees. Today? He drove here from the airport by himself, along the twilit back roads of Georgia, and for thirty minutes he was followed by a car that slowed when he slowed, accelerated when he accelerated.

Paranoia, he thinks, but he also thinks of his great-uncle Byron, who had his skull fractured during the Freedom Rides back in the early sixties.

Pierce walks outside and tenses up as a car drives right up to his motel unit, lights bright, and there's his service pistol back in his luggage—which he's fired a total of three times, on the range—but the engine and lights switch off, and Major Jeremiah Cook's voice cuts through the Georgia darkness.

"Good to see you, Captain," he says. "Let's get to work."

After retrieving his legal pad and laptop, Pierce follows Major Cook and Special Agent Connie York past two other rooms in this motel, which is L-shaped, with an office at the junction of the L and a coffee shop at the far end. Connie unlocks the door of the next room—marked 11 in stick-on numbers—and leads them in, switching on the lights. "It's a hole, but it's workable," she says. "Allen, give me a hand, will you?"

The motel room looks like it's part storage facility, and he works a few minutes with Connie to push the beds against the walls and get a row of folding chairs and a table set up. Connie then digs around in the remaining clutter of boxes and shopping bags and emerges with a large whiteboard, which he helps her hang up on a wall. Connie is an attractive woman, and Allen not only enjoys working with her but also just likes being in her presence. Not enough to ask her out—one piece of advice he did take from Pop was never to dip one's pen in the company ink—but he can still admire a smart and good-looking woman.

Pierce takes a seat and says, "What do we have, Major?"

Cook's face is red and strained, and Allen recalls their last deployment, to Germany, where Cook insisted on going for a run every morning, despite his scarred and wounded leg. Allen wonders how his boss keeps it together.

"Just a quick brief until Huang and Sanchez show up," he says. "When they do, we're each going to fire up our laptops and check out each Ranger's service record. Connie, will you put up the photos?"

York arranges the booking photos of four Army Rangers on the left side of the whiteboard and then writes the names of seven civilian dead on the right side. Allen keeps pace, taking careful notes on the details of the case and the soldiers' arrest, pausing just once at hearing that a two-year-old baby girl is among the victims.

His writing hand stills. Part of his JAG training at the University of Virginia School of Law in Charlottesville after his six weeks at Fort Benning involved looking at past incidents when Army personnel went beyond the normal bounds of civilized actions—No Gun Ri, My Lai, and Abu Ghraib—and he knows he shouldn't be too surprised to see a case in which Army Rangers apparently went berserk and killed civilians.

But a little girl? Two years old?

"And that's it so far," Connie says, recapping her black marker. "Sir? Anything you'd like to add?"

Cook struggles to his feet, goes to the whiteboard, taps at the photos and then the list of victims.

"Here's the gap," he says, pointing to the clear section between the photos and the writing. "We need to fill it in. Find out what possible connection could exist between these civilians"—a tap to the board—"and these Rangers."

Allen says, "Do we know when Huang and Sanchez are arriving?"

Connie says, "Just before midnight, if their flights are on time. There's a rental car waiting for them at the airport. Sir?"

Cook goes back to his chair, sits, winces, and stretches his left leg out. "The three of us are about to find out what kind of meal this motel's coffee shop serves. Then tomorrow, bright and early, we're going to send Huang and you, Allen, to the jail where these four are being held. It's in Ralston, next town over."

"Sounds good," Allen says.

"Connie, you and I, along with Sanchez, we're also getting an early start tomorrow."

She looks confused. "You mean the 8:00 a.m. meeting with Sheriff Williams?"

"No," he says. "I mean the three of us are going over to the murder scene. The so-called Summer House."

"But she said we couldn't gain entry," Connie says.

Allen takes notice of that. The locals are already pushing back hard, even before they've been here a full day?

"That she did," her boss replies. "Let's just show up and see what happens."

Connie says, "She'll be pissed. Sir."

Cook nods, and Allen likes the tone of his boss's voice.

"I'm counting on it," the major says.

CHAPTER 9

I LOOK AT the red numerals on the little digital clock on the nightstand. I've been awake for an hour. At night, when the dreams and the memories come back, it seems like the walls and ceilings and floor are conspiring to close in on me, choking out my breath, choking out my life.

I get out of bed and drape a sheet and blanket around my shoulders, unlock the motel room door, and go outside. There's a lawn chair, and I sit down, wrapping everything about me.

Outside it's still warm and muggy, and flying insects are swarming around the motel parking lot lights. The lot is nearly deserted. It's just about 2:00 a.m., and the other two members of my squad are delayed due to flight problems.

Typical hurry up and wait.

I shift and tug the sheet and blanket closer. Army planning. Still hard to believe I'm now Army, through and through. For years I was with the NYPD, climbing the ladder, making good collars, going from precinct to precinct, and putting in my time in the Reserves. I was just out of high school when the Towers came down, and after graduating from the Academy I felt I could do a bit of payback while still wearing the shield, if luck came my way.

But luck and payback came to somebody else first on a dirt road in Afghanistan. A place that still haunts me but where I will never return.

The drone of an approaching car jolts me back to my present assignment. I think of Colonel Phillips, still not liking the depth of his cough during my last talk with him. Nearly a year ago he called me into his office at Quantico and said, *I'm setting up a special squad. You're going to lead it. It's going to have CID investigators, a JAG lawyer, and a psychiatrist. Your job is going to take on major crimes, here and abroad, make sure justice gets done, that there are no cover-ups, and most of all, that the locals don't frame our folks.*

And I said, *Yes, sir,* and now I'm in Georgia. In 1864 General William T. Sherman made his march from Atlanta to Savannah, and just before Christmas Day he sent a message to President Lincoln:

I beg to present you as a Christmas gift the city of Savannah, with one hundred and fifty heavy guns and plenty of ammunition, also about twenty-five thousand bales of cotton.

Up there in Quantico, my Colonel Phillips is waiting for a gift, and I know it cannot wait until Christmas, or even until next week.

A car pulls into the lot and parks near me. The headlights switch off. Two doors open up, and the men inside get out and approach me.

"Major Cook," the first one says. It's Lieutenant John Huang, US Army Medical Corps, psychiatrist.

"Sir," the second one says. Special Agent Manuel Sanchez, US Army CID, former LAPD officer.

I say, "Glad to see you, gents." I swivel in my chair and add,

"You're in room 9. It's unlocked. Two sets of room keys on the bureau. Agent York and Captain Pierce are in room 8. We'll be getting up at 0600 later this morning. We'll check the service records for the four Rangers and prep the rest of our day. Get organized and try to get some sleep."

Both say, "Yes, sir," and they get their gear and head to their room.

I sit and wait, the parking lot quiet again, and the bugs continue surging around the bright lights.

More sounds of cars approaching.

At this hour?

I think about our meeting with the county sheriff and how she described the last murder in this county, years back, when the abused Millie Porter took her vengeance against her Barry.

A common secret among us cops is that most murders get cleared in just a day or so. They're easy, they're blatant—drug deal turns bad, husband or wife gets tired of abuse, an armed robbery goes south.

Two cars and a rental van pull into the lot, come to a stop. Doors fly open, there are loud conversations, and I see two men go to the rear of the van, haul out television equipment.

The members of the Fourth Estate have rolled in, ready to pass sentence and convict with a few chosen words or sixty seconds of videotape, always able to duck out with that blessed word *alleged*.

Not me. I'm old-fashioned, I know, but I still want to see where the evidence leads us.

I get up from the chair, blanket and sheet still over me, wanting to get back to my room before one of the reporters decides to see who this odd man is. Once inside, I plan to stay awake.

As for Sheriff Williams and myself, we don't have a crime to solve but a mystery.

And I hate mysteries.

CHAPTER 10

IN HIS CELL at the Ralston town jail, Staff Sergeant Caleb Jefferson is awake, sitting up against the concrete wall, legs stretched out, listening to one of his squad mates snore. It sounds like Specialist Ruiz, originally from El Paso and a good man to have at your side in a foxhole. Ruiz is a great shot and a great scrounger on post, and he has the amazing ability to fall asleep at any place or time, whether in a cold, ice-crusted trench high up in the mountains or in an FOB shelter with mortar rounds dropping in.

A groan and Corporal Barnes seems to come awake. He whispers, "Ah, crap, not again, Ruiz. Hey, Ruiz, knock it off." The snoring increases, and Barnes kicks the barred door to his cell, making it rattle. "Ruiz, wake up! Or roll over! Christ…"

Jefferson keeps an eye on the situation. The jail here consists of six cells, built back when black-and-white television was still the rage. Old-fashioned bars and locks, concrete beds with thin foam mattresses, single wool blankets, foam pillows with a case thin enough to see through. Stainless-steel commodes and sinks. His orange uniform is starched, smelling of detergent.

"Sergeant, you awake over there?" Barnes asks.

"I am."

Another voice comes out of the darkness. "Me too. Jesus, when Ruiz starts sawing wood..."

The fourth and youngest member of his squad, Specialist Vinny Tyler, is from Idaho. Skinny but, by God, can that kid hump the gear when need be, especially climbing those rock escarpments that seemed to rise klick after klick, right up into the clouds.

A cough and a hack. Ruiz—originally from personnel re-covery—snorts and wakes up. His cell is across the corridor from the other three. "Hey, what's going on?" he says. "What did I miss?"

Barnes says, "Nothing much. Miss Sullivan County trotted through here in a see-through nightie, handing out coffee and doughnuts."

Ruiz yawns loudly. "Fine by me. I hate doughnuts."

Jefferson smiles as there's low laughter from his men, and he thinks, *Hey, cops out there surveilling us with hidden cameras, try to figure that mood out.* It's a good fire team, handpicked by him, one of the best, roughest, and finest in the company. He knows their strengths, their weaknesses, and, most important—right now—their family status. None are married, none have kids, and that's a good thing not to have in the back of one's mind when chasing the Taliban through ravines.

Or facing serious trouble stateside.

Save for him. His wife died two years back from ovarian cancer, and her daughter—his stepdaughter, Carol—is under the care of an aunt in Savannah and is mending at a treatment center in Hilton Head.

His team is lean and mean, just the way he wants it.

Tyler calls out, "Staff Sergeant Jefferson?"

"Right here," he says.

"Everything...everything's gonna be fine, right? You're sure, right?"

Jefferson thinks of that old house with the filth inside and the yells and shouts, and he knows Tyler is scared. It's one thing to fly hot into an LZ or to take fire from a tree line or to make a dynamic entry into some rock-and-dirt farmhouse over there in Afghanistan.

But this is here, this is CONUS, this is the blessed safety zone.

"Everything is going to be fine," he says. "Don't you worry none."

Ruiz says, "Hey, Specialist?"

Tyler says, "Yeah, Ruiz, what is it?"

Ruiz swears in Spanish. "You second-guess the sergeant one more time, the first chance I get, I break your freakin' nose."

CHAPTER 11

SPECIAL AGENT MANUEL SANCHEZ is sitting next to Special Agent Connie York as she drives the rental Ford sedan down a bumpy dirt road, and Manuel is holding on to the door handle, trying very hard not to upchuck his morning breakfast of greasy sausage, eggs over easy, and grits. Grits! He has yet to figure out the attraction of grits—just a fancy name for mush. And beans for breakfast? Not here, not in this place.

At the entrance to this dirt road was a wrought-iron metal pole—pockmarked with rust—and dangling to the side was a very worn wooden sign with painted carved letters saying THE SUMMER HOUSE 1911.

In the rear of the sedan, Major Cook—sitting so his injured left leg is stretched out—says, "Connie, you can slow it down."

"Sir, we're running up against the clock. I think we're almost— yep, there it is."

Manuel knows what Connie means about the clock, because he's been here in Georgia less than six hours, and after the rushed briefing before breakfast, he already feels like he and the rest of the squad are a day behind. Four Rangers in jail, seven civvies dead—including a two-year-old baby girl!—and pretty soon reporters will be dogging their every step.

Connie brakes the Ford to a halt and dust rises, then they all get out, Major Cook struggling for a few seconds with his cane. Connie and he pretend not to notice, though he enjoys noticing Connie. In the morning heat she's discarded her black jacket, and the slacks are pretty tight around her curvy bottom, and the white blouse is clinging nicely to her torso.

But Manuel knows better than to look too much at his fellow special agent, because he's still deeply in love with his wife, Conchita, back home in East LA with their three girls, a sweet little home in a relatively quiet neighborhood.

Besides, Connie is wearing her Army-issue SIG Sauer in a waist holster and is a better shot than he is.

As he and Connie wait for the major to join them, Manuel examines the old two-story house. At one time it was probably a destination to be proud of, a place to unwind from the city. Two wooden pillars at the front, black roof and black shutters, wide wooden door in the center. But the paint is faded, shingles are missing from the roof, and the pillars are cracked and sagging. There's yellow-and-black crime-scene tape fluttering across the door, along with an official sheriff's department adhesive seal pressed against the doorjamb.

Two pickup trucks are parked nearby, along with a Sentra whose trunk is being held closed by a length of frayed clothesline. A light-blue Volvo sedan with a Delta Air Lines parking sticker on the windshield is set some meters away, like the driver was concerned the run-down vehicles here would somehow infect it.

In every direction, except the dirt road they just came down, there's nothing save brush and tall pine trees, though through the brush at the far end of the lot there looks to be a body of water. Manuel frowns. Too much emptiness, too many trees. He grew up in a crowded LA neighborhood, joined the Police Academy, and went over to the Army when the police department was shedding personnel to balance its budget, plus the Army at the time was promising a hefty enlistment bonus.

"Looks damn empty and quiet, Major," he says.

"True," Cook says. "Connie?"

She glances down the dirt road. "Odd. Only one real entry in and out. You come in for a hit, and you leave yourself open for trouble if a UPS truck or some lost soul comes down the road. It could block you, get people curious why you're here."

In the distance a dog barks.

"Let's take a look around," Cook says, and he leads the way, leaning heavily on his cane. Manuel and Connie follow.

It doesn't take long. The perimeter is trashy, with discarded tires, rusty fifty-five-gallon drums, piles of lumber and chicken-coop wire, and sodden pizza boxes. Manuel wonders if the ghosts of the rich folks who built this place mourn the once-perfect yard. On the far side of the house one of the windows is open, and from another window a rusting air-conditioning unit is sagging on supporting two-by-fours, looking like it could fall at any moment.

One and then two helicopters roar overhead.

The other two windows on that side are closed, and so are the ground-floor windows on both sides. One of the windows is covered with plastic.

After returning to the front, Manuel says, "I don't like that single door, Major."

"Tell us why."

He says, "Like the dirt road. Only one way in or out. With a dynamic entry, rolling in, you'd think they'd use a ladder, smash one of the first-floor windows, come in through both the door and the windows."

Cook says, "This is Georgia. Lots of firearms in private hands. Maybe they thought rolling in through the windows exposed them more. That door looks like it was breached by explosive charges. You do that, folks in tight quarters like this, in a small house like this, they might run to the rear when the door blows open. That means you're funneling your targets into one area."

"Maybe," Connie says, and Manuel knows she's looking at the scene with the same cop eyes he is, though her earlier time was with the Virginia State Police—not as difficult or as tough as the LAPD. "I wish the sheriff hadn't been such a bitch. I'd love to go inside."

Manuel turns at the sound of a loud car engine, getting louder, and roaring down the dirt road is a brown-and-white Sullivan County Sheriff's Department cruiser, bouncing up and down in the dust, and Cook says, "Well, let's see what happens if we talk nice to the sheriff."

The cruiser skids to a halt, and Manuel sees a woman in her fifties jump out, face red with anger, wearing jeans and a black polo shirt, and she yells out, "Damn it, Major, I told you I wasn't going to let you into the goddamn crime scene! What the hell do you think you're doing here?"

Cook looks pretty damn calm, and he says, "You told us we couldn't go inside. We're not. We're outside, looking in."

The sheriff strides forward, fists on her hips. "You like to play games, Major, is that it? Well, tell you what. I got some friends in DC, and I can play games, too, including getting your whole goddamn crew out of my county and back on the first plane to Dulles!"

CHAPTER 12

LIEUTENANT JOHN HUANG of the US Army Medical Corps gets out of the rented Ford sedan, pulled into a narrow parking space in front of the Ralston Police Department. On the small front lawn, memorials listing Ralston's war dead from the Revolutionary War to the Civil War and all the way up to Vietnam share space with poster-board campaign signs for various offices.

Captain Allen Pierce joins him on the cracked pavement. It's not even 8:00 a.m. and the shade of the large oak in the park across the street is not large enough to protect them from what is going to be one hell of a hot day. Down a ways is a Southern Baptist church, and exuberant singing is coming from the building. John shakes his head. Twice in the past five years he's gone to overcrowded Hong Kong for extended family reunions and thinks the residents there would smile in delight at seeing so much empty and available space.

"What do you think, Allen?" he asks. Officially Allen outranks him as a captain, but since Allen's a lawyer and he's a psychiatrist, they decided months ago they could drop the ranks and the *Yes, sir* and *No, sir* while working in the field.

"Think?" Allen asks, reaching into the car, retrieving his

briefcase. Like him, Allen is wearing a two-piece dark-blue suit with black shoes and a white shirt, no necktie. "I think you and I have just increased this town's diversity by twenty percent. Come on, Doc, let's see if someone's awake at the jail."

There is a single dark-blue Ralston police cruiser parked in the lot, along with a red Dodge Colt stained with rust and mud. A narrow concrete path takes them to the rear of the brick, two-story building, where RALSTON POLICE DEPARTMENT is painted in gold on a glass door.

John tries the door. It's locked.

"I like the look of that," Allen says, coming up next to him, reading aloud the paper sheet directing emergency, after-hours, and weekend contact to the Sullivan County Sheriff's Department. "Small town, small crime."

"Except for the four Rangers, stuck in there, charged with slaughtering seven civilians," John says, still not wanting to believe on an emotional level that Rangers could do something so horrid in the States, but also knowing from cold, clinical experience that anything is possible.

Including the slaughter of civilians.

"There's a doorbell," John says. "Give it a push."

Allen pushes it twice, and before his third try a shadow appears behind the door. The door is unlocked and pushed open, and a plump young man wearing black-rimmed glasses, gray trousers, and a blue uniform shirt with no name tag or shield says, "Yeah? You guys lost or something?" He has keys in one hand and a coffee mug in the other, bright red with yellow letters saying OFFICIAL BIKINI INSPECTOR.

John thinks, *Yeah, lost in time, about five decades,* and Allen says, "I'm Captain Allen Pierce, United States Army, and this is Lieutenant John Huang. We're here to see the four Rangers."

The door is being held open by the man's hip, and he takes a sip from his coffee mug before saying, "You guys have an appointment?"

John says, "No, we don't."

"You've spoken to Chief Kane about coming here?"

Allen says, "No, we haven't. We got in late last night."

The man says, "You got badges or something?"

John takes out his leather badge case from an inside coat pocket, shows it to the jail attendant, and Allen does the same. The jail attendant rubs his chin with the hand holding his keys and says, "Well...I guess the chief needs to okay this. But he's not here."

Allen smiles, but John sees how his fellow investigator is nearly gritting his teeth. "So where is he? Can you call him?"

The young man looks surprised, like both he and Allen should know what's going on. "Fellas, it's deer-hunting season for muzzle-loaders. The chief is out by Sweeney's Tract by now...and there ain't no cell phone coverage out there."

Allen's smile is getting icier, and John says, "Sir, if I may...We're not here to cause any trouble. We're here to help those four men. Now, we know they've been charged with horrible crimes. We understand that. But the captain here is an Army lawyer, and I'm an Army doctor, and we've been ordered to see the men, to talk to them, to send a report back to Washington."

John knows what he's said is 50 percent true, 50 percent bullshit, but he hopes the magic words of *Army, ordered,* and *Washington* just might work.

The jail attendant says, "You're here to help, then?"

Allen says, "Sir, absolutely."

John has a guilty thought that this is probably one of the few times this pudgy young man has ever been called *sir*.

He says, "You stay here. I'll be right back." With coffee cup still in hand, he steps back in, locks the door, and then disappears from sight.

Allen says, "Looks like it worked."

"Yeah."

"Tell me again, how do you do it?" Allen asks. "Me, I've got law books and online records to help me puzzle out legal crap, years of precedents, and judges out there to kick me in the nuts if I stray too far. But you?" Allen taps the side of his head. "All between your ears, Doc, trying to figure out what's going on with some other guy's brain. Don't know how you do it."

"There are degrees and learning on our end, too," John says, feeling uncomfortable in the heat.

"Yeah, but I know enough about psychiatry to know that every ten or so years there's a big upheaval that turns everything upside down. Lawyers? Man, we're still working off a document that King John signed more than a thousand years back. How do you do it?"

Like a PowerPoint presentation, faces of past patients he talked to after joining the Army come to him, men and women, young and old, privates to colonels, all sizes and shapes and colors, but one thing is the same for each of them: their eyes. Each has the same dull, blank look of someone who has gone into the abyss and is trying so desperately to climb out.

And he, Dr. John Huang of Stanford and the US Army Medical Corps, is lying along the lip of a precipice, reaching a hand out, anxious to rescue his patient down there in the darkness, and also desperately hoping that, listening to the bloody horrors they took part in and witnessed, he won't also be pulled down.

John says, "I don't know. It's a gift, I guess."

The shadow reappears, the door is unlocked, and this time it's opened only a foot or so.

The jail attendant stands in the gap, nervous, face pale, no longer holding the kitschy coffee cup.

"Sorry, fellas, none of them wants to see you," he says. "You need to leave. Now."

CHAPTER 13

I WAIT FOR Sheriff Williams to take a breath and I step forward, keeping my voice soft and low. "I'm sorry you feel that way, Sheriff, and with all due respect, I'm not here to play games."

"You got one funny goddamn way of showing it," she says, nearly spitting out the words.

I say, "Sheriff, you have to admit you placed us in a box. You told me we couldn't get access to the crime scene. I respect that. If I didn't, then I would have had Special Agent Sanchez"—I gesture to him, standing about three meters away—"knock that door down and let us in. I didn't do that."

The sheriff folds her arms. "A goddamn good thing you didn't or you and yours would be getting processed right now in my county jail."

I smile, nod, trying to maintain a reassuring look. "I respect that, and appreciate that, Sheriff. Now, if I may, we're all here. It's still early on a Sunday morning. You've been active-duty, you've been exposed to enemy fire and danger in Iraq. Not many people can say that, now, can they? And you know that out in the field you have to bend sometimes to get your job done."

Sheriff Williams lifts an eyebrow. "Like me bending to let you into the crime scene?"

"Sheriff, my detachment and I are here on official business. We need to get into that house. And I'm just asking you—from one Army vet to another—to allow us in."

I wait, then a slight smile appears on her previously hard face, and she lets her arms fall free. "You're a slippery and smart one, I'll give you that. All right, we go in, but no photos, nothing taken from the house, you follow my lead."

"Absolutely."

She nods to me. "And don't forget, Major, I'm a slippery and smart one, too."

I follow her to the wide wooden steps leading to the door of the old home, and she removes the yellow-and-black police tape and gently drapes it on a railing. Up at the door she turns and says, "Years and years ago this was a famous place in our little town. It belonged to a rich fella named Callaghan, owned a shipping company over in Savannah. There's a little lake nearby, and he and his family and rich friends loved coming here during the summer, 'fore air-conditioning came here." She shakes her head. "Yeah, a nice little historical place. Poets, writers, politicians— they all made their way here. Including FDR, like I said earlier. And then the Callaghan family got hit hard during the Great Depression, had to give it up and other properties, and from generation to generation, it came to this. Being rented to a bunch of losers by some property management company. Okay, let me give you a bit of a timeline before we go in."

Behind me, Connie and Manuel have notebooks and pencils in hand, both starting to scribble. She says, "This past Thursday Whitey Klamer, a friend of one of the deceased and a student at Savannah Technical College, came by for what he said was a random visit at about 7:00 a.m. Right. At that hour of the day? Based on what we've found in the house, he was probably coming for a drug buy. Nobody answered his knocks, the door was partially open, he went in, saw what he saw, came out and puked, and then called Dispatch. First unit responded, saw the extent of the crime scene, and I was next, along with everybody else on the force, including retirees."

She squats and points to the hinges, where I note familiar-looking scorch marks and bent metal. "One of the first things I spotted. Look. The Rangers used det cord or some other explosive device to get in. Very quick, very pro." She stands up and takes a folding knife from her pocket, opens it up, and cuts through the seal blocking the entry. "Give me a hand, will you?"

She drags the door to one side, and I do the best I can with one hand, the other one holding on to my cane, and I think, *Good job, Sheriff, putting me in my place and showing us who's still in charge.*

Williams says, "You can bet how much the shit hit the fan when we saw what was in here. My investigators got right to work, and we started canvassing the area."

I ask, "Did you call for help from the Georgia Bureau of Investigation?"

She scoffs. "The GBI? The vampires? Nope, no thank you."

Connie says, "Why do you call them vampires?"

The sheriff turns to Connie and Manuel. "Legend has it vampires can only come into your house if you give 'em permission. Same with the GBI. State law says they can only come in to work with local law enforcement if you let them in. Believe me, not many sheriffs in Georgia want that. Not going to happen in my county. Okay, let's take a look-see."

We cluster just beyond the entrance. My eyes adjust to the dim light. The first thing I see is an overturned couch. There are yellow and orange triangular evidence markers on the scuffed and worn wooden floor, now stained with blood.

Without notes—which I admire—Williams starts reciting the facts of the crime scene, pointing to different areas in the room.

"This is where we found the first three victims," she says. "Gordon Tilly, Randall Gleason, and Sally Tisdale. This TV here was still on when their friend stopped by Thursday morning, paused on some kind of shoot-'em video game. Ironic, huh?"

"Yes," I say. "Very ironic."

We go farther into the home, and I spot more of the plastic triangles on the floor. The counter in the kitchen area has fingerprint dust residue, and the same is on the wooden walls leading to the stairs going up to the second story.

Williams says, "We recovered from the residence two 9mm pistols, a shotgun, and a .308 hunting rifle, along with scales, plastic bags, and about twenty pounds of marijuana. And before you ask, the pistols had not been recently fired."

Manuel says, "Were these people known to you?"

The sheriff shrugs. "Some. But from what I heard from my sources and others, they were strictly small-time, not on my top ten. Upstairs?"

To me, the wide stairs look as daunting as the first time I saw a climbing rope, dangling in a gym when I was in seventh grade at PS 19.

"You go first," I say. "I don't want to hold you up."

Six minutes later, I'm at the top of the stairs, with Williams, Connie, and Manuel all pointedly looking away from me, as I feel how warm my face is, the trickle of sweat down my neck and back, and the burning and screaming coming from my insulted left leg. Fingerprint dust is on the doorframes to both bedrooms.

"Thanks," I say to no one in particular. "Sheriff?"

She takes an audible breath. "Worst scene is in here."

"Then let's get it over with."

We cluster at the entrance to the bedroom while the sheriff goes in, points to a group of evidence triangles on the floor and stains on the floor and against the cracked plaster wall.

"Gina Zachary," she says. "She was found here, shot in the back of the head. Looks like she was trying to protect her little girl... and, well, that's her bloodstain over there."

It's small and cramped in this bedroom, the smells deeper and fouler. I'm breathing through my mouth.

"The bed," she says, not bothering to point. Blood spatter is on the wall where the mattress butts up against it. "Stuart Pike. Shot dead here in bed. His name's on the lease."

Manuel speaks up. "He was in bed?"

"Yes," the sheriff says.

"Okay," Manuel says after a moment.

The sheriff says, "Something wrong?"

"No," Manuel says. "Seems funny, that's all. Downstairs the door gets blown open, there's shooting, running up here, the Rangers are chasing up after them... and he's still in bed."

I keep quiet, and so does Connie.

Williams shrugs. "Maybe he was drunk. Or doped up." She glances at her watch. "One more, right across the way."

We go into the other bedroom, which has two beds. The air is only slightly better in here.

Williams points to blood spatter on the floor. "Last victim. Lillian Zachary. Older sister of Gina. Looks like she was hiding under the bed when she was dragged out and shot."

I look at Manuel and Connie, and they're just taking in the scene. A few seconds pass.

"Sheriff, anything else you can tell us?" I ask.

She rubs at her chin, checks her watch again. "We got two witnesses who put your boys on the scene or heading to the scene. Lady up the way was walking her dog Wednesday night, heard some shouts and gunfire. There's a utility light at the end of the driveway. She saw a pickup truck come down the driveway, haulin' ass. It stopped, and she saw the driver and a passenger. She got a partial plate number 'cause she was spooked by all the noise. We managed to trace it to a Ford F-150 Supercrew registered to Sergeant Jefferson, and she IDed him and another Ranger from a photo lineup we were able to later pull together. After we put out a BOLO for 'em, a Ralston police cruiser spotted the Ford at the Ralston Pub & Grub Friday night, and all four were inside, getting drunk."

"All right," I said. "And the other witness?"

"There's a Gas N' Go about a mile down the road. Owner of the store remembered two of your Rangers coming into the store, kinda wired up. They were dressed in regular Army camo gear, not civilian clothing. Two other fellas were out in the parking lot, smoking. Then they got into the F-150 and headed out, going in the direction of this place. Time stamp says they were at the store 'bout twenty minutes before the lady walking her dog heard the shooting."

Manuel and Connie maintain their composure, but I can sense what they're feeling. This is not looking good for the four Rangers.

I say, "That's very thorough. Thank you, Sheriff."

One more look at her watch. "I'll tell you two other things before I get going. One is that we dusted the area and found prints belonging to two of your Rangers, Staff Sergeant Jefferson and Corporal Barnes. And we recovered shell casings, and they're—"

A chiming sound cuts through the thick air, and the sheriff digs a cell phone out of a rear pocket, slides a finger across the screen, and brings it up to her face. "Sheriff Williams," she says. I can make out the murmur of someone talking to her, and she nods and says, "Okay, okay...Thanks, Bobby, for pushing this one through. Appreciate it. You take care. Best to Mary and the kids."

Her face looks worn as she puts the phone back into her pocket. "That was Bobby Pruitt over at the GBI's forensics lab in Savannah. We seized Sergeant Jefferson's 9mm Beretta pistol when he was arrested Friday night, and Bobby did me a favor, put the pistol right on top of the test list."

"I thought the GBI were vampires."

The sheriff says, "Not when they're staying put in Savannah and helping me out with a solid."

I think we all know what's coming next, which doesn't make it sound any better.

"Sorry, Major," she says. "The shell casings we found here are a match to Sergeant Jefferson's sidearm. The truth is, your Rangers were in this house that night and killed all these people, including that little girl."

CHAPTER 14

AT HUNTER ARMY AIRFIELD—just south of Savannah—Special Agent Connie York parks their Ford rental in front of a three-story brick building, headquarters for the Fourth Battalion, Seventy-Fifth Ranger Regiment, and home to the four Rangers who are in a town jail in Ralston, nearly an hour away. The water tower for the post is visible nearby, and while most of the facility is open land with palmetto trees and southern oaks draped with Spanish moss, the Ranger complex is a post within a post, with high brick walls enclosing it, complete with wire and spikes on top to discourage any unofficial visitors.

Next to her, Major Cook stays silent. He's been quiet on the drive over here after that horrid search of the kill house, although he was quick and pleasant during their earlier meeting on post with Colonel Brenda Tringali, head of the Third MP Group of the CID. She gave them additional information about the four Rangers—the usual and typical complaints of them being drunk and disorderly while off duty, though the initial complaints were never followed up because local law enforcement agencies didn't want to get the Rangers into trouble. When they left her office, Connie said to Cook, "She seemed fairly cooperative, Major."

And he said, "Of course she was cooperative. This case is

white-hot and is going to cause one hell of a mess for the Fourth Battalion here and everybody else on post. Better we outsiders take the heat than her and her MPs."

Connie switches off the car engine. Cook remains quiet, holding his cane in his hands.

"What are you thinking about, sir?" she asks. There have been times when she's felt comfortable enough to banter and joke with him, but not this time.

"I'm thinking about what Sanchez asked, back at the murder house."

Connie says, "About the civilian, Stuart Pike? The one found dead in his bed?"

"That's right," Cook says. "Sanchez made a good point. Why was he still in bed?"

"Maybe the sheriff is right," she says. "Maybe he was drugged, drunk, or passed out."

"Passed out enough so he doesn't at least get off the bed when his girlfriend runs screaming into the bedroom, after the front door gets blasted open?" Cook replies, opening the door. "Come along. We've got work to do."

An hour later, she and Major Cook are still waiting outside the office of Lieutenant Colonel Vincent Marcello, commanding officer of the Fourth Battalion. They are in a small outer office, sitting on a black leather couch, while at his desk an apologetic Major Frank Moore keeps on making excuses for his commanding officer.

Moore says, "I'm sure he'll be free in just a few minutes, Major. I'm so sorry for the wait."

Cook says, "No apologies necessary," but Connie knows exactly what's going on. She and Major Cook are just Army cops, dressed in civilian clothes, and the commanding officer here is putting the two of them in their place. All around them on the walls are photos of the Rangers with the Fourth Battalion, in action in places like Iraq and Afghanistan as well as earlier deployments to Panama and Grenada.

Several helicopters thrum overhead, and not for the first time as a CID agent, Connie thinks of herself as a fraud. She's a tough cop, a good investigator, but she's not a real soldier. She knows that. She and Sanchez are both warrant officers, an odd and mostly overlooked rank between an NCO and an officer, and even though they're supposed equals, Sanchez always likes to rag on her that he's got more field experience with the LAPD and six months more in the CID than she has.

This airfield and those photos and the men and women out there in this hot Georgia heat, they're the real Army. The records of the four Rangers they all examined this morning were certainly eye-opening, with the listings of their duty stations, schools attended, and deployments conducted. The records also displayed what the four accused Rangers overall have achieved: Combat Infantry, Pathfinder, Parachutist, and Air Assault badges, ribbons denoting the Purple Heart and the Bronze Star Medal, plus various other recognitions.

At the time, Connie felt embarrassed. She's known as a *slick sleeve,* her uniform bare of service medals and overseas campaign ribbons. Waiting now for Lieutenant Colonel Marcello, that feeling comes back, of being an imposter among these real soldiers.

Major Moore is wearing camouflage fatigues, and his ink-black hair is closely trimmed. He says, "I still can't believe you're here, and that Sergeant Jefferson and his fire team were arrested. It must be some kind of mistake."

After seeing and hearing all the evidence this Sunday morning, Connie doesn't want to burst the major's bubble, but Cook says, "That's what we're hoping, too. Tell me, do you know them well?"

Moore shakes his head. "They're in Alpha Company. I never interacted much with them, but, man, the stories about them...They're called the Ninja Squad."

"Really?" Cook asks. "Why's that?"

Moore says, "They're superb at moving at night. I mean, everyone can move at night; with NVGs on, it's hard not to. But Sergeant Jefferson and his crew, they take it a step further. It's like...like they're goddamn shadows or something. And Sergeant Jefferson, he's tight with his men. All teams are tight, but Jefferson, his men trust him and follow him, no questions asked. Once I heard how he weeds out newbies who want to be in his section. They go on a night hike, through some deep woods, and Jefferson marches right off a cliff...into a swamp. Fall isn't much, but for Sergeant Jefferson, those who fall with him into the swamp with no hesitation, no questions, they get in. The others...don't."

Connie says, "Sounds impressive...for training."

Moore shakes his head. "Same thing out on deployments. His fire team always gets the tough jobs because they can get them done, no bullshit. He and his team can approach a target farm-house, even with dogs and Taliban guards around, and they can still slip into a compound without anyone noticing, breach the door, and kill everyone before someone can pick up a weapon."

Shit, Connie thinks, *doesn't that sound familiar,* and Moore says, "Thing is, when they get stateside, wow, can they get into—"

When his phone buzzes Moore gives the two of them a big smile. He picks up the receiver and says, "Moore," and after a few nods, he says, "Yes, sir, straightaway."

He hangs up the phone.

"The lieutenant colonel will see you now."

*   *   *

Lieutenant Colonel Vincent Marcello is standing behind his desk, an impressive piece of furniture that Connie thinks is bigger than her bed back at Quantico. The desk is brightly clean, and Marcello continues to stand as he looks down upon a piece of paper. There are the typical in and out baskets, two telephones, and a computer monitor. It's a corner office, filled with light, and souvenirs, plaques, and photos are up on the wall.

Marcello is huge, bulky, like under his camo uniform there are slabs of muscle, and he's bald, the only hair being two bushy black eyebrows.

Without lifting his head, he says, "Major Cook, why are you here?"

After half a beat, Cook says, "Colonel Marcello, my team and I were ordered here to conduct an investigation into—"

"I know that, Major," he cuts in, voice louder, head still bowed down. "But I have a very competent investigator here, Colonel Tringali of the Third MP Group. I trust her and her CID investigators. She even has a positive working relationship with Sheriff Williams over there in Sullivan County, the scene of the crime. So why are you here?"

"Orders, sir."

Marcello finally lifts his head. There's a pink scar running down his right cheek. Connie is suddenly glad that her boss is the focus of the colonel's anger and attention.

"A special squad for a special case?"

"You could say that, sir. We investigate those matters of high priority and high attention, to make sure the accused's rights are preserved but also to ensure that justice is done. Sir."

Marcello stares at her boss. "In other words, you big-foot right in and take over the investigation."

"Not entirely accurate, sir."

"If you say so."

Marcello picks up a pen, signs the document before him. "Well, you're here. You have questions, I'm sure. Ask away."

"Sir, we'd like to interview fellow members of their platoon, to see if—"

"Not going to happen."

From Connie's vantage point, it seems like Cook is really leaning on his cane. The pain in his left leg must be awful this afternoon, with all the walking and standing.

"Sir?" Cook asks.

"Oh, didn't I make myself clear? You cannot and will not interview members of that team's platoon."

"May I ask why, sir?"

"Certainly," Marcello says, opening his center drawer and carefully putting his pen inside, then closing the drawer. "Because we are this nation's firefighters, ready to go anywhere when the president tells us to go. We're trained and equipped to deploy to anywhere in the world within eighteen hours. And in approximately"—he glances at a large watch on his large wrist—"two hours Alpha Company is boarding C-17s to go overseas. And those men don't have time to talk to you. Nor do I, for you see, Major Cook, I'm leaving with them, to join them and Bravo and Charlie Companies."

Connie is growing angrier and angrier with each passing second, hating how the lieutenant colonel is completely ignoring her.

Cook says, "With your deployment, sir, who will be assigned as rear detachment commander?"

A long second or two passes. Marcello says, "Not bad for a former NYPD cop. The rear detachment commander will be Captain Rory O'Connell. He has a few months left before his ETS, so he'll be handling personnel issues and other routine matters for the battalion."

"I'd like to arrange to interview him, sir," Cook says.

"You don't need my permission, Major. But he'll be a busy man, dealing with the battalion's affairs." Another glance at his watch. "You have time for one more question, Major. Make it a good one."

Cook says, "Sir, these four men under your command, they are in serious trouble, having been arrested in connection with the violent deaths of seven civilians. At some point in our investigation would you consider being a character witness for them?"

Connie is surprised at how quickly and violently Marcello delivers his one-sentence answer. "Not on your life."

Cook says, "Sir…if I may…why is that?"

Marcello looks at his watch one more time. "In the field, there is no squad that I'd rather have at my back than Sergeant Jefferson's. But we're not always in the field. Since they've been CONUS, they've been a constant pain to me. Some years ago, Major, a predecessor to my battalion command saw his career ruined because his Rangers acted wild on post and off. That's not going to happen to me. As far as I'm concerned, the quicker those four are convicted and sent off to prison the better."

Cook says, "I see, sir."

"Glad you do," the colonel says.

CHAPTER 15

EVEN WITH HIS rental car's air-conditioning, Special Agent Manuel Sanchez has sweated through his suit coat, shirt, and trousers, and his miserable day out in rural Georgia is not even close to being over. Following the tour of The Summer House—now forever to be known in their official paperwork as *the murder house*—Major Cook and Special Agent York headed off to Hunter Army Airfield. Lieutenant Huang and Captain Pierce were sent to the nearby town of Ralston to interview the four jailed Rangers.

Cook said to Sanchez, "The sheriff said a woman witness was out walking her dog the night of the killings. That means she's around here. Go find her and talk to her."

But as Sanchez quickly learned, *around here* is a pretty wide swath of mostly empty land.

The nearest two dirt roads off the main road led to nothing but dead-end turnarounds, sprinkled with empty beer cans, broken cardboard boxes, and plenty of shot-up targets and broken bottles.

The third dirt lane led to an empty house.

The fourth dirt driveway ended at a worn and sagging gray house, where a heavyset, tattooed, bearded man wearing cut-off jean shorts and rubber boots up to his knees—and no shirt—came out onto the leaning porch with an old couch taking up most of it, eyed Sanchez as he identified himself, and then said, "You're not one of those Jehovah's Witness types, are you?"

"No, sir," he said. "Like I said, I'm a special agent in the US Army, conducting an investigation."

"About what?"

"The people who were murdered up the road, at the place called The Summer House."

The man scratched at his hairy belly and said, "Don't know nothing about that. But if you do see any Witnesses in your travels, tell 'em not to bother knockin' on my door. My soul ain't worth saving."

Now he's at a third house, going down a short but wide dirt driveway that has a campaign sign at its entrance—REELECT SHERIFF WILLIAMS—and when he gets out of the silver Ford sedan, he hears a dog barking from inside the single-story ranch-style home, with yellow clapboards, black shutters, and peeling paint.

A good sign.

He walks up to the wide front porch, taking everything in. There's a parked Volkswagen Beetle—a new model, though rusted and battered some—and a sagging clothesline, and an old washer-dryer combo dumped to the side. He takes a step up onto the porch, the dog barking even louder, and knocks on the door. The porch has two chairs whose upholstery is torn, letting some stuffing dangle out. There's a water bowl on the wooden planks, and the door leading into the house has deep gouges, like a dog is used to scratching it, begging to come inside.

He knocks twice more before a woman cautiously opens the door. "Yes?" she asks.

The woman is in her late forties or early fifties, face worn and tired, her gray-black hair pulled back in a ponytail. She's wearing a floral housecoat that she's grasping around her neck, and she's keeping the screen door closed.

"Ma'am, sorry to bother you, but I'm Special Agent Manuel Sanchez of the US Army."

Her tired eyes widen. "The Army? For real?"

"Yes, ma'am," he says. "Here's my badge and identification."

He holds his leather wallet up to the screen, and the woman gives it a quick glance and says in a voice that's almost a hoarse whisper, "What's the Army doing around here?"

"I'm part of a team investigating the murders of seven civilians who lived up the road, at The Summer House," he says. "Four Army personnel have been arrested."

The woman looks uneasy, and Sanchez says, "I've talked to Sheriff Williams about her investigation. She said a woman walking her dog saw a Ford pickup truck leave the house right after the shootings. It was you, correct?"

He waits.

Behind the woman the barking dog is louder and louder.

Sanchez wonders if he should press her when she says, "That's right."

Finally, he thinks, and he opens the screen door and gently presses himself into the house. "I promise, this will only take a few minutes."

Inside the house, a large dog that looks to be a brown mongrel with large floppy ears leaps up and nearly knocks Sanchez on his ass. He backpedals as the woman says, "Toby, Toby, you knock that off, right now!'

A large smear of dog drool hits Sanchez's pants leg as the dog barrels past him and bursts through the open front doors, howling and barking in apparent joy after breaking free.

She closes both doors and says, "That Toby. He sure has a spirit 'bout him. When he wants to run, he runs. When he don't want to come in, he don't come in."

Sanchez quickly takes in the house. Before him and to the left is a kitchen area, and to the right is a small living room. Behind him is a small coatrack with a light jacket, a raincoat, and an umbrella hanging from pegs. There's another water bowl and a half filled dog bowl below the coatrack.

He's still looking around when he says, "Ma'am, I'm sorry, I don't recall your name."

"Oh," she says. "Wendy. Wendy Gabriel. Would you like to sit down?"

The interior of the house is relatively cool after spending the last couple of hours traipsing outside in the hot Georgia sun, but Sanchez isn't sure how to reply. The interior of the house is so crowded and cluttered that he can't believe it's still standing. There are piles of newspapers, magazines, stuffed cardboard boxes, folded-up clothes, more newspapers, and more magazines, and mail...hundreds of pieces, it looks like. A hollowed-out area in the living room reveals a worn couch and a television set, and a nightstand piled with bags of dog treats and candy.

A hoarder, he thinks, but he gives the woman credit: she's a neat hoarder. Everything seems to be in its place, though there are lots of places.

"This way," she says, and they go into the kitchen, where there's a lonely uncluttered chair. Wendy picks up thick piles of *Newsweek* magazines—the top one has a photo of Ronald Reagan on the cover—and he sits down.

"Thank you, ma'am. I promise I won't stay long."

She sits down, too, hand still holding the housecoat closed. "Those killings...horrible, simply horrible. My God. Is the Army going to arrest them, too?"

"The crimes were committed off post, ma'am, so it's under civilian police authority," he says, taking out a small notebook and pencil. "But the Army still wants to know what happened, the how and the why."

She says, "But how come you're not in uniform?"

Which is approximately the nine hundredth time Sanchez has been asked this, and he says, "I'm with the Army's Criminal Investigation Division. We usually wear civilian clothes because it helps us blend in while we're doing our job. Now, if I may . . ."

He flips open to a blank page in the notebook and says, "Sheriff Williams told me that you witnessed a Ford F-150 pickup truck leaving the residence sometime Wednesday night. Do you recall what time it was?"

She says, "Oh, yes, without a doubt. A bit after 8:00 p.m., right after *Jeopardy!* was over. I was taking Toby for a walk."

"Along the main road, then, right?"

"That's right," she says.

"And what did you see?"

She shifts in her chair. "We were heading home. We were on the side of the road where the dirt path leads into that place where the college kids were stayin'. The one everyone calls The Summer House. Is it true, they was all shot? And a baby girl, too?"

He nods. "True, I'm sorry to say. What did you hear? Or see?"

Wendy wipes at her eyes. "So sad. So very, very sad . . . Well, it wasn't sad then, it was just strange, that's all. I was with Toby, and I heard a loud bang, like a truck was backfiring. Then a bit of gunfire . . . not loud, but like . . . well, like they were shooting from the bottom of a well. Now, I know what regular shooting sounds like, but maybe it sounded different because it was inside, not outside? You know what I mean?"

"That I do," he says. "And did you hear anything else?"

"Well, before the shooting happened, a helicopter flew over. And after the shooting stopped, we walked another minute or two, and just by that dirt road, this Ford pickup is driving real fast and nearly runs me and Toby down. They stopped for just a second, and then they sped off, went north."

"Did you see who was driving?"

"This real angry-looking black man, and there was another fella sitting next to him. They both looked at me, and, Christ, I was scared. I don't know why, but the way they looked at me, they frightened me some."

"Had you ever seen those men before?"

"Nope."

Sanchez is taking notes, mind dancing along, knowing that when this case comes to trial, she's going to be one hell of a witness for the county.

"Ma'am, Sheriff Williams says you remembered the license plate of the truck. Is that right?"

"That's right."

"Well, excuse me for saying this, but did you write it down?"

"Nope."

"Had you seen the truck before in the area?"

"Nope."

"Then . . ."

The first smile of his visit appears. "You're asking me how I remembered what I saw? Easy. I like doing them puzzle books, you know, fill in the blanks and the crossword puzzles? Letters and numbers, they stick with me. I remembered the first three letters and the first number . . . afraid I didn't catch the rest."

"And what was that?"

"The letters *T-B-B*, followed by the numeral 3. The sheriff later told me, when she thanked me for being a witness and picking those photos of those two fellas, she said she was able to trace down the letters and number and match it to that angry black guy driving the truck."

"But the letters and the numeral 3? Why did you remember that?"

"Easy," she says. "*T* for Toby. And *B-B* because I call him Baby all the time. And the number 3—that's how old he is. Toby Baby 3."

Sanchez writes that down, as Toby Baby remains outside, howling and running.

"Ma'am, when did you learn about the murders?"

"When Deputy Coulson, when he came by the next day, asking me if I saw anything in the area the night before. I told him and gave him the license plate letters and number, and a few hours later, I was at the county building, talking to the sheriff."

There you go, Sanchez thinks, and he says, "Ma'am, is there anything else you can tell me? Anything else at all?"

She shakes her head, the smile fading, still looking tired and discarded. "No, I can't think of anything."

Sanchez takes out his business card, passes it over. "Ma'am, thanks so much for your help. I greatly appreciate it. This card has the number for my cell phone and my office. You think of anything, anything at all, call me at any time."

He gets up, and the woman looks at both sides of the card and says, "Is there a reward?"

Sanchez says, "If I find out there's one, you'll be the first to know."

He gives the place one good last glance, from the piles of dirty dishes in the sink to the endless piles of mail and other junk to the two coats and umbrella hanging from the coatrack to the water bowl and bowl of food. There are also three doggie chew toys, neatly lined up. Two covered plastic bins neatly filled with dry dog food. A shelf that holds a grooming brush and small boxes of dog vitamins and pills.

Wendy opens the door, leading the way out, and yells, "Toby! Toby Baby! Come back home now! You come!"

He goes to his car, gives the woman a pleasant wave, gets into the car, and starts up the engine, letting the cold air just wash over him.

Sanchez makes a turn and then heads away from the woman's home, wondering why Wendy Gabriel lied to him.

CHAPTER 16

CAPTAIN ALLEN PIERCE is lost, a feeling he hates, and he turns around once more in the town of Sullivan, looking for the district attorney's office. Twice he has parked at the county courthouse, which also holds the sheriff's department and is next to the county jail, and both times the doors were locked, even though an earlier phone call to the district attorney said he would be waiting for Allen in his office.

What the hell is going on here? Are the locals making fun of the Army outsiders and laughing while seeing them go around in circles? There's been a group of residents sitting on benches across the way at a park that proudly boasts a Confederate Army soldier statue, and Allen is feeling that's exactly what's going on.

He looks at his iPhone, checks the address for District Attorney Cornelius Slate, sees the address, and—

The numbers don't match.

On the wooden sign near the parking lot is the number 44, noting the street address for the county buildings.

Slate's address is listed as 62 Sullivan Highway, also known as Route 119. Not in the county buildings after all.

He pulls out of the parking lot.

Fool, he thinks. Overreacting.

And lost to boot.

Fifteen minutes later, Allen's in a renovated, light-yellow Victorian house where Cornelius Slate shares space with a dentist's office. The heavyset, cheerful man putters around his crowded office, offering him coffee from a Keurig machine, talking about the weather, and inquiring about Allen's travels. On a hardwood floor covered with dusty Oriental rugs sit bookshelves and filing cabinets, and framed black-and-white photos of what looks to be downtown Sullivan hang on the wall.

Slate is in his sixties, paunchy, wearing dark-green trousers with suspenders and a striped shirt, sleeves rolled up his beefy forearms. His head is fleshy, white hair combed back in a pompadour, and his black-rimmed reading glasses are perched halfway down his nose.

"Sorry I'm late," Allen says for the third time since arriving.

"Ah, don't worry about it," Slate replies, making a dismissive wave of his hand. "Not all district attorneys in Georgia are high-paid employees of the county, hanging out in fancy courthouses. You get out of one of those urban counties like Chatham, where Savannah is, it gets rural real quick. There's not enough crime around here to maintain a full-time district attorney, so I have my own practice and step up to the plate when need be. Which is an honor but can also cut down on some of my billable hours, not able to defend a client 'cause of the conflict of interest."

"Have you been district attorney that long?" he asks.

"Ten years, and two more, God willing, if the good folks here in Sullivan County decide to return me to office."

Allen holds the warm cup in his hands. "I've seen the campaign signs. For you, the sheriff, the congressman, others."

"It's that time of year," he says. "Tell me, young fella, you seem a smart sort. Where did you go to school? How did you end up in the Army?"

"I went to Columbia," Allen says. "One of my professors...he had been a first responder on 9/11 before going to law school. He died young of cancer, probably from working at the Towers after they came down."

Slate nods. "Revenge, then."

Allen corrects him. "Justice. And have you always practiced law here?"

The district attorney grins. "Sure looks like it, the messy office I got, the town where I live. Nope, I went to George Mason and then worked corporate law for Georgia-Pacific for lots of years. Ended up with a fat paycheck and sleepless nights. Quit Georgia-Pacific. Now I have a small paycheck and I sleep like the proverbial baby."

Then he shakes his head and says, "Well, what a mess, eh? All those murders, those four Rangers arrested. And at The Summer House at that. What a goddamn shame, to see a lovely place like that get run-down and dirty, and then have all those folks get shot inside. A real damn shame."

Slate leans back in his old-style office chair, which loudly creaks. "I can see why the Army sent a fella like you down here, but what's your job? To defend them?"

"No," Allen says, sipping the coffee, which is one of those vanilla blended-spice types he despises. "I'm part of an investigative unit assigned to high-profile crimes like this. We're looking to gather information, ensure that all the facts are known."

"I see," Slate says, his hands folded over his belly. "You also had a Chinaman with you this morning, over at the Ralston jail. Where is he now?"

Allen has never served overseas in either Iraq or Afghanistan, but he's sure the hair rising on the back of his neck is coming from knowing he and the others are under constant surveillance.

"He's on other duties," Allen says, still hating the coffee, wanting to correct this small-town, small-minded lawyer about using an ethnic slur to describe a fellow officer, but right now he needs information.

"Well, what can I do for you? What do you need to know?"

"I don't know much about Georgia criminal law, so I'm looking for a quick guide," Allen says. "I know it's early, but do you anticipate indicting the four of them for first-degree murder or second-degree murder?"

Slate has a cheery smile on his face. "Neither."

"Excuse me?" Allen asks, feeling warm, like the older man is enjoying putting him in his place.

"I guess you do need some guidance after all," Slate says. "In Georgia, we don't have first-degree or second-degree murder. We have malice murder, felony murder, and voluntary manslaughter, among others. Of course, it all depends on the grand jury meeting after the official arraignment for your Rangers."

"When do you expect the arraignment?"

"Thursday or Friday of next week. Grand jury will take a bit longer."

"On my flight down I read that most Georgia counties have grand juries that meet every Wednesday. True?"

Slate shakes his head. "Haven't you figured out yet, we're not a usual county? In Sullivan County we meet every six months for a grand jury."

Allen is stunned. A half year wait for an indictment?

"For real?" he asks.

"Do I look like I'm joking, son?" Slate asks. "Nope. Six months is typical, though I imagine with a case like this one, we'll be able to rearrange things, move it up some. In the meantime, those four fellas will have an opportunity to have a bond hearing, to see if they can be released prior to the indictment. Which I doubt. But any way you look at it, these fellas won't be going to trial for a year to eighteen months. We're a busy state down here."

"I see," Allen says.

Slate says, "Those four Rangers, they sure didn't want to talk to you this morning."

"That's their right," he says. "Since they were arrested outside their post, they'll have to arrange for their own civilian defense."

"But would you advise 'em if they asked?"

"Not me personally," Allen says. "But I'm sure someone in JAG could lend assistance. But JAG lawyers are trained to deal with the military justice system, not the civilian system."

"Sounds complicated," Slate says.

"It can be," Allen says.

Slate is still smiling, and then—like a flash of lightning illuminating a night landscape—the smile disappears and Slate frowns, his eyes narrowing and darkening, his fingers clasping tighter across his stomach.

"But know this, and know this well, and tell your boss, son, whoever the hell he or she might be," Slate says, his voice low and steady. "Sheriff Emma Williams is one tough and smart investigator, a real bitch on wheels. If she's arrested those four Rangers so quick after all those boys and girls and that baby was killed, then she's got a solid case that she's gonna give to me when the time is right."

Allen stares quietly at the old man.

The district attorney says, "So, son, I'm gonna tell you this. It might take a year, eighteen months, or even two years, but I'm gonna find those Rangers guilty, and I'm gonna make sure they end up on death row and someday get a needle in their veins. You got that?"

"I got that," Allen says.

"Good!" The smile returns, and Slate moves his chair forward. "Anything else?"

Allen stands up, reaches over, puts his barely touched coffee cup on the district attorney's desk.

"Just one more thing," Allen says. "I'm a commissioned officer in the United States Army and an attorney admitted to the New York and Virginia bar. Unless you spent some time wandering around Long Island thirty or so years ago and had a brief affair with my mother, don't call me son, ever again."

He turns and quickly walks out.

CHAPTER 17

LIEUTENANT JOHN HUANG is sitting on a park bench across the street from the Ralston Police Department, just waiting. It's been several hours since he and Allen Pierce visited the police department's jail and were turned away, and when Allen said he was going to visit the district attorney, John said he would stay behind.

"And do what?" Allen asked.

"Talk to the Rangers."

"How?"

And John said, "By using my wily Asian ways. How else?"

The day has been long, sitting here in the shade, reading articles on his iPhone from back issues of *Journal of Psychiatric Practice,* and once going into the nearby small convenience store to grab lunch. The young lady wearing jeans and a blue smock with ADDY on her name tag took his money and passed over a wrapped ham-and-cheese sandwich and a bottle of Lipton iced tea, then she said, "Mind if I ask you a question?"

"Go ahead," he said, knowing what was coming next.

"What are you?" she asked. "Huh? Do you mind? Japanese? Korean? What are you?"

He scooped up his lunch and change and said, "Californian."

Now he waits.

Earlier and separated by thirty or so minutes, two different sets of dark-blue Ford vans pulled up across the street, with film crews and correspondents tumbling out and, nearly just as quickly, tumbling back in, having been turned away by the ever-vigilant jail attendant and bikini inspector.

John sips from the now-warm Lipton tea.

The guy was doing a pretty good job.

A white Dodge Ram pickup truck comes down the road, turns into the lot, stopping next to the red Dodge Colt. A tall, thin woman gets out, wearing the same type of uniform as the male attendant, and she sprints to the rear door of the jail.

John checks the time. It's 5:10 in the afternoon.

He's thinking someone's late and—

There goes the bikini inspector, into his Colt, and his tires squeal as he gets out onto the main street, back into whatever Sunday afternoon life awaits him.

John dips into his soft leather briefcase and pulls out a necktie, which he quickly secures around his neck.

Now it's time to get to work.

It feels good to walk across to the jail, stretching his legs, and he goes up to the familiar door with the sign and rings the doorbell, and rings it once more.

A shadow appears as before, but it's the woman attendant now, red hair tousled, face flushed and perspiring, and she says, "How can I—"

He grabs the door, opens it wider. "Sorry I'm late," he says. "I'm here to see Specialist Tyler."

"Hey, uh, what—"

He pushes past her and says, "Is he ready? I won't take long."

The woman steps in front of him. "Hold on. Just who the hell are you?"

John lets her stand for a few seconds and then shapes his face into surprised anger. "You don't know? Honestly? Before he went hunting today, Chief Kane told me it was going to be all arranged. Hold on."

He grabs his regular wallet, takes out his Virginia driver's license, flashes it in front of the poor young woman, and says, "I'm Dr. John Huang of the US Army Medical Corps. I flew in a while ago from Washington, DC. I'm here to personally interview the four Rangers, starting with Specialist Tyler."

The woman bites her lower lip. John chose Tyler for a reason, for according to the briefing he received last night at the motel, Tyler is the youngest of the four.

"Why are you here?" she asks.

"Ma'am, that's medical information, and that's confidential," he says, putting an edge into his voice. "Now, will you bring Specialist Tyler to me, or are we going to have to wait here until Chief Kane returns from Sweeney's Tract and have him order you directly? And then have another conversation with you later? Ma'am?"

Her shoulders slump. "Hold on."

"Don't mind if I do," John says.

Ten minutes later, he's in a small meeting room, with one-way glass built into the wall, a table bolted to the floor, and two black plastic chairs. He's sitting in one chair and Specialist Vinny Tyler is sitting in the other, wearing an orange jumpsuit that says RALSTON PD JAIL in faded black letters on the back.

John is smiling and gracious with the young man, who's got a lot of muscles and strength under that jail clothing. His red hair is trimmed short, and there's stubble on his chin and cheeks. His eyes look green. His face is pale, but he constantly looks around the room with suspicion, like he's waiting for a net to drop from the ceiling or for the sprinklers to start spraying out water.

John says, "Specialist, I'm Lieutenant John Huang, a psychiatrist with the Army's Medical Corps. How are you doing? How's the food? Are the staff treating you well?"

His eyes continue to flick around the room. "Doing okay. Food sucks, but I've eaten worse. And the staff seems to be just one guy or gal, so that's about it. Why are you here?"

"Here to talk to you."

"About what?"

John shrugs, leans back in his chair, and relaxes his legs and arms in an open position, wanting the Ranger before him to see John not as a threat but as a possible ally or even friend.

"About whatever you'd like," he says. "Where you grew up. Why you joined the Army. Why you became a Ranger...I've seen the training courses you guys have to go through. Incredibly difficult, aren't they?"

The specialist doesn't take the bait. His eyes have stopped flickering. They're boring right into John.

He continues. "Or you can talk about your deployments. The missions you were on. What you saw, what you did."

Tyler moves his wrists, like he still can't believe he's manacled.

"Or why me and the team got arrested for what happened over in Sullivan," the Ranger calmly says, like he's reading out a map grid of numbers and letters. "You want me to talk about that?"

Defiance, John thinks. *He's talking but there's will and defiance there.*

"If you'd like," he says.

"Sure," he says. "Then you'd use it against me. Right?"

"Not exactly," he says. "But I need to inform you, Specialist, that I'm here as a psychiatrist, attached to a special investigative CID unit. I'm not here to represent you as a patient."

"Meaning what?"

"Meaning that what I learn in talking with you will be part of the CID's investigation into what might have happened that led to your arrest."

"A cop."

"No," Huang says. "A doctor who's looking for truth."

"To use against me."

"To be used in seeking justice," Huang says. "To find out who you are, what you're thinking, to see if there are any extenuating circumstances. To make this CID investigation fair and complete. You have my word."

The young man's eyes continue to drill into him. John doesn't yet know the specifics of his service, but he knows from experience the outline of what this hard young man has done. Rangers are the proverbial tip of the spear. They go in hard and fast and get the job done. They are sent into the hottest and most dangerous places, and even though in another life Specialist Tyler could have been an automotive technician or a home contractor, John is under no illusions.

This young man before him has killed in the service of his country, and has seen friends of his wounded, maimed, and killed right beside him.

"Your word..." Tyler says, dragging the two words out. "You think I'd trust the word of a pogue?"

Pogue, John recalls—person other than a grunt.

"I would hope so."

"What do you know about me, 'bout what I do?" he starts demanding. "You ever go overseas? You ever been in a pit in a forward base, hearing the mortars whistle in? You ever shove wads of combat gauze into a buddy who's bleeding out? You ever been up against some sandbags, and all of a sudden sand pours down on your head and you hear the gunshot from the sniper who almost drilled one into your forehead?"

John says, "I don't think that really—"

Tyler quickly changes the subject. "You a virgin, Doc?"

"That's something I'm not here to talk about," he says.

A jingle-jangle of the handcuffs as Tyler moves his hands. "Oh, yeah, it is. You know what I mean. There's a whole lot of difference 'tween reading about having great sex with a hot chick and actually doing it. No books, no magazines, no porn videos, nothing is like the real deal. That's the difference between you and me, although we're both Army. You just don't know what it's like out in combat."

John has heard this before, and he says, "Then why did you agree to talk to me?"

Tyler struggles, sits back in the chair, blinks his eyes, looks down at the dirty tiled floor, and then looks up again.

"Sometimes the guilt just gets so hot and raw you need to talk to someone other than your team buddies," Tyler says, his voice softer. "When things don't go right . . . when innocents pop up . . ."

His voice softly dribbles away to heavy silence.

"Please tell me more," John says, putting as much sympathy and empathy as he can into his voice. *We've made progress, we're opening him up, this is going to work.* He's looking forward to reporting back to Major Cook what he's about to find out.

"Please," John repeats. "Talk to me."

Tyler gets up, chair scraping, cuffed hands before him.

"No," he says. "I've changed my mind."

CHAPTER 18

TIME PASSES SLOWLY, but Staff Sergeant Caleb Jefferson is in no rush. Earlier, when Specialist Tyler unexpectedly left, he whispered quick orders to Barnes and Ruiz, the other members of his fire team, about what to do next, and like the good men they are, they followed his orders.

A door opens up with a metallic *clunk,* and the woman jail attendant—Marcy—brings Ruiz in, putting him back into his cell, and Jefferson stands up.

Marcy comes to the old-fashioned barred cell door and says, "Your turn, Sergeant Jefferson, if you wish."

"Yes, ma'am."

"You promise to be a gentleman, like before?"

"Absolutely, ma'am."

"You know what's next."

"I do, ma'am."

He puts his hands through a slot in the bars so Marcy can handcuff them, and after the shackles snap into place, he steps back, as she uses a large metal key on a wooden stick to unlock the door.

With the cell door open, she gestures him forward, and he follows her direction. She and the other jailers seem in awe of him and his team, which is just fine, because they are widely ignorant of what he and they are capable of.

Jefferson thinks that in under a minute he could hurt and disable Marcy, free himself, Barnes, Tyler, and Ruiz, and get out of this small town in under ten minutes, never to be seen again.

It's certainly something to think about.

In the small interrogation room, he stares at the Army psychiatrist as he pulls his chair up close to the small table and lets his handcuffed hands and thick arms stretch across the tabletop, invading Dr. John Huang's personal space.

Jefferson knows a lot about shooting people, leading men, and blowing things up, but he also knows a bit of how an officer's mind works.

Huang is slim, well dressed, and of Chinese descent. To Jefferson, this means he's come from the kind of strict Asian upbringing in which Mom and Dad force their children to be 100 percent at all times. Tiger moms and tiger dads. He, on the other hand, grew up in Gilmor Homes in Baltimore, living with his grandmother, Mom in jail and Dad gone, and the street education he got there was probably one hell of a lot rougher and to the point than what the good doctor experienced.

"So," Jefferson says, "what do you want?"

Huang is leaning back in his chair, trying to look cool and inviting, and Jefferson will have none of that. His brown eyes are tight and intelligent, and the staff sergeant is going to be cautious with this bright man, even if he's probably never picked up a weapon since Basic.

"You came to see me," the doctor says. "Why is that?"

Jefferson says, "You came here and specifically asked for Specialist Tyler. That's why I'm in this room with you. To see what you did to him. He's the youngest member of my team. You trying to tempt him, break him?"

The doctor says, "I just wanted to talk to him."

"How did it go?"

"It went fine."

Jefferson smiles. "How did the other two interviews go? Not as well?"

"They went fine," the doctor repeats.

Jefferson slightly shakes his head. "Oh, come on, Doc. It didn't go well so don't bullshit me. I've got one hell of a good bullshit detector, built and polished over the years, working with upstanding officers like you. Don't tell me otherwise."

He says, "Fair enough. I won't bullshit you. And I'll say the other two men—Barnes and Ruiz—were quiet. And formidable. They barely went beyond name and rank. And said you were the best staff sergeant they've ever served with."

"Not surprised," Jefferson says. "They're the best I've ever led. Now. Back to the original question. What . . . do . . . you . . . want?"

"To talk to you and your men," Huang says. "You've been arrested. All four of you are facing serious charges."

"That's like telling me the sun just set," Jefferson says. "You've got to do better than that."

Huang tries to maintain his composure, but Jefferson knows he's getting under the doctor's skin. Jefferson says, "You want to talk to me. Fine. I'll save us all a bunch of time and tell you what's what."

Huang says, "All right. I'm curious to hear what you have to say."

Jefferson makes a point of leaning over a bit more. "Just a question before I begin. You ever been out in the field?"

"I don't see how—"

"Lieutenant, I get an answer or I'm out of here."

Huang doesn't look happy. "No," he says.

"All right, let's put it out there. My men and I, we don't fight for God, country, or whatever clown is sitting in the Oval Office. We fight for one another or our platoon or our battalion. That is *it*. When you're in a trench in the middle of the night and the *muj* are coming through the wire, sending RPG rounds your way, you may hate the guy next to you for stealing your clean socks last week, but by God, you've got his back."

Huang sits quietly, and Jefferson says, "And who's got our back? The Army? JAG? CID? You? Anybody else?"

The doctor says, "I can help. You tell me what's going on, what happened, I might be able to—"

"Help in what way?" Jefferson asks. "Are you going to get that county sheriff to set us free? Think the district attorney won't indict us? You think the families of those folks in that old historical house are going to forget what happened? You going to tell CID that it was all a mistake and put pressure on the county sheriff to let us go?"

Huang snaps to. "You're telling me that you and your squad were in that house, Staff Sergeant?"

Jefferson withdraws his hands, puts them in his lap. That was stupid, getting angry like that.

"That's enough," Jefferson says. "Enough."

Huang slowly unfolds himself from his chair and leans over the table. "Tell me, Sergeant. Tell me what happened in that home. Why were you there? Did they shoot first? Did you respond automatically, not able to stop?"

Jefferson says, "You like being a doctor?"

"What?" Huang asks, confused. "Yes, yes I do."

Jefferson slowly stands up. "I love docs, honest to God I do. Combat medics in the field, shit, they are the goddamn best. Mortar rounds exploding around you, grenades flying overhead, rounds whipping near you…you hunker down so hard you want to dig a hole eight meters deep with your hands. But when a guy gets a piece of shrapnel in his neck, when somebody screams out, 'I'm hit, I'm hit, Medic,' those guys jump up and run out and do their job. God, I love 'em and respect them."

He turns, anger building in him. "But not you, Lieutenant. You're a goddamn head doc, worthless. And if you come talk to my squad again without my permission, one of these days I'll track you down and hurt you. Bad."

CHAPTER 19

SPECIAL AGENT MANUEL SANCHEZ pulls over to the side of the road in his rented Ford sedan, yawns, rubs at his eyes. It's been one long grueling day, for after his interview with Wendy Gabriel he decided to continue going up and down Route 119, interviewing other households that might have witnesses to what happened on Wednesday night.

Not surprisingly, the interviews went bust. He's talked to two men, three women, and two young boys, in a variety of rural houses and mobile homes, up and down this lonely stretch of Georgia state highway, and no one saw a thing. Lunch was a bottle of orange Fanta and two packages of peanuts from a service station's vending machine just outside Sullivan.

He checks the car's clock. It's just after 8:00 p.m., the time when Wendy said she saw the pickup truck owned by Staff Sergeant Jefferson leave the kill house four nights ago. The dirt driveway to The Summer House and a utility pole with a single streetlight are up ahead.

Time to see what Wendy claims she saw.

He puts the car in drive, goes to the driveway, and backs in a couple of meters. Sanchez leaves the engine in park, gets out, and walks in the glare of the headlights, out to the road.

He turns around, looks at the Ford sedan. Even with the glare of the headlights it's easy to make out the license plate. He goes back to the car, flicks off the headlights, leaving the amber parking lights on.

There.

Still visible.

He stands on the road, looks up at the streetlight. It's an old streetlight, the kind with a large bulb screwed into a metal dome. The light is yellow and weak, gradually fading in and out.

Interesting.

He looks around at the scenery. So dark, so empty. Just brooding, heavy trees. The bare pavement. So quiet, save for insects out there, and night birds and a dog barking. Toby Baby? Maybe. So very, very different from the constant lights, noise, horns, engines, and music back home in LA.

Sanchez goes back to the car, switches off even the parking lights, and then returns to the road.

The overhead utility light is still bright enough to make out the license plate. Not crystal clear but enough to do the job, for someone to get the first three letters and a number.

"There you go," he whispers.

His jacket feels clammy and confining on him, so he takes it off, folds it in half, and then stops.

A car or truck engine, out there.

He turns.

No headlights.

He looks back at the sedan.

Walks to it, opens the door, drapes the jacket—a Brooks Brothers coat with shiny buttons his wife, Conchita, bought for him when he got a promotion last year—over the driver's seat, so the buttons are facing up.

He switches on the headlights.

Goes back to the road.

The license plate is clear. The color of the car is easy to make out, as well as the car brand.

That's it.

He returns to the car, switches off the headlights, puts on the parking lights once more.

Goes back to the road.

Waits.

The overhead utility light fades in and out, the yellow light faint.

An engine loudly starts up, and his LAPD instincts kick in as he leaps away from the road, just as a pickup truck roars by, so close he feels the warmth from the exhaust pipe. The truck races down the road and brakes, squealing rubber.

The truck's lights are doused.

It waits, somewhere down the road.

Sanchez's SIG Sauer is in his hands. He doesn't remember pulling it from his holster. He quickly goes to the Ford, switches off the parking lights. He drops to one knee, holding the pistol in both hands, over the hood of his rental car.

The truck is still there.

Engine running loudly.

No lights. No voices. No honky-tonk tunes coming from within. He's pretty sure the driver switched off the engine some ways back and coasted down here before roaring by, to catch him by surprise.

Sanchez wishes he could trade the rented sedan for one of the unit cars he used back when he was a cop. Then at least he'd have some heavier firepower, a Remington 870 pump-action shotgun or a Bushmaster .223 semiautomatic rifle with a thirty-round magazine.

The driver revs the engine.

Sanchez whispers, "Come on, *pendejo,* come on back and let's play."

Another squeal of rubber and the truck roars down the highway, and a few seconds later, its headlights and taillights flick on, like the driver is taunting him.

Sanchez stands up, puts the SIG Sauer back in its holster.

The overhead streetlight is still weak, and he looks into the car interior and sees not a thing.

CHAPTER 20

STAFF SERGEANT CALEB JEFFERSON stares at his late-night visitor and says, "How the hell did you get in here?"

Major Frank Moore, executive officer for the Fourth Battalion, says, "I spun a tale. What else? I told the jail attendant I really, really needed to see you, and she wouldn't let me in, and then I pulled the weary war vet who needs help bullshit story."

Jefferson says, "And that got you here?"

Moore shakes his head. "Nah. I had to promise to give her a helicopter ride next week."

"Sir, you need to leave, right now," Jefferson says. "This isn't helping."

"But you need to know a couple of things, and I sure as hell don't trust the phones here or at the post," Moore says.

The major is a good guy and has run interference for him several times with the battalion commander, Lieutenant Colonel Marcello, but Moore's exposing himself, being an hour away from post and at this town jail.

"All right, sir, but please, make it quick."

The major is still in his fatigues, and he lowers his voice. "The battalion commander was interviewed earlier today by two CID investigators."

"I'm sure Marcello told the investigators what fine, upstanding troopers we are."

Moore smiles. "I had my ear to the door. He threw all of you under the bus, you know, the heavy-duty one with spiked tires."

"You drove out here to tell me this?" Jefferson asks.

"Staff Sergeant, I'm an officer, but I try not to be stupid," he says. "The crew that's here, looking into things...it's not a typical CID investigation. They're here from Quantico, and they're going to poke into anything and everything."

"I know that," Jefferson says. "My guys and I were interviewed a few hours ago by a shrink, trying to find out what makes us tick."

"What did you tell him?"

Jefferson says, "I told the nosy little shit I wet the bed a lot when I was a kid and had mommy issues. What do you think?"

"This isn't a joking matter, Sergeant."

"Again, you drove out here to tell me that, sir?" he asks. "Major Moore, did they talk to you as well?"

"That they did," Moore says. "I told them I hardly knew you and your squad."

"Good job, sir," he says, pleased that this officer, at least, is on the beam. "Is there anything else?"

"Your aunt Sophie called me," he says.

Oh, shit, Jefferson thinks. "No."

"Yes," Major Moore says.

"Is everything all right with Carol?"

Moore says, "Oh, yes, Carol is doing fine under the circumstances. What we talked about earlier is all set. But Aunt Sophie knows you and yours are in trouble, and she wants to—"

"No," Jefferson says.

"Sergeant, all she wants—"

"Sir, no," Jefferson says. "It's all under control. Everything is under control, thanks to you. But if my aunt starts making a fuss, it'll be all done. Game over. You call my aunt on your way home, tell her to keep quiet. Please. Keep quiet."

"Sergeant, are you sure?"

"A hundred percent," he says, scraping his chair back. "Call my aunt when you can. Tell her I'm fine, tell her thanks for taking care of my girl. And that I'll come over for a visit when I can. But be careful. Call my aunt from a pay phone on your way back."

"Might be hard to find one."

"Sir, no offense, you better find one," he says.

Ninety minutes later, Major Frank Moore pulls up to his town-house in Georgetown, his late-night dinner—fried chicken from a Publix store nearby—sitting on the car's passenger seat.

Besides a quick meal, this Publix also offered a rare public pay phone outside, which he used to call Staff Sergeant Jefferson's aunt, Sophie Johnson. The strong-willed and strong-voiced woman seemed to reluctantly agree to her nephew's request to keep quiet and not stir up a fuss about what was happening to the staff sergeant.

Moore gets out of his Honda CR-V, goes up the brick pathway to the front door. It's a nice, quiet development, and his wife, Patricia—four months along with their first child—is spending the week visiting her mom in DC. He gets to the door, puts the plastic bag on the steps, and, as he takes the key out to unlock the door, hears rustling in the shrubbery over by the living room windows.

Damn white-tailed deer, he thinks, *are getting more and more brazen, coming out and chewing up everyone's yard,* and as he steps back to take a closer look, a man emerges from the shrubbery and says, "Hey, Major Moore."

Before Moore can reply, the man pulls a pistol with a sound suppressor from his waistband and shoots the Army major in the forehead.

CHAPTER 21

IT'S EARLY EVENING and I'm leaning so heavily on my cane that I think the metal might split. My left leg feels like it's a carved roast sizzling under an infrared restaurant lamp. My leg throbs and throbs, seemingly in pace with my heartbeat, and what's keeping me going is knowing that this is our last visit of the day, and when I get back to my motel room, it'll be time for my early evening ration of Extra Strength Tylenol.

Earlier Connie and I visited the Route 119 Gas N' Go convenience store, and an eager young Indian man working behind the counter who didn't speak much English managed to tell us that we needed to speak to his uncle Vihan in the morning to get access to the store's surveillance system.

Now we're at the side entrance of Briggs Brothers Funeral Home after a bit of sleuthing—all right, maybe ten seconds' work on Connie's part—revealed that the Sullivan County coroner is Ferguson Briggs, owner of the largest funeral home in this part of Georgia.

The building is white with black shutters, with a mini steeple to make it look like a house of worship, and a three-car garage is off to the side of a large paved parking lot. There's a lot of shrubbery and a wooden sign out on the road painted black and a faded maroon color.

Without asking for direction from me, her commanding officer, Connie picks up the courtesy phone.

"Hello?" she says. "Yes, who's this, please? Jim Briggs, thank you. Could you meet me at your door, please? I'm Special Agent Connie York from the US Army, here with Major Jeremiah Cook. Yes. We're Army investigators and—thank you, we'll wait."

Connie's face is red and shiny with perspiration, and strands of her blond hair are sticking to her forehead, but she still looks great. She catches me looking at her and says, "What?"

"Been a long day," I say.

"Yeah, and not much progress," she says. "I hope the others have something to show for it."

"When we're done here, send out a group text," I reply. "Time for a session back at the motel before we call it a night."

Connie looks over my shoulder at a nearby brick building with a concrete chimney and then the three-car garage and says, "Think that's where they keep the hearses?"

"Watch your language," I say. "They're called coaches."

Inside the funeral home lights click on.

"Duly noted," Connie says. "Funny thing, the county coroner being a funeral director."

"Lots of funny things here in Sullivan County," I say. "And it's an elected position. Meaning the good citizens of this county didn't vote him in just because he's got a degree in forensics or forensic anthropology. He's here because probably he treats the locals with respect, sympathy, and doesn't overcharge them for pretty boxes with shiny handles."

"Aren't you the cynic today," she says, smiling. "Sir."

Flying insects are hammering themselves against two yellow light bulbs when the rear door is unlocked, and a young man steps out, straightening his thin black necktie.

To Connie I say, "It's a day ending in *y*...Thank you, sir, for coming to see us. Mr. Briggs, I'm Major Cook, and this is Special Agent York. We're with the Army's Criminal Investigation Division."

He's about a half foot taller than me, early twenties, skinny, and he runs one hand through a thick tangle of brown hair while trying to tighten the knot on his necktie with the other. He has on black trousers, black shoes, a white dress shirt that's wrinkled, and I have three quick assumptions: one, he's wearing this clothing on a Sunday evening because his father told him to; two, like it or not, he's going to inherit this family business one of these days; and three, he's probably not alone back there in the funeral home. He's either with someone else or a video game. I know I wouldn't want to be alone, with bodies being stored in the building's basement.

"Ah, heck, you can call me Jimmy," he says. "But I need to ask to see your IDs. A couple of months ago some guy from the Georgia State Patrol came by and I was fixin' him coffee, and Daddy nearly tore my head off when he came over and found out I didn't know if the guy was official or not."

Connie displays her shield, as do I, and she says, "Was he official?"

"Oh, yeah, but that didn't mean anything," he says shyly. "Daddy was still upset. What can I do for you folks?"

I take a breath as a new, stronger wave of pain radiates up and down my leg. "I understand the county coroner's office is located here. Am I right?"

Jimmy nods. "One hundred percent. Daddy's been coroner for twelve years, and in less than two weeks he's going to be reelected."

"Do you have the bodies of the...folks who were murdered this past Wednesday, here in storage?" I ask.

His face seems even more yellow in the light. "Blessed Jesus, that we do. We're lucky that two of the guys were pretty skinny. We were able to put them together on one tray, and the mom and her kid..." He swallows, revealing a prominent Adam's apple. "Bless 'em all."

"We'd like to examine them, please," I say.

"Now? You mean... right now?"

"That's right," I say.

He shakes his head. "Can't do it, sir. Can't."

I say, "You've seen our shields. We've identified ourselves. Four Army Rangers have been arrested for those murders. We'd like your assistance in our investigation."

Another shake of the head, and he takes a step back into the funeral home, like he'd rather be in a place storing seven dead civilians than be out here with us.

"I can't do that. Honest, I can't," he says. "Daddy would have my hide."

I don't have to say anything, but Connie steps into play, smiling.

"I appreciate what you're saying, Jimmy, but we're from the Army, trying to do a very hard job," she says, her voice sweet and calming. "I know you don't want to disappoint your father—he does seem very strict—but he did leave you in charge, didn't he? And I know this area of the country is very, very patriotic. Don't you want to help us? Support the troops right here by letting us into your business?"

I think Connie is on the mark, but Jimmy shakes his head and starts closing the door. "Daddy'll be here tomorrow, after 9:00 a.m. You can try him then."

The door gets closed and locked, and one by one, the lights here on the first floor switch off.

Connie sighs, wipes her face. "Once, boss, I saw this horror movie about a funeral home, where the dead all rise during the night and tear the funeral home owner to pieces. Before they get really nasty, that is."

"Sometimes dreams don't come true," I say. "Send out the text. Let's get back to the motel."

In the car, I sit down with a grimace and buckle up. Connie works her phone a moment before starting the Ford Fusion, then switching on the air conditioner and headlights. Just as she gets us back on the road, another car up the street pulls out.

I grip my cane, occasionally glancing at the side-view mirror, as we drive along, taking a turn or two.

Connie checks her phone quickly and says, "Done, sir. Everybody is coming back in. Should be ready in about thirty minutes."

"Good," I say. "Anything else?"

"Yes, sir," she says. "Ever since we left that funeral home, we've been followed. I even made a slight detour, and those headlights never left us."

"Good call, Agent York," I say, looking again in the side-view mirror. "Let's do something about it."

"You want me to lose them?" she asks.

I painfully shift in my seat, remove my SIG Sauer.

"No," I say. "I want you to stop them."

CHAPTER 22

SPECIAL AGENT YORK has worked long enough with Major Cook to know that when he makes a request like this one, he doesn't want to get a lot of questions in return. Just get the job done. Connie likes working for a supervisor who has confidence in his employees without micromanaging them.

Connie says, "Yes, sir. I'm on it. Make sure your seat belt is nice and tight."

"It is," he says, holding the pistol and the door handle. "Just don't crash us."

Connie starts accelerating. "What, you don't like my driving?"

"I don't like filling out motor vehicle accident paperwork," he says. "Go."

Connie goes, speeding up even more.

The car behind them speeds up as well.

The lights from the small businesses and homes flash by as she quickly exceeds the forty-mile-an-hour speed limit and goes right up to sixty, which is as much as she dares on this narrow road.

A look in the rearview mirror.

Still there.

She thinks of saying that maybe those are cops back there,

but she keeps her mouth shut. The major certainly isn't afraid or concerned about being pulled over, so why mention it?

Focus on the driving.

The road sweeps to the left, and there's a squeal of tires as she handles the Ford nice and tight, keeping it in their lane, making sure they don't drift over the solid yellow line.

Sixty-three.

Sixty-four.

The road is a straightaway now, and the pursuing lights are getting closer, like they're egging her on. She quickly wishes she was back with the Virginia State Police with backup only a radio call away.

In a calm voice, Cook says, "Intersection coming up. Light's still green."

Connie's tempted to slow down with all that civilian traffic crowding up the intersection, but no, she's getting angrier that she and the major are being chased at night in this rural town in Georgia, like moonshiners being chased by the cops.

"Light's turning yellow," Cook says.

"No worries," Connie says.

They race through the intersection, horns honking and screaming at them, Connie expertly passing a blue van slowing to make the stop. Up ahead the road swerves hard to the left, and she lets her foot off the accelerator, switches off the headlights. Turning hard, Connie pulls into the parking lot of a McDonald's, quickly halting the Ford between a parked pickup truck and a mud-spattered Toyota, using the emergency brake to prevent any brake lights from popping on back there.

She turns and sees a black Dodge Charger roar by, and then she slips the Ford out of the parking lot and soon pulls up behind it, keeping the headlights off for a moment.

Cook says, "Well done, Connie."

Even with the adrenaline rush from this ongoing chase Connie feels a spark of pleasure from her boss's praise in a tight situation like this. She turns on the headlights, flicks them to high beams, and says in a heavy drawl, "The Virginia State Police aims to serve, suh."

No answer, but that's fine.

She barrels up right to the rear of the Charger, and she can see movement inside, like the passenger or driver is looking out the rear window, trying to see who's now chasing them.

"Sucks to be on the other side," she says.

And the major says, "Keep at it, keep hammering them."

The Charger makes an abrupt right onto a narrow road, and Connie swears, missing the turnoff. She slams on the brakes, the Ford sedan shivers and comes to a halt, and she slams the shifter into reverse, the transmission grinding a complaint.

Cook looks behind and says, "Clear."

Into drive.

Down the narrow road.

The Charger's lights are now off, but she catches a brief glimpse of it as it passes under a utility light, and she punches the accelerator down. The Ford roars into life as she resumes the chase, everything narrowed and focused into a tube before her, looking at the Dodge speeding away, barely noticing the *flick-flick-flick* of objects passing by, like trailers and dirt driveways and utility poles.

As the road gets emptier, the taillights up ahead come on, and she knows the driver of the Charger is concerned about crashing into something in the dark, sacrificing stealth for safety.

The lane gets narrower. No more driveways. No more distant lights.

A yellow-and-black sign is visible for a second.

DEAD END.

"Good," Cook says.

A thump as the pavement gives way to dirt.

"Sir," she says, "I think—"

The taillights up ahead drop from sight.

Something moves across her field of vision.

Connie slams on the brakes, the Ford sedan fishtailing as the tires try to grip the dirt-and-gravel road and—

For the briefest of moments, a chest-high white metal pipe blocking the road snaps into view, and Connie closes her eyes as the car hits it hard.

CHAPTER 23

IN THE LAST few seconds of our chase I try to focus on Connie's superb driving skills as we force the Dodge Charger into a dead-end lane, but my mind is racing back to last year, and the voices come to me:

Move, move, move.

Faster.

We're taking fire.

Connie slams on the brakes.

The Ford skids.

Then a loud bone-shattering *thud* and metal scraping and screaming and—

Not there.

Here.

We've hit a metal pole set across the dirt road, and my chest hurts from slamming against the shoulder harness. My cane is on the floor, but my hand is still holding my SIG Sauer.

Dust clouds settle in front of us. The hood of the sedan is scraped and dented, the heavy white metal pole just a few inches away from the windshield. Any faster or lower, the pole would have shattered the windshield and taken off our respective heads.

I hold the SIG Sauer with both hands so Connie can't see the shaking. But my left leg, still quietly howling in pain, starts a series of tremors.

"You all right, Connie?"

"Sir . . . yes. Sorry, are you okay?"

Fire, I think. Slight chance, but what if that collision tore something in the fuel line and there's a spark? We're trapped here and Connie can easily get out, but—

I take a breath. "Can you back us out?"

She shifts the car into reverse, backs us out, metal groaning and moaning. The headlights pick up a large dip in the road, explaining why the taillights from the speeding car ahead of us had seemingly disappeared.

Trees and brush are close by, and I see the bent metal pole, set across the dirt lane. At one end is a chain lock, and on the other side is a large bolt mechanism, allowing it to be raised and lowered at will.

I take another breath, squeeze my hands tighter around the comforting grip of the pistol. "This is how it happened," I say. "One of the guys in the Charger calls a friend. 'We're being chased.' The friend says, 'Go down this road, get a bit of a lead, and I'll take care of it.' The Charger races past the open gate, their friend drops the gate, almost in time to take our heads off. Just like in the 'stan. Villagers and the Taliban, out there keeping watch, talking on cell phones, ready to hit us when they're good and ready."

Connie rubs her face with both hands. "Seems like a good explanation, sir."

My heart rate is calming down. I look around at the darkness about us, imagine men hidden there, watching us, considering us, armed and waiting.

At least we're not on fire.

"Ask you a question, Connie?"

"Certainly, sir."

"Your first marriage. To George. Why did it end?"

She says not a word, which I expected.

CHAPTER 24

CONNIE TURNS AND stares at Major Cook. After this chase and the collision and nearly having both of their heads torn off, why in God's name is he asking her about her first failed marriage?

What the hell is going on?

Cook is quiet, but Connie gives him a good long look, sees his cane on the floor, his left injured leg shaking, his hands gripping his SIG Sauer, and his eyes looking straight out there into the darkness.

Now she knows.

He's not all here.

Part of him is back in Afghanistan.

Asking her about her first failed marriage…something safe, something domestic to talk about after this violent chase reminded him of a war zone.

He's trying to get back here, all of him.

"Boxes, sir," she says, noticing the Ford's engine is running rough.

"Go on."

"After we moved in together, he had about twenty cardboard boxes filled with books, clothing, all that stuff," she says. "And when he got it all unpacked, he kept the empty boxes in the basement, all neatly piled up. Month after month I bugged him to get rid of the boxes, they were taking up so much space. And when he didn't do that . . ."

Her boss says, "You knew that deep down, where it counted, he wasn't committed to the marriage. And Walter? What was his deal?"

She tightens her grip on the steering wheel, lifts herself up a bit from the seat, peers ahead. The dust has settled and there's nothing more to be seen.

Connie says, "Walter was one for setting traps. Like cleaning out the dishwasher, folding the laundry, getting the oil changed in the car, all without me asking. And those were his traps. 'Connie, didn't you see what I did? Why don't I get credit? Why don't you notice me?' And I told him, 'Walter, you're so big into ambushes, why the hell don't you transfer from CID to an infantry unit?'"

"Did he?"

"No," she says. "Left the CID and joined the FBI. Last I heard he was in Des Moines, chasing down farmers cheating on their government subsidies."

The engine is running even rougher. Cook reaches down, picks up his cane, and sets it across his lap.

Connie says, "Sorry about the accident. I'll do the paperwork."

"No," her boss says. "My job. I'll take care of it. But you can turn us around and head us back to the motel. We've still got lots of work to do."

Connie shifts the car into reverse again, and after a bit of careful three-point turning, she heads back up the road.

"I'm also sorry I lost them," she says.

"Nothing to apologize for."

The Ford bumps some as they get back onto asphalt.

"Sir?" she asks. "I don't understand."

Cook puts his SIG Sauer back into his holster. "I wanted whoever's out there to know we're aware of them following us and that we're going to do something about it. You did well, Connie. No worries. But do get us back to the motel without hitting anything else."

Connie smiles. "Can do, sir."

They drive on for a few more minutes, and she looks up in the rearview mirror, makes a quick turn, and then looks again.

"Major."

"We're being followed again," he says.

"That's right."

"Let them follow us," he says, the SIG Sauer coming back out into his hand. "But if they come too close, or try to do anything funny, throw us into a U-turn."

"And then try to shake them off?"

"No," Cook says, lowering his window with one hand, pistol firm in the other. "I have other ideas."

CHAPTER 25

THE DRIVE GOES smoothly after that, with the not-so-friendly lights still behind us, and as we near our destination, I roll the window up. When Connie gets us back to the Route 119 Motel and Coffee Shop, there's a huddled group of men and women outside our room 11. Connie parks our damaged Ford as close as she can, and she says, "Sorry, boss, the Fourth Estate has arrived, in all their assumed glory."

Damn it, I think, because I wanted to get to my room first to secure some painkillers, but I'm not in the mood to maneuver my way twice through that enthusiastic mob. No pain relief any time soon.

"As before, Connie," I say, grabbing my cane. "I'll take the lead."

She unsnaps her seat belt. "You'll take the lead in answering questions, sir. I'll take the lead in blocking us a path."

The next few seconds are a mess as I stay close behind Connie while she forces her way through the dozen or so men and women, dressed in everything from jeans and T-shirts to carefully styled suits, for the network correspondents, and lights from three television cameras glare at us as we get to the door.

"Are you the Army investigators here about the murders?"

"No comment," I say.

"Are the four Rangers being defended by the Army?"

"No comment."

A younger voice screams out, "You've got blood on your hands, killers! Blood on your hands!"

That doesn't deserve any kind of response, so I keep my mouth shut and we finally get into our meeting room.

The room is still small, still crowded with furniture. I find the first available chair and sink heavily into it. Up on the whiteboard are the list of civilian victims and the booking photos of the four Rangers.

"Before we start," I say, "just a reminder when it comes to talking to the news media. Don't."

My crew all nod, and Captain Pierce comes over with a cardboard cup of coffee, which I sip. It's cold. No surprise.

Connie takes a chair, joining Special Agent Sanchez and Dr. Huang.

"We'll go first," I say. "Connie?"

Connie removes a legal pad from her shoulder bag and starts off.

"Major Cook and I met this morning with Major Frank Moore, the executive officer for the Rangers' Fourth Battalion at Hunter Army Airfield. He was stunned that these four would have been arrested for such a crime. He said Sergeant Jefferson and his fire team are known as the Ninja Squad, for their ability to enter a house full of hostiles and kill them all."

Captain Pierce frowns. "That's a hell of a precedent. I mean no disrespect, Major, but if that's what they're known for in Afghanistan, it certainly complicates things."

I say, "It certainly does. Connie?"

She nods, flips a page. "After meeting with Major Moore, we had a brief session with their CO, Lieutenant Colonel Vincent

Marcello. He also repeated Major Moore's point, that these are highly skilled, professional, and decorated soldiers. But he would not go out of his way to praise them. He said that while on post, out of a combat zone, they can be a disciplinary problem, even though no law enforcement agency has officially filed a complaint against them."

"Anything more than that?" Sanchez asks. "Can we talk again to the colonel?"

I say, "Marcello is currently airborne with three companies of the Fourth Battalion, heading out for a deployment. The best we can do is talk to a Captain Rory O'Connell. He's the rear detachment commander, handling battalion affairs while they're deployed, but he's gearing up for ETS, so we need to get to him quick."

Huang looks around, looking embarrassed, and says, "What's ETS, Major?"

"Expiration of term of service," I explain. "Meaning Captain O'Connell is a few months away from being discharged."

Connie continues with another flip of a page. "The major and I also went to the convenience store the four Rangers visited prior to the killings. The worker said we need to talk to the store's owner before viewing any surveillance recordings."

When Connie pauses, I say, "We also visited the coroner's office to examine the victims. In this county, the coroner is an elected position. And he's also the local funeral director. His son was working alone tonight and refused us entry. We'll try again tomorrow. And just so all of you know, Agent York and I were followed after we left that funeral home. No big surprise, some folks around here are curious about what we're doing. Anybody else encounter anything similar?"

Sanchez quietly says, "A truck with its lights and engine switched off tried to scare me away while I was out working on

Route 119 at the driveway to The Summer House. Sped by so quick I could feel its breeze."

This gets everyone's attention. I say, "You all right?"

He shrugs. "I've experienced nastier work in the Rampart Division. It's okay."

I make it a point to give everyone a quick look so I know they're paying attention. "All right, folks, stay alert out there, and make sure all of you have your tac vests handy. And, Pierce and Huang, I know lawyers and psychiatrists don't always walk around armed, but make sure you carry your service weapons. Lieutenant Huang?"

My psychiatrist says, "This morning Captain Pierce and I tried to gain access to the Ralston town jail. The attendant wouldn't let us in. I stayed behind while Captain Pierce went to visit the district attorney. At about 1715 hours I got into the jail and interviewed the four Rangers."

Pierce looks impressed. "Doc, when I left, you were taking it easy in the park across the street. How the hell did you get in?"

Dr. Huang seems pleased with himself. "Trade secret. Anyway, I got in, and I interviewed two of the Rangers—Corporal Barnes and Specialist Ruiz—and they stuck to a script. Mostly name and rank, and that Staff Sergeant Jefferson is the best leader they've ever served under."

Sanchez nods. "Hanging together. Big surprise."

Huang says, "But I started off with the youngest squad member, Specialist Vinny Tyler. The other two were calm and collected. Tyler...he was defiant. But he wanted to talk, especially about the difference between frontline troops like him and rear-echelon soldiers like us. But before he left...there was guilt there. Serious guilt. I plan to go back tomorrow, see if I can take that further."

I ask, "And Staff Sergeant Jefferson?"

Huang pauses, then says, "He was the surprise. I didn't expect him to talk to me, but he did . . . and he wasn't happy I was there. Threatened to hurt me if I came back and talked to the Rangers again. But he let something slip in our talk, when he was getting angry with me. Major, he practically admitted he and his Rangers were there that night."

We all get quiet. Someone's pounding at the door, claiming to be from the *New York Times*. Or the *Washington Post*. I'm not sure and I don't care.

"Go on," I say.

"I told him that we were here to find out the truth, especially if it might be able to help him and his men," Huang carefully says. "And he threw that right back in my face. Said something to the effect that the families of those who resided in that old historical house wouldn't forget what happened that night."

Silence in our little room.

Huang shakes his head. "Major, they've been there. They know what the location looks like. Sir, based on what we've learned so far, the matched empty shell casings and the fingerprints, I think they were at that house and slaughtered those civilians."

That hangs in the air for a moment, and then my cell phone rings. ANONYMOUS CALLER, the screen states.

"Cook," I answer.

The man's voice is low and to the point. "Your goddamn killers butchered our neighbors. You think you're going to help 'em get away with it, you're wrong. Pack up and go back to DC, assholes."

I say, "We're actually from Quantico."

By then the man has hung up.

CHAPTER 26

I BRUSH OFF the phone call—I heard much worse said to my face working Midtown South—but my doctor's considered statements have made my stomach do a slow flip.

"It seems the locals love us," I say. "Is there anything else, Doc?"

"No, sir," he says. "I'll report back tomorrow after I try to interview Specialist Tyler again."

More pounding on the door. This time it's CNN. Then they go away and it's quiet again.

"Captain Pierce," I say, "did you meet with the district attorney?"

"Affirmative, sir," he says. "Cornelius Slate. Runs the county's business out of his office. Looks like the stereotypical small-town lawyer, but he's got serious legal chops. Graduated from George Mason and was a high-priced corporate lawyer for years before retiring to Sullivan. Bad news for the Rangers is that justice moves slowly in this county. It might be weeks or even months before an indictment is prepared, and in the meantime, he's told me that he's gung-ho to put all four of them on death row."

"Anything else?"

Pierce frowns. "He didn't come out and say it, but I have a sense he might be the local chapter head of the Sons of the Confederacy. And that's all I got for now."

"Good to know," I say. "Agent Sanchez? You're up."

Sanchez leans forward in his chair, clasps his hands together. "Sheriff Williams said there was a female witness out walking her dog who saw a pickup truck depart the crime scene the night of the murders. I tracked her down. Wendy Gabriel. She confirms what the sheriff said, recalls seeing a truck after hearing some gunshots, and spotted two men in the cab when they stopped under a utility light." He waits, then says, "But she's lying."

A second ago Huang was doodling on his pad, Connie was rearranging her bag, and Pierce was tearing apart a doughnut and eating it.

Now they are all staring at Sanchez.

"How?" I ask.

"I went to the road where she says she was walking her dog and saw the truck stop and then depart. I parked my rental underneath the utility light, near the driveway that goes to The Summer House. It's barely working. I folded my jacket, draped it over the seat of the car. Major, I couldn't see the buttons on my jacket. How could she see two men and later ID them in a photo lineup?"

Connie says, "Maybe their interior light was on."

Sanchez sits up, shoots back, "After committing multiple homicides? You think so, Connie? You learn that chasing down speeders outside the Beltway?"

Connie starts talking—I know Sanchez doesn't have much respect for her previous service in the Virginia State Police—and Pierce and Huang try to interrupt.

Sanchez raises his voice. "But that's not all!"

I hold up a hand. "Cool it, folks. Sanchez, what else is there?"

Sanchez's voice gets louder, firmer, and I see the old LAPD cop in him come out.

"The woman is a hoarder," he points out. "Lives alone except for her dog. She loves her dog. Her house is a mess except for the area where the dog food, water, treats, toys, and medicine are kept. It's spotless. But she said to the sheriff and to me that she was walking her dog that night, along the state road. She wasn't."

Huang asks, "How do you know?"

Sanchez says, "There was no leash. There was no leash on the porch, there was no leash by the door, there was no leash by her dog's area. There's no way she was walking her dog along that state road at night without her guy on a leash. I'm telling you, she's lying about what she was doing that night."

I smile at my guy. "Good catch. Tomorrow pay her another visit. See what she has to say about that."

In the next few minutes there's more pounding at the door from various journalists, which we all continue to ignore. Sanchez is in the corner, speaking Spanish to his wife, three time zones away. Huang and Pierce discuss the challenges of finding a way to get a pizza delivered past the reporters, Connie works on her computer, and I stare at the whiteboard.

We're starting to get evidence, which is a good thing.

But between the photos up there of the Rangers and the list of the dead civilians, there's still a wide and visible gap.

What's the connection?

Why were the Rangers there?

If Staff Sergeant Jefferson knows the layout of the property, doesn't that put them there? Especially with the forensic evidence of fingerprints and shell casings?

My cell phone vibrates and I dig it out of my jacket pocket. The ID says ANONYMOUS CALLER once more.

I answer it, thinking if I'm lucky this time I'll be told my Microsoft computer needs repairs, when a woman's voice says, "Major Cook?"

"Here," I say.

There's the sound of music and people talking in the background, and she says in a louder voice, "It's Sheriff Williams. I know it's late and all, but I was hoping we could talk."

"Certainly," I say. "What's going on, Sheriff?"

She says, "I just found out why your Rangers killed all those people."

CHAPTER 27

THE PARKING LOT of the Sullivan Memorial Baptist Church is nearly packed, and Special Agent Connie York wants to drop off Major Cook and Special Agent Sanchez at the entrance, but from the rear seat her boss says, "No. We'll all go in together."

Connie finds a spot after a couple of minutes circling the parking lot, like a Predator drone seeking targets of opportunity. When they get out of the battered Ford Fusion and start toward the church, Sanchez looks at the hood and shakes his head.

"Great driving there, Connie," he says. "I'm sure it'll buff right out."

Before Connie can shoot back a comment, Cook says, "I told her to go down that road, to follow the car that had been tailing us. Unless you want to try fixing it when we get back to the motel, knock it off, Sanchez."

Inwardly Connie smiles as Sanchez takes the hit from the major, and the three of them slowly make their way to the side entrance of the church hall. Amplified voices come from inside the building, followed by applause and cheers. Two extended black vans pull up into open handicapped spots and the doors pop open, TV camera crews and reporters sprinting out.

"Incoming Fourth Estate," Sanchez says.

Through a grimace—no doubt from his aching leg—Cook says, "Just ignore them."

Connie gets to the church door first and opens it up, and a plump woman in a pink dress holding a clipboard and a deputy sheriff in a brown-and-tan uniform are standing there. The deputy sheriff—LINDSAY, according to his name tag—says, "Help you folks?"

From behind them Connie hears voices say, "Hold on, just a moment, please, we have some questions..."

Cook says, "Major Jeremiah Cook, Army CID, with Special Agents York and Sanchez. We're here to see Sheriff Williams."

The woman frowns as she looks down at the clipboard, but the young uniformed man says, "Bonnie, it's okay, the sheriff told me they were coming in."

They slip inside, and Connie looks back as the TV crews and reporters try to come in, but Bonnie—raising the clipboard like a shield—holds them back, saying over and over again, "I'm sorry, you're not on the list... I'm sorry, you're not on the list..."

The interior of the hall is hot and crowded, with rows of folding chairs packed with people, and at the other end of the hall— flanked by US and Georgia state flags—a ruddy-faced man with carefully set black hair, wearing a gray suit, white shirt, and red tie and standing on a small stage, speaks into a wireless microphone, an arm around the shoulders of Sheriff Emma Williams. Four male deputies stand to the other side of the man speaking, all four looking embarrassed to be there.

"And I know you people well, and your brothers and sisters, serving overseas, for whom I pledge my undying assistance, many of whom I've met firsthand. And I thank Sheriff Williams and everyone here in Sullivan County for your continuing and deep support, which I'll take with me to the United States Senate! Thank you and God bless!"

Whoops, hollers, and applause, the flashing of cameras, and the man hands off his microphone to an aide, turns and gives the sheriff a handshake and a peck on the cheek, and then moves into the crowd.

Major Cook raises his voice to Deputy Lindsay. "Who's that?"

"Him?" Lindsay answers. "That there's Representative Mason Conover from Georgia's First District, and in less than two weeks he's gonna be one of our new senators. Come along, folks, I know Sheriff Williams wants to see you."

The large, muscular deputy sheriff clears a path for Connie, Sanchez, and the major, and Connie has the oddest feeling she's met Lindsay before, which is impossible. But there's that little itch at the base of her skull that tells her she knows him from somewhere.

Large campaign signs, including Conover's, are tacked up around the walls, naming other candidates, from potential Congress members to potential sheriffs—and there's Williams's name, and sure enough, there's Briggs, the local funeral home director, running again for county coroner.

What a way to run a county, she thinks, and then she, Sanchez, and the major are ushered into a kitchen area, with sinks, refrigerators, stoves, and metal countertops. Sheriff Williams is sitting on a stool near a shiny metal preparation table, and she takes off her round dark-brown uniform hat, revealing a band of sweat above her brow.

"Politics," she says. "Ain't it something?"

The three of them take stools around the preparation table as the sheriff turns to the deputy and says, "Clark? Do me a favor and ask Zell to come in here with my business case. Thanks."

After he departs, she smiles and says, "My deputies, all good boys. So proud of 'em."

With just the four of them now in the kitchen, Williams says, "Can I get you folks something cold to drink?"

Sanchez keeps his mouth shut. Connie could use something to cut the dryness in her mouth but senses tension from her boss and waits for him to take the lead.

"No," he says. "We're fine."

Another deputy sheriff comes in, carrying a soft brown leather satchel, which he hands over to the sheriff, and, damn it, Connie has the very same feeling as before. She has the oddest sense that she knows this man, too, just like the other deputy. Or at least has seen them before.

What is going on with her? The heat? The lack of sleep? The meals that aren't anything but deep-fried?

The sheriff reaches into the case, slips out a manila folder, and then pulls a photo from the folder. "This fella. He sure looks familiar, now, doesn't he?"

Williams slides the photo across, and she and Cook give it a look. It's a Savannah Police Department booking photo of a young man, and she instantly recognizes him.

"That's Stuart Pike," she says. "The man found in the second-floor bedroom, still in bed."

"That's right," Williams says. "He's the official renter for The Summer House, and he was involved in a bit more than moving marijuana." She taps her finger on the photo. "Seems he was arrested last month, for selling fentanyl near Savannah State University. Out on bail. We here in the county didn't know about this sideline of his, 'cause if we did, we would have gotten to him earlier."

Another photo comes out and is placed on the table, next to the booking shot. This is a formal color photo, of a young and, Connie notes, very attractive African American woman wearing a light-blue formal dress. Her smile is wide and confident, and her eyes seem bright with joy and intelligence.

Sanchez asks, "Who is this young lady?"

"Carol Crosby," Williams says. "A junior at Savannah State. She's studying marine biology, did an internship last year up in Maine, at the Shoals Marine Laboratory. Perfect 4.0 grade-point average. A couple of weeks ago, though, poor Carol was at an off-campus party. Looks like her drink got spiked, maybe as a joke, maybe by mistake."

Connie says, "An overdose, then."

Williams nods. "Oh, yes. It was touch and go for a while, but now she's in recovery over in Hilton Head, taking some time off from school."

Cook says, "What's the connection?"

Another tap of the finger. "This girl here. Carol Crosby."

"I'm sorry. I don't understand," Cook says.

"Oh, I'm sorry," Williams says, though her voice is definitely not sympathetic. "I thought you Army investigators would have known all of this. Carol Crosby, she's the stepdaughter of Staff Sergeant Jefferson, the head of that Ranger squad. Her mamma died a few years back from cancer, and Staff Sergeant Jefferson, he's been a proud single parent ever since."

Even with what's going on in the adjacent function hall, Connie feels like it's gotten awfully quiet.

Williams says, "Detective Josh Gregory, over in Savannah, when he heard about the Rangers being arrested, he dug back some and came up with Mr. Pike here. You see, Pike was arrested by a drug squad headed by Josh's crew near the college campus, and a while later some guy called up, asking for information about whether Pike was the source of the fentanyl that nearly killed young Carol Crosby. The caller said he was calling from Hunter, and the detective who answered the phone, he used to be stationed there...Well, it ended up the detective bent investigation protocol and told this caller that, yes, Pike was the supplier."

Cook looks down again at the two photos. "And?"

"And the caller said, 'Well, that man and whoever's working with him, they're gonna pay a price.' And hung up. Josh did some additional digging around, couriered these photos over to me, with one other bit of information."

"What's that?" Connie asks.

Sheriff Williams picks up the two photos—one of a now dead man, the other of a nearly dead woman—and puts them back into her satchel. "That call came from Staff Sergeant Jefferson's cell phone."

The sheriff zippers the bag shut, then looks at Connie and Cook with a sad but determined look.

"That's what happened," she says. "That sergeant and those Rangers, they went into that house, all angry and fired up, and killed every living soul there. Even that little innocent baby. You know it, and I know it, and one of these days all four are gonna get a needle in their veins. You can count on it."

CHAPTER 28

AT NEARLY 2:00 A.M. on Monday morning, following a very busy Sunday, the woman is very pleased to be out of her uniform, in civvy clothes, her body relaxing from not wearing all that damn gear. She's carefully driving her civilian car on a narrow dirt road that borders a swampy area near Hunter Army Airfield, and when she comes to a wide part of the road, she stops the car, switches off the engine and lights, and steps out.

The damn wild area here is full of noise, from frogs to insects and birds, and speaking of birds, a Black Hawk helicopter and then another one fly overhead, going to the lit area on the horizon marking the runway for Hunter.

She leans against the fender of the car, the metal still warm, and pulls out a burner phone she purchased with cash and with a hat pulled over her eyes from the Walmart Supercenter on Abercorn Street.

Time check: 2:00 a.m. on the dot.

The phone rings, and she puts it up to her ear and says, "Yes?"

The connection is lousy, full of static and random pops and hisses.

"How's it going?" comes the demanding male voice. It sounds like he's on his way to the other side of the world.

"It's going all right," she says.

"You call that all right?" A louder burst of static and "...told me it would be open-and-shut, that the Army would come in for a day or..." More static. "...but they're still there, aren't they?"

"Yes, sir, they are," she says. "But it's a big case. I didn't think they'd send down a special squad to work it."

"Well, they did, didn't they?" And his voice fades out. For a moment, she hopes he's out of range.

No such luck.

He comes back and says, "What now? How much more coverage is this going to get?"

She shakes her head. "I'll work it, don't worry. We'll get it wrapped up soon. I promise."

"...better," he says. "This Major Cook. You've seen and talked to him..." Another pause. "...next?"

"Excuse me, sir?"

He says, "I said, when are you talking to this Major Cook again?"

"Tomorrow," she says. "I'm sure it'll be tomorrow."

"Tuesday? Tuesday?"

Shit, she forgot about the time.

"No," she says. "Monday, later today."

"Handle it, all right? Or you can forget ever..."

The line goes dead.

"Sir? Are you there? Sir?"

Dead air.

All right, then.

She switches the phone off, takes a penlight out of her pocket, switches it on, and removes the back of the burner cell phone, removes the SIM card, and snaps it in two. Then she walks to the edge of the road—damn it, thorns just scratched her left hand!—and tosses the broken SIM card and phone into the swamp.

For a moment, in the heavy air with the loud noises of the swamp, she looks over at the lights of Hunter.

Men, she thinks, shaking her head and going back to her civilian car. *So damn weak.*

CHAPTER 29

MY RINGING CELL PHONE wakes me up in the dim light, and I switch on the bedside lamp and grab the phone, resting on Bruce Catton's *Glory Road*, which has traveled here with me and so far remains unread. At my side, my Panasonic Toughbook— my Army-issued laptop with which I've been reviewing and re-reviewing the four Rangers' service records—falls to the floor. Which is fine, since the laptop is designed to perform even after being nearly blown up.

Like me.

"Cook," I answer, and my caller replies with a series of heavy, deep coughs. When the coughing stops, I say, "Colonel Phillips?"

A weak voice says, "Good guess. Maybe you should be a god-damn detective or something."

I check the time. It's 6:00 a.m.

"You're up early, sir," I say.

"Got a lot going on," he says. "I've read your email. Anything else to add before I brief the provost general?"

I rub at my sleep-encrusted eyes. "Nothing much except the news media are down here like sharks, smelling chum in the water after being starved for a week. They didn't stop knocking on my door until about 1:00 a.m."

"Gotta love the Constitution, don't you?"

"All the time, sir," I say.

He laughs and coughs twice, then says, "Game plan for today?"

"First I'm going over to Hunter to talk to Captain Rory O'Connell," I say. "The entire Fourth Battalion has been dispatched, and he's been assigned as rear detachment commander. I want to find out more about our four arrested Rangers."

"What about the battalion commander? Or his XO? Or their platoon leader? They should be passing on that information to you, not a rear echelon officer."

"They've all been deployed overseas. Sir. Just after we arrived."

I can hear his labored breathing over the phone.

"That's damn convenient, isn't it?" he says. "Having the entire Fourth Battalion deployed. Making it damn near impossible to interview fellow Rangers and witnesses."

"My thoughts exactly," I reply.

"Good," he says. "More you follow the way I think, the better your career will be. Get the job done."

"Yes, sir," and Phillips disconnects.

I swing out of bed, careful of my left leg, and damn if I don't smell coffee. Not unusual since the coffee shop is just down at the other end of this strip of motel rooms, but it smells awfully close.

I toss a blanket over my shoulders, walk over, and see little squares of paper on the floor, like some odd cyclone dropped them off before I went to sleep. Bending over and catching my breath, I gather them up.

Handwritten notes from desperate journalists wanting interviews. *Atlanta Journal-Constitution. USA Today.* MSNBC. *New York Times. Savannah Morning News.*

And a sweet little scribbled note in red ink from Peggy Reese, of the *Sullivan County Times,* complete with phone number:

Dear Army officer,

It would really make me happy to talk to you about what happened at The Summer House.

Sincerely,
Peggy Reese

I crumple up the notes, toss them into a wastebasket, unlock the door, and peer out. It's still dark outside, and there's a shape of something in front of my door, and the sputtering and flickering of a small gas stove. My eyes adjust, and it's Special Agent Manuel Sanchez, stretched out in a sleeping bag on top of a foam mattress, leaning against the wall, wearing a simple black T-shirt. Near him is the gas stove with a coffeepot gently boiling.

"Morning, sir," he says, picking up the pot with a folded-over handkerchief. "Care for some fresh brew? Not sure what the shop over there is serving us, but it sure as hell isn't good coffee."

I drag one of the motel's lawn chairs over and sit down next to my CID investigator. He's smiling a good-natured smile, with his dark skin and perfect white teeth, but his eyes are always on alert, scanning back and forth. Sanchez is a man of reserved strength and violence. There's a lot going on behind his eyes, and I'm glad he's on my team.

He pours the coffee, and I say, "You're the reason I stopped having people hammering at my door a few hours ago."

"That's right, sir," he says, deftly lifting the cup to me. "Thought you needed a good night's sleep after all the work yesterday."

The coffee is hot, spicy, and sweet. "What is this?"

"It's café de olla, Major," he says, settling back with his own coffee cup in hand. "It's a nice medium roast, but there's cinnamon in there, along with an orange peel."

I gingerly take another sip. I like it.

I ask, "How did you convince the news media to stop banging on my door?"

"Not just your door, sir," he says. "Everyone's."

"Damn uncomfortable out here."

He shrugs. "No worries. Besides, the doc, he snores something awful."

"The reporters give you any trouble?"

Sanchez looks like I've just asked him if he cheated on a final exam. "Oh, no, they were quite sweet and cooperative. I love the press, and once they get to know me, the love comes right back."

Right, I think.

I curl my hands around the ceramic cup, warm them. "What do you think?"

Sanchez frowns. "It's a crap show for sure, Major. I don't envy whoever's going to rep those four... The evidence seems pretty overwhelming. You know? Lots of evidence and pieces... but..."

I wait. Sanchez will talk when he's ready.

"It's like, you know, we got a big puzzle and lots of pieces. The fingerprints. The shell casings. The witness supposedly seeing them drive out, even if her story's kinda weak. The store surveillance tape. And now we find out from the sheriff that it looks like the Rangers killed all those folks for revenge. Lots of pieces."

"Agreed," I say.

Sanchez puts his cup down on the cracked concrete. "But the pieces aren't fitting. Like, to make 'em fit, like a jigsaw puzzle, you have to do what my *tio* Pepe would do. When he'd get pissed doing a jigsaw puzzle, he'd take a pair of shears and cut the pieces to fit. That's what I feel like. To make everything fit, we need to trim stuff."

"You're not liking the evidence?"

"Oh, no, Major, I'm loving the evidence. Makes me think we

can wrap this up in a few days so I can go home to my *familia*. But still...I can't see the Rangers killing all those innocents. Maybe the dealer, maybe a couple of others if they came after them with guns. But it looks like the civilians were surprised. A few of them were playing video games. The oldest woman, she was hiding and was dragged out from underneath the bed."

I say the words I hate saying. "Then there's the little girl."

"Brrr," he says. "That's stone-cold, it is. I can't see that. The Rangers, 'cept for the youngest one, they're hanging tough. You'd think if they didn't do it they'd be screaming that they're innocent. So why aren't they doing that? And then there's my dog walker, who claims she saw that crew leave the house after all the shooting. Major, no way did she see that."

I nod in reply, sip from my coffee, enjoying the dark pre-morning before the sun rises, before more phone calls and messages and questioning.

"After another briefing and a breakfast, you're off to the dog walker again," I say. "Get her story straight. Pierce is going back to the district attorney, get a read on when the first court hearing will be held. I'll have Dr. Huang reinterview that young Ranger, and Connie and I, we're off to that convenience store that caught surveillance footage of those four the night of the murders. And then we're off to Hunter. When we come back, you'll join us to examine the bodies at the funeral home."

Sanchez nods. "Sounds like a full day."

Recalling what I found earlier in the Rangers' service records, I say, "By the end of the day, I want more pieces. And I want them to fit."

CHAPTER 30

DESPITE ITS NARROW AISLES, the Route 119 Gas N' Go is well stocked. Its overflowing shelves boast everything from motor oil to fishing lures to canned goods to paper products, with coolers and freezers at the far end. Special Agent Connie York is up at the front of the store with Major Jeremiah Cook.

Behind the checkout counter topped with dispensers of cigarette packs and tins of chewing tobacco is Vihan Laghari, the store's smiling owner dressed in jeans and a pink Lacoste polo shirt. He has a thick black moustache, two gold chains around his neck, and three gold rings on his hands, which he constantly rubs as he speaks. He says in barely accented English, "A bad deal, what happened. A very bad deal."

"It certainly was," Cook says, smiling. "And for the third time, please, Mr. Laghari, may we see the video surveillance from that evening?"

"Of course, of course. Right this way, good sir, good ma'am," he says, going to the other end of the counter and gesturing them in. A young boy and girl look up from their cell phones, smile, and go back to whatever games they're playing. They're wearing khaki shorts and bright-yellow T-shirts printed with the store's logo.

York takes in the crowded work area. More cigarettes, large

plastic bins with lottery scratch-off tickets—or, as they're called here, *scratchers*—and, underneath the counter and cash register, a color television with a bright, sharp picture. She's not sure what the program is, but it's some sort of musical number with young Indian men and women in bright clothes dancing in a meadow somewhere.

On the side counter, a large computer screen displaying four surveillance video feeds is hooked up to a laptop. One shows the store entrance, the second shows the outside with the four gas pumps, the third shows the rear of the store, and the fourth focuses on the cashier area. She sees herself, Cook, and Laghari on the screen.

"See?" he points out. "Recording all the time, twenty-four/seven. For two days, then records over. When we heard about those dreadful murders, dear me . . . Sheriff Williams, she asked me if I saw anything that night, and I said no, the usual customers." Laghari shakes his head. "But later she came back and asked to review that Wednesday night. She was looking for something."

Cook asks, "Did she tell you what?"

Another shake of his head. "No, no, no. Just a review of a few hours, and she spotted it. She thanked me very much for my help. Would you like to see that Wednesday night? I kept a copy of what I gave to the sheriff."

"Very much so," Cook says.

"My boy, Prince, he will help," the store owner says. "He knows all this computer stuff."

Laghari speaks loudly in a burst of Hindi, and the young boy gets off his stool, puts down his handheld device, and comes over. "Sure, *bapu*," he says. The young boy works the keyboard, and the live feed of the surveillance cameras shrinks to a small square in the corner. His fingers rapidly go to work, and then . . .

Up comes a recording.

"Here," the boy says. "Here's what the sheriff copied."

York's throat thickens as she watches the footage, and she feels her heart rate increase.

A pickup truck pulls up to the front of the store. Four men get out, and she recognizes the four Rangers: Staff Sergeant Caleb Jefferson, Corporal Curtis Barnes, Specialist Vinny Tyler, and Specialist Paulie Ruiz. Jefferson and Barnes go to the store's rear cooler section, grabbing some type of power drinks. As they're in the store, Tyler and Ruiz remain outside, smoking cigarettes and having a heated discussion, lots of finger-pointing and arm-waving.

Connie checks the time stamp. The day is last Wednesday. The time is 7:40 p.m.

Twenty minutes or so before they're seen leaving the site of the killings.

Jefferson pays cash for the drinks. Barnes is behind him, face hard and determined.

Laghari works the cash register, and then the two Rangers leave. Tyler and Ruiz drop their cigarettes on the ground.

"See?" Laghari asks. "Just what I saw that night . . . soon before the dreadful murders."

Cook says, "Connie? Get a copy of this, will you?"

"Yes, sir," she says, going into her bag, fumbling around for a second, coming out with a thumb drive.

But she knows she won't need it.

What she's just seen in the surveillance tape will remain sharp and clear in her mind for years to come.

The four Rangers, all dressed in fatigues, boots, and MOLLE harnesses.

Jumping into their truck and quickly driving away.

Off to perform a mission.

CHAPTER 31

CAPTAIN ALLEN PIERCE finds the law offices of Cornelius Slate busier this Monday morning than during yesterday's visit. It's already been a grueling time since he arrived here, and he hasn't gotten much sleep. At first he thought it might be a treat—okay, sexist and rude, but he's male after all—to share a room with Agent York, but she has been brisk and no-nonsense, and goes to bed in shorts and a T-shirt. Nothing untoward has happened.

Which is fine.

He yawns repeatedly and barely has enough energy to do his job.

Slate's waiting area has five chairs, and all of them are occupied. A man holding metal crutches stares at the cast on his lower left leg. A young man in jeans and a T-shirt sits slumped, fingers working on his cell phone, baseball cap sideways. An older couple sit stiffly next to each other, one periodically turning a head to whisper harshly to the other.

The interior door opens. A woman in a floral dress belted in slim black leather steps out. Her brown hair is cut short, and her round glasses look vintage 1985.

"Captain Pierce? Attorney Slate will see you now."

"Thanks," he says, getting up and grabbing his case, following the woman into Slate's office. He sees her belt has missed a loop at the rear and decides to keep that observation to himself.

Slate is better dressed today—blue shirt with a white collar, red necktie, gray slacks—and he comes around his desk to say, "Captain Pierce! Good to see you again. Glad I could make time to fit you in. Have a seat, have a seat. Coffee?"

Remembering the vanilla swill he had yesterday, Pierce says, "No, thanks. I've already had my morning allotment."

Slate grins, goes back to his desk, and says, "Well, I've got some news for you, Captain Pierce."

Great. No more *son*. At least Slate didn't call him *boy* instead, which Pierce sees as a small victory. He says, "What's that, Mr. Slate?"

Slate looks down at his desk. "We've got the arraignment hearing set up for those four Rangers this coming Thursday, only three days away. Circuit judge Howell Rollins shuffled his schedule, so the judicial process is starting to grind its way along."

"But not much is going to happen at the hearing, correct?"

"Nope, not at all," Slate says. "Official reading of the charges and pleas entered. That's about that."

"How about representation?" Pierce asks.

"That's a funny thing," Slate says.

There's a line from a Joe Pesci movie Pierce is tempted to use—*Funny how?*—but instead he says, "Could you explain?"

"Sure," the district attorney says. "I visited the prisoners this morning, just to see where things are. And those four are refusing outside representation."

"But . . . you're saying the hearing is still scheduled for Thursday? Even without representation?"

Slate nods. "That's right, Mr. Pierce. You see, the thing is, these four plan to represent themselves."

CHAPTER 32

SPECIAL AGENT MANUEL SANCHEZ pulls his Ford sedan into the front yard of Wendy Gabriel's home and sees the Volkswagen is still there. Good. He gets out of the car and starts up to the old, sagging house, which looks exactly the same as it did yesterday.

But he slows as he approaches the porch.

It looks the same, but it sure doesn't sound the same.

No noise is coming from inside the structure.

No dog barking.

No dog?

Sanchez steps onto the porch, knocks on the door.

"Ma'am?" he calls out. "Are you home?"

Quiet.

Two more heavy knocks, and he stops, listening.

Nothing.

What now?

In another time and place he would contact the locals for assistance, explain what's going on and how he needs to reinterview a vital witness.

But here and now?

Sanchez has a flicker of suspicion that just won't go away.

From his nearly being run down last night to Agent York and Major Cook being trailed to the sharp looks he and the others get from the civilians, he knows the locals are not his allies. They are up to something.

He looks at the door and its lock. Typical pin tumbler. He goes back to the trunk of the Ford, rummages through his go bag, filled with all sorts of technical goodies, chooses a small zippered black case, and carries it to the front porch.

Sanchez looks again at the lock, then removes from the case two tools: a small tension wrench and an even smaller tool called a short hook. He gets to work, and in less than fifteen seconds, he unlocks the door.

He pushes it open. Puts the lock-picking tools in his coat pocket. Takes out his SIG Sauer.

"Mrs. Gabriel? Are you here?"

No reply.

He steps in and says, "Toby! Toby Baby!"

No sound of paws thumping on the rug or nails rattling on the linoleum floor. Sanchez steps farther in, takes a breath.

With the door and windows closed to the outside heat, the stench inside nearly knocks him back.

The smell... rotten fruit, greasy food, piles of bagged trash decaying in the far corner.

He moves slowly through the crowded living room, clearing the place as best he can without any backup, and as he walks, he's able to separate some of the stench.

He doesn't smell something he's expecting: the smell of a bloated, decaying, and putrefying body.

A narrow staircase is packed on both sides with piles of books and magazines. He takes his time, but upstairs he does what he can. There's a bathroom that is so filthy and jammed with towels and soap bottles that he doesn't even bother to enter.

The bedroom has a narrow path to the bed and a bureau that has just a few papers on top—what a surprise—and that's it.

When he gets out of the house, back onto the porch, he takes a deep, cleansing breath.

The house was locked, the car is still here, and there's no sign of violence or a struggle.

But Wendy Gabriel is gone.

Sanchez holsters his pistol, walks back to the car.

Check that.

The witness is gone.

CHAPTER 33

SPECIAL AGENT CONNIE YORK is with Major Jeremiah Cook in the small and nearly empty office of Captain Rory O'Connell, the officer in charge of the Fourth Battalion's paperwork, family issues, and supply matters during any overseas deployments.

O'Connell's in his early thirties, trim, with black hair streaked with gray, narrow black eyebrows, and tired yet alert brown eyes. He has on an Army combat uniform, and the cinder-block walls of his office enclose a desk with a phone, a computer terminal, and piles of papers and file folders stacked on either end.

O'Connell's voice is quiet and whispery, and only when he starts talking does Connie note the scar tissue around the base of his throat. "Let's make this as quick as we can, all right? In a half hour I've got a Ranger wife coming in, scared to death her husband's truck is going to be repossessed, and thirty minutes later, I need to check in on a sick ten-year-old girl who's afraid Daddy's never coming home. And then I need to find out where in hell the battalion XO has gotten himself. He's due to leave here in twelve hours, and I have a shitload of paperwork for Major Moore to sign before he heads out. What a goddamn mess. I was hoping the deployment would stay on schedule, but it was moved up, which meant I got picked to initially take care of things while they're gone."

Cook looks at her and gives her the slightest of nods.

She has the lead.

"Captain, with the battalion deployed, any soldiers we could possibly interview about the four arrested Rangers are now overseas. We're hoping you can help us fill in the blanks."

O'Connell shifts in his seat as a bout of pain slides across his face. Connie sees him now as someone who has wounds like Cook, struggling to get through every day.

O'Connell says, "I'll try, but I was in Bravo Company. They're in Alpha."

Connie says, "We know they're called the Ninja Squad. True?"

O'Connell sighs. "Yeah. Over in the 'stan they were known for being able to target and hit Taliban sites—sometimes little farmhouses—without being detected. Hard and fast at night, got the job done, never injured on their part. I was even in their operating area for a few months during my last deployment, where I saw their work firsthand. Very impressive. Thing is, they believed their own headlines. Which can lead to trouble."

"What kind of trouble?" York asks.

"They think they're invincible. That's fine, but other Rangers, they get infected. If the Ninja Squad can slide through without getting hurt, well, why not us?"

York's not sure how to reply to that, but the major moves his cane for a moment and says, "The Humvee I was in got nailed by a roadside bomb. You?"

The slightest of nods, one warrior acknowledging another. York feels both admiration and jealousy.

"Mortar rounds at our FOB," he says. "I was caught outside with our local interpreter. Killed him, injured me. Which is why I'm out of here in a few months. My body...just can't take it anymore. But those Ninjas. Ninjas over there, Ninjas back here."

Cook says, "I think I know what you mean."

No, she's not going to let that one slide, the two men ignoring her. York says, "Sorry, I don't know what either of you means. Please explain, Captain. What do you mean, 'Ninjas back here'?"

"Well, it's the way Rangers think when they're deployed," he says. "There's an intensity and pure raw thrill of being under fire, returning fire, trying to kill someone who's trying to kill you. It's a kind of...a high. And having experienced that high, of having everything on the line, of being exposed and seeing death around you, coming back to the post and dealing with what's called chickenshit—polishing your dress boots, having all the forms filled out and checked off, keeping your uniforms properly ironed—it can push combat soldiers over the edge."

Connie says, "Ninjas here, then?"

He nods. "They look for action, they crave action. Staff Sergeant Jefferson's squad, they looked to raise hell here. Either on post or off. Sometimes it made for long nights and weekends for the MPs and local law enforcement within about a thirty-mile radius. But because the locals love the military, no charges were officially filed against them."

Cook says, "What did these Ninjas do stateside?"

O'Connell shakes his head. "Assaults, drunk driving, breaking and entering private quarters while drunk, vandalism, petty theft. Stunts and pranks against other companies in the battalion. It got to the point where other Rangers here in the Fourth Battalion got a real hard-on against them, thinking those four could break the rules and mostly get away with it."

York says, "That includes their battalion commander, Lieutenant Colonel Marcello, am I right?"

"Quite right," O'Connell says. A helicopter roars overhead, causing some of the desk files to vibrate. "A number of years back a previous battalion commander here had his career ruined because another Ranger squad raised hell like Staff Sergeant Jefferson's Ninjas. Marcello vowed it would never happen to him."

York thinks, *Hold on. This is something.*

The odd evidence, the weird occurrences, the outstanding questions...what Marcello told her and Cook earlier, and now what this officer has just confirmed.

Staff Sergeant Jefferson and his squad were heartily disliked by their fellow Rangers. Sliding through. Never really punished. Never really disciplined.

Until now.

A frame job? Could this be a frame job?

Cook says, "Sorry to interrupt, Captain O'Connell, but something's caught my attention."

Yes, York thinks. *The major sees what I see.*

But Cook has another question.

"Staff Sergeant Jefferson's squad, they were last deployed to Afghanistan two months ago. From what I'm able to puzzle out from their soldier record briefs, they were supposed to be in their area of operations for six months, not two."

The helicopter sound fades away. O'Connell is staring hard at her boss.

"But I can't see anything else about their deployment," he goes on. "Their area of operations. Any missions they went on. Any after-action reports. Why is that?"

O'Connell shrugs. "I don't know. I wasn't there."

York waits. There's some sort of new tension between O'Connell and her boss.

Cook says, "Captain O'Connell, I think you do know."

O'Connell's eyes flash. "You think shit."

"Some days, yes," Cook says, his voice calm but hard. "This is a small base. The Rangers are a tight unit. If something odd happened to them while deployed, you'd know. Not all of the details. But you'd know."

York waits, wondering what O'Connell will do. His face is firm, his eyes set, and she can feel the anger coming off him, like vapor rising from a hot sidewalk after a rainstorm.

"I've got nothing to say," O'Connell says.

"That's not going to be an option for you, Captain," Cook says. "We're CID. You're going to answer my questions completely and truthfully or we'll leave and come back. And come back again. And maybe you'll miss your deadline of being discharged in a few months because hearings have to be held."

O'Connell looks like he's about to come across the desk and grab Cook's cane and beat him with it, but he waits some more. York thinks the Ranger is struggling.

He says, "A couple of the guys in my company got screwed up because they thought they were Ninjas, too. One's blind. The other's in a wheelchair for life. That wasn't good."

Cook says, "That's understandable."

"You can see I don't particularly like them," O'Connell says. "But I'm not about to snitch on them."

"Whatever you say to us will be confidential, Captain O'Connell," her boss says. "Nothing in print, nothing official."

O'Connell looks at her, as if for reassurance. York remains silent, not wanting to shatter this mood.

Sorry, Captain, she thinks. *No sympathy from me.*

The Ranger captain says, "I believe the reason you don't see any paperwork from their last deployment is that they weren't under the command of Fourth Battalion. They were temporarily detached elsewhere."

York says, "The Afghan National Army?"

With disgust, O'Connell says, "As if. No, our friends up in Langley. Staff Sergeant Jefferson and his squad are so good, the Company borrowed them."

The air seems heavy and threatening. *Now,* York thinks, *now everything has changed in this investigation.* What have she and the major stumbled across? The CIA?

Cook says, "All right. The Company. But why were they sent home so early?"

O'Connell rotates slightly in his chair, back and forth, like he's hoping the longer he waits to reply, the quicker Connie and her boss will leave.

Connie thinks, *To coin a phrase, Captain, "As if."*

"There was an incident," O'Connell finally says. "Staff Sergeant Jefferson and his squad were sent straight home."

"What was the incident?"

One more pause from O'Connell.

"Staff Sergeant Jefferson and his squad hit a house," he says. "It was the wrong house. No Al-Qaeda, no Taliban, no ISIS, no insurgents. A house full of civilians."

Another helicopter comes overhead, and then the noise eases off.

O'Connell says, "And the Rangers slaughtered them all."

CHAPTER 34

THE NEWS FROM Captain O'Connell hits me so hard that for a few blessed moments I can't even feel the pain in my left leg.

"How do you know this?" I ask.

"Like you said," he says, "I hear things. I hear rumors. But this rumor . . . so nasty I had to double-check, to verify. I made a call, to an Army intelligence officer I met when I was deployed to Afghanistan. Captain Amy Cornwall."

"How did she know? Was she there?"

"Beats the hell out of me," O'Connell says. "But she's with Langley now, and she did a favor and confirmed it. The squad was in a village called Pendahar, in Khost province. Amy told me that after that house was wiped out, the CIA wanted to cover their big butt and so they sent the Rangers home. Things are so fragile over there, the story about a squad of Rangers committing a war crime would screw up the peace negotiations big-time . . . Yeah, that's something the CIA would want to bury deep."

A glance over at Connie. She looks as shocked as I feel.

York says, "Is there anything else you know about the killings over there?"

"No," he says.

"Does Colonel Marcello know?" I ask.

"I can't see how he doesn't."

I ask, "Were they facing disciplinary action? Was the incident investigated?"

O'Connell says, "To answer both of your questions, I don't know. Look, whatever happened took place half a world away. I wasn't there. Officially, the Army says the squad wasn't under their control. They belonged to the CIA. And if you think the Company is going to come forward and reveal all without a busload of subpoenas, you're crazy. Nothing is going to happen from Langley's end."

"And their fellow Rangers in Alpha Company and Fourth Battalion?" I ask. "Do you think they know what the men did in that village?"

O'Connell's hand gently taps on his clean desk. "It's certainly possible."

Something comes to me. "Wait. A few minutes ago you said the rest of the battalion was going to be deployed when you had gone through your discharge. But their deployment date got moved ahead. Right?"

"Correct," he says.

"But why? Why was the battalion ordered to deploy earlier than scheduled?"

"I don't know."

The pains in my leg decide to come back for their usual visit. "But don't you think it's an incredible coincidence...that these same Rangers are accused of killing a houseful of civilians in an Afghan village, and then of doing the same thing some weeks later in a Georgia town? And just when we arrive to conduct an investigation, any witnesses we could talk to are out of reach because the battalion's deployment schedule is suddenly changed?"

"Yes," O'Connell says. "One hell of a coincidence."

"I don't like coincidences," I say.

"Me neither," the captain says.

As we're leaving Hunter, a white MP police cruiser with flashing blue lights comes up behind us, and I say, "Connie, do pull over. I don't think this poor rental can take any more."

She does just that, and the cruiser stops. The woman who steps out of the driver's side is someone I recognize.

It's Colonel Brenda Tringali, head of this base's Third MP Group. She comes to my side of the car, I roll the window down, and she leans in, putting both hands on the open window frame. One hand has a small bandage on it.

She says, "How's your day going, Major?"

"Fine, ma'am," I say. "Our investigation is continuing."

Her skin is a light brown, and she has ink-black hair and sharp dark-brown eyes. "Good to know. I'd appreciate a briefing at some point as to how your work is progressing."

"If I have something to share, ma'am, I'll certainly consider that," I say.

She has a slight smile, but there's no warmth or humor in it. "That wasn't really a request, Major Cook."

I say, "Since you're not in my chain of command, ma'am, that's how I'm taking it."

Her eyes lock onto mine and then she slaps the open window frame and steps away. "Speed limit on post is thirty miles an hour," she says. "Is that clear?"

"Very," I say, and she heads back to her cruiser. I tell Connie, "All right, let's go."

She eases our way out into traffic, and I say, "Speed it up, Agent York. I don't want to be late to the county coroner's."

"With pleasure, Major," she replies as we quickly get up to forty miles an hour.

CHAPTER 35

I'M ON THE PHONE with Colonel Phillips, our superior officer, as Connie speeds us west on Interstate 16, back to Sullivan County and Briggs Brothers Funeral Home. The engine of our Ford grinds here and there, and the battered front hood vibrates hard against its latch, threatening to break free.

"Colonel, I'm sorry," I say. "I didn't make that out."

There's a hiss of static, and his voice seems distant and quiet. He says, "...do what I can, but that's one hell of a bit of news. Ranger squad accused of killing civilians overseas and then here...Damn, it'd be like if those My Lai soldiers came back from Vietnam in 1968 and shot up a 7-Eleven..."

He coughs and coughs.

"Colonel," I say. "We're going to need information about what happened in that Afghan village. What connection there might be between here and Hunter. There's got to be something."

More coughing. "...see what I can do." The colonel disconnects the call.

I look at Connie, whose hands are firmly gripping the steering wheel.

"Sir, I'm getting some thoughts here, and I hate to bring them up."

"Speak, Connie. Don't hold back."

"You've got a Ranger squad that raises hell in the States. Other platoon members and Rangers in their company don't like them. They think this squad gets away with everything. Even their CO won't back them up...That's what he said, right, when we met him?"

"You're right, Connie," I say. "Go on."

She passes a Walmart tractor-trailer truck and keeps on speeding.

"Then the rumors start, the stories, the tales," she says. "Other Rangers get drunk at local pubs and roadhouses, swap tales about what they heard the staff sergeant and his squad did in Afghanistan. 'Can you believe it?' they say. 'Jefferson and his Ninjas got away with it again.'"

I keep my mouth shut. When an investigator who works for you starts talking, you let them talk. You don't want to disturb whatever slender thread their mind and gut have come up with.

"There's resentment," she says. "Anger. They know what happened in Afghanistan. They think the Ninjas got away with it. *All right,* a couple of them think. *Let's set them up here in the States. Do something that can't be overlooked, can't be ignored.*"

I say, "So another squad of Rangers committed the murders?"

"That's right," she says.

"A hell of a stretch," I say. "There's a lot of evidence pointing to this squad. The fingerprints. The woman with her dog. The shell casings matching Jefferson's pistol. The surveillance video from the store. One of the men in the house being the drug dealer for Staff Sergeant Jefferson's stepdaughter. Jefferson telling Dr. Huang he knew what The Summer House looked like. The younger Ranger, Tyler, expressing guilt to Huang."

Connie nods. "But the fact they were accused of exactly the

same crime in Afghanistan, Major...there has to be a connection. Something."

My phone rings and I pick it up, seeing the ID marking AGENT M SANCHEZ.

"Cook," I say. "What do you have, Sanchez?"

His voice is clear and right to the point. "Nothing, Major," he says. "Wendy Gabriel is gone from her house. And so's her dog."

I close my eyes for a brief second. "Anything else?"

"Yes," he says. "Her car is still there. I gained access to the interior of the house and didn't find any blood spatter or signs of a struggle or any evidence something bad happened. She and her dog...they're gone."

"All right," I say. "Agent York and I are en route to Briggs Brothers Funeral Home. Meet us there."

"Yes, sir," he says, and we both disconnect, and Connie gives me a quick glance.

She says, "Sir?"

"Still here."

"We've just found out that the Rangers were accused of a war crime in Afghanistan, something similar to what happened here in Sullivan County. I think we should be trying to find out more about what happened over there. See if we can talk to those few Rangers who haven't deployed. Ask Captain O'Connell to revisit his sources. I don't see why we're still going to look at those bodies in the funeral home."

I move my leg, and miracle of miracles, there's no harsh spasm of pain.

"We're going there because that's our job."

CHAPTER 36

ONE OF THE REASONS Special Agent Sanchez likes working for Major Cook is because deep down he's still an NYPD detective, and once Cook got the news about the missing witness, he didn't waste precious minutes grilling Sanchez on what happened and where Sanchez thought Wendy Gabriel could have gone. There are other matters to address, and now he and the major and Connie York are in the cool basement of Briggs Brothers Funeral Home.

With them is the owner, Ferguson Briggs, who's also the duly elected coroner for Sullivan County. He's a slim, gaunt man with a thick head of black hair combed back and basset-hound eyes and jowls. He's wearing a white knee-length smock over his black pants, white shirt, and black necktie, and for the fifth time this grim day, he says, "Have you folks seen enough?"

Sanchez certainly has, but he's not going to say a word. Before him and Agent York and Major Cook are the fifth and sixth victims of the shooting at the civilian house, and Sanchez sees that York is having trouble keeping it together.

He doesn't blame her. This slide-out metal drawer has the young mother—Gina Zachary—and her two-year-old daughter, Polly. Like the other victims, the dead woman has been stripped of her clothing and her body has been washed. Her body is slightly bloated, and her skin is a dead gray-white color. A white sheet is pulled up to her shoulders.

Thankfully, her little girl is under a smaller sheet, completely covered.

But Cook surprises him.

"No, not yet," he says. "Let's see the little girl. Polly."

It's like the room has chilled down another ten degrees. Briggs looks surprised, and York says, "Sir, are you sure?"

"Yes," he says. "We're here to find justice. No matter how grim. Mr. Briggs?"

The funeral home director stiffly walks over, pulls down the sheet. The little girl's head is turned, thank God. There's a wound in the center of her little chest, and someone has dressed her in fresh white little-girl panties.

His eyes tear up, thinking of his own little girls. All that innocence, sweetness, pure little-girl joy…snatched away with a brief, harsh moment of violence.

The passing seconds hammer hard, and Sanchez waits, hoping to hear something from the major, until thankfully he says, "All right. Pull the sheet back up."

Thank God for small favors.

Briggs steps forward, pulls the sheet back over the dead girl, and slides the drawer back into the opening, closes the door. The basement is tile and steel and has the heavy smell of formaldehyde and other chemicals. There are two metal examining tables in the center of the room, with drains underneath, and cabinets and shelves on the other side. The room is well lit.

"Now," Briggs says, "here's the last of 'em. Stuart Pike. He's the gent who was renting The Summer House and who was found in his bed up on the second floor. That girl Gina and her poor little girl, they were both on the floor near the bed. Too bad about that place...all that fine history that happened there and now it's only gonna be known for all these killings."

Sanchez looks at the body and then over to Connie. Her face is almost the color of the dead young man in front of them, probably still in shock at having seen the dead little girl. Sanchez doesn't think Connie has had much experience with homicide victims, having worked most of her police career with the Virginia State Police. He thinks she probably saw a fair amount of traffic accident victims, but there's a hell of a lot of difference between looking at someone who was killed in an accident— a tire blowing out at a high rate of speed, for instance—and someone like this guy, shot right in the forehead by someone intent on killing.

Cook says, "And are the county investigators finished with their examination?"

"That they are," Briggs says. "We've heard from all the families, and with the investigation complete, we expect we'll be releasing to them shortly. The poor folks."

Sanchez says, "No offense, but the bodies haven't really been autopsied, now, have they?"

Briggs shakes his head. "What, you want me to cut them all open and check their stomach contents? Or saw off the top of their heads, take out their brains and weigh them? What the hell would that prove? You've seen it with your own eyes how these poor folks died. What else do you want?"

Sanchez thinks, *A complete autopsy and investigation, that's what we want,* and Cook is staring at something. Sanchez tries to see what.

The sheet has fallen off the left side of the drawer, exposing Pike's right arm.

"Excuse me," Cook says. "I want to look at this."

The major limps over and leans his cane against the metal tray.

He peers down at the right arm, and Sanchez steps in next to him. Connie stands on the other side of the major.

Sanchez sees a slight lump on the man's forearm. Cook gently picks up the arm and runs his fingers up and down the cold gray skin. He says, "Do you see it?"

Connie says, "No," but Sanchez thinks he knows what the major has learned.

"Let me try, sir," Sanchez says, and like handing off some dreadful prize, Cook holds out the arm to Sanchez. The skin is cold indeed, but there's something wrong with the wrist. He can actually move it from a midpoint down the length of the forearm.

"It's broken," Sanchez says. "Midway down."

Cook limps around the body of the dead man and goes to his left arm. As before, he lifts up the arm, running his fingers across the forearm.

"Same here," the major says. "Broken." He looks at the funeral director. "Were his lower wrists bandaged in any way?"

Bragg rubs at his chin. "I remember so. Both wrists were wrapped up tight with those brown ACE bandages, you know? But no hard cast."

Cook places Pike's left arm back onto the metal tray, pulls the sheet over.

Connie says, "Both arms broken."

"Like someone was sending a message," Cook says.

Sanchez looks at the single bullet hole in Pike's forehead. "This guy was on the second floor, in bed. Now we know why he didn't get out of bed when the door blew open and the gunfire started. He probably couldn't move quick enough."

Sanchez follows the major's lead, replacing the dead right limb back under the sheet. "Breaking both arms . . . I can see that, boss. You want to hurt someone for hurting your daughter."

Connie cuts in. "That's a fair message, for an Army Ranger who's going after the drug dealer who hurt his stepdaughter. But killing everyone in the house ... what kind of message is that?"

Cook limps back, retrieves his cane, leans on it, and then nods to the funeral director. "All right," he says. "Now we're done."

CHAPTER 37

AT THE RALSTON town jail, Police Chief Richard Kane isn't having a good day, and Dr. John Huang really doesn't give a crap. The two are in Kane's office—both standing, since the chief didn't take a chair and Huang wasn't about to do so and have this beefy cop with a thick moustache stand over him—and Kane says, "The hell do you think you're doing, coming in here again, wanting to see one of them Rangers?"

Huang says, "My job—what else?"

Kane says, "You embarrassed me by coming in yesterday and foolin' one of my jail attendants. You think you can come back here today and do the same thing?"

"Not at all," Huang says.

"Then why are you here?"

"To interview Specialist Tyler," he says.

"Why should I let you do that?" Kane says, his voice louder. "Why should I show you that courtesy when you faked your way in here on Sunday?"

"Because I already did it once."

Kane shakes his head. "Don't mean I have to let you do it again."

Huang says, "Your choice, of course. But I'm here as part of an official Army investigation as to what happened over in Sullivan, and you've got the four suspects in custody. How do you like all the news media attention, Chief? There's about a half dozen reporters camped out in your parking lot, all wanting to talk to you and find out how the Rangers are being treated."

Kane crosses his thick arms over his dark-blue uniform shirt. "I can handle them."

"I'm sure you can now," Huang says. "But what do you think would happen if I were to go out there and tell those reporters that the Ralston police chief is now blocking an official Army investigation? And that the day before, his staff allowed me to do my job but now he isn't? What do you think those reporters are going to think? I'll tell you what they'll think. One of the nastiest words a politician or police official never wants to hear: *cover-up*. You think there are a lot of reporters out there now, wait until I go out and have a press conference, accusing you and your jail staff of blocking the Army's investigation."

Kane looks like he's about to gnaw on his moustache in his anger.

Huang goes on and says, "Or you let me see Specialist Tyler, like I did yesterday, and when I'm through, I'll go out and have a quick press conference with the news media, tell them that Chief Richard Kane is treating his prisoners perfectly and that you are bending over backward to cooperate with the Army. How does that sound?"

Kane's eyes are still glaring at Huang, but he says, "You're a goddamn slippery one, aren't you?"

"Only if I'm coming out of a pool."

Kane says, "You think you're so smart, then? Huh? Like all those Asians, all you do is study twenty-four/seven, don't have a dating life, don't do anything outside of schoolwork and books. Couldn't even change a car tire if you had to."

With a smile, Huang says, "I started dating girls when I was fourteen, I run marathons four times a year, and I can cook the best cheeseburger you'll ever taste. Chief Kane, may I see Specialist Tyler?"

The chief still looks like he's having a crappy day, and then he grins and says, "Damn, you're the first Chinese fella I've ever met. Glad you're an American and on our side. Come along, get your ass to the interview room. You already know where it is. I'll get him out to you presently."

Specialist Vinny Tyler is sitting up against the concrete wall in his small cell. Across the way is his fellow specialist Paulie Ruiz, and no surprise, Ruiz is on his side, sleeping and gently snoring. Among other things, Ruiz is known in his squad for always complaining about not getting enough sleep, and when there's downtime—like here in the Ralston jail, for example— he says he's going to catch up on a year's worth of sleep and does just that.

The rest of the cell area is quiet. Corporal Barnes is barely visible over in his cell, reading a paperback, and Staff Sergeant Jefferson can't be seen.

That's a good thing. Staff Sergeant Jefferson is one of the strongest and most powerful men he's ever known—both physically and mentally—and Tyler knows he won't be able to do what he has planned with Jefferson staring him down.

He picks up a single sheet of paper that's on top of the metal sink-and-toilet combination. The words have been printed out large. With a pencil he writes in the last sentence:

I'M SO SORRY.

Then he scrawls his name and rank.

Having paper and any writing materials is supposedly forbidden here in this small jail, but one of the jail attendants, Marcy, seems to have taken a liking to him, and when he asked for a sheet of paper and a pencil to write something important, she quietly slid them into his cell.

And last night, when he told her that the pencil needed sharpening and he didn't want to bother her and could she provide him with one of those little pencil sharpening tools, she had given him that as well.

The sheet of paper goes back on the metal commode. He takes the pencil sharpener from under his bunk, thinks of the long days ahead of him, the weeks, the months. He trusts Staff Sergeant Jefferson, believes in Staff Sergeant Jefferson, but Tyler is still so very frightened.

What if the staff sergeant is wrong? And he goes to prison for the rest of his life? And nearly as bad...suppose he's dumped out of the Army? What then? A life ahead of changing oil in cars, being a greeter at Walmart, going to a grocery store and deciding which of a dozen cereal brands to buy, while some overweight civvy notes his Ranger cap and wants to butt in and say, *Thank you for your service*? Never again having that pure rush of being out on some rocky ridge, a bud on your left and a bud on your right, all of you firing and shooting and defending one another?

No longer?

Tyler sighs, takes the pencil sharpener, and puts it in his mouth, biting down hard, cracking open the plastic.

He spits out the remains into his hand.

Among the broken blue plastic shards is a shiny little razor blade.

He thinks it will be sharp enough.

Huang is in the interview room, waiting, legal pad in front of him and pen in hand, thinking of how he's going to proceed with this morning's interview. He made progress yesterday morning with the young Ranger, getting him to open up just a bit, and in that brief opening, Huang saw a way forward. Today he will tell Tyler about other soldiers he's interviewed in the past, about what those soldiers have seen and done, and the guilt and dreams they've carried. Huang will tell Tyler that the guilt and dreams will never fully go away but, with Huang's and others' help, the burden can be eased.

And Huang is desperately hoping at some time in the next hour or so Tyler will give him details of what the burden is and how it came about.

A siren gets his attention.

Shouts.

He puts his pen down.

Hears men or women running by. More shouts.

Doors being slammed.

Huang wants to get up and see what's going on, but he knows better. He's gotten back into the jail for an interview by spinning a good story with a sprinkling of medical and Army bullshit, and he doesn't want Chief Kane to start pushing hard—

The metal interview door opens, banging into the wall.

Kane is standing there, breathing hard, face red and beads of sweat running down his cheeks.

"Sorry to tell you, Dr. Huang, but I can't arrange your interview with Specialist Tyler."

It feels like that metal door has also slammed into Huang's chest, but he needs to ask the question.

"What's wrong?"

Kane says, "That young Army Ranger just done slit his wrists and killed himself."

CHAPTER 38

IT'S A GRIM MEETING of my investigators when Huang arrives and tells us what's just happened over at the Ralston jail. He's followed by Sanchez, giving us an update about his missing witness. Then I ask Connie to brief the others about our funeral home visit—learning one of the victims had broken wrists—followed by a report on our earlier viewing of the convenience store's surveillance tape, and I take over at the end, passing on that the four Rangers were accused of committing exactly the same type of civilian massacre in Afghanistan during their last deployment.

The room is quiet and the air thick with disappointment. York, Huang, Sanchez, and Pierce all are downcast, looking at the worn carpeted floor. Huang shakes his head, looks up, face drawn.

"Major, it was my fault," he says. "I pushed Specialist Tyler too hard. His suicide is on me."

I raise my voice. "Knock it off, Lieutenant. You were doing your job. That's it. The specialist was fighting demons. You were trying to help him. Show him a way out. A chance to recover. This time, the demons won. Aided by a jail attendant who should have followed procedures."

Huang's expression doesn't change.

"Captain Pierce," I say. "The district attorney told you the Rangers are planning to represent themselves at the upcoming hearing on Thursday. Any details?"

"No, sir. He told me the Rangers would speak for themselves, and that was all."

Huang lowers his head. I think I know what he's feeling. In his own and final way, Specialist Tyler has already done that, spoken for himself.

"Sanchez," I say. "Was there any evidence our dog-walking witness left that house under duress?"

"No, sir," he says. "Door was locked and secured, like she left and expected to come back. The inside of the house was a mess, but no sign that items were tossed around, no sign of violence."

York asks, "How did you get in, then?"

Sanchez shrugs. "The usual way. You got a problem with that?"

Before Connie can snap back at Sanchez, I say, "But her vehicle was still there."

"Yes, sir."

"Neighbors?"

"None within easy walking distance, sir," he says.

I heave myself off the chair, go to the whiteboard. The innocents on one side, the accused on the other. I uncap a marker, draw a line between Staff Sergeant Jefferson and the dead Stuart Pike, drug dealer and renter of the kill house.

"This is the connection," I say. "The man who supplied the fentanyl that nearly killed Jefferson's stepdaughter, Carol Crosby."

I put the pen down, and then with my right index finger I erase parts of the marking so what remains is a dotted line.

"I don't like it," I say. "The man has two broken wrists. That I can see. But killing him and everyone else...a little girl, her mother, kids playing video games, dragging a woman from underneath a bed to put a round in her head?" I turn away from the whiteboard. "I don't like it."

I go back to my chair. "Huang, Pierce, go out to that coffee shop. See if you can find something for us to eat that isn't deep-fried."

Pierce says, "Yes, sir," and Huang is quiet as they both step out of the room.

I say, "Sanchez, do what you do best. Go out and make friends with the news media, and make sure they leave us alone. With Tyler's suicide, we're going to have reporters dogging us every foot, every mile, every minute of the day. Get us some breathing room."

"On it, boss," he says, and leaves, and there's just Connie and me.

I get my phone and dial a number. A sturdy male voice says, "Sullivan County Sheriff's Department, Deputy Crane speaking."

"This is Major Cook, Army CID. Is Sheriff Williams available?"

"Not at the moment, sir."

"Please have her call me at her earliest convenience."

With that task completed, I disconnect the call and sit still in the quiet room. Connie is quiet as well. I hear a few voices outside, think it's Sanchez, on the job.

"Sir?" she asks.

"Yes?"

"Are you going to call Colonel Phillips?"

"Not at the moment," I say.

"Why?" Connie asks.

"Because I'll have to tell him that one of the four Army Rangers is dead, that we've got overwhelming evidence putting those Rangers at the scene of the murders, and that this evidence sucks. Too convenient, too helpful, and too screwy. I do that right now,

I'll be on the phone with him forever, and we don't have the time. There are too many things moving too quickly."

I turn at the sound of the door unlocking, and Pierce and Huang are coming in, hands empty. I'm wondering what went wrong when Sheriff Williams follows them in, with Sanchez right behind her.

Not a problem. Food can wait.

Williams is wearing a worn camo jumpsuit, zippered up the front, hands covered with black leather shooting gloves. She's holding her carrying case in her right hand and says, "Major? Heard you were looking for me."

I stand up, left leg complaining once more. "I am."

"Good," she says, holding up her bag. "Same here. And sorry to say, because I love the Army and such, I've got the final nails in those Rangers' coffins."

CHAPTER 39

WILLIAMS SITS AT the near table, takes a laptop out of her bag, and says, "I was on my way to have a peaceful afternoon at the range when I got a phone call and then an urgent email." She powers up her laptop. "Then you contacted my office, and here I am."

Chairs are pulled in, and I try to keep my leg out of the way.

As the sheriff's computer comes to life, she says, "I see a hell of a lot of reporters out there. I bet it's gonna get worse for you once the news gets out about that Ranger who just died. When I leave, I can send a couple of my off-duty deputies to set up a little cordon—at least they'll keep the reporters at a distance."

Huang looks like he's been gut-punched, and I say, "No, we'll be fine. What do you have, Sheriff?"

I know I should feel grateful to the sheriff for coming by, but it's unsettling. I wanted to talk to her over the phone, on my terms, not have her barrel in, like she's once more showing off that this is her town, her county, and ultimately her investigation.

Biting her lower lip, she works the keyboard and says, "Harold Blake, over at the GBI, gave me a frantic phone call and a screamer email a while ago about our Stuart Pike and his merry gang of drug dealers."

I say, "You said earlier you considered the Georgia Bureau of Investigation vampires, that you never let them into an investigation because they'd take it over."

"Yeah, I did say that, didn't I?" she says. "But that's if I invite them. And this was no invite. This was a sharing of information. Big difference."

Sanchez—my former LA cop—says, "Cooperation is nice, when it happens."

Williams flashes a smile at Sanchez. "Who said anything about cooperation? It was a sharing, that's all. Investigator Blake and I go way back...including a weekend at Myrtle Beach when we were both younger and he was married. Okay, here we go."

From the laptop's tiny speakers comes a burst of static, and she says, "All right. This is what we have. My buddy Harold, he's working on the South Georgia Drug Task Force. It's a mix of GBI, the FBI, the DEA, and even the State Police. They've been doing a lot of investigating, tracking, and surveillance of drug dealers in this part of the state."

Connie leans over the table. "Stuart Pike was being watched, then."

"That's right, young lady. They had The Summer House wired. Stem to stern. And Harold sent me—strictly on the QT—an excerpt from what was being recorded in Pike's room the night of the shootings. I've listened to it three times...and by Christ, I get the chills each time. Now it's your turn, I'm afraid."

Williams rotates the laptop, and there's an icon in the center of the screen, depicting a recording system. She puts her finger down on a button, and the hiss of the static gets louder.

Muffled voices. Music and little bursts of fake gunfire and explosions.

"Got you, you..." one of the voices calls out.

A low squeaking noise and a slight moan, and a louder

man's voice: "Will you shut up down there? Trying to get some rest..."

Williams says, "That figures to be Pike, in his bedroom. The other noise is from the two guys and gal downstairs, playing that video game. Okay, in about two seconds..."

I think, *One one-thousand, two one-thousand...*

A loud *thump* bursts out of the speakers. In my imagination I know what's just happened: using det cord, the assailants have blown open the door.

Shouts.

Screams.

Muffled *pop, pop, pop.*

I know that sound.

Pistols with sound suppressors.

More screams.

Footsteps pounding on stairs.

"Go!" a woman screams. "Go!"

Sound of a door slamming open.

Man's voice: "Gina, what the hell—"

"Stu, please, please—"

A little girl is crying.

I know I'll never forget that sound, ever.

Two more muffled shots, then a low voice murmuring a sentence, and one more shot.

A few seconds pass by.

Williams swallows. "We're sure that's Gina Zachary and her little girl, Polly. That third shot was for Stuart Pike."

Just the faint murmur of voices, and then one last muffled shot.

"The older sister, Lillian," Williams explains. "She was the last one."

I say, "There are a few words on the recording, just before Pike gets shot. Can you play that back, louder?"

Williams says, "Sure. I know exactly where to replay it...and I know what it says, but I want you folks to make up your own minds on what you hear."

We're all leaning into the laptop that is offering so much, and Williams touches a few keys. The sound is louder, with the hissing of the static, and the sound of the gunshot is so loud it seems like it's coming from inside the room, and then a man's voice, low and full of anger and strength:

"This is what you get when you screw with a Ranger's family."

I slowly sit back.

Williams scratches at the back of her head. "Sorry, folks, this about wraps it up, doesn't it? Those Rangers are guilty as sin, and we all know it now, don't we?"

CHAPTER 40

IT'S EITHER LATE at night or early in the morning—depending on one's point of view—and Special Agent Connie York is awake in her damn uncomfortable bed, sitting up, her laptop in front of her.

Her temporary roommate, Pierce, is only three feet away, but he's sleeping soundly, which is a gift. She has foam earplugs that she always brings with her on trips, to deaden any noise out there that would prevent her from sleeping, but she could be in the middle of a dead desert tonight with no sounds and she still wouldn't be able to get to sleep.

Too much is going on.

Since Sheriff Williams left with that one last and compelling piece of evidence, and after a lousy evening meal and even lousier discussion about what to do next with the major and the rest of the crew, she's now here in her shared room, watching and rewatching the convenience store surveillance tape.

Something is bugging her, and she can't figure out what it is.

The lights are off in their cruddy room. Occasionally she hears voices outside, from either drunks leaving the town's few bars after closing time or members of the press, still hovering around them like the vultures they are.

The only illumination comes from her laptop, and the brief bit of surveillance tape she views again and again.

Outside the store, near the gas pumps, Specialist Vinny Tyler and Specialist Paulie Ruiz are smoking, talking, pointing at each other. Voices seemingly raised. An argument going on.

"Oh, damn," she whispers. "Too bad there's no audio. I'd love to hear what you fellows are saying."

Inside the store, Staff Sergeant Caleb Jefferson and Corporal Curtis Barnes move briskly and efficiently, going to the rear to get energy drinks and then coming up to the counter to pay for their purchases.

Money is passed over and change is received. Outside Tyler and Barnes are still talking, and it seems like Tyler is on the defensive. Hard to pin it down, but it looks like poor Tyler is making an argument to Barnes and is losing.

Poor Tyler indeed, his life ending not on some foreign battle-field in the service of his country but in some steel-and-concrete cell in a small Georgia town.

She goes through the surveillance tape two more times. Yawns.

Something is still wrong.

Again, she goes back to the beginning and sees the big pickup truck roll in, and the owner, Vihan Laghari, is sitting on a metal stool, smoking a cigarette, watching the television set underneath the counter.

When the door opens up, Laghari stubs out the cigarette, stands up, and—

She rewinds the video.

Watches.

Rewinds the video.

Even in the poor black-and-white quality of the video, she can make out what Laghari is watching on the hidden television.

It's not a Bollywood program.

It's one of those reality housewives shows on the Bravo network.

"Damn," she whispers.

She opens a browser window, gets to work, and there's a pounding on the door that goes on and on and on.

York instantly slaps the cover down on her laptop—getting rid of a light source—then she rolls over onto the floor and thrusts her right hand into her open go bag.

On the other side of the room Pierce wakes up and says, "What the hell is going on?"

The pounding is heavy, hard, determined.

"Keep your voice down," she says to the JAG lawyer. "Somebody either wants in or wants our attention."

She slides along the wall, SIG Sauer in hand, and she quietly unbolts the chain to the door. There's a peephole in the door, but there's no way she's putting an unguarded eye up to it. Too many memories of horror movies with ice picks driving through the peephole into dumb victims . . . which she most certainly is not.

York grabs the doorknob, gives it a good spin, and quickly pulls the door open.

Outside an angry-looking Major Cook is there, metal cane in hand, dressed in gym shorts and a gray-and-blue NYPD T-shirt, and he says, "Choir practice. Now."

He limps off to room 11, and after grabbing her laptop she follows him, with Pierce right behind her, yawning and scratching at his head.

Pierce says, "Mind telling me what 'choir practice' means?"

The laptop is warm under her arm. "Old cop slang. An after-hours meeting, unofficial, no records kept. Usually it means an after-shift party. Or an ass kicking. Care to guess what we're in for?"

"No," Pierce says.

Inside room 11 it's warm and stuffy, and it smells of sweat

and old grease, just like her own room with Pierce. If there's housekeeping at this motel, Connie has yet to see it.

Huang and Sanchez are there, sitting next to each other, wearing shorts and T-shirts. Sanchez has a number of tattoos on his large upper biceps. The major waits until everyone is seated and then slams the door shut.

Nobody says a word. Everyone is paying attention. Cook's face is mottled red, and York thinks this is the first time she and the others have seen his wounded leg. She's shocked at how pale and thin it is, and how the flesh is puckered and ridged with scars and burn tissue. The pain her boss goes through every day must be tremendous.

He says, "Listen up. Look around. This is a special unit, coordinated by the Criminal Investigation Division of the goddamn United States Army, tasked to investigate crimes of high interest and severity. That means Colonel Phillips and myself thought at one point you had the experience and guts to get the job done."

York's computer is on her lap, and she's slowly manipulating the keys, wanting to take a closer look at what the new browser window is revealing.

Cook leans into his cane, and she thinks he's standing here, leg exposed, to shock all of them, and the major's doing a good job. Even though she's quietly working on something else, his words shoot out at them like chunks of cold stone.

"Right now, damn it, you're failing. All of you. You've done some preliminary work gathering information and evidence, but you know what? It's all been fed to us! All of it! The police reports, the witnesses, the surveillance tape, the forensics, the county coroner...everything has been set up on the proverbial goddamn silver platter, and right now it stops!"

York freezes the browser.

My God.

Can this be true?

Cook nearly shouts, "Sanchez!"

He sits up. "Sir!"

"Wendy Gabriel, the witness who has the dog. Find her or find someone who knows why she's gone, or where she's gone. You hit every mobile home and shack within five miles of that place. You go back to her home and you look it over, see if there's anything there that says why she left and where she went."

"Sir, she's a hoarder and—"

"I don't care if she collects her dog's urine in mason jars. You get back into that house and find something. Pierce."

"Sir," Pierce says.

York slowly moves her fingers, the digits feeling fat and clumsy, because she can't believe what she's just found.

"Pierce, you get your ass back to the Ralston jail. Do whatever you have to do to talk to the Rangers. Why in hell are they planning to defend themselves without outside counsel? Are they being pressured? Blackmailed? And when you go to Ralston, you take Huang with you."

Huang says in a tired voice, "But, sir, I mean—"

"Doctor, shut up and do your job," Cook says, his face even more red. "You suck it up and get back to Ralston, and you do your damn professional best and get in there and talk to those Rangers. What happened to them in Afghanistan with that civilian house they supposedly hit? What rivalries and jealousies do other members of their battalion have against them? What do they think drove Tyler to kill himself?"

York is staring at her computer screen, hoping she's right, hoping she's—

"Agent York!" Cook yells. "What the hell is so goddamn important on your goddamn computer? Have you listened to a goddamn word I've said?"

"Sir, I—"

A phone rings. York feels warm and ashamed, like a high school student caught cheating on a test. Everyone looks around the room to see which one of them has interrupted the major, until he curses, reaches into his shorts, pulls out his phone.

He glances at the screen.

"Colonel Phillips," Cook says. "Good. Let's see what he's found out about our Rangers and the CIA."

The major brings his phone up and says, "Cook, here. Sir, could I—oh."

Then, amazingly and frighteningly, his red face drains of all color, becoming pasty white.

Something is wrong, York thinks.

Cook says, "But, sir—"

No.

Something is very seriously wrong.

CHAPTER 41

MY LEFT LEG feels like the femur inside is a piece of old wood blazing with white-hot heat, and I do my very best to ignore the pain when I say, "I'm sorry, sir, could you say that again?"

Even though the caller ID said PHILLIPS CID QUANTICO, it's not our commanding officer speaking to me.

It's his deputy, Lieutenant Colonel Broderick, and he says, "Colonel Phillips is in the hospital. We're not sure how long he's going to be there, or when—or if—he's getting out."

"Can I ask what's wrong, sir?"

"No," Broderick says. "I've been placed in command. Major, how long before you can wrap it up and report back to Quantico?"

I find for a moment that I've lost my voice.

The pain is rippling up and down my leg, like an inferno that just goes on and on.

My crew are all staring at me in their shorts and T-shirts, sitting in this warm and pungent motel room in rural Georgia.

"Colonel, I'm sorry...come back to Quantico?" I ask.

"That's right," he says. "I'm shutting you down. All of you. Pack your bags, pay your bills, and get back to Quantico. When you get here, you're going to write up a summary on how you dicked everything up down there, and then it's over."

"Sir, we're right in the middle of—"

"Major, you're in the middle of one of the biggest domestic Army screwups since we spied on demonstrators back in the sixties. Since your alleged investigation has started, you've pissed off the locals, gone places where you shouldn't have gone, insulted elected officials, and—oh, yeah—you went down there with four Army Rangers in custody. Now one's dead because your idiot doctor pushed him to kill himself."

I can't believe what I'm hearing, and I say, "Colonel, that is way out of line, sir, and—"

Broderick says, "You don't get it, do you? Not only is this investigation over, you and your unit are over. Paperwork is being drawn up right now to disband it. Your lawyer is going back to JAG to defend enlisted men stealing MREs, the doc is going to be investigated for malpractice, and your two other CID investigators are also going to face disciplinary hearings. As for you, Major, I think a quiet request to retire will be looked upon favorably."

I clench my hands, a fist on my cane, a fist holding my phone. "Our job isn't completed, sir. There's a lot to be done."

"And it's going to be done as it should have been, by the book, by the locals," Broderick says. "Those Rangers committed their crimes off post. Face it, Jeremiah, your unit was an experiment. And most experiments fail. I expect to hear about your travel plans by noon today."

He disconnects the call.

I slowly lower my hand.

Expectant faces look up at me, their boss, their major, their leader, waiting for me to say something, waiting for me to make it all right.

What I've heard from Colonel Broderick is ricocheting around in my mind, but I need to get us out of this room.

"Outside," I sharply say. "Now."

I open the door and limp out into the darkness.

The air is thick, hot, and warm. It's like I can't remember ever being cool.

I stop at the front end of our battered Ford, and my crew gather around. Their faces and attitudes are barely visible in the parking lot lights. Fortunately for us, it seems like the ravens from the news media are finally sleeping.

"Face in," I say. "Huddle up."

I see Connie has her laptop firmly under her arm, and I feel a shot of anger but let it slide for now.

"That was Lieutenant Colonel Broderick," I say. "Colonel Phillips is in the hospital. Broderick has taken over. He called to say he's shutting us down. Period. End of discussion...and probably the end of our respective careers."

Almost as one, my four team members seem to take a small step back, as if in shock.

I say, "I've been told to submit my retirement papers, and all of you are facing disciplinary hearings and probable punishment or reduction in rank. None of your futures look bright, I'm sorry to say."

Sanchez says, "This is bullshit. Major."

Pierce says, "High-quality bullshit, sir."

"Whatever it is, Broderick wants our travel arrangements made by noon today. There won't be a debriefing or hearing on what we've found. I'm to write a report in Quantico, which will be buried, and the rest of you are to go home. Now, we have some things to discuss."

York puts her laptop on the hood of one of the Fords. "Sir, if I may—"

I lose it. "For God's sake, York, put that damn thing away!"

Even in the dim light, I can see anger flare across her face. "No, sir, I won't do that. Not on your life. Look at this, and look at it now, Major."

"Agent York, you're about to—"

"Damn it, Jeremiah, listen to me!"

My anger is sliding right up there, but a rational part of me knows something is driving my ex–Virginia state trooper, and I keep my mouth shut.

She taps a key on the laptop, and a familiar video pops up, the surveillance video stream from the convenience store.

"The store surveillance video," she says. "It's a fake."

CHAPTER 42

SPECIAL AGENT CONNIE YORK is feeling a lot of emotions right at this moment, but the one that secretly pleases her the most is knowing that all these strong and capable men—including Cook and especially Sanchez, who likes to whip out his LAPD background at every opportunity—are giving her 100 percent of their attention.

Pierce stares at the screen. "Fake? It looks pretty real to me, Connie."

"The Rangers are real, the store owner is real, but this"—and she taps the lower right corner of the screen—"this time stamp, it's fake. You see what it says? It says 7:40 p.m. Presumably about ten minutes before the killings started, twenty minutes before they were seen leaving The Summer House."

They are all staring at the white numerals, and Sanchez says, "Sorry, I don't see it."

"That's right," York says, an edge of triumph in her voice. "Because you're missing it."

She moves her finger, taps the area that shows the television set hidden underneath the counter. She plays the video back and forth, back and forth, and on the screen within the screen, there are faint images of a man and two women arguing, and then one woman pushing the man into an in-ground swim-ming pool.

"That," York says. "See that?"

Nobody says anything, and from the look in their eyes, they don't have to.

"Anybody recognize the program?" she asks.

Again, silence.

York takes a deep breath. "It's one of those reality television shows. This one is on Bravo. It follows a group of rich and spoiled housewives. This particular episode ends with a fight be-tween two women, with one woman pushing the other's husband into the pool. I went back online, checked the local television listings, and found out when it was aired in this area. Guys . . . the time stamp's been played with. The episode showing that fight scene was at 6:40 p.m. last Wednesday night, not at 7:40. The Rangers . . . maybe they were leaving to go visit that house, maybe even break the arms of the drug dealer. But the timing is off. And somebody did it on purpose."

She waits.

She runs the video once again, and the four men lean in. She warms inside when Cook says, "My apologies. You did one hell of a good job."

And he quickly changes the subject.

"Sanchez?"

"Sir," he says.

"You got into that dog owner's house with your usual bag of tricks, correct?"

"Yes, sir, I did. No excuse."

"None needed," Cook says. "Get back into that bag of tricks. I know what you carry, based on our last trip to Germany. Go on back to all of our rooms, especially room 11. Tell me if you locate any ears or eyes."

"On it, sir," he says, and he goes over to the other rental car, opens the trunk, moves things around for a minute or two, and then quickly walks back to the row of doors, holding in his right hand a small black box that has two stubby antennas.

Even in the heat, York feels frozen. Just a minute ago it seemed like everything was done, finished, she and the crew heading back to Quantico in humiliation and disgrace, her Army career crippled. Being called home, following orders, nothing else to do.

Now?

This pure mystery—of whether or not the four Army Rangers murdered a houseful of civilians last week—has now grown darker, more complex.

And more dangerous—no doubt about it.

Sanchez comes back, takes one more look at his device.

"Confirmed, Major," he says. "We've got GSM listening devices in each room, and two in room 11, our workroom. No doubt about it. We've been spied on since we got here."

CHAPTER 43

WHILE SANCHEZ WAS doing his work, I was already deciding what was going to happen next.

Again, my squad is looking at me, seeking answers, seeking direction.

I'm not going to disappoint them.

"Decision time," I say. "Lieutenant Colonel Broderick has ordered us to shut down. He also told me he wanted to know about our travel plans by noon today. That's in about six hours."

I pause for a moment and continue. "You're going to continue talking and discussing in all of the rooms like normal. You're not going to set any traps or talk for twenty minutes about the weather. Nothing that will raise suspicions. But make sure you don't reveal exact times or places where you might be going. And that includes the interior of the rentals. Those might be bugged as well. They just may have GPS surveillance trackers stuck to the undercarriages. Sanchez, check them out."

Sanchez nods.

Huang says, "But...what's the point? If we're supposed to leave in six hours?"

I shake my head. "No, you didn't hear me right, Lieutenant.

I'm supposed to tell Colonel Broderick of our travel plans by noon. Not anything else."

Again, a moment of silence. I say, "This is where it's going to get interesting, gentlemen. And lady. You know what's ahead for all of you. You can retire to your rooms and take the rest of the day off. That might be the right choice. Or you can keep on working this . . . this case, whatever the hell it is."

Sanchez from the LAPD is the first. "I'm in, boss."

"Me too," comes Huang, the psychiatrist, followed by Pierce, the attorney, who says, "You can't keep me away from this one."

Connie nods. "We've just broken something here, with the listening devices and doctored surveillance tape, the CIA involvement. This lady's not for turning."

I'm surprised at how quickly overwhelmed I am, at seeing this diverse group of Army folks come together so easily, right after I chewed out their collective asses. I'm not sure if they know exactly the career black holes they've committed themselves to entering, but I'm so damn proud of them that I can't talk for a moment.

I cough. "All right. A few more items on the to-do list. Connie, you go back to that convenience store, and you grill that owner, you grill him hard, about what happened to that tape. Who was behind it, and why. Sanchez, I know that house belongs to a hoarder, but like I said before, I want you to go in and find something to lead you to where she is. All right? *Find something.* Then I want you and York to get back to that funeral home. See if the family of Stuart Pike has called to make arrangements. I don't know how you're going to do it, but I want you to grab that body for a future autopsy by someone who doesn't run a funeral home. I want to know more about when his wrists were broken, and how. It seems like the Rangers did it on purpose. Let's make sure."

About ten minutes ago this group was low-key, dispirited, unsure of what to do next. I'm happy to see fire in their respective eyes.

"That's not all," I say. "Lieutenant Huang, you're going back to the jail. I want another conversation with the three surviving Rangers."

Quietly my doctor says, "I don't know if they're going to want to talk to me."

"Then find out," I say. "Do your job. For all you know, one of those Rangers might be shook up by Tyler's suicide. And I want Captain Pierce to go along as well. Again, see if you can find out why they're insisting on no representation. What in hell is driving them?"

"Sir," Pierce says.

"Finally," I say, "Sanchez and York, I want you to go back to The Summer House. Supposedly there are listening devices in there, ones that recorded the dynamic entry, the shooting, and those last words, about not screwing around with a Ranger's family. All of that was fed to us. I want some evidence that the house was really bugged. Got it?"

More nods around the half circle of my brave folks.

"Sir?" Huang asks.

"Yes?"

"Are you going to call Colonel Broderick at noon, then?"

I smile. "I'm afraid not."

My crew looks puzzled.

I go on. "By noon I plan to be on my way to Afghanistan."

CHAPTER 44

SPECIAL AGENT CONNIE YORK is shocked by what she's just heard and says, "Major... Afghanistan?"

"That's right," he says. "The Rangers being over there, their deployment being cut short, them being accused of committing the same crime in Afghanistan as they supposedly committed here in Georgia last week... that's where it all began. It needs to be looked into. And that's why I'm going."

"But..." York stops what she's about to say, knowing it's going to sound foolish out here in this dark parking lot, with the other investigators around her.

"Go on," Cook says. "What were you going to say?"

"Sir... you've always said you would never, ever go back to Afghanistan."

The major just nods. "I have said that, haven't I? Good memory. Things change, don't they? All right, any other questions? Concerns? Connie, you're going to drive me off to Hunter Army Airfield in fifteen minutes. I'm going to try to grab a flight from there."

She says, "Yes, sir. Good luck."

"It's up to the Army and my convincing skills. Not sure if luck is going to be a factor. But Agent York... and everyone else, pay attention."

His confident words just flow right out and nearly shake her to the core.

"While I'm in transit, I'm going to be in and out of contact for a couple of days," he says. "In my absence, Agent York is in command. Questions?"

And damn him, there is a question, from Sanchez!

He steps forward, tattooed biceps prominent and bold, and he says, "Sir, if I may, no disrespect to Agent York, but I have more street experience and—"

"Shut it," Cook says. "Anything else?"

Silence, so quiet York can hear the flying bugs bounce against the closest streetlight.

"Get to work," he says, and he limps back to his room.

Sanchez catches her eye, and she wonders if he's going to apologize, but he turns and goes back to his room.

Just over an hour later, York pulls the rental Ford into the parking lot of the Fourth Ranger Battalion headquarters building. Dawn broke just a few minutes ago, but the base is already busy with vehicle and pedestrian traffic.

Here the parking lot is nearly empty. The battalion is now overseas, Iraq or Afghanistan, checking their gear, loading weapons, ready to move out and act on their training to be the tip of the proverbial spear.

York says, "Are you sure, Major?"

"No choice," he says, dressed casually, in khaki slacks and a short leather jacket, his metal cane at his side. "It started in Afghanistan. We need to find out what and how it started."

"No, I meant—"

"You mean, why did I put you in command?" he asks. "Don't insult me, and don't insult yourself. Anything else?"

"Sat phone?"

"In my bag," he says. "I'll be out of touch here and there for the next day or two. It's going to be yours. You heard what I said back at the motel. Follow through hard...but be flexible. Whatever new leads you develop, they're yours. But work quickly...you probably have twenty-four hours before Quantico comes down and crushes you."

"Nice thoughts," York says.

"You seem pretty calm, considering your career will probably be over by the end of this week."

York knows those words should freeze her with fear, but instead she feels almost exhilarated, knowing she is on a knife edge. She thinks maybe this is what the Rangers over in that building felt like, going into combat. Everything exposed, everything on the line.

"The only thing I'm concerned about is that we're all out here, alone," she says. "No support from the locals and definitely no support from Quantico. It feels like we're the Light Brigade, charging out all alone with cannon fire roaring at us."

Cook passes his room key over and says, "Go through the trash in my room."

"What?"

He says, "There's a piece of paper, a note. From a local newspaper reporter. Peggy something or other. She wants an interview. Talk to her. She'll be your local intelligence agency. Find out if she has anything to offer. When I get a chance to call, I will."

Cook gets out, shuts the door, and then opens the rear door and grabs a black knapsack. He starts limping to the front door of the battalion building.

Something both warm and cold seems to settle into her chest.

York knows she should get to work, but she can't take her eyes off her handsome and struggling boss, limping like he has the entire hopes and fears of the squad riding on his shoulders.

The major opens the front door, walks in, disappears from sight.

Connie sighs, starts up the Ford's engine, and then jumps with fear as the passenger door opens and a soldier gets in and sits down.

"How's it going, Agent York?" asks Colonel Tringali, head of the base's Third MP Group.

CHAPTER 45

SPECIAL AGENT MANUEL SANCHEZ is back at the home of Wendy Gabriel, famed dog walker.

"Wendy?" he calls out. "Toby? Hello?"

No answer, but once he expertly picks the lock, he still enters the house with his SIG Sauer pistol out in a two-handed grip, just in case.

He blinks his eyes. The stench is burning them.

The voice from the major returns to him:

Find something.

The search is slow, methodical, and sickening.

In the living room thirty-three minutes ago, seeing handwriting on a thick manila envelope hidden underneath two old copies of *Glamour* magazine, he picked up the envelope and opened it.

Revealing plastic-wrapped stool samples from Toby from a month ago.

That led to a vomiting match out on the porch, soiling his Brooks Brothers jacket, and he has a foul thought of that ice queen, Connie York, being in charge of the unit while the major is in Afghanistan. Sure, according to the records, she is senior to him by about two months, but based on his street experience, he should be running this case, not her.

Now he's up on the second floor, head light, guts sour, and feeling like he needs an hour-long shower, wishing he could burn his clothes—save for his jacket—when this is done.

But he won't give up.

Not with the major flying over the Atlantic toward a place so filled with horrors he swore he would never return there.

Sanchez spends just a few minutes in the bathroom, wishing for the light-blue latex gloves he had back in the LAPD, but he finds nothing but old cosmetics and prescription bottles.

From there he goes into the bedroom, follows the same cluttered path leading to the unmade bed, sees two impressions in the stained, crumpled sheet, one smeared with dog hair and what looks to be dog spit. Wonderful.

Sanchez turns, follows a narrower path cleared through the waist-high piles of junk to the bureau at the other end of the room, the top of it clean save for some sheets of paper.

"Idiota," he whispers. Here, at least, are some things Wendy likes to keep ordered. Recent bills from Georgia Power, Comcast, and AT&T. Envelopes in a neat pile, with handwriting noting, "Pd 8/24, ck #1119."

One other envelope is apart from the others. Cream-colored and thicker.

The typewritten address is Wendy's, and the return address is an embossed blue seal and SULLIVAN DISTRICT ATTORNEY.

Sanchez opens the envelope, reads the message on a nice thick piece of office stationery, whereupon one *WENDY GABRIEL of Sullivan, in and of Sullivan County, is charged with numerous violations of Georgia Code 16-12-4: Cruelty to animals; said complaint brought to the District Attorney's Office by ...*

He quickly folds the sheet of paper, returns it to the envelope, and puts it in his jacket pocket just as his cell phone rings.

CHAPTER 46

FOR THE LAST forty seconds Captain Rory O'Connell's stare at me has been steady and unyielding.

"Lucky you," he finally whispers, "we do have a C-17 Globemaster taking off within thirty minutes, end destination Bagram, carrying additional equipment, but why in hell should I allow you to get onto that aircraft?"

"I need to get to Afghanistan," I say.

"Why?"

"I'm convinced there's evidence over there concerning the Rangers from Alpha Company."

"What kind of evidence?"

"I don't know," I say.

"All right," O'Connell says. "Do you have orders from your superiors in Quantico?"

"No."

"Travel authorizations?"

"No."

"Have you had a recent medical exam and immunization update?"

"No."

The Fourth Battalion's rear detachment commander waits

another long second. "I don't see a helmet, body armor, gas mask, or anything else you need for an overseas deployment, Major."

"I'm hoping you'll help me out."

O'Connell shakes his lead, leans back a bit in his chair, and I see him wince from his old injuries. "Major, why in God's name would I even consider letting you on that aircraft? No orders, no authorization, no equipment. What, you think this is an episode of *NCIS,* you can just hitch a ride into a combat zone? It's a career ender for both of us. Now, please...leave me be. Fourth Battalion's XO is still not available, there's a missing pallet of equipment that should be in Bagram, and I've got a shitload of paperwork to get through. All because someone decided Fourth Battalion needed to be deployed nearly a month ahead of schedule."

I lean on my cane. "You don't like the Ninja Squad, do you?"

"Not many around here do."

"But if you were in an FOB with them, with Taliban coming at you in waves, and they were next to you, and they were running low on ammo, you'd help them out, right? Even if you don't like them, out there you'd have their backs. And vice versa."

O'Connell's face winces once more. "That's different. That's over there. Not here, in Georgia."

I limp toward him. "That's where you're wrong, Captain. Something happened to them in Afghanistan. And it's followed them to Georgia. That's what I'm trying to tell you. Afghanistan has come home here to Georgia, and those guys are low on ammo and need your help."

I hear a distant whine of jet engines, wonder if that's the C-17, ready to take off and make the long flight to Afghanistan, the dusty and torn-up country that has sent so many of our finest back home in shiny metal caskets.

O'Connell looks down, picks up a pen, and in one harsh move tosses it across the small office. He gets up.

"Follow me," he says. "And even with that cane, haul ass."

Nearly thirty minutes later, I'm practically stumbling across the flight line, leaning heavily on my cane, wearing freshly washed ACUs tagged COOK and carrying one heavy rucksack with a helmet bouncing along against my hip. Helicopters and other aircraft are lined up in neat rows before us.

The engine noise gets louder as we approach the C-17 Globemaster—dark green, squat, fat, and ugly, with four engines slung underneath its large wings—and O'Connell leans close and yells, "It's about thirteen hours to Ramstein, and from there, another seven or so to Bagram. There're no first-class or business-class seats aboard, Major, just the fold-down seats along the fuselage. Going to be damn uncomfortable."

"I'll make do," I say, knowing there's nothing else I can say.

He says, "Not sure where the Fourth Battalion is going to be deployed—orders change all the time—but you'll want to get transport from Bagram to the village of Pendahar. That's near where the . . . event happened with the Ninjas."

"Got it," I say.

"It's the Old West in the Middle East, Indian country out there," he says. "So watch your ass and do your best to hook up with anybody that's got heavy firepower. And no offense, that sure as hell ain't the CID."

I just nod, knowing that I have nearly twenty hours of flying time ahead of me to think of where I'm going and what I'll do when I get there.

He grabs my elbow. "You sure you can do this, limping like you do?"

The engine noise is louder. "I've got to."

He says, "That IED...what happened to you over there?"

"Usual story," I tell him, raising my voice. "Was out on a mission, three-vehicle convoy, we got hit. I was trapped in the wreckage. Took a while for me to get pried out."

O'Connell tries to smile. "Hope it was an important mission."

"Sure was," I say. "I was going out to interview a goat herder whose flock was raided by an airborne unit for a cookout."

He shakes his head, and I can tell his own pain is really riding him today.

Then he laughs. "Thanks for your service, Major."

"And you?" I ask. "Looks like you're still carrying a bit of shrapnel in you."

"Nope," he says. "Not a single piece of metal." I'm sure he notes the confusion on my face, and he adds, "Oh, I was wounded when that mortar round struck my FOB. But I wasn't injured by that. Our interpreter, Nadir, he took the full force of the blast. Pulverized him. And I was nearly shredded into pieces by his bone fragments."

He slaps me on the shoulder. "Get going or you'll miss your flight."

I don't tell the captain that despite my brave front, that's exactly what I want to do. Instead I take a breath and go forward to the large aircraft that's returning me to a deadly nightmare. Off by the airfield service buildings I see the flashing blue lights of MP cruisers.

I try to pick up my pace, ignoring the MP arrival back there, and move right along to what's ahead for me.

CHAPTER 47

THE CELL PHONE belonging to Special Agent Connie York begins ringing and she ignores it as Colonel Tringali gives her a steady look.

"Good morning, Colonel," she says.

"Agent York," comes the calm reply. "Looks like your major is going off on a trip."

"I wouldn't say that," she says, thinking, *Not sure what's going on, but I can't let you delay the major.*

Her cell phone stops ringing. The colonel says, "Not bothering to answer it?"

"Not at the moment, ma'am."

A few seconds drag by. "Where's Major Cook going?" Tringali asks.

"Into Fourth Battalion headquarters, ma'am."

"I can see that," she says sharply. "Who's he going to see in there?"

"I would imagine someone from the Fourth Battalion, ma'am."

"Considering ninety-nine percent of Fourth Battalion is now overseas, that doesn't leave very many possibilities, does it, now?" Tringali says. "Your major is seeing Captain O'Connell, the rear detachment commander."

"That sounds like a good guess, ma'am," Connie says, and her cell phone starts ringing again. Months ago she selected a standard old-fashioned ringtone for this new handheld and is glad for the solid choice.

"Still not going to answer your phone?"

"It would be rude, ma'am," she says.

"Why did your major go to see Captain O'Connell carrying a knapsack?" the colonel asks.

Caught, she thinks, *caught.* All it would take would be this hard-ass MP officer going in and mucking things up. But what can she say?

Stall.

She says, "The major likes to be prepared."

The cell phone stops ringing.

Tringali says, "If he's so goddamned prepared, that must be the same for his little squad of investigators. Right? Tell me, Special Agent, does the name Wendell Connor ring a bell? Colonel Wendell Connor?"

Damn it, the name does sound vaguely familiar, but before Connie can think further, Tringali says, "Colonel Connor is the goddamn garrison commander of this post. Tradition and common courtesy would mean your major should have at least met with him to brief him on this investigation."

"I can't speak for the major, ma'am," she says.

"Certainly," Tringali replies. "But that's how you've operated. Outside normal rules, regulations, and procedures. Just like the goddamn Ninja Squad you're so eager to clear. But a little birdie from Quantico told me that you and the rest of your squad are being called back and are going to be disbanded. Nothing can save you folks now. You've crossed a lot of lines. Just like those Rangers. They've crossed the line, and nobody—not even you and your precious major—can save them."

Tringali opens the door, steps out, and turns around, putting her hands on the roof of the Ford rental and lowering her head to look back inside, just as Connie's cell phone rings once more.

"How long will your major be in there?"

Just long enough, she thinks. "I don't know, ma'am."

"He seems to be a capable fellow, am I right? Able to hitch a ride back to Sullivan when he's done?"

"Sorry, ma'am, I don't understand."

She says, "Then understand this. Get your ass off my post, and don't ever come back. And answer that goddamn phone already."

CHAPTER 48

CAPTAIN ALLEN PIERCE is sitting in the front seat of their Ford rental, with Lieutenant John Huang sitting next to him, silent, parked on a side road underneath the shade of two old oak trees. Earlier they spent a rotten hour at the Ralston town jail, being harassed by the news media, then yelled at and threatened with arrest by tomato-faced Chief Richard Kane.

Pierce says, "Rough morning, am I right?"

Huang softly says, "Not as rough as yesterday."

Sure, Pierce thinks, when Specialist Tyler slit his wrists and bled out all over his concrete cell floor. He says, "Doc, again, it wasn't your fault. You were doing your job. That's it."

Huang sits up and looks at Pierce with something Pierce has never seen from the doctor before: pure anger.

"Shut up, will you? Captain? Look, if you screw up, that means a defendant is having a bad day, maybe he goes away to Leavenworth until an appeal is made. Or you do something wrong in court and maybe a guy as guilty as sin walks free. But you know what? They're still goddamn alive, aren't they? I screw up, a decorated and brave man opens up his veins and bleeds out in a small Georgia town."

"His choice, Doc, not yours."

"What kind of doctor was I, then? Was I doing the best I could for him as a patient? No, I was doing what was best for the Army."

"In case you've forgotten, you're an Army officer, John."

He shakes his head in disgust, plucks at his trousers. "Me? An officer? I'm just a goddamn underpaid psychiatrist who's never heard a shot fired in anger, has used his service weapon four times—all at the range—and I can't remember the last time I wore my dress uniform."

Pierce doesn't know what to say. He hates to admit it, but Huang is making a good point. He remembers the initial shock of going through the six-week Direct Commission Course at Fort Benning, in this very state, and the tough trial of transferring from a civilian life to a military life. There, the slogan was "Soldier first, Army always."

But Huang is right. What kind of soldier is he, compared to the Rangers? What can Pierce say to convince Huang that he is a soldier, that he was doing his job?

He takes his cell phone out, dials Sanchez, and Sanchez answers on the first ring.

Pierce says, "How goes it?"

"I've wrapped up at this woman's place. Is Agent York with you?"

"I've called her three times. No answer. She must still be at Hunter."

Sanchez says, "Look, the major told York and me to hit the funeral home, try to grab that kid's body for a real autopsy. With her out of reach, I'm going over there in a few minutes, and I could use you as a backup. Find some legal way for us to grab the remains."

Pierce says, "What legal way?"

Sanchez says, "You're the damn lawyer in this group. Find one."

He says, "All right. I'll meet you there. And the doc is coming with me as well. We're not getting any cooperation from the Ralston police chief to see the other three Rangers."

"Fine by me," Sanchez says. "Maybe he can counsel the funeral home director to cooperate with us. See you in a bit."

"Hey," Pierce says. "You say you're done at that woman's house. Did you find something?"

"I sure as hell did," Sanchez says, and disconnects the call.

CHAPTER 49

INSIDE HIS CELL at the Ralston town jail, Staff Sergeant Caleb Jefferson is sitting cross-legged on his bunk, waiting, thinking, pondering. There's a fresh smell of soap and bleach in the air, and he knows it's from yesterday, from cleaning up the adjacent cell after Specialist Vinny Tyler—his man, his responsibility!—ended his life.

A good leader always takes care of his men, always brings them back, the best he can, and he feels bone-deep inside that he's a failure. Not that he hasn't lost men before, but that was overseas in the 'stan, where a sniper's bullet, a mortar round, or an RPG could end a life in the blink of an eye. That was the job. That was the risk everyone took.

But not here. Not in this pissy little cell. Not in Georgia.

Corporal Barnes whispers, "How are you doing, Sergeant?"

"Shut up," Jefferson says.

The other surviving member of their squad pipes up as well. "Sergeant, we all agreed about what happened. Vinny...he just couldn't hack it anymore. That's all. It's not your fault."

"Ruiz?"

"Yes?"

"You can shut up, too."

They quiet down.

He continues to sit, brooding.

Out there is his other responsibility, his stepdaughter, Carol, though truthfully, he never really uses the word *step*. The two of them bonded almost instantly when he started seeing her mother, Janice, with none of the fighting and griping about "You're not my real daddy," and she was his daughter as much as any biological father's out there.

He wonders how she is. He wonders about Major Moore, the battalion's XO, if he got to Aunt Sophie in time.

The planning, the agreements, everything else must stay in place.

Jefferson realizes he's clenching his fists.

But what if he's wrong?

And what if all this ends up killing the last two members of his squad?

CHAPTER 50

SHE CAN'T SEE Hunter Army Airfield, but the noise of the air-craft taking off and landing can be heard just beyond the thick grove of pines and messy swamp. Mosquitoes fly around her in clouds, and after a minute she gets back into her civilian car, waits, slapping and killing two of the little monsters that got into the car with her.

Today she has on her uniform, and it feels good. Even though it's nice to get into civvy clothes when one's shift is done, it's also nice to wear the uniform and to have people look at it, connect her to a powerful organization, and, for the most part, give her the respect and attention she deserves.

She checks the time just as her burner phone chimes.

Right on schedule.

"Yes?" she answers.

Again there's a burst of static and a harsh whine, and the caller's familiar voice comes on and says, "Tell me what's new."

"The investigation has been officially closed," she says. "They've been ordered to wrap up and go back to Quantico. Within a day everything here will calm down. The Army can screw up here and there, but one thing they're good at is following orders."

Even with the bad connection and the distance, she can

sense the relief in the man's voice. "Good news indeed. Finally. Jesus."

She shakes her head, not happy she has to spoil his good mood.

"But there's a complication," she says. "Cook is on his way to Afghanistan. Somehow he found out what happened to the Rangers over there."

Her desperate man swears for a long minute, and he says, with more bursts of static interrupting him, "...never should have trusted you...gone along with this scheme. Damn it, we're both going down!"

She says, "Shut up and listen good. We both agreed to this, and we're both going to see it through. It's going to take Cook nearly a day to get over there. Lots of time for me to continue cleaning things up on this end. And when he gets there, it's going to be one crippled CID officer with no orders, no backup, in a combat zone. Lots of bad things can happen to him."

Hiss of static.

"Like what?" he says.

"Like never you mind," she says. "But things are getting more complicated. No more calls. Just see it through. In a few more days, it will be fine. Trust me."

The signal wavers some and then the call is over. *Damn him,* she thinks. What creature has she hooked her wagon to, anyway?

She gets out of the car, takes the burner phone apart as before, breaking the SIM card, and she scoops out some mud with her dress boot and buries the phone and pieces.

Then she hears the sound of a vehicle approaching.

From the narrow dirt road behind her a mud-spattered black jeep with a black canvas top grinds up through the brush, engine rumbling. On the front bumper a faded sticker is barely visible, showing the bars and stars, and the words THE SOUTH SHALL RISE AGAIN.

Two men get out of the jeep, bearded, wearing worn jeans and hooded sweatshirts.

"Hey, sweetie," the one on the right says, grinning. "Howzabout moving your crap car so we can get by? Hughie and me are in the mood for some four-wheelin'."

She says, "I was here first. Why don't you back up and let me get by?"

The two men laugh. The other man says, "Shit, sweetie, you think that uniform impresses us? You're out of your jurisdiction, hon, so why don't you move your hunk of junk so we can push on by?"

The driver says, "Yeah. I don't reverse for no one, and especially some broad who thinks she's all that."

She nods. "All right," she says. "I was just trying to be nice."

Her pistol slides easily right out of her holster, and she shoots them both in the head.

CHAPTER 51

SPECIAL AGENT MANUEL SANCHEZ is sitting alone inside his rental car in the parking lot of Briggs Brothers Funeral Home and spots another silver Ford sedan pull up next to him. Sanchez gets out, walks over, and opens the rear door, taking a seat. Pierce and Huang are sitting up front.

The interior of the car stinks of sweat and well-worn clothes.

Sanchez shuts the door. "Any word from the ice queen?"

Pierce's hands are draped over the steering wheel. "I don't like that nickname."

"Tough," Sanchez says.

Huang says, "We got a text from her a while ago. Seems like the major got himself a flight out of Hunter to Bagram. York's on her way back, to meet us here."

Pierce says, "So, what did you find at the dog walker's house?"

Sanchez says, "Since York is now in command of this little detachment, I'll wait until she gets here. I don't want her to get upset that I'm going behind her back."

Huang shakes his head. "She's been a warrant officer longer than you. Cook put her in charge. What's your problem?"

Sanchez says, "I know things. I've seen things. Especially when an inexperienced woman takes charge and people get hurt or killed. I don't mind women being in charge. Only if they've got the background. York doesn't have it. She's been a state trooper, traveling the mean streets of the Beltway. And—"

Pierce says, "Here she is."

Sanchez sees the Ford with the battered and scraped hood pull in next to them, and Pierce says, "John, you know, you don't have to come in here."

Huang doesn't wait. "Captain, I'm coming in."

Sanchez joins the JAG lawyer and the psychiatrist outside as York emerges from her own rental. She looks worn, tired, over-whelmed. *Good,* he thinks. Maybe later the two of them can have a come-to-Jesus meeting and she'll do what's right for the good of the group, letting him take the lead.

York says, "The major is on his way to Bagram, best as I can tell. After I dropped him off, I had a brief talk with Colonel Tringali, the head of the MP unit at Hunter. She knows we've been ordered to head back to Quantico, and if she knows, the word will get back to Virginia that we're not currently packing our bags. We don't have much time."

Sanchez says, "Connie, I—"

"It's Agent York, if you please," she says. "What is it? We don't have time to dick around."

He feels his jaw tense. "Nothing, ma'am, it can wait."

"Good," she says, "let's see what we can get from Mr. Briggs. Pierce, you got some legal mumbo-jumbo that will allow us to grab Stuart Pike's body?"

"I think so," he says, rubbing at the stubble on his chin. None of the men had time to shave this morning, and Sanchez is still steaming over York's put-down.

"All right, let's do this. Huang, you can stick behind if you want."

He manages a smile. "Strength in numbers, ma'am. Maybe we'll scare him straight or something."

"Maybe," she says.

With each passing second, each passing minute, York is aware that Major Cook is farther out there over the Atlantic Ocean, heading into a combat zone, while she's taken command in a little combat zone of her own. Not only does she have to deal with an angry Army MP colonel who wants to see the three surviving Rangers have a date with an executioner's needle; she also has somebody who's bugged their rooms and one CID investigator who's being a royal pain in the ass.

After brushing past the younger Mr. Briggs, she and the others are in the director's office. Ferguson Briggs looks the same as he did the other day, save the knee-length white smock he previously wore over his black suit, and his dark-brown basset-hound eyes look surprised at seeing his office crowded with four Army personnel. York is sitting in one leather-upholstered chair, Sanchez is sitting next to her, and Pierce and Huang are against the near wall. Hidden speakers air soft classical music.

The place is carpeted, somber, with unread leather-bound books in a bookcase. One wall holds a display of casket styles, complete with finishes and handles, and various framed certificates hang opposite. Briggs's desk is neat and orderly, with file folders and a thick black binder Connie thinks must contain the pricing options he shows the grieving. About the only object out of place is a plain brown cardboard box, tied together with string.

And speaking of grieving families, Briggs gets right to the point.

"I'm sorry, ma'am, but you've come at a very bad time," he

says. "I have the Parnell family arriving in a few minutes. You need to be out of my office by then. You see, their poor son died last night, in their garage."

"Suicide?" Connie asks.

"In a manner of speaking," he says. "The young lad died of an overdose, like so many others in this county. One of the hardest parts will be writing the obituary. We often say 'died suddenly at home,' but most folks know what that means nowadays. Now, again, tell me why you're here?"

"The bodies of the victims," she says. "We'd like to examine them again."

And grab one on our way out, she thinks, *until we can figure out what to do next.*

"I'm sorry, but all save one have been turned over to their respective families."

Sanchez butts in. "For real? Why so soon?"

Briggs still looks mournful. "Why not? With regard to the bodies, the county sheriff has told us her investigation is complete. She authorized me to release the remains. The last family left about thirty minutes ago, the Gleason boy."

Connie says, "Hold on. You said 'all save one.' Who's left?"

"The poor gent who had his arms broken," Briggs says. "Arrangements for his remains are still up in the air."

"That's good," Connie says, "because our investigation isn't complete, and we'd like to view him again."

No need to mention taking Pike. She trusts Pierce, the JAG lawyer, has a strategy to use when the right time comes.

"All right, I suppose you can do that, for all the good it will do you."

A little shiver of cold caresses the back of Connie's neck. "I'm sorry, what do you mean by that?"

Briggs points to the cardboard box. "I received directions to cremate his remains, and there they are, waiting to be shipped to Savannah."

The room falls silent. Connie thinks she hears the quick intake of breath from Pierce and Huang.

Briggs says, "Is there anything else I can do for the Army?"

CHAPTER 52

SPEEDING INTO THE parking lot of Route 119 Gas N' Go, Special Agent Connie York nearly runs into a motorcyclist pulling out from the pumps—a woman with a helmet and leathers flipping her the bird as she roars out onto the state road—and Connie thinks, *Sure. Why not?* One more piece of bad luck to maintain the tone of her day.

She pulls into an empty space, and the second Ford, driven by Sanchez, who was determined to tailgate her all the way over here, pulls in next to her. Then Huang parks, in the third rental car. Beside her in the car, Pierce says, "Don't let Manuel get you down."

"I won't," she says, taking the keys out of the ignition. "But when I get a chance, either later this week or during our respective disciplinary hearings, I plan to ring his bell."

"You do that, you'll get free representation from me."

York gets out, Sanchez and Huang exit their cars, and they all go into the convenience store, thankfully empty of customers. Behind the counter is an older Indian man, with a thick moustache and bright eyes and a big smile, wearing gray slacks and a pink polo shirt with the store logo. He says, "Good day, ma'am," as York goes up to the counter.

"Good day to you," she says. "Where's Mr. Laghari?"

He looks at each of them. "Good day to all of you."

York says, "Yes, thanks for your courtesy. Where is Mr. Laghari?"

A nod. "Help you?"

"Vihan Laghari, where is he?"

The man keeps smiling. "Can I help?" he says.

Sanchez says, "Looks like we've got a language problem here, boss."

She swears to herself and then sees a photo of the owner in a frame nearby, along with a woman and his two children.

"Here," she says, picking up the photo, holding it in front of the man. "Where are they?"

She motions to the rear of the store, and then outside, and the man vigorously nods. "Ah, Vihan, he's gone."

"Gone where?"

"Gone home," the man says, still smiling. "To Mumbai."

Huang says, "The store owner leaves with his family, and there's one guy left behind. Doesn't sound good, boss."

Then Sanchez moves in next to her, flashes his leather wallet with his CID badge, and says, "Police. Got that? Police?"

The man isn't smiling anymore, and York says, "Sanchez, what the hell are you doing?"

"My job," he shoots back. "You should try it sometime."

Not fair, but Sanchez thinks of the times back in the LAPD when he came up against people like this clerk who smiled a lot and pretended to know just a few words of English. More than two hundred languages are spoken in his home state of California, and in investigating cases, Sanchez has run into everything from Albanian to Urdu and has no patience to wait for an interpreter.

He goes around the counter, still holding his badge out like he's facing a vampire with a cross, and the guy shuffles back, lifts up his hands, and York says, "Knock it off, Sanchez. Get your ass back over here."

Pierce says, "Whatever you're doing, Sanchez, it's illegal and it won't be admissible in any court," and crap, even Huang jumps in and says, "If your intent is scaring a guy who can't speak English well, congratulations, you're doing a great job."

He ignores them all, sees a pile of receipts, invoices, and other paperwork. All in English, thank you very much, and he starts flipping through the yellow and pink invoices, the other bills from snack suppliers and soft drink distributors, and, yes, yes, right there.

Buried deep in the pile, another envelope with the return address of SULLIVAN DISTRICT ATTORNEY.

The clerk says something in Hindi or whatever, and Sanchez gives him a look, sees the cheery smile and happy face are gone, and there's the look of one hard man who would probably take him on if there weren't other people in the store.

He pulls out the sheet of paper within the envelope, gives it a quick glance. The language is almost identical to what he read back in Wendy Gabriel's house of trash and smells. *VIHAN LAGHARI, DBA ROUTE 119 GAS N' GO, of Sullivan, in and of Sullivan County, is charged with numerous violations of Georgia Code 3-3-23: Furnishing to, purchase of, or possession by persons under 21 years of age of alcoholic beverages; use of false identification; proper identification; dispensing, serving, selling, or handling by persons under 21 years of age in the course of employment; seller's actions upon receiving false identification; said complaint brought to the District Attorney's Office by...*

Sanchez takes the envelope from his coat pocket that he lifted from the top of Wendy Gabriel's bureau, pulls out that sheet of paper, turns and holds them both up so Pierce, Huang, and especially York can see them.

"See this?" he says, thrusting out his left hand. "Criminal complaint filed against Wendy Gabriel from the district attorney. Charging her with cruelty to animals."

And he puts out his right hand. "And this? Criminal complaint filed against this store and its owner, for selling alcohol to minors. Maybe Pierce can tell us later the punishments, but I bet the animal cruelty one would mean the woman's dog being seized, and here, the store's liquor license being pulled, which is just as good as shutting it down."

Sanchez folds up both sheets of paper, returns them to their respective envelopes.

He says, "Agent York, both complaints were brought forth by Sheriff Emma Williams. Get it? And if she's put you at risk for losing what's precious to you, what would you do to prevent that?"

Huang says, "Good God. You'd do anything, anything at all."

Sanchez nods, feeling great, feeling on top of the world.

"Like cooperating in putting out false evidence," he says.

CHAPTER 53

SPECIAL AGENT CONNIE YORK is pushing the damaged Ford rental up Route 119 as fast as she can, with the dented and scraped front hood shaking and vibrating like it's seconds away from tearing off. She feels like she's in a race for her life, for justice, for everything, and some damnable folks are up ahead, pulling the finish line away from her.

Next to her, Pierce, the squad's JAG attorney, gets off his smartphone and says, "No joy, Connie. District Attorney Slate is in meetings all day, can't be disturbed."

"Big surprise," she says, looking up in the rearview mirror, seeing the other two rentals in a train right behind her, Sanchez hanging close again with Huang not far behind. "All right, get on the phone with Briggs, the funeral home director. And put him on speaker."

She checks the time as Pierce starts making the call. At this point Major Cook is still hours short of arriving in Germany for a refueling stop and, even with the satellite phone, is probably out of reach.

No matter.

She's seeing this one through.

"All right, sir. Hold on, please. I'm going to put you on

speakerphone," Pierce says. A flick of the finger on the screen and a voice booms out, "This is Ferguson Briggs."

"Mr. Briggs, thank you," Connie says, keeping her eye on the narrow state road. "A quick question, if I may. This morning you said something to the effect that you received directions to cremate the remains of Stuart Pike, the man who had been renting that home."

Briggs says nothing for a moment, and then, cautiously, he says, "Yes, that's true. I did receive instructions to do that."

"From his family?"

"No," he says.

"Who, then?"

Another pause and she glances at Pierce, who glances right back at her with a look of expectation upon his face. Briggs clears his throat. "Why, Sheriff Williams contacted me and told me to go ahead with the cremation. She told me that a family member had contacted her."

"You just went ahead and did it, then," Connie asks.

"Why not?"

Connie makes a chopping motion with her right hand, and Pierce disconnects the phone call. Up ahead is the now familiar dirt road off to the right, leading to The Summer House.

She makes the turn, speeding right by the old sign, the other Fords following behind her, and then she sees a haze, some parked vehicles with flashing lights, and when the smell of something burning comes to her, she knows once again she's too late.

York slows down and approaches the house as Pierce says, "Oh, shit, look at that."

On the scene are two brown-and-white cruisers from the Sullivan County Sheriff's Department and two fire engines from the town's volunteer fire department. About a half dozen firefighters wearing bright-yellow turnout gear and helmets are wetting down what's left of the house, which is a smoldering, smoking pile of collapsed wood, shingles, and broken windows.

She parks the rental behind the nearest cruiser and steps out, the smell of smoke thick and disappointing. Even with Pierce next to her, and quickly followed by Huang and Sanchez, never has she felt so utterly alone. Even doing traffic stops along the highways of Virginia, back in her state trooper days, she was never entirely by herself if something went south. If she got into something desperate or dangerous back then, help was one quick radio broadcast away.

Not here.

This entire place is against her and the CID team.

Two men and a woman dressed in the brown and tan of the Sullivan County Sheriff's Department are talking to an older man who has ASST. CHIEF lettered on the back of his coat, and then the woman—Sheriff Williams, of course—breaks away and comes over, a very happy and satisfied smile on her face.

Even with the thick Georgia heat, York is taken aback by the confidence in that woman's smile.

She's getting away with it, whatever the hell *it* is, and she's not showing any fear or concern.

"Morning, folks," she says, stepping closer. "Hell of a thing, isn't it? A nice old historical home like this burning down. A real pity."

York shakes her head. "Arson?"

A shrug. "Could be. We'll have to wait for the fire inspectors to figure it out. Might take a month or two."

One by one, the other members of her squad line up next to her, tired, beat down, and now seeing another piece of evidence literally go up in smoke.

"How convenient," York says.

Sanchez says, "Yeah, damn convenient."

Something seems to crackle in the air. The sheriff steps in closer, and her two deputies do the same. Williams's face seems to change, from the open cheeriness of earlier to something hard and dark, and then she changes again.

Smiles.

She reaches out, touches the damaged hood of the Ford. "Wow, will you look at this. Recent collision damage. Looks like you hit something hard."

York keeps quiet. A piece of the shattered roof of the house collapses, causing a flare-up and another billow of smoke. The sheriff says, "You know, funny thing, the other night Randy Poplar, he runs a private shooting club over on the north side of town, he reported that somebody ran into his pipe gate. Dented it all to hell."

The sheriff rubs the hood of the car. "His pipe gate is painted white, and look what we got here. White paint scrapes. Damn coincidence, I'm sure."

"I'm sure," York says.

"Still, to be certain, I might want to investigate further," and again her tone changes, becoming slow, threatening. "Seize this vehicle. Match the paint scrapings here. Hell, the more I look into this, there might be charges down the road. Know what I mean? Failure to report an accident. Leaving the scene of an accident. Causing an accident resulting in excess of a thousand dollars in damages. Lots of potential criminal liabilities out there."

The smile pops back. "But, Agent York, I hear you folks are being called back to Virginia. Packing up and leaving. Wrapping up your work here. Looks like the only problem you'll have is facing the rental company when you get back to the Savannah airport."

York smiles back. "Sorry, Sheriff, you've heard wrong."

That startles the sheriff. Good.

"What did you say?"

York says, "You heard wrong. We're not leaving. Not today, not tomorrow. We're leaving when our job is done. No matter what burns down, who disappears, or who flies back to Mumbai, we're staying on this case. If you've forgotten, we're the US Army, and we don't back down."

Williams makes the slightest shake of her head, and the two strong-looking and armed deputies move as one to back her up.

The sheriff says, "This county ain't for you."

York heads back to the open door of her car.

"Oh, you're wrong, Sheriff," York says. "I love it here. It's a great, charming place. You know, when I retire, I might even move down here and find a little place to live. Get used to it, Sheriff. My squad and I are going to be here for a long time to come."

CHAPTER 54

BACK AT THE Route 119 Motel and Coffee Shop, York brakes hard, taking up two spaces and not really giving a shit. The two other sedans pull in, and she takes out the key to Major Cook's room, walks in, and—

The place is clean.

Fresh linens on the bed.

Carpet cleaned.

His suitcase on the floor next to the door.

She goes over to the trash bin.

Empty as well.

She clenches a fist, rubs it against her forehead.

What did Major Cook say, just before he left?

There's a piece of paper, a note. From a local newspaper reporter. Peggy something or other. She wants an interview. Talk to her. She'll be your local intelligence agency.

She turns, and Sanchez, Pierce, and Huang are inside the room.

"Quick," she says. "Anybody know where they dump the trash for this place?"

Huang says, "I went out for a run early yesterday morning. There's a Dumpster out behind the coffee shop."

She brushes by them, goes out, and, damn it, a herd of

reporters is out there, with cameras, notepads, pens, and they pepper her with questions as she makes a quick walk to the coffee shop.

"Excuse me, do you have any comment on the suicide…"

"Will the Army defend these killers of innocents…"

"Do you think the Army is responsible for the death of that little girl…"

She pushes through, gets around the corner of the building, and Sanchez is behind her, and bless Pierce and Huang, they hang back, block the reporters, trying to give her a few seconds to herself.

There's low brush, plastic bags of trash, broken bottles, wooden pallets leaning up against the concrete-block wall. Ventilation fans hum in the side of the building. A dirt lot bordered by brush and saplings. A green Dumpster is next to the rear entrance of the coffee shop. She stops, sees a puddle near the bottom of the metal container, where grease, waste, and other nasty fluids have seeped out. Clouds of flies are buzzing around the open cover.

Sanchez says, "Damn," but he's smiling at her, like he's daring her.

Dare taken.

She steps up to the Dumpster, grabs the greasy metal edge, hauls herself up, and falls in, losing a shoe in the process.

York tries breathing through her mouth, but it's hard to keep focused. She's knee-deep in trash, sludge, bottles, empty cans. No recycling program here in Sullivan County. There are vegetable peelings, cold mashed potatoes, clumps of grease, chewed rib bones, crumpled and soiled napkins, chicken bones. So many flies are buzzing and hovering that she's afraid she's going to swallow some.

Get to work, she thinks. *Get to work.*

Using bare hands—damn it, why didn't she get a pair of gloves before diving in so quickly?—she moves piles of trash, broken green bags, more trash and peelings and sludge tumbling out, and she makes a mistake, breathing through her nose, and her mouth starts filling with saliva. Nausea is coming at her in waves.

"You okay in there, Agent York?" Sanchez asks from outside.

She's afraid if she tries to talk, the vomiting will begin, and she doesn't want to give him the satisfaction.

In a corner is a pile of smaller, white plastic trash bags.

Like the ones motel and hotel maids use on their carts. She trudges over, breathing hard, something sharp poking her left leg, and she tears open the near bag. Crumpled paper towels, used tissues, scraps of plastic, and—

Bits of paper. Note paper.

Sopped through with coffee.

Connie carefully unfolds the notes, laying out the little bits of paper on a nearby piece of cardboard. CNN, the *New York Times*, *Atlanta Journal-Constitution*.

A note in careful cursive, with a phone number at the bottom.

Dear Army officer,

It would really make me happy to talk to you about what happened at The Summer House.

Sincerely,
Peggy Reese

Connie memorizes the phone number, folds up the wet paper, puts it into her coat pocket. The flies are so thick that it looks like ashes are falling from the sky. She stumbles through the piles again, gets to the wall, and hauls herself up and over, falling to the ground. Sanchez is there and steps back, bringing a hand up to his face.

"God, Agent York, you stink."

She sits up against the Dumpster. "Nice powers of observation. Get me my bag, will you?"

There's just a passing look in Sanchez's eyes—*What am I, your gofer?*—but he does as he's told, and he brings over her bag. She digs out her cell phone and makes the call to Peggy Reese of the *Sullivan County Times.*

No answer.

She can hear the voices of reporters out there, beyond the brush and piles of trash.

Sanchez squats down next to her.

"We'll try later," she says.

"I don't like it," Sanchez says. "You talk with reporters, you always get screwed."

"Well, good for the investigation that I don't agree with you."

York goes back into the bag, takes out her Iridium 9555 satellite phone, powers it up. Waits a moment, and then dials a preprogrammed number.

Ring.

Ring.

Ring.

Nothing.

Sanchez says, "I thought these phones have worldwide coverage."

"Most times," she says. "Most times."

Damn it, she thinks as the crowd of reporters plows its way through and starts asking questions, taking photos, pushing and shoving.

A horrible thought comes to her. The last time she saw their boss he was walking into Fourth Battalion headquarters. But that doesn't mean he got on a transport to Afghanistan, now, does it? Maybe the reason the sat phone isn't getting answered is that it's not in his possession. Maybe he's in detention somewhere back at Hunter.

Where's Major Cook?

CHAPTER 55

IN HIS CELL at the Ralston town jail, Staff Sergeant Caleb Jefferson makes a decision and then gets off his bunk. Funny, when the decision is made, then it's done. You go out and do the job, and respond to emerging threats and situations, but there's no second-guessing, not in the Rangers. You learn lessons at some point, but when you set off on a mission, there's no looking back.

Ever.

At the other end of the block, one of the jail attendants with a meal cart is passing out an early supper—usually barely warm hot dogs in untoasted buns, a bag of chips, a mustard packet, a juice box. Jefferson raps the old metal bars with his hands and says, "Hey, you down there. I need to see the chief. Straightaway."

The attendant is a chubby, surly young boy wearing a tan uniform and light-blue latex gloves. He says, "I'll get to him, soon enough. I'm doing my job here."

"And doing it *so* fine," Jefferson says, and he goes back and sits down on his bunk. A couple of minutes later, the young boy comes back, drops a paper plate with the supper on it, and shoves it into Jefferson's cell with a foot. Then he leaves, pushing the meal cart before him.

The Ranger picks up the two cold hot dogs, makes sure they've not been spit upon or tampered with, and in a few minutes, supper is finished.

Corporal Barnes calls out, "Everything okay, Sergeant?"

"It's perfect," he says, wiping his hands with two brown paper napkins.

Specialist Ruiz says, "You sure, Sergeant? I don't remember this part coming up, you seeing the chief."

Jefferson crumples up the napkins, steps up to the bars. Both Barnes and Ruiz are standing close to the bars of their respective cells, wearing the same dull orange jumpsuit as Jefferson. He tosses a crumpled napkin at each, and both go through the bars and strike their heads.

"No turning back now, gentlemen," he says.

He hears a metallic clatter of a door opening, and a still-angry-looking Chief Kane strolls in. Jefferson has a funny thought that if the poor chief were to have a coronary and die right now, that angry look would probably stay on his face all the way through the funeral.

"What is it?" Kane asks.

Jefferson says, "Chief, we've been here a few days, and I've made a decision."

The chief hitches a hand on his utility belt. "What decision is that?"

"I want to meet with that Army lawyer who's been trying to see me and the rest of my team. As soon as can be arranged. I want to meet him, and I want the district attorney to be here at the same time."

Kane looks suspicious. "Why the hell should I do that? You had your chance before. You turned it down. Why should I let you do it now?"

Jefferson drapes his big hands over one of the crossbars of his

242

cell door. "Because having us around here is a royal pain in the ass, isn't it, Chief? And wouldn't you like to get rid of us as soon as possible? Stop all the phone calls, all the news media banging on your door at all hours of the day? Get me that Army lawyer and the district attorney, and I'll make it happen."

"How?" Kane asks, and in addition to the suspicion on his face, Jefferson sees something else in the man's eyes: hope that this whole mess will go away.

Jefferson grins, steps back from the barred door. "Just you wait and see."

CHAPTER 56

WHEN I WAKE UP, my Bruce Catton book on the Civil War is on the floor of the C-17 and I hear the whine of the engines as we prep to leave Ramstein after the hour-long refueling stop. I would love to bend down and pick up the book, but right now my body is in dull-ache mode, and it's the best I've felt in the last few hours, so I stay still.

The interior of this transport aircraft is huge, eighty-eight feet in length and eighteen feet in width, and most of the inside is taken up with pallets and containers of equipment for the Fourth Battalion, tied down with webbed straps. Also along as cargo are three Rangers from Beta Company of the Fourth Battalion, and in the flight to Germany, they sat as a group on the starboard side of the aircraft. Only once did they pay attention to me, when they realized I had no food or water, and one of the specialists gave me a bottle of water and three energy bars.

The aircraft sighs to a halt.

We wait.

Wait some more.

In a forward area is a door marked LAVATORY, and beyond that is a small corridor leading to a galley. Next to that, a steep set of stairs leads up to the flight deck. The overhead curved ceiling is crammed with wires and conduits.

On this mission the craft has a loadmaster and three pilots, one acting as a reserve so each one can get some sleep, and across from me, one Ranger nudges another, who nudges the third.

I look over.

One of the pilots is coming down the stairs from the flight deck, not looking happy. I check my watch. It's almost 3:00 a.m. in Ramstein, on Wednesday.

The pilot comes over to me, leans down. He has captain's bars on his Air Force flight suit.

"Got a problem here," he says, voice loud over the sound of the four idling engines.

"What's wrong?" I ask, knowing that whatever it is, it's all on me.

He says, "Got a flash message from the control tower. They want to know if I've got an Army officer aboard named Cook. What did you say your name was again, back at Hunter?"

I don't know why I do it, but there's something in the pilot's tone of voice and I casually move my left hand over to the right side of my chest, give it a good scratch.

"I didn't."

The pilot stares at me hard.

"Mind telling me just what the hell you are, Major?"

"I'm an investigator with the CID. I need to get to Afghanistan because…"

Why is a very good question. I've thought about it, over and over again in the long hours above the Atlantic, running through the investigation and what my crew and I have learned, and I've come to some sort of conclusion, but this will be the very first time I dare to say it aloud.

I lift myself off the seat a bit, so the pilot can hear every word, and even through the sudden pain, I make myself clear:

"I need to get to Afghanistan because a team of Army Rangers is being railroaded, and I need to find evidence they're innocent before they get executed."

The pilot looks over at the three Army Rangers, ready to go into combat in Afghanistan, and turns back to me, nods.

"Glad we got that cleared up," he says. "Major."

He turns around and climbs up the steps to the flight deck. One of the Army Rangers sitting across from me gives me a brief nod, unbuckles from his seat, and comes over. He doesn't say a word but picks up my Bruce Catton book and hands it over to me. I nod in thanks, and he goes back to his place. I suppose if I was the investigator the NYPD and Army think I am, I would go over and try to interview these Rangers, to see if they have any knowledge or feelings about the Ninja Squad, but I know in my gut that the real truth and evidence are not here but where I'm headed.

The engines roar louder, and the large, lumbering C-17 maneuvers its way to take off. I'm ashamed to feel regret, regret that I wasn't pulled from the aircraft.

It would have been the easier, and safer, outcome.

But ease and safety aren't in my future.

Within a few more minutes, we're airborne again, heading for Bagram.

CHAPTER 57

CAPTAIN ALLEN PIERCE is leaving the interior of a cluttered and busy restaurant called Four Corners BBQ—located at the intersection of Route 119 and a local country road—when his smartphone rings. He puts down the plastic tray holding cold drinks for the squad and checks the phone's caller ID, sees the call is coming from SULLIVAN DISTRICT ATTORNEY.

"This is Pierce," he answers. Most of the restaurant's seating is outside on worn, splintering wooden picnic tables, and the Army personnel are sitting at a far table, underneath a large hickory tree. For once they don't have the news media hovering around.

"Hey, Captain, glad I caught up with you. How's your day going?"

"It's going well, Mr. Slate."

"I hear you and your folks might be leaving soon, heading back home to Virginia. That true, son?"

Pierce works his jaw as the old insult comes across his phone, said in a polite and soothing voice, a descendant of the master class establishing the correct order of things.

"First, we're not leaving any time soon, Mr. Slate, and second, I told you not to call me son. Understand?"

Slate says, "Oh, sorry to offend you, snowflake. That's what all you entitled members of society do nowadays is look for ways to be offended. Isn't that right? Or is *snowflake* one of the forbidden words nowadays? Should I make a list, then? Make sure I don't hurt your tender feelings?"

"What do you want?" Pierce says, struggling to keep his voice steady.

"Well, it looks like the head Ranger, Staff Sergeant Jefferson, has changed his mind. He wants to talk to me, and he demanded that you come along as well when we meet."

It feels like a sudden hot wind is buffeting him. "Are you sure?"

"Damn, I'm not going to win reelection in a few days because I'm not sure of my work. 'Course I'm sure. He told Chief Kane over in Ralston that he wants a meeting as soon as possible with you and me. Now"—and Pierce hears the sounds of paper shuffling—"I've got a couple of appearances over in Chatham County Superior Court tomorrow, but I think I can manage to get over there this evening. Say . . . 8:00 p.m. Does that work?"

Pierce could have had an appointment with the Georgia Lottery Corporation to receive a payout at 8:00 p.m., but there is no way he is going to miss this meeting.

"I'll be there," he says. "At the Ralston jail?"

"That's right."

"Do you know what Staff Sergeant Jefferson is considering?"

"Not a clue, but I bet we'll know soon enough, now, won't we?" The district attorney chuckles and says, "See you then, son."

CHAPTER 58

LESS THAN THIRTY MINUTES after Captain Pierce has told them the news of Staff Sergeant Jefferson's change of heart, Special Agent Connie York and her squad are still at Four Corners BBQ, seated at an outdoor picnic table sipping way-too-sweet iced tea and thinking through options and strategy, when her smartphone rings.

The number is ANONYMOUS, and before she answers, York says, "It's settled, then. Pierce, when you go to Ralston, I want Huang to go along. Another set of eyes and ears will prove helpful."

Huang says, "Glad to be there, ma'am."

Nodding, York turns around on the picnic table bench, accepts the incoming call, and says, "Hello?"

"Who's this?" comes a suspicious-sounding woman's voice.

"This is Special Agent Connie York, Army CID."

"Oh," the woman says. "Just wanted to make sure. I saw that you'd been calling me all day, leaving messages and such, but I wanted to make sure. This is Peggy Reese, *Sullivan County Times*."

York gets up and walks away from the table where Pierce, Sanchez, and Huang are still sitting, wanting to focus entirely on this call.

"Mrs. Reese, I can't tell you—"

She laughs. "Ah, hell, ma'am, I ain't no missus. You can call me Peggy."

"And you can call me Connie," she says. "I would love a chance to talk with you."

"Oh, wouldn't that be nice," she says. "I'm afraid I'm busy for a bit with my Walmart shift."

"But you said you were from the newspaper."

"I am from the newspaper," she says. "In fact, I was out this afternoon trying to sell ads and I left my damn cell phone at home. I also do photo work and most of the typesetting, and with all that, I still can't make a living. But I'm a damn good reporter."

"I see," York says. "Then let's make an appointment. I'd be open for an interview if that's what you're looking for."

"You know it," she says. "How does tomorrow afternoon sound? Say, around this time?"

No, no, no, York thinks. We don't have the time.

"Can't we do it earlier? After you get out of work?"

A slight pause. "I guess we can, if you don't mind meeting with me late. You see, my stocking job, it usually gets me off at about 2:00 a.m. Think you'll be up to seeing me then, 'fore I go to sleep?"

"I'm sure I will be," York says.

"Tell you what, we get off the phone here, I'll send you a text with directions to my place. How does that sound?"

"Sounds great," she says. "We'll be there."

The tone instantly changes. "Whoa, whoa, whoa. Who said anything about 'we'? Who's this 'we'? Your boss?"

York quickly thinks and comes up with an answer. "No, he's working the case elsewhere. I was planning to bring one of my other investigators along."

"Nope," she says. "Not going to happen. Either you by yourself or there's no meeting. Got it?"

York looks over at her three men. "All right, then it'll be just me. Alone."

"Fine."

A pickup truck pulls in, sending up some dust from the restaurant's unpaved parking lot. York says, "May I ask you why you only want me there?"

Peggy says, "You may," and then disconnects the call.

York goes back to the picnic table, sits down. The three men look at her, and she says, "That was the reporter from the local paper. I'm talking to her later tonight."

Sanchez says, "What the hell do you want to do that for? I thought it was a mistake the first time you called her, back when you climbed out of the Dumpster. Dealing with reporters is always a mistake. They all have an agenda, and they always screw up the story."

She picks up a plastic cup filled with sweet tea, takes a sip, and decides she's never drinking tea, ever again. "Because the boss thought it would be a two-way street, me giving her a story, her giving us an idea of what the hell the local landscape is like. Right now we're operating in a fog, only getting information that someone is tossing in our direction."

Pierce says, "I think you're right, ma'am. Even with Staff Sergeant Jefferson changing his mind, it'd be helpful to know the background of the players around here. Finding out our rooms were bugged, seeing how two main witnesses have fled, and having the kill house burn down...it all points to trouble."

Out on Route 119, a brown-and-white Sullivan County Sheriff's Department cruiser slows down and comes into the restaurant's parking lot. It stops in the middle and sits there. A male deputy sheriff in the front seat looks at them.

Sanchez says, "There's our trouble, right there. That sheriff and her staff. You know, maybe talking to that reporter is a good idea after all."

York turns her head and stares at the deputy sheriff. A stocky, broad-shouldered young man, who locks eyes with Connie.

She stares right back and says, "Well, Agent Sanchez, so nice to have you on board."

Huang says, "Should we leave?"

Connie says, "No. We stay. Let him leave first."

Pierce says, "Might take a while. Huang and I need to get to Ralston eventually."

She won't break the stare. To the JAG lawyer, she says, "You two can head out. Me, I don't have a bus to catch."

The men stay put for the time being, and the wait goes on.

Then the cruiser slowly turns around and leaves the parking lot. York turns back to the three men and rubs her eyes.

"Looks like you won that round, ma'am," Pierce says.

"Maybe so," she says. "But I'd love to know how many more rounds are waiting for us out there."

CHAPTER 59

IN A SMALL waiting area outside Chief Kane's office, the chief comes from a corridor leading into the jail's interior and shakes his head. "Sorry, Dr. Huang, the Ranger won't see no one but Captain Pierce here and Mr. Slate."

Huang just gives a slight nod of his head, but Pierce feels bad for the doc. Maybe it was the staff sergeant's decision, but the tone of the chief's message was that of the old voice telling those with a different skin hue in this part of the world to stay in their place.

"All right, Doc," Pierce says, standing up and taking his briefcase with him. "I'll be back shortly. Don't do anything untoward and find yourself in one of these cells."

Huang manages a smile. "Maybe the food is better."

"Hate to say it, but you might be right."

He walks down the short and narrow concrete-block hallway with Chief Kane and asks, "Any idea when the district attorney is arriving?"

Kane says, "Just a few minutes. He called me from his car. I'll make sure he gets in with you and Staff Sergeant Jefferson."

They're outside a heavy metal door with a sign saying ALL CONVERSATIONS SUBJECT TO AUDIO AND VIDEO RECORDING. Pierce says, "Staff Sergeant Jefferson has requested me to be here. You'll make sure that all recording devices are switched off?"

"They already are," he says.

"You sure?"

His eyes flash with anger. "Positive."

"Glad to hear it," Pierce says as the chief unlocks the door. "Again, any idea what's on Jefferson's mind?"

"Not a clue."

Pierce enters the interview room, and it seems the chief takes great satisfaction in slamming the door shut.

The small room is depressingly similar to others Pierce has visited over the years, although those were always at Army posts. But this one would fit right in, with its pale-green concrete-block walls, scuffed tile floor, and round table with four light-orange plastic chairs.

The door opens and Cornelius Slate comes in, smiling, wearing a seersucker suit with a white shirt and a red bowtie. He looks like the stereotype of a Southern lawyer, complete with sweat stains around his armpits.

Pierce so wants to punch that older man in the face, but he restrains himself, and after a brief handshake, Slate takes the seat across from him and drops his black leather briefcase on the table.

"Damn hot today, isn't it?" he says. "Last week of October and Election Day is next Tuesday, but it still feels like the middle of August."

"I didn't notice," Pierce says.

The district attorney opens his briefcase, smirks. "That makes sense, now, don't it?"

It doesn't make sense, but Pierce knows what the lawyer is driving at: *Your ancestors worked the fields, so I'm sure you're used to the heat.* He says, "This is a bit of a surprise, the staff sergeant asking to see us both. Do you have any idea what he's seeking?"

A shake of the head. "Nope. But I imagine we'll find out— well, like, now."

One more opening of the door, and Kane escorts Staff Sergeant Jefferson into the interview room. This is the first time Pierce has met with the Ranger, and he's immediately impressed with his size and bearing. Even wearing an orange prison jumpsuit and with his hands cuffed in front of him, Jefferson looks like a man at ease, entirely comfortable with who he is and where he is.

Pierce wishes he had Huang next to him, looking and observing with his psychiatry skills.

Jefferson takes a seat.

Kane says, "Staff Sergeant, I'll leave you be with these two gentlemen. Mr. Slate, Captain Pierce, if either of you wants to leave, just knock on the door. One of my folks is stationed right outside and they'll take care of you."

The chief leaves, closes the door behind him, and Jefferson says, "You're Captain Pierce, the JAG lawyer?"

"That's right," Pierce says, taking out a yellow legal pad and pen. "Now, before we begin, I need to tell you, Staff Sergeant, that if you're requesting me to represent you, then—"

Jefferson says, "I don't want your counsel. I still plan to represent myself."

Pierce slowly puts the legal pad and pen down on the dirty round table. "I'm sorry, Sergeant, I don't understand. Then why did you want me to be here?"

The large Ranger nods in the direction of the district attorney. "Because I want you to hear what I'm going to say to this fine gentleman here and make sure there are no misunderstandings or future disagreements. You think you can do that for me, Captain?"

Pierce says, "This is very...unorthodox."

Jefferson grins. "I'm an unorthodox Ranger. You're Mr. Slate, right? The district attorney?"

"That's right," Slate says, and Pierce is pleased to see that the man looks as confused as he is. "What do you have in mind?"

Jefferson says, "Remind me, my guys and I are facing a judge in two days, on Thursday, right?"

"That's correct," Slate says.

"And what kind of hearing is it?"

"An arraignment," Slate says. "You could also make a request for bail, but due to the circumstances of this case, you shouldn't waste your time."

"Then what?"

Slate says, "Next step will be a hearing before a grand jury, the indictment, and then the entire process gets going. I expect you and your fellow Rangers will face trial eight or nine months down the road. If not longer."

Pierce knows all of this due to his research but wonders what the Ranger is planning. This is all straightforward, all by the book.

And in the next ten seconds, Pierce is stunned at what he hears.

Jefferson says, "Yep, I knew all that. But I also know that there's a way to short-circuit this whole process."

Slate says, "Sergeant Jefferson, I don't have time for your amateur lawyering. I suggest you work with Captain Pierce here and—"

Jefferson says, "Nope. Not going to happen. But I will tell you what will happen this Thursday, when I appear in front of that judge. I plan to stand there and look him right in the eye and plead guilty to all charges."

CHAPTER 60

STAFF SERGEANT CALEB JEFFERSON enjoys seeing the shock and confusion on both of these lawyers' faces, even the Army one, who's supposedly looking out for his interests. They may be high-priced and highly educated lawyers, and he might be an Army grunt and in handcuffs sitting in front of them, but he has the sweet, sweet feeling of being totally in charge.

Pierce says, "Sergeant Jefferson, I'm not your official legal representative, but that—"

Slate cuts him off. "Just like that? You want to plead guilty?"

"I certainly do," Jefferson says. "In open court and in front of that judge and the world. But I want something in exchange."

The district attorney still looks shocked. "Like what?"

This is it, and Jefferson recalls a time back in Afghanistan, early one morning, responding to a Taliban ambush on a narrow mountain trail, and letting the training kick in. Anyone else, facing the incoming AK-47 fire and RPG rounds, would run away or go to ground. But Jefferson did what he had to do, what was right, which was to charge straight at the attackers, not giving up an inch.

Like now.

"You'll get a guilty plea from me, Mr. District Attorney, and in exchange, you'll let my two guys go free. Completely and one hundred percent off the hook. Got that?"

The JAG lawyer says, "Sergeant Jefferson, you can't do this."

"Sure I can," he says, smiling. "Mr. District Attorney here, give him some time. He can draw up all the legal papers and I'll sign them. But you, Mr. JAG, I need you to look over them, cut through the legal mumbo-jumbo, and you tell me, in straight Army talk, that what I'm signing is what I want. I plead guilty to the murders, take my sentence like a man, and my two guys get freed, and nothing happens to them down the road. Not a damn thing."

Slate says, "I can't guarantee that the Department of Justice won't want to look into it if there's a public outcry. The other two Rangers might be charged with federal offenses."

Jefferson says, "That's out of your control. That's okay. I'm a reasonable guy."

The JAG lawyer turns to Slate and says, "You can't be considering this! This isn't justice!"

The district attorney doesn't say anything.

Jefferson says, "Sure he's considering it, Captain Pierce. Why not? He can say he got a conviction without the pain or expense of a lengthy trial, I take the fall, he looks good to the voters, and justice is done."

"But the forensic evidence..." the JAG lawyer says.

Jefferson says, "I've heard some about the forensic evidence. All points to me, right? Nothing connecting the squad."

The district attorney nods. "Seems that way."

"Wait," the Army captain says. "There was a witness, seeing you leave that place with at least one other Ranger."

The district attorney says, "Well, that's true, Captain, but...just because he was at the scene doesn't mean he took part in the killing."

Jefferson nods, feels that the district attorney is coming his way. "My fingerprints are in that house. Empty shell casings from my weapon. And what those clowns did to my stepdaughter...the district attorney can step up before the judge, say he got a deal, and I murdered all those folks because I snapped. Right? Every time there's a war, there are always stories about the crazy vets who come back and lose it. I'm just the latest one. Right? I found out my daughter nearly died from an OD, and I snapped. Went in there and murdered everyone. The end."

Jefferson waits.

The JAG attorney says, "This isn't right."

The district attorney says, "You heard the staff sergeant. You're just here as a witness, not to act as his defense, Captain Pierce."

Jefferson says, "That's right, Captain. And if you don't co-operate, well, I'll get somebody else in here to do the job. But one way or another, it's going to happen. The district attorney is going to draw up a plea agreement that I'll sign, and he's going to write up some official papers that my guys are going to be cut loose, with no chance of any prosecution, today or tomorrow or fifty years from now."

A pause. He adds, "What do you say, Mr. District Attorney? Want to get my guilty plea? Save the county the expense of a trial? Get this case put away day after tomorrow when I appear before the judge? Help you get reelected?"

The district attorney smiles.

"Son, you got yourself a deal."

CHAPTER 61

SPECIAL AGENT CONNIE YORK is in her motel room, sitting cross-legged on the saggy and scratchy platform that claims to be a bed, when there's a heavy knock on the door. Her laptop is in front of her, and she's trying to figure out what time Major Cook is getting into Bagram—and why in hell Afghanistan insists on having their time zone thirty minutes off, instead of on the hour like other countries. She puts her laptop aside and goes to answer the door.

Standing outside by the door is the motel's manager, a squat, greasy-looking man named Farnsworth wearing dark-green pants, a white T-shirt, and suspenders. A taller, skinnier man wearing stained gray dress pants, a white dress shirt, and a blue necktie is standing next to the manager, and a uniformed deputy sheriff is standing just a few feet away.

"Yes?" she asks.

Farnsworth rubs his chubby hands together, looks embarrassed, and says, "Well, er, Mrs. York, I—"

"Special Agent York, please," she says. "What's wrong?"

The manager looks at the other men for support. "Well, I'm sorry, we have a situation here. This is Henry Abbott, the health inspector for the county, and he's got an official order, and I'm sorry, I have to follow what he has to say."

Connie knows exactly what's coming and says, "What is it, Mr. Abbott? Mold in the walls? Poor electrical connections?"

He shakes his head, holds out a folded sheet of paper. "Sprinkler system out of order in this wing of the motel. Sorry. It's a health hazard indeed. If a fire were to break out, you folks could be seriously injured. Or worse."

The door next to hers swings open, and Special Agent Manuel Sanchez comes out, yawning, scratching at his lower back, and then instantly stopping at seeing the three men outside Connie's room. He steps over and says, "What's going on?"

Connie says, "We're being kicked out. For health reasons. It seems the sprinkler system in this place is out of order, and the county is ordering us to leave our rooms."

Sanchez looks at the deputy sheriff. "And that fella in the nice brown-and-tan uniform is going to make sure we comply. Right, Deputy?"

The deputy says, "Just the law, folks. You need to depart the premises straightaway. Please don't make any trouble."

Connie thinks of her meeting with the local newspaper reporter, only a few hours from now.

"No, at the moment we won't do that," she says. "Mr. Farnsworth, any chance you have some spare rooms on the other side of the motel?"

He shakes his head. "Not a one. Not with all those damn reporters."

"And can you recommend any other place in the county where we can stay?"

For the briefest of moments, she sees the manager look at the deputy, and the deputy looks back, and there, without a word, is the answer.

"I see," she says. "Sanchez, start packing. When Pierce and Huang get back, they'll do the same."

*   *   *

An hour later, after Pierce has briefed her and the others on Jefferson's plan to plead guilty in less than two days—*Good Lord, what a day this has turned out to be*—she and the men are outside in the dark of the parking lot, luggage at their feet, standing next to their rental Fords. While the motel manager and the health inspector have left, the deputy sheriff has remained, casually leaning against the front fender of his cruiser.

Sanchez says, "Sorry, Connie—I mean, ma'am—there's not a single damn motel room available anywhere near here. The nearest is in Georgetown."

York stares at the deputy sheriff. "Remind me, is Georgetown in Sullivan County?"

"No," Sanchez says as Huang and Pierce look on. "It's in Chatham County."

Connie picks up her bags, goes to the trunk of the nearest Ford. "No. We're not leaving Sullivan County. Not tonight, and not until the job is over."

She opens the trunk, and Pierce says, "Ah, ma'am, what do we do…I mean, what do we do in the meantime?"

Connie slams the trunk down. "I once pulled a twelve-hour surveillance on a drug mule who was supposed to show up at a welcome center in Fredericksburg on I-95. But my relief never showed up, and I had to spend a whole day and night in my car."

She gives her squad a good, hard, determined look.

"You get used to it."

CHAPTER 62

STAFF SERGEANT CALEB JEFFERSON is lying awake on his bunk sometime after midnight when a shadow passes by outside in the dim light, and Chief Kane appears in front of the barred door to his cell. Across the corridor Specialist Paulie Ruiz is doing what he does best when he's sleeping: snoring.

"You have a visitor," Kane says.

"Pretty late."

"Don't care," he says.

"Well, I'm your guest at this fine facility, and I care." Ruiz's snoring goes on, and in the darkness, Jefferson smiles. Some would hate the noise, but after months of serving with the specialist, Jefferson finds it comforting, soothing, something that's part of his life.

"Don't matter," the chief says. "Your visitor wants to see you. Now."

Jefferson crosses his legs. "Sorry. It's after visiting hours and I'm pretty damn comfortable where I am."

Kane says, "Okay, Sergeant Jefferson, I—"

"Staff Sergeant."

"All right, Staff Sergeant Jefferson, you're a badass. I know that and you know that. Nothing to prove. But if you don't get up and prep for a visit, I'll call in my two brothers-in-law. They always wanted to be police but were too dumb to pass the test. But they'll come in if I call them, and then I'll open this cell door, pepper-spray you hard. And then my two idiot brothers-in-law will Taser you until you wet your pants. Then I'll put you in restraints, and then you'll make your visit, and at the end, you'll still be a badass, and we'll all know you're a badass."

Jefferson laughs, swings off the bunk, and comes over to the cell door. "Chief, that's pretty good. Okay."

Kane moves around and there's a rattling noise, and something is slid underneath the door. Jefferson bends over, picks up a wide leather belt with manacles and chains, two long enough to reach his ankles.

"What's this?" he asks.

"Your visitor knows you're a badass, too," Kane says. "Just taking precautions."

A few minutes later, as Jefferson shuffles along the corridor with his ankles shackled, his cuffed wrists secured by chains to the wide leather belt, Kane opens the interview door, and Jefferson shuffles in.

Sitting across the table is Sullivan County sheriff Emma Williams. She's in civvy clothes, blue jeans and a black T-shirt, but her hard face and sharp eyes remind Jefferson of a Pashtun woman he once saw who had her burqa accidentally torn off when it got caught in a bus door. The look on her face toward the US soldiers standing around her was the same as he sees here from the sheriff: a raging anger barely held under control, a face failing to hide the thoughts of revenge, sharp knives, and flesh being carved out.

"Sit down," she says, and he gives her that victory, sitting a bit clumsily with all the shackles fixed to his waist, ankles, and wrists.

"Good to see you, too," he says.

The stone-cold angry look on her face doesn't change. "We had an arrangement, a deal, an agreement."

"We did," Jefferson says. "An arrangement with me and my three Rangers. Now there's only two other Rangers. The circumstances have changed. The deal has changed."

Williams says, "No, it hasn't."

"Well, so says you," Jefferson says. "But right now there's signed paperwork with your district attorney, witnessed by an Army lawyer, that says otherwise."

"The district attorney, he works for me," Williams says. "You won't get away with it."

He smiles. "Give it your best, Sheriff. But it won't work. Guarantee it."

She moves her chair over so she's closer to him, lowers her voice. "You signed those papers, you signed the obituary for you and your Rangers. This is my county, my land, and I make the rules. Remember that."

Jefferson scrapes his chair closer, too. "Here's a story for you, Sheriff. Non-PC, so I apologize in advance."

"I don't have time for your tales," she says.

He says, "Oh, you'll love this story. Once upon a time an Air Force plane was flying over a remote part of New Guinea when it crashed in a storm. There were three survivors: an Air Force airman, a Navy seaman, and an Army Ranger. They were captured by a tribe of headhunters—see, I told you it wasn't PC—and the chief said that they were trespassers on his sacred soil and that they were all sentenced to death. But the method of their deaths was up to them. The chief said if they each committed suicide, their skins would be tanned and turned into sacred canoes, and their spirits would live forever among the tribe. If not, then they'd suffer weeks of torture before dying anyway.

On a wooden table were a number of weapons. Faced with this horrible choice, the airman picked up a poison capsule, took it, and said, 'Hurray for the Air Force.' The seaman saw a rusty revolver with one round in it, and before shooting himself in the head, said, 'Hurray for the Navy.'"

Jefferson grins at seeing the sheriff hanging on his every word. "Then it came to the Army Ranger. He saw the table full of weapons and then went to another table, which had kitchen utensils, picked up a long two-tined fork and started stabbing himself furiously, up and down his arms, legs, even his chest and abdomen, punching it in, and soon he was bleeding from dozens of wounds. Just before he passed out from blood loss, the tribal chief said, 'Why did you pick such a painful way to die?' And the Army guy looked up and said, 'I'm an Army Ranger. Fuck you and your sacred canoe.'"

Jefferson stands up, heads to the door, where he will hammer on the door and ask to go back to his cell.

"Same to you, Sheriff," he says.

CHAPTER 63

SPECIAL AGENT CONNIE YORK spots the correct street number on the mailbox marking the home of Peggy Reese of the *Sullivan County Times,* and she parks the Ford sedan a few yards up the road. They are in a small housing development of double-wide trailers with carports.

After Cook's orders hours back, Sanchez spent some time under both vehicles, searching the undercarriages with a flashlight, and said, "Looks clean. I don't think they're tracking us in our rentals." As she switches off the engine and hands the keys over to Sanchez, she thinks this was at least one bit of good news before they all started this early Wednesday morning.

"I've got my phone, and I've got my service weapon," Connie says.

"I still don't like it," Sanchez says. "For all we know, that woman is a cousin of the sheriff and is ready to take a wrench to your head. You know how everybody down here is always somebody's uncle, aunt, second or third cousin."

York opens the door. "Well, if that's true, let's hope she's estranged."

She walks up the asphalt and then along the driveway. A dog is barking somewhere, and up ahead, a light is on over the front door. Flying insects are making a moving halo around the globe.

One knock on the door is all it takes, and a slim woman with cotton-white hair opens the door. "Right on time," Peggy Reese says, smiling. "I like you already, Agent York. If that's who you are."

Connie digs out her wallet and badge, shows the identification. "This is who I am."

"Then come right in."

The inside of the home is clean and orderly, with two couches forming an angle, a kitchen off to the left, bookcases filled with hardcovers and paperbacks, and a coffee table with newspapers on top—*Wall Street Journal, New York Times, Atlanta Journal-Constitution.* Peggy is wearing black slacks and a yellow-and-blue Walmart smock, which she tugs off and tosses to the floor. Underneath she has on an old Allman Brothers concert T-shirt, and two large black-and-white cats come tumbling into the living room, hitting each other with their paws.

"Roscoe, Oreo, knock it off!" she says, scooping them up in her arms, giving each a quick nuzzle, and then tossing each onto a separate couch, where they land safely and expertly.

She turns and says, "You know what you call two cats?"

"I don't know," Connie says, liking the woman. "A herd? A pride? A duo?"

Peggy smiles. "A crazy cat lady starter kit. Get you a drink before we begin?"

Connie shakes her head. "No . . . it's too late, and officially, I'm on duty."

"Hon, wasn't going to offer you liquor," she says. "I like a cold lemonade after a shift. Cleans out the dust and bullshit in my mouth."

"I'd love one," she says.

"Be right back," Peggy says. "Sit on a couch. Hope you like cats. Roscoe and Oreo don't think I get enough visitors, and they're right. As long as you're here, they'll be either sniffing your hair or biting your feet."

A few minutes later, she's sipping on a glass of cold, fresh lemonade, the best Connie's ever had, and Peggy has a reporter's notebook and pen in hand. She says, "Mind if we get to work? Won't make Wednesday's paper, but if all goes well, it should appear in the Thursday one."

Connie stifles a yawn. "I'll do the best I can. But some things I can't comment on."

Peggy flips a page in the slim notebook. "Fair enough. Mind telling me your official rank and name, and where you're from?"

"Special Agent Connie York, US Army Criminal Investigation Division. Stationed in Quantico, Virginia."

"And you got a major running the show down here," she says. "Older fella who's limping. Where is he?"

Connie says, "He's been . . . called away."

"I see," she says. "Where?"

"I can't tell you."

The reporter smiles. "Oh, this is gonna be fun."

Connie says, "You might not think it's fun when your part is done."

"Oh?"

"I need some information about this county," she says. "Right now, you're it."

The reporter's smile fades. "Let's just wait and see, all right?"

Fifteen minutes later, Connie is exhausted. Despite the woman's age, and the rural county she lives in, and the small paper she works for, Peggy is good. Sharp, inquisitive, and when Connie dodges a comment, the older woman doesn't complain, she just nods and circles back, and a while later tries again. Connie has dealt with reporters over the years, during her time in the Virginia State Police and through her Army service, but this woman—who has one of the black-and-white cats sitting on her shoulders throughout—is one of the best reporters Connie has ever encountered.

Peggy scribbles some more, looks up, and says, "Well, seems like that's about as much as I'm gonna squeeze out of you this morning 'bout what happened at The Summer House, the poor place." The notebook slaps shut.

Connie says, "My turn now."

"Not sure if I can help you."

"But you know this county, you know the people."

Peggy carefully says, "Not as much as you'd think."

"But you're a reporter here."

"Not always," Peggy says. "I've only been here five or so years."

"Aren't you from Sullivan?"

Peggy bursts out laughing. "Crap, no. Gad, is my accent that thick? No, I'm from North Carolina originally. This double-wide belonged to a distant uncle who passed on, and I was the nearest relative it was awarded to. Nope, went up to the University of Richmond for my degree in journalism, got my master's at Columbia, went to work for the *Times-Dispatch* in Richmond, did some bureau work for the Associated Press, and then went to the *Washington Post*."

The other cat jumps into her lap, and she scratches its head. Even from across the room, Connie can hear the loud purrs.

Peggy says, "You're too polite to ask, so I'll answer it for you. Special Agent York, I'm a drunk. Or alcoholic, if you prefer. Time came at the *Post* when early retirement was offered, and it was gently suggested that I depart, so I did. And when I woke up and dried out a couple of years later, here I was."

"I see," Connie says.

The woman keeps on rubbing the cat's head. The purring stays constant.

"Peggy, what can you tell me about this county?"

The reporter doesn't meet her eye, just keeps on rubbing and rubbing. "It's a county. No better and no worse than most counties, I guess."

"Then Sheriff Williams," Connie says. "You've been here long enough to know her quite well. What's she like?"

"Our blessed Emma Williams, high sheriff of Sullivan County?" Peggy asks. "She's a fair, loving, and incorruptible law enforcement officer who is devoted to public service."

The words say one thing; the woman's tone says quite another.

"Peggy…"

"Oh, what does it matter?" Peggy says. "In a day or two you Army folks will be gone from Sullivan County. Those of us who stay here, who can't or won't move, we'll still be around to have Sheriff Williams as our local and friendly chief law enforcement officer."

"It matters a lot," Connie says. "If it can make a difference in our investigation…please, Peggy, tell me what you know."

Peggy looks up, eyes strained and worried. "Any way you can protect me?"

Connie says, "Truthfully? Probably not."

She slowly nods. "The truth. A pretty rare jewel in this county." Peggy takes a breath. "All right. Emma Williams is sheriff of Sullivan County, and she runs the biggest criminal enterprise in this part of Georgia. Not a gallon of moonshine, bale of marijuana, or kilo of crystal meth gets moved around or sold here without her knowledge, approval, and cut of the proceeds."

The room is silent. The cat's purrs are still loud.

Peggy says, "Think that'll make a difference?"

CHAPTER 64

AFTER CONNIE YORK gave him the keys, Special Agent Manuel Sanchez switched to the driver's seat and started up the car, then drove down the road a number of yards, turned around, and headed back up to the house where the newspaper reporter lives. When he was at a point where he could see the house and where the car wasn't lit up by a streetlamp, he pulled over and switched off the engine. Now he waits.

Something they never show in cop shows or movies is just how much waiting there is. You wait for a warrant to be delivered from a judge. You wait at a suspect's house. And most of all, you wait for a shift to end so you can go home safe to your family.

A cop's most important job.

Lights appear at the end of the street, coming this way. Sanchez slides down so he isn't silhouetted by the approaching headlights. They grow brighter and then dim as the car enters a driveway, backs out, and then returns the other way, parking right in front of the newspaper reporter's house.

He sees the light bar across the roof of the car. A near streetlight illuminates a cruiser from the Sullivan County Sheriff's Department.

How about that, Sanchez thinks.

He slides up and takes a better view. Looks like one deputy in the front seat. Just sitting, watching.

A flare of light, and the deputy lights up a cigarette.

That just pisses off Sanchez. It's bad enough the sheriff's department here is up to some nasty business concerning the Rangers, but this is just insulting, blatantly parking in front of the reporter's house where York is, letting her know that every trip, every interview, is being tracked.

Insulting, it is.

Sanchez reaches up, switches off the dome light, and then opens the door, steps out. In the darkness, he smiles. Just like the old days, not like most of his past cases in the CID, tracking down a missing M240 machine gun or checking payroll receipts to see if some Army clerk has been skimming. This is going to be fun.

He smells cigarette smoke, gets closer to the open cruiser window. From his coat pocket he pulls out an object and shoves the hard edge against the deputy's neck.

"Hands on the steering wheel, right now," he snaps out, and the cigarette is dropped on the pavement, where Sanchez stubs it out.

"Hey, hey, do you know—"

"Shut up," Sanchez says, pushing into the deputy's neck harder. "Hands on the steering wheel. Don't you do anything else but breathe."

The deputy follows the instructions, and in the faint light from the interior it seems like his hands are shaking. Good.

Sanchez says, "You got poor training and situational awareness going on there, Deputy. You wouldn't last an hour in any big-city department. What's your name?"

"Dix," the deputy says.

"What the hell are you doing here?"

The deputy's voice is shaky. "I was ordered here."

"Who gave you the order?"

"Sheriff Williams."

"What are you supposed to do? Arrest the people in the house?"

"No, no, just keep an eye on the place. Make it public so they know they're being watched."

Sanchez says, "What's the point?"

The deputy falls silent. Sanchez knows he's treading on thin ice and makes it quick. "Answer me, and then I'll let you be. Why does the sheriff want the people there to know they're being watched?"

Dix says, "Sheriff Williams wants the Army out of here. Period. The end. Put enough pressure on them, she figures they'll leave."

"Why?"

The man emits a nervous laugh. "Mister, go ahead, pull the trigger, blow my brains over the windshield. A year ago some deputy was giving her a hard time about paperwork, overtime, shit like that, and he said he was going to make a complaint to the GBI. We never heard from him again. Never. He just got up...and disappeared."

Sanchez thinks he's pushed his luck and this guy too far. He says, "Time for you to slip out, Deputy. You just leave and tell the sheriff you did your job, that you were seen and that you're doing your part to spread hate and discontent."

Knowing he's going to live, the deputy seems to find a stronger voice. "And who the hell are you?"

"A concerned bystander," Sanchez says. "Now get going or your sheriff will get a call that you screwed up the job. Take one hand off the steering wheel, start up, and drive away, nice and slow."

The deputy's right hand goes down, the cruiser starts up, and he says, "Mister, you better hope I never run into you again. Threatening a police officer with a gun is serious business."

Sanchez pulls his hand back, gently slaps the deputy on the cheek. "What's the charge for threatening a cop with a smartphone case? Get going."

He steps aside, and the cruiser speeds off. He turns and looks at the house where Cook and the journalist are talking about the case and, more important, what the hell is going on here in this county.

Sanchez puts the smartphone back into his coat pocket, removes his SIG Sauer from his waist holster, goes over to the Ford.

But instead of getting back into the rental, he sits on the damaged hood, weapon in hand, doing what most cops do.

Waits.

CHAPTER 65

AFGHANISTAN

FOR THE PAST half hour or so, the acid knot in my stomach has been outweighing the pain in my left leg as we make the final approach to Bagram. I've been running through various options and scenarios in my mind of how to get off this aircraft once it lands and comes to a halt, and what to do afterward.

Bagram has grown tremendously since we got here post-9/11, and I remember talking to some old hands who were here back then, looking at all the broken-up Soviet aircraft that had been left behind. "When we eventually get the hell out," this old Reserve colonel told me, "I can guarantee we'll do a better job cleaning up."

But what's waiting for me now—

I stop thinking as the huge aircraft makes a sharp dive and turn, and I grab on to a seat strap to keep from falling over. One of the Rangers spots me and yells out, "Nothing to worry about, sir! Just a bit of evasive maneuvering, keeping any Taliban out there on their toes!"

I nod in thanks, my stomach clenched, and I think again of what's waiting for me, which is going to be trouble. Without the proper travel authorizations and other paperwork, I'm going to be in-country quite illegally. Not only that, I'm also going to have to figure out a way of getting out of Bagram and to a village called Pendahar.

Lots of figuring. No ready answers.

The engine noise changes pitch, and there's a heavy *clunk-clunk* as the C-17's landing gear is deployed. I hold my cane in my hands. My rucksack is on the deck, my Bruce Catton book tucked back inside. Across from me, the three Rangers look to be talking among themselves.

Thump.

On the pavement. No windows to see what's out there, but in my mind's eye, I remember, from a Black Hawk helicopter ride I took here during my last deployment. Rows of CH-47 transport helicopters, Apache attack helicopters, Kiowa reconnaissance helicopters. Hangars. Clusters and clusters of square buildings. Heavy equipment. Concrete blast walls with rolls of concertina wire on top. Mountains in the distance. And at nearly five thousand feet in elevation, the air here is cool at night and thin.

The engines change pitch again as the pilots slow down.

What now?

Out there in Bagram is a small CID satellite office I once used for a few weeks during my last tour. If I can get there, and if Quantico hasn't contacted them, I might be able to do some razzle-dazzle, get some cooperation from the CID warrant officers stationed here. Like back when I was in the NYPD. There were also procedures and directives to follow when interacting with other detectives in other precincts, but they were mostly ignored. You needed help, you needed information, you either picked up the phone or dropped by the other precinct house.

The C-17 continues to slow down, maneuvers again. My breathing quickens.

The small CID office is on Putnam Road in Bagram, some distance from this main runway.

I'll be walking with a cane.

How long to get there?

And will I make it?

The C-17 sighs to a halt.

Lights flicker on inside the huge fuselage.

I unbuckle the straps and move, and I clench my teeth in agony. My cane falls, and I lean down to pick it up, breathing hard. When I sit up, the three Rangers are standing in front of me.

One squats down—African American male, a sergeant—and he says, "That true, what we heard back in Germany? You're here to help out some Rangers from Alpha Company?"

"That's right."

"They being railroaded?"

"Looks possible," I say.

"Which ones?" he asks.

"Staff Sergeant Caleb Jefferson and his team."

Another Ranger snorts. "Assholes," he says.

But the sergeant says, "Yeah, but our assholes. Come along, Major. We're gonna help you off."

"You don't have to," I say.

But he nods to the other two men and says, "You can't hardly move. And you got something important to do."

The other two Rangers come to me and lift me out of my seat, and the sergeant grabs my rucksack.

"Let's get moving, Major. Time's a-wastin'."

The next long minutes drag by in a painful blur as the three Rangers manhandle me off the parked C-17, as we pass the secured pallets of equipment while the aircraft's loadmaster lowers the rear ramp. Instantly the wind and the harsh smells of Afghanistan batter me, and I try not to panic at the memories of being in that shattered Humvee, the vehicle burning, trapped, smelling my own flesh starting to cook off...

It's near noon local time, and in the distance two twin-rotor Chinook helicopters are taking off. I find it hard to catch my breath because of the thin air, but the bulky and armed Rangers move like they're college boys on spring break, relaxed and strong. I fade in and out, and there's talking, more soldiers around, and we pause outside a hangar. I want to ask what's happening, and the sergeant returns to me and says, "We've got an open window of about ten minutes, Major, before somebody official comes over to check us in. Where can we take you?"

"Putnam," I say. "Putnam Road."

He strides away with confidence, and I take in the sheer size and noise of Bagram, then the other two Rangers flank me, holding me up, and a minute or two pass before I'm bundled into an unarmored Humvee, and we drive away.

Eventually we're traveling down Baskin Road, and there's traffic going back and forth, and civilian workers walking by, wearing orange reflective vests, lanyards holding their identification, bouncing around their necks.

I'm in the rear with one of the Rangers who's been holding me up, and he says, "Can you believe this damn place has a Pizza Hut? Can you believe that?"

The Humvee comes to a halt at the intersection of Baskin and Putnam. The sergeant turns away from the steering wheel and says, "End of the line, Major. We need to get our asses back 'fore we get in the shits. Good luck, sir."

Some hustle and bustle, and now I'm alone at this dusty intersection, my heavy rucksack on my aching back, cane in my hand, and my breathing is still labored as I turn and limp my way down Putnam Road.

As I move along the narrow road, past tan-colored ribbed cargo containers, squat concrete one- or two-story buildings, blast walls, and utility poles, I run through my mind what I'm going to say, and how I'm going to say it, when I arrive at the CID office.

Two heavyset bearded contractors walk past me, nodding, and both have sympathy in their eyes at seeing me struggle along. Probably think I'm one dedicated trooper, sticking to his job, and I know that's not true. Months ago I left this place and attempted to put everything away in a box and on a shelf, but the smells and the wind and the constant noise of generators and aircraft taking off and landing are bringing it all back.

I even remember the last time I was here in Bagram, working with local MPs, an FBI agent, and two women investigators from SIGAR, Special Inspector General for Afghanistan Reconstruction, as we arrested two National Guard engineers from Alaska who were faking invoices and work orders so they could sell fuel oil to local Afghan merchants.

A long time ago, a simple crime. I don't know if I'll ever again recognize a simple crime.

Up ahead now. To the CID office and maybe I can get some coffee, something to eat, as I try to convince them to get me from here to the village of Pendahar.

I stop.

The familiar tan-colored concrete cube of a building is right where I remember it, but there's been a change.

The metal front door is padlocked shut. The two small windows have metal shutters drawn down. The colorful sign marking the CID presence is gone, leaving just four empty bolt holes in the concrete.

Damn it!

A male voice speaks up behind me. "Sir? Is that you, Major Cook?"

I pretend not to hear the inquiring voice and do my best to quickly limp down a side alley.

"Sir," another voice barks out. "You need to come with us."

I grit my teeth, increase my walking speed.

It's all I can do.

CHAPTER 66

ACROSS FROM SPECIAL AGENT Connie York, Peggy Reese says, "There. You made me talk. Proud of yourself? Just remember. You can do your job and then leave, and we few innocents will be around to face whatever wrath will rise up."

"I'm glad you said what you said," York says. "But I'm surprised that—"

"Surprised? I thought an Army investigator like you wouldn't be shocked by nearly anything."

"You'd be wrong," she says. "It's just that in these times, I can't see how—"

"You can't see how a woman like her could get away with it?" Peggy asks, scratching the chin of one of her cats, her voice harsh. "There's 159 counties in the great state of Georgia. What, you think all of them are run on the straight and narrow? You don't think there are opportunities for graft and corruption?"

"But your newspaper, I mean—"

Peggy says, "My newspaper is owned by Tyron Bogart, an old fogy who believes in one thing and one thing only: the bottom line. A good chunk of the paper's advertising comes from the county: printing legal notices, court settlements, stuff like that. His printing plant also prints up county documents. How long

282

would the paper last if the county pulled its business? And if the county pressed on other advertisers to do the same if he ran stories that he should?"

"The internet—"

"Sure," she says. "When I've had bouts of bravery here and there, I've tried contacting other news organizations, from the *Journal-Constitution* to *USA Today* to every TV station that broadcasts in Sullivan County. No dice. Haven't you read the news, Agent York? Newspapers and real reporting are dying. Nobody cares anymore about local news. It's all scandal, all the time, whether from DC or Hollywood. Meanwhile, Sheriff Williams builds her little empire and staffs it, and only a few care, and those few keep their heads down. Otherwise they get pulled over for going a mile over the speed limit or their construction permits get turned down or their electricity gets shut off for no good reason at all."

York feels like she's been dropped into one of those old black-and-white movies with the cliché of the corrupt Southern sheriff running a criminal enterprise, and she quickly remembers that every cliché has a basis of truth.

"How can she do it alone?"

Peggy sighs. "She doesn't do it alone. Haven't you noticed her big manly deputy sheriffs? She recruited them carefully and—"

It snaps to for York, how she thought she knew the deputies from somewhere before.

"The military," Connie says. "They're all from the military."

"Half right," Peggy says. "Her deputies are all ex-military, but not the ones who've served and been honorably discharged. No, she picks up those who've been quietly separated by something called a failure to adapt discharge."

York says, "Enlistees who can't make it through the first six months, even if they've gone through their training and been deployed overseas. They can't, or won't, adapt to military life. They have discipline problems, mental problems—situations like that. They're discharged...not a dishonorable discharge, but something close to it."

"You've got it right, Agent York," she says. "Sheriff Williams picks up those fellows who have Rambo fantasies. When she gets them, they're upset, disappointed, ashamed. And the good sheriff offers them a gun, a uniform, and a good job, respect and all that. She pays them well above the going rate, from her cut of the various criminal enterprises that go on in the county. These losers get a second chance. And they will do anything for her. Anything."

Anything, York thinks. *Anything.*

"But how can she do that? How does she know how and where to get these soldiers?"

Peggy says, "Politics. How else? It's in her blood, it's in her family. The Williams family has been prominent in this county for more than a hundred years, from Atlanta to—"

"Washington," she says. "I was in her office a few days ago. I saw lots of photos up on the wall, her meeting with lots of politicians. But there was one black-and-white photo, some man in a suit, standing on the Capitol steps."

Peggy nods. "Her great-uncle, Whitney Wilson Williams, United States senator. Served two glorious terms back in the 1950s. His great-niece Emma always wanted to go to Washington, but her one try for Congress six years ago finished with her in third place. Sheriff Williams doesn't like losing, but she knows the facts. She can't go to DC on her own."

York says, "I saw her the other night at a campaign rally for...what's his name again?"

"Conover," she says. "Mason Conover. A dim bulb among our congressional delegation, which means he'll go far when he's elected senator next week. And rumor has it that Sheriff Williams is on tap to be his chief of staff once he moves to better quarters."

"But her background here, I mean—"

Peggy says, "Damn it, Roscoe, how can you get heavier by just sitting here?" She picks up the cat and gently puts him on the floor. "Oh, who's going to investigate her? Me? The *Washington Post*? Nope. She has a clear path to Washington, where she's always wanted to be. Which will be nice for me and this county, not having her looking over us day after day, like some bloodthirsty medieval queen."

York just stares at this older woman's calm and nearly relaxed face.

Peggy says, "Why, she told me last year she planned to get to DC no matter how many bodies she had to step on along the way."

CHAPTER 67

THE HONORABLE EMMA WILLIAMS, sheriff of Sullivan County in the state of Georgia, strides through the crowded interior of Babe's Breakfast in Tanner, a town in the western area of her county, smiling and nodding to its customers, either sitting at the counter or in booths, until she gets to the last booth in the row and sits down.

Across from her this early Wednesday morning is a surprised Cornelius Slate, district attorney, a full breakfast plate of scrambled eggs, toast, grits, and sausage links in front of him.

"Hey, Corny," she says, knowing just how much he hates the nickname. "Fancy me finding you here."

"Uh..."

A heavyset waitress in a stained pink uniform comes over, and before she can say anything, Williams holds up a hand. "Ah, just coffee. Black. And put it on Corny's tab. I'm sure he won't mind."

The waitress shuffles away, and Williams takes off her campaign-style hat, puts it on the padded seat next to her, and says, "You know, Corny, I don't know how anyone can start a day with something so filling and heavy. I put away a breakfast like that, I'd be snoozing for half a day."

Slate doesn't say anything, but his face is ashen, and Williams says, "But, if something is in front of me, I can't stand the temptation. 'Scuse me." Williams picks up a sausage link, takes a healthy bite. "Yum. Boy, this is something, isn't it? Sure doesn't taste like one of those tofu or turkey sausages. It's the real deal."

Slate says, "Er..."

She finishes the sausage link, picks up another one from Slate's breakfast plate, and takes another pleasing bite. "Corny, just what in the hell are you up to?"

"My job, Sheriff. You know how it is."

She shakes her head. "No, I don't know how it is. What I do know is that you went behind my back last night and made some sort of criminal plea deal with that Sergeant Jefferson. Corny, why in hell did you do that without clearing it with me?"

The flush on his face deepens. "Ah, Sheriff, with all due respect, I am the senior law enforcement officer in this county. I really don't have to, ah, clear anything with you."

She eyes him coldly as she chews on the sausage link. Slate stays quiet. Williams reaches out and takes the last link off his plate. "Corny, with all due respect, do I really need to reaffirm the facts of life for you? Do I? Remind you of the times my boys drove you home from the American Legion or the Trackside Roadhouse when you had too much to drink? Or the time that your nephew Bobby Tim beat the crap out of his wife, a real embarrassing mess for you, and I took care of it? Or other times we helped out your office in finding last-minute evidence that let you prosecute cases that were dead-enders?"

Slate picks up a forkful of scrambled eggs, changes his mind, puts the fork back down on his plate. "Ah, that's all in the past now, isn't it? The truth is, I don't have to clear anything with you now, Sheriff. What happened is the staff sergeant agreed to plead guilty at the hearing tomorrow. That gets that case out of here, saves time and money for the county. Everybody wins."

Williams takes her time chewing the last of his sausage link. "Win? What kind of win is that? Those two other Rangers go free."

"But you know there's no forensic evidence linking them to the crimes. It all goes back to the staff sergeant. He's taking the blame, and it's still a win."

She chews some more. "I don't see it that way."

"Well, I do, Sheriff."

"You know what I see? I see you up for reelection next Tuesday, running against that Falconer fella, and you want to crush him. You had the votes, Corny, to win...but that wasn't enough. You want to go into Tuesday's election with this high-profile case behind you. The case of The Summer House murders. Impress the voters. Make it a landslide instead of a decent win. Make up for all your shortcomings."

Slate lowers his eyes.

Williams says, "Hell, that's not a bad strategy, Corny, but you should have cleared it with me first. You know it, and I know it. But you had to go rogue, go off the reservation, and I can't—and won't—stand for that. Pretty soon I'll have to square accounts with you, and I warn you, it won't be pretty."

He lifts his eyes, looking defiant. "How's that, Sheriff? Word we get is that when Mason gets elected to the Senate, he's taking you along to Washington. Good for you—you're heading out, going to your dream job and place of residence. That means those of us back here, we're on our own. We need to look out for ourselves. That's the truth."

She picks up a napkin, wipes the grease off her fingers. The truth is the truth, and she has hitched her hopes and dreams to Representative Mason Conover, doing what it takes to get him elected to the Senate—even putting up with his whiny phone calls these past few days—but why admit it to this clown?

"Aw, hell, Corny, what makes you think that? Sure, I might be leaving Sullivan County if the congressman wants me to come along after he wins, but I intend to keep my organization in place, humming along, even with me gone. Deputy Lindsay, he'll be taking my place. Just you wait and see."

Slate's eyes widen. "That boy Clark Lindsay? Are you kidding? He's the one who shot and killed Mrs. Gendron's dog."

"The dog charged him."

"The dog was blind!" Slate says.

"Still, it should have known better," Williams says, tossing the used napkin on the district attorney's plate. "Thing is, Corny, if everybody knew their place and stayed in their place, it'd be a better world."

The waitress from earlier comes over, puts down a white mug of coffee. Williams picks up the coffee cup, gently blows across it.

"Ah," she says, taking a sip. "Nice and black. Just like our souls, Corny."

CHAPTER 68

AFGHANISTAN

MY NOT-SO-GREAT ESCAPE ends with me coming up against a smooth concrete wall, maybe a blast barrier or something separating this part of the compound from another set of buildings. I turn, and two male corporals in standard ACUs and carrying holstered pistols approach me, wearing patrol caps and very serious looks on their faces.

"Major Cook?" the one on the left asks.

"Yes, that's me," I say, returning their salutes, feeling tired, defeated, and just worn-out. All the way here and to be picked up in a narrow alley by two MPs, no doubt dispatched from Quantico, way on the other side of the world. Mission definitely not accomplished.

I'm in deep trouble, and with the pain and the exhaustion coursing through me, I also feel shame, that I'm letting down not only my investigative squad but also the three imprisoned Rangers.

The one on the left says, "Sir, would you come with us? Please?"

The other one steps forward, holds out a hand. "I'll take your rucksack, sir."

Then I notice the special skill tab on the soldier's shoulder: RANGER.

*   *   *

We're traveling on one of the access roads paralleling the main Bagram runway when the corporal driving says, "Sir?"

I'm sitting in the rear of the uncomfortable Humvee, my muscle memory roaring back, reminding me of a previous ride in a Humvee and how it nearly killed me and—

"Yes?"

"Do me a favor, sir, huddle over and pretend you're napping, okay?"

"Why?"

"Because there's a checkpoint up ahead. I think they might be looking for you . . . and I got my orders."

Shit, I think, and I lower my cap and hunch over to my right, like I'm resting against my rucksack. The Humvee slows. The front door opens. Some voices.

I try to ease my breathing, like I'm really asleep, instead of being moments away from being arrested for a variety of charges.

The door is shut.

The Humvee resumes its motion.

The corporal says, "Boy, the MPs sure are stirred up about an Army major named Cook who smuggled himself into this shithole. Lucky for me, I didn't spot your name tag back there."

I slowly sit up. "Some luck."

A few minutes after the checkpoint, I'm in a cluttered cubicle made of plywood, in a secure area near the runway. The sounds of jets taking off and landing and the deep *thump-thump* of helicopters roaring overhead is constant, and before me is an Army Ranger captain talking to someone on a phone. The plywood walls are covered with maps, calendars, charts, and a Dallas Cowboys cheerleaders poster.

The captain says, "Yes, ma'am. Yes, ma'am...I understand, ma'am."

He suddenly stands up, a frown on his weathered face, and says, "This call is for you, Major. Excuse me while I step out."

I take the phone and wait until the captain leaves the cubicle, a thin squeaky wooden door closing behind him, and I say, "This is Major Cook."

A strong woman's voice comes across the phone line. "This is Major Fredericka West, Special Troops Battalion, Seventy-Fifth Ranger Regiment, out of Fort Benning. We need to talk."

I feel like a wide-eyed young rookie out on his first real street patrol back in the NYPD, facing real trouble for the first time. "Major...about what?"

"I don't want to do it over the phone," she says. "Has to be face-to-face."

"Here?" I ask as an overhead helicopter makes the plywood walls shake.

"Hell no," she says. "Where I am. At an FOB near Khost. Close to a village called Pendahar. Interested in seeing me now?"

"Very much so," I say. "But, Major...how did you...I mean..."

Her voice is filled with steel and determination. "I'm with the battalion's Military Intelligence Company. And one bit of interesting intelligence has come my way in the last twelve hours. You know Major Frank Moore?"

Instantly I reply, remembering the pleasant man I met a few days ago with Connie, before going up before the Fourth Battalion's colonel. "Certainly. The executive officer for the Fourth Battalion."

"That's right," she says. "His body was pulled from the Savannah River last night, local time, with a bullet to the forehead. It looks like he was murdered right after an unauthorized visit to Staff Sergeant Caleb Jefferson over in Ralston, in Sullivan County."

Damn, I think.

Her voice changes in tone. "Major, do you remember a specialist from the Eighty-Second Airborne named Conner? Brad Conner? He was charged with stealing a crate of 7.62-millimeter ammunition and selling it to a gang in Charlotte."

The name pops up in my memory, and I say, "Yes. Nearly three years back."

"Right. Your investigation cleared him."

"Well, Major, my investigation went to the evidence. That's what cleared him."

She says, "That's your point of view. You knew that Specialist Conner's dad was an Army Ranger, correct?"

"Well...yes, I did learn that during the course of my investigation, but that's about it. It didn't matter."

The major on the other end of the line says, "Well, it matters to us. His father is Trent Conner. Former command sergeant major at the Ranger Training Brigade at Fort Benning, and prior to that...well, I don't have the time to tell you his service record and list of awards and decorations. Let's just say Command Sergeant Major Conner is a goddamn legend in the Ranger community, and you earned a solid, helping out his son."

I know this is an exaggeration, but I'm not going to correct the major.

She adds, "So let's you and me get together to figure out what the hell is going on with Fourth Battalion and that damn Ninja Squad."

I say, "Yes, let's."

CHAPTER 69

EVEN THOUGH IT'S his day off, Dwight Dix of the Sullivan County Sheriff's Department—known to family and friends as DD—is not having a good morning. He pulled an unexpected late shift last night on direct orders from Sheriff Emma, and he's still humiliated by how he was chased away by that slick spic who fooled DD into thinking he had a pistol in his hand.

He paces back and forth in the small kitchen of his double-wide, barefoot, wearing blue jeans and nothing else, drinking a cold cup of coffee. Out in the living room with the orange shag carpeting that stinks because his wife Penny's two cats keep on pissing there, his son, Morris, and daughter, Tina, are yowling and tussling over some broken plastic toys.

"Penny!" he calls out to his wife. "Will you tell those two to settle down?"

Penny murmurs, "Tell 'em yourself," and goes back to her late morning, hell, her now daily routine of lying on the couch with the scuffed and worn cushions, watching one of those damn chick chat shows on TV, balancing a bowl of cheddar snack crackers on her swelling stomach, where their third child is coming along.

DD pours the cold coffee down the sink and stares out the grease-stained kitchen window. He doesn't belong here. He's never belonged here. But after he was dismissed during his first deployment for some crazy reason due to his temper, he found himself working as a fry cook outside Savannah before Sheriff Emma recruited him. It was a sweet gig when it started—nice pay, bennies, and for once his temper was seen as an asset instead of a liability—but now it's different.

Oh, he doesn't mind doing shit for the greater good, like tuning up suspects or planting crystal meth in some toad's pickup truck, making it easier for the district attorney to get a conviction, but the stuff he did and saw in The Summer House, the shooting, the screaming, and . . .

That poor baby girl. Why her?

He shakes his head. Enough is enough. It's time to man up and get a deal, get the hell out of here and bring along Penny and the kids, and if she doesn't want to move her fat ass off the couch to go with him, well, he'll figure it out.

DD ducks into the bedroom, past piles of clothes, socks, and panties on the floor, and quickly gets dressed. He grabs the keys to his truck from an ashtray loaded with old coins and paper clips and heads back out to the kitchen.

"Where you going, DD?" Penny asks.

"Out," he says, tugging on a pair of sneakers.

"Why?"

"'Cause I got to."

"Got to do what?"

He doesn't even look back at her when he heads to the door. "Out to finally make things right."

Penny Dix waits until she hears DD's truck roar out of the trailer park and then picks up the bowl of snack crackers, puts it on the cluttered coffee table, and, with an "Oomph" and a heavy sigh, gets off the couch. She moves into the kitchen, takes her cell phone out of her purse, and makes a call.

"Sullivan County Dispatch. What's the nature of your emergency?"

"I need to speak to Sheriff Williams."

The snotty-sounding woman says, "She's in a meeting and can't be disturbed."

Her bratty kids are screaming again, and Penny sticks a finger in one ear so she can hear better. "Look, missy, this here is her cousin Penny calling, and I need to talk to Sheriff Emma right now."

The woman says nothing. The line goes quiet.

A *click* and a reassuring voice comes on the line. "Hey, Penny, hon, what's going on?"

"Sheriff Emma...it's DD."

The reply is quick. "What's wrong?"

"I don't know," she says. "Something's been botherin' him these past few days. He's been using the chaw more than he does, drinking more, and at night he gets these awful dreams. And right now he left the house without even much saying good-bye."

Her cousin says, "Did he say what was wrong? Or where he was going?"

Penny hesitates. She never got good grades in school, not ever, but she's not stupid. She knows how Sheriff Emma runs the county and knows DD has to do some things that others would refuse. But if DD is in some kind of trouble...why wouldn't Sheriff Emma help?

"Sheriff, he said he was off finally to make things right, something like that. Do you know what it means? Is it important?"

Even with the TV on and the damn kids screaming, she can hear her cousin just breathing on the phone.

"Emma, did I do right, calling you?"

And before the call is disconnected, the cold voice of her cousin says, "Penny, you have no idea."

CHAPTER 70

SPECIAL AGENT CONNIE YORK is desperately trying to keep her yawning under control, but based on last night and the previous nights, it's a damn losing battle. Her worn and dented rental Ford is parked at the end of a dirt road, and the other two Fords are parked a few feet away. Huang and Pierce arrived just a few minutes earlier with their late breakfasts: plastic-wrapped doughnuts, coffee, and orange juice in plastic containers, all purchased a while ago from a convenience store in Chatham County.

Sanchez says, "You sure you two weren't followed?"

Pierce takes the lid off his coffee. "Look up the road. You see a cruiser coming down?"

Huang joins in. "Maybe there's a black helicopter coming."

"Shut up," Sanchez says.

York says, "All of you, knock it off."

Cold quiet comes to the group. York feels like a failure. All of them slept in the three cars overnight, though it wasn't much of a sleep. Tired, achy, and facing a day of...

What?

What to do? Major Cook ordered her to push the investigation, but what was left to push? The dog-walking witness is missing, and so is the owner of the convenience store. The murder house and whatever evidence was inside are a pile of burnt rubble. Staff Sergeant Caleb Jefferson has cut a deal to plead guilty and is about to make it permanent at tomorrow's court hearing, and, oh, yeah, the sheriff is corrupt and a criminal to boot, and her deputies are following them wherever they go.

Sanchez says, "You haven't heard from the major, right?"

York says, "I've tried twice. No answer."

"You sure you're using the sat phone, right? Agent York?"

Just before she's about to use her voice to tear off that arrogant cop's head, her phone rings.

Her cell phone, not the Iridium satellite phone.

She digs into her bag, pulls it out.

BRODERICK CID QUANTICO.

York lets the call go to voicemail, like she's done three times prior.

Huang asks, "Colonel Broderick, ma'am?"

"The one and only," she says.

Sanchez says, "One of these days you're gonna have to answer."

"Maybe I'll give the call to you, Agent Sanchez."

Sanchez looks like he's going to say something when the phone rings again.

Pierce says, "The colonel's being persistent this morning."

York is about to say the same thing when she sees her screen: BLOCKED CALL.

She steps away and answers the phone. "Hello?"

An unfamiliar man's voice. "Is this the Army cop?"

"Excuse me?"

"I said, is this the Army cop? The one looking into The Summer House killings, the one the Army Rangers been charged with?"

"I am," she says. "I'm Special Agent York of the Army CID. Who's this?"

"Someone who knows what really happened that night, lady. Someone who wants to let you know."

"Why?"

"'Cause I was there, and I helped, and it made me sick," the man says, his voice quivering. "I want to make it right. I want to talk to you, lady. Confess it all. Get a deal and get the hell out of this county."

"How did you get my number?"

"Peggy Reese, that bitch reporter. But I made a deal . . . she gave me your number, and I promised to give her the whole story a day later, give you folks enough time to do your job."

Some of her crew are whispering, and York takes a few steps farther away. "How do I know you're for real? That you're not just making it up?"

The man sighs. "I'll tell you something that's not in the papers. How's that? Up on the second floor of the house, right-side bedroom, older lady was drug out from under a bed."

York says. "Okay . . . that's a start."

"Oh? Then how about this, then? The bedroom across the hall, there were three dead folks. A guy in the bed with bandages on his arms, a chunky woman on the floor, and . . . a poor dead little girl, right there. Like her momma was trying to protect her."

The air around her suddenly feels chilled. York says, "I need to see you. Right now. Where?"

The man says, "Shit, not in this county. There's a Waffle House across the north county line on Gateway Boulevard West, just off Route 204, on the way into Savannah. I'll see you there in ninety minutes. How's that?"

"That sounds fine," she says. "How will I know you?"

The man says, "I'll be the scared son of bitch sitting by himself at the far end. And you, lady, you come by yourself. Okay? I'll make sure I'm sitting near an exit door, and if you come by with anybody else, I'm outta there."

He disconnects the call.

York walks back to her crew, tells them what's just happened. Not surprisingly, Sanchez makes a fuss. "Damn it, York, this whole county is wrapped up and under that sheriff's thumb. And you're going off to meet some clown who said he was there?"

"He told me things that haven't been made public."

"Sure," Sanchez says. "And if the sheriff is in on whatever happened, then she might have fed this guy this info. Set you up. Get you going to that Waffle House, and arrest you for crossing a double-yellow line. You could end up in the county jail and never come out."

"Good point," she says. "Which is why you're going to be in charge when I'm gone, Sanchez, so the investigation continues. You're going to protect those three surviving Rangers. Make sure nothing happens to them until we hear something from the major. Got it?"

Sanchez finally nods, and Huang and Pierce both say, "Yes, ma'am."

York nods, too. "Good. Now transfer your gear from that rental. I've got places to go, and sorry to say, I'm not driving the one with the dented hood. Based on our luck, the damn thing will pop off about halfway there."

Twenty minutes later, York pulls over for a quick moment, reaches into her bag, comes out with her SIG Sauer. There's a round in the chamber, of course, but she wants to make sure she has two spare clips nearby when she goes into the Waffle House.

If it is a trap, she's going to be ready.

CHAPTER 71

AFGHANISTAN

I'M IN TEMPORARY QUARTERS for the night, waiting for a convoy to leave Bagram at 5:00 a.m. tomorrow, heading south to Khost to meet up with Major Fredericka West. Earlier she said, "These are supposed to be secure phone lines, but we're not taking any chances. I'll set up transport for you. See you late tomorrow morning, Major. Safe travels. Stay low."

The quarters are an old concrete-block building, subdivided into small plywood cubicles. I've had a dinner at the local DFAC, and a quick washup, and I've stretched out on a borrowed sleeping bag with a wool blanket over me.

A small lamp on a stand is next to the bed, and close by is my trusted Bruce Catton book, along with my Iridium satellite phone.

I grab the phone, power it up, dial the digits.

Ring, ring, ring.

No answer.

Ring, ring, ring.

Still no answer.

Where's York? What's she doing? How's the rest of the crew?

And the investigation there in Sullivan?

I shut the Iridium down, restart it, and then dial the numbers once more.

Ring.

A crackle of static and I sit straight up, ignoring the bolt of pain that shoots right through my leg and into my skull.

"Major?" comes York's voice. "Are you all right?"

Her voice is fading in and out, and I go right to the condensed version of what I've been doing.

"I'm fine," I say. "I'm in Bagram, heading off to Pendahar tomorrow. Look, remember Major Frank Moore, the XO of Fourth Battalion? Got word from a Ranger officer here that he was murdered after visiting Staff Sergeant Jefferson. Bullet wound to the head, pulled out of the Savannah River."

"Damn," York says. "Major, things are also moving quickly over here. Witnesses have disappeared, the murder house was burned down, and it looks like Sheriff Williams is running the county as her own personal criminal enterprise."

Now it's my turn to swear. York goes on, her voice strong and in charge. "That's not all. Staff Sergeant Jefferson's cut a deal with the district attorney. He's..."

Her voice fades out and there's a hiss of static, and her voice comes back and says, "So there's that."

I raise my voice. "That's what?"

Her voice cuts through. "He's pleading guilty! In exchange for pleading guilty, the district attorney is cutting the other two Rangers loose!"

More static and she says, "Hold on, making a turn now."

"A turn? Where are you?"

A nervous laugh. "On my way to a Waffle House for a very late breakfast! With a witness who says he was at the shooting! Sorry, Major, I think we're gonna break this case stateside..."

I rub at my aching leg. "Who's the witness?"

"Don't know."

"Is Sanchez with you?"

Her voice fades out again. "...alone."

"York, don't you dare go there without backup!" I yell. "I want Sanchez with you!"

There's silence, not even a whisper of static.

I admire York, I trust York, and I'd love to see York in a bikini, but Sanchez has a more down-and-dirty outlook about humanity, having worked some very mean streets in LA when he was a cop. If York is off to meet somebody claiming to be a witness at a Waffle House, I want Sanchez sitting in a nearby booth, with a cut-down AR-15 across his lap.

"York!" I yell.

One more hiss of static, and her voice fading out. "...I'll be okay, Major."

Then the call is disconnected.

For the next half hour, I try again to call Connie, and none of the calls go through.

I finally stop when someone in the adjacent cubicle pounds the thin plywood and yells, "Hey, some of us trying to sleep over here! Knock that shit off!"

I turn the light off, stretch out, and I don't go to sleep, not at all.

York seems to be right. The case is breaking open in Georgia, and here I am, alone and clueless, stuck in Afghanistan.

CHAPTER 72

SPECIAL AGENT CONNIE YORK spots the familiar shape and logo of the Waffle House just off Route 204 leading into Savannah, and she has a tinge of anticipation, knowing that the airport she arrived at a few long days ago is just a quick drive away.

It'll be wonderful, she thinks, *to get this damn thing wrapped up, get back on a silver bird, and get the hell out of Georgia.*

She parks beside the bright-yellow-and-red building with its black lettering and gets out of her car, thinking of an article she read once that said FEMA had a "Waffle House index" with which it determined how damaged a community was after a hurricane or tornado passed through it. The sooner the local Waffle House opens after a natural disaster, the quicker a local community would recover.

York opens the door and steps in, wondering what kind of index the CID could establish if she broke this case in the next several minutes at this particular Waffle House.

The interior is like every other Waffle House she's been in, with bright lights, a counter, and booths with red cushions. There's a good mix of customers here at midday, locals and workers, and in the last booth, sitting by himself, is a nervous-looking male who nods at her as she approaches.

He's in his late twenties, light-brown hair buzzed short, with deep-blue eyes that are flickering around, like old memories are haunting him. He has on blue jeans and a soiled white T-shirt that is tight against his torso and bulky upper biceps.

York steps up to him and says, "Let's change seats."

"Huh?"

She takes her soft leather bag off her shoulder, gestures with her free hand. "Move around. I don't know you, I don't know where you're from, all I know is that you told me you have knowledge about a mass killing that took place less than a week ago. Move it. I want my back against the wall."

The guy gets up and does just that, and she thinks, *Good. Score one for the team.* Him moving shows he is malleable, weak, and she will use that to her advantage.

When he is settled, she sits down, content with knowing that from this last row of booths, she has a good view of the restaurant's interior. A young blond waitress comes over and drops off the multicolored menus, and Connie barely gives the menu a glance as she looks closer at the man across from her, with his muscles and close-cropped hair.

Something comes to her.

A gamble, but what the hell.

"What unit were you in before being discharged?" York asks. "And how long have you been working for Sheriff Williams?"

Her questions seem to stun him, because he stares, nods, and says, "How do you know?"

"We know a lot more than you think," York says. "Answer the question. Starting with your name."

He clasps his hands in front of him on the clean table. "Dwight Dix. Before I became a deputy in Sullivan County, I was in the Tenth Mountain Division, out of Fort Drum. Did part of a tour overseas in Afghanistan before..."

Dix seems ashamed, and York won't push it, not now. "Something happened, you were discharged, at loose ends...and Sheriff Emma Williams offered you a job. Right?"

A quick nod. "That's right."

She takes out a white legal pad and pen, sets them before her.

"Very well, then, Dwight. You told me you had information about those killings. I believe you. You gave me details only someone who was there or intimately involved would know. What happened?"

Dix shakes his head. "Nope, we're not gonna do it this way."

York feels tense, part of her wanting to grab this fool by his T-shirt neck and slam his thick head onto the table. *You had something to do with a two-year-old girl being killed!*

She takes a breath. "What way is that, Dwight?"

He taps her legal pad. "I want you to write something legal for me. About immunity. About me telling you what happened that night at The Summer House and who did the shooting, and why. I get that piece of paper promising not to prosecute, and then I'll talk."

York keeps her voice even. "You like watching those *Law & Order* marathons on TV, is that it?"

"Huh?"

She says, "Dwight, I'm a law enforcement officer with the US Army. I don't have any pull with county or state law enforcement, and not much with federal law enforcement."

His face falls, and she adds, "I mean, I could write something up like that, but it wouldn't be legal, it would be a lie, and that's not how I operate. Understand?"

"But I need something..."

York uncaps her pen. "This is the best I can do, Dwight," York says. "I'll write out a statement and sign it with my name, rank, and service number, and—"

"How about your badge number?" he interrupts.

"CID agents don't have badge numbers," she says. "I'll make a statement saying that in my professional opinion you have expressed remorse and have offered invaluable investigative assistance, and that in any future dealings with state or federal law enforcement, I will be willing to speak up on your behalf to protect your legal interests."

As she narrates this to Dwight, she writes down the words, and she signs them with a flourish. After tearing off the sheet, she passes it over to Dwight, keeping her face calm and impassive, because that piece of paper is total and utter legal bullshit.

But he bites.

He folds it up and puts it in his pocket. "Okay, what do you want to know?"

"Were you there the night of the killings?"

"Yes," he says.

"Who ordered them to take place?"

"Deputy Clark Lindsay, but I'm sure Sheriff Emma was behind it. Hell, nobody in the sheriff's department can take a crap without her say-so."

"Who was there?"

"Me, Clark, and Teddy Collins."

"Why did you do it?"

He shrugs. "We did our jobs. We were told that in this house was a bunch of low-life drug dealers that had skated over and over again on various charges. We were told to clear the place out. Clark said not to worry, these guys had competitors—it'd eventually be pinned on some rival drug gang."

York again thinks of two-year-old Polly Zachary. "Did you shoot that little girl?"

"Shit no!" he says, raising his voice, causing some customers in the nearby booths to turn their heads and look at him. "There were two guys sitting on a couch. I took them out. Clark and Teddy...they took care of the rest, the girl downstairs and the folks upstairs."

"But the Rangers were arrested two nights later," she says. "You're telling me they weren't involved?"

Another shake of the head. "Nope."

"But there was evidence from the scene. Fingerprints, shell casings."

Dwight says, "I heard later from Clark that the Rangers were there about an hour or so 'fore we got there. That'll take care of the fingerprints, I guess. And Clark...he's got another job working as a civilian attendant at the shooting range at Hunter. I bet he could get some empty shell casings from a certain Ranger's pistol if he had to."

York is writing so hard and fast that she is sure the pen is close to shredding the paper. She has a memory of once working on a computer jigsaw puzzle, with none of the 128 pieces fitting, until she used the Help feature of the program and reduced the number of puzzle pieces to 24. Then the puzzle was solved within seconds.

This deputy, this disgraced soldier, this killer sitting so calmly across from her, he is her own Help feature.

Damn, won't the major be happy when she calls him later.

"But here's the big question, Dwight," she says. "Why? What was the real reason to frame the Rangers for those killings? What was it?"

He seems to be wrestling with something, and she says, "Dwight, what I signed there, I'm behind it one hundred percent. I won't let you be by yourself. I promise."

The man squeezes his hands together. "It had something to do with Afghanistan, when they was there."

Afghanistan, she thinks, *just like Major Cook thought.*

"Dwight," she says, "tell me."

*   *   *

In the parking lot of the Waffle House, Bo Leighton carefully parks the stolen Honda Accord that he and his cousin Ricky lifted a few minutes ago after they had tailed the guy earlier from Sullivan. Lesson he learned a long time ago is that if you need wheels, get something dull-looking and ordinary that doesn't stand out, and then use it quick, 'fore the owner makes the call and the stolen car is sent out over the wires.

He and Ricky are both wearing black wrestling sneakers, loose khaki pants, and short black hoodies. Each has a ski mask on his head, ready to be pulled down in the next thirty seconds when they start dancing.

Bo switches off the engine, leaving the keys in the ignition. He says, "You ready?"

His cousin says, "Damn it, now that I'm here, I'm kinda hungry. Why can't we get something to eat and then do the job?"

Bo feels the usual frustration bubble to the surface. His cousin has dead-aim with a gun and is quick with his fists and boots, but most times he fails to see the larger picture. Like the time when he was first picked up on an adult charge that got reduced, and he was on work release, with two weeks left on his sentence, and he left a county lawn-mowing job to get a beer at a nearby tavern. In doing so, he got an extra twelve months tacked on for attempted escape. And why? *I was thirsty for a beer,* he said.

Bo swivels in his seat and picks up a black gym bag, unzips it, and hands over a Desert Eagle .45 semiautomatic pistol. "Because we were told by Sheriff Emma that the job has to be done now, as soon as possible."

"Funny thing, what we're about to do to that deputy, 'cause of his boss." Ricky works the action of the Desert Eagle, sits up, and slides it into his waistband.

Bo does the same with his. "Don't worry, he'll get a nice cop funeral. Make his family so proud."

Before Bo opens the door, Ricky says, "What happens if some other cop or do-gooder gets in the way?"

Bo says, "Kill 'em all."

CHAPTER 73

THE DEPUTY BEFORE York is about to speak when two men burst through the door at the far end, wearing ski masks over their heads and brandishing pistols. One yells out, "Nobody moves! This is a goddamn robbery!"

York instantly thinks, *No, no, it isn't*—she doesn't believe in coincidences—and lowers her right hand to her open bag to grab her SIG Sauer. She says, "Stay put, Dwight, stay put."

But Dwight's flipped his head around, spots the two men. "Shit," he says.

The first gunman is pointing his pistol at the cashier, making her put cash into a small green plastic bag. The nearer gunman is slowly walking down the center aisle. He yells out, "Hands on the table! Now! Hands where I can see 'em!"

Some whispers and words from the customers as they all follow the shouted directions, and the gunman says, "Freeze! I want everybody to stay put. We'll be outta here in a minute!"

York doesn't believe him. She quickly grabs a napkin, covers her right hand with it, and in a moment has both hands on the table, the napkin concealing her pistol.

In a low voice she says, "Dwight. Slide under the table, now."

With the man at the other end focusing on getting the money—a cover for what they're actually here for, York has no doubt—the approaching gunman is looking at each customer as he comes down the aisle.

But the mask is screwing up his peripheral vision.

They have a few seconds of grace.

"Dwight," she says again. "Slide under the table."

But Dwight says, "Screw this."

He jumps up from the booth, runs to the door marked EXIT, and York pulls her gun hand free as the nearest gunman says, "Gotcha, Dwight!"

He fires twice, and York fires just as quickly.

Screams, shouts.

Dwight collapses against the closed door, his white T-shirt torn and bloody, and York stands up, both hands on her pistol, and approaches the gunman sprawled out on the floor as his companion whirls and dives out the front door.

"Federal agent!" she yells. "Everybody, stay where you are!"

Screams, shouts, dishes falling to the floor and breaking. She gets closer to the gunman, looks down at him, then quickly glances around at the frightened customers, making sure there isn't a third gunman hidden out there.

York points to a bearded man with a John Deere cap and yells. "You! Call 911!"

The gunman has three wounds right in the center of his chest, and his legs are crumpled underneath him, like all the muscles and ligaments have turned to jelly.

His pistol is on the floor.

A young boy in a nearby booth turns around and reaches to pick it up.

York yells, "Kid, no, don't touch the gun!"

And the second gunman comes back in the front door.
York lifts up her pistol—
A gunshot and a hammering blow to her head.
Darkness.

CHAPTER 74

SPECIAL AGENT MANUEL SANCHEZ is on his way to the Ralston jail, the other Ford behind him, Pierce driving, Doc Huang sitting next to him.

After York left for her trip to the Waffle House—*How in hell can anybody seriously eat at a place that sounds like it belongs in a Disney park?* Sanchez thinks—they went back to the convenience store to see if they could get the current manager to say anything more about the indictment that's put the store in danger, but the manager they talked to last had been replaced by a gracious woman with about a half dozen English words in her vocabulary.

Another visit to the funeral home revealed the director is gone on an unexpected trip to Atlanta, and District Attorney Cornelius Slate is in the middle of a trial and can't be disturbed.

The sky is overcast, and Sanchez feels, yeah, a big-ass storm is coming, and everyone's heading for the hills.

Sanchez is in a hurry, but he's keeping his speed right below the limit. No use giving Sheriff Williams and her criminal gang an opportunity to pull them over for speeding. He did the same back in LA as a cop, when looking for any excuse to—

The other Ford is flashing its lights, honking its horn, and his phone starts ringing.

Damn it, he thinks, *something must be up.*

He pulls over the Ford, braking hard, tossing up a cloud of dust from the side of the road. Around them are nothing but trees, fields, barbed wire, and skinny cows.

Sanchez gets out as Huang and Pierce come over to him, both looking worried.

"Give," he says.

The dust settles. Huang gives him his phone, set to the home page of an Atlanta TV station.

Two killed, one seriously wounded at Waffle House robbery.

Sanchez tries to scroll through the screen, but he does it wrong, and a goddamn weather app shows up.

Pierce wipes at his forehead. "They're not identifying the two dead," the JAG lawyer says, "but the seriously wounded is a woman. We've been calling Connie's cell ever since the story broke. No answer."

"What now?" Huang says. "Manny, what do we do now?"

Sanchez gives the smartphone back to Pierce. "I'm heading to Savannah. You find out what hospital York's been taken to, let me know. If she learned anything before the sons of bitches started shooting, I want to find out."

"And what about us?" Pierce asks.

Sanchez walks back to his rental. "You two stay on the job. Get to the Ralston jail. And—"

He stops.

Their original goal was to try to see the Rangers again, to find out why in hell the staff sergeant is planning to plead guilty tomorrow.

But the ambush of York changes everything.

Sanchez quickly walks back. "You two get to the jail. I don't know how you're going to do it, but you're going to protect those three Rangers. Got it? All the witnesses in this county are gone, and now they're going after us. The Rangers are next. Get to the jail, do what it takes to protect them."

Pierce says, "How?"

"Figure it out."

From Huang: "But..."

"But what?" Sanchez says. "We've got no time."

Huang looks at Pierce. "We're...a lawyer and a doctor. That's all. How can we do this?"

Sanchez says, "You're wrong, Doc. You're both armed officers of the United States Army. Act like it."

Then he heads back to the rental and, after his first two steps, starts running.

CHAPTER 75

SHERIFF EMMA WILLIAMS is having her photo taken with a crew of young volunteers for the Conover for Senate campaign late that Wednesday afternoon when the day's burner phone starts vibrating in her right-hand trousers pocket.

She keeps her smile frozen in place as the photographer for the *Sullivan County Times,* a young pimply boy who's taking himself way too seriously, maneuvers the young boys back and forth, making sure their handmade cardboard signs are held up at the correct angle. KIDS FOR CONOVER they say, and there are also a few of her own, REELECT SHERIFF WILLIAMS, in the mix.

As her cell phone continues to vibrate, Williams wants to shout to the photographer in this Baptist church hall in Sanders, a small town at the western end of the county, *Move your skinny ass!*

But that would earn the wrath of all assembled here, she's sure.

For God's wrath, well, he hadn't sent a lightning bolt yet to scorch her butt, so either he's ignoring her or he doesn't exist.

Finally, the young boy in a T-shirt and long shorts that go below his knees lifts his camera to his face, and after a quick series of *click-click-click,* he says, "Now, y'all stay in place so I can get your names straight, okay?"

The kids seem excited that their photo will end up in the paper, and Williams squeezes the shoulder of an older woman volunteer and says, "Do you mind? I have to take a phone call."

The woman smiles and points. "If you need some privacy, the food bank pantry is right over there, Sheriff."

Williams nods in thanks, walks quickly over to the small room with shelves stacked with canned foods and boxes of macaroni and cheese, and answers her burner.

Congressman Mason Conover says, "My latest polling shows we're going to win by at least ten points next Tuesday. Tell me you've got everything under control."

Williams says, "I've got everything under control."

"Good," he says, his voice suddenly sounding cheerful, a tone she's not heard in months. "That being the case, Emma, you can start packing your bags in the morning."

He disconnects the call, and Williams needs to lean against the nearby concrete wall for relief.

So close, so very, very close.

She jumps as her burner phone rings again.

"Yes?"

"You know who this is," comes another familiar male voice.

"I do," she says. "How did it go?"

"We did what you asked us to do, but there's..."

Her sense of relief flashes away, like a sliver of ice dropped on the sidewalk in the middle of August. "What happened? What went wrong?"

"Ah... Sheriff, like I said, we did what you asked us to, but there was more... shooting. Seems like DD was talking to this woman, and she was armed, and she shot back. My poor nephew Ricky, he got himself killed."

Williams says something extraordinarily foul and obscene about the man's nephew Ricky and then says, "Go on. What else."

"Well, his cousin Bo, he fired back, and he shot that woman in the head. Near enough killed her. And later I found out...Damn it, Sheriff, that woman is some sort of agent or investigator with the Army."

Williams feels like the concrete-block wall she's leaning against is now pushing back at her, threatening to collapse and bury her at this very moment.

Her mouth suddenly dry, Williams says, "How long was DD with her?"

"I don't know," the man says. "It's just that DD and her were sittin' in a booth when Ricky and Bo went in."

"But she's alive."

"Barely, I guess," he says. "Took a round to the head. I tell you, Bo must have been some angry and spooked to miss like that, not take the top of her head off."

She stands up from the wall. "Then Bo will have a chance to make it right."

"What's that, Sheriff?"

Williams closes her eyes, concentrates. "The shooting took place outside Savannah. Gunshot wound to the head. Nearest trauma unit is...Memorial Health University Medical Center, in Savannah. Tell Bo to get over there and finish the job. I can't have any loose ends out there, especially if that bitch wakes up."

"Sheriff..."

"And another thing," she says. "Your idiot brother. Tell him to be home tonight and all through the morning. I need to talk to him about a job. Got it?"

A pause from the other end of the line.

"I said, got it?"

The man's voice changes to a pleading tone. "Sheriff, I don't know if Bo is up to it. I mean, he's good at tuning folks up if they do you wrong, making a truck delivery down to Mobile, or lifting whatever car you might need, but getting into a hospital and—"

She takes a step. "You listen to me, you squirmy little peckerwood bastard! Those two nephews of yours, I sent them on a job, because you told me they could do it and do it well! And they screwed it up! Now that Bo of yours is going to get over to Savannah as quick as he can, and he's gonna end it! You understand me? I said, do you understand me?"

The voice is meek. "Yes, ma'am."

She won't let it go. "Well, just to make it clear, you slimy little toad, I want that woman gone. Got it? I want her out of the picture this afternoon, and I want confirmation. And it better be a firm and complete confirmation or I'll send you in next time to saw off her goddamn head and give it to me as a trophy! Do you get it now?"

"Yes, ma'am," the man replies again, sounding like he's six years old and he just peed in the bed.

"Good!" she says. "I didn't work and sweat and bleed to get where I am just to throw it all away 'cause of idiot men like you! Get the job done!"

Williams disconnects the call, turns, and is horrified to see two young girls there, maybe eleven or twelve, dressed in sweet little pink and yellow dresses. The girl on the left is holding one of her campaign signs, and the one on the right is holding a black marker clenched in her tiny hands.

"Sorry you girls had to hear that," Williams finally says, taking the black marker pen from the one girl and scrawling her name on the poster held by the other. "You'll learn soon enough what I was talking about, how important it is not to depend on men."

CHAPTER 76

SPECIAL AGENT MANUEL SANCHEZ is speeding east on Interstate 16, about fifteen minutes outside Savannah, when he glances up at the rearview mirror and sees a dark-blue police cruiser right on his tail, blue lights flashing.

Sanchez looks at the speedometer.

One hundred two miles per hour.

It'll be hard to talk his way out of this one, but he's going to try.

He switches on the Ford's directional and slowly pulls over to the side, where there is nothing around save for tall pines and flat swampy areas, while recalling the text he got a few minutes ago from Pierce, back at Sullivan.

YORK IN CRIT CONDITION, ICU, MEMORIAL HEALTH UNIV MED CTR, SAVANNAH.

A thought comes to him. If he's lucky and can spin a good tale, maybe this trooper will let him go. Hell, almost everyone down here is a huge supporter of the military. Say the right words, Sanchez thinks, and maybe the trooper back there will give him a police escort to the hospital, shave off some of the desperate minutes left in his travel time.

The cruiser pulls to the side as well, comes up to him, and in Sanchez's rearview mirror, he spots that it's from the Georgia

State Patrol. The cruiser sits there, and Sanchez taps his fingers on the steering wheel, impatient for the process to start. From the glove box he pulls out the rental agreement and takes his driver's license out of his wallet.

The door to the cruiser opens up. A heavyset African American woman steps out, putting on her gray campaign-style hat, and starts walking in his direction. She has on a light-blue uniform shirt and gray trousers with a black stripe down the side.

Sanchez lowers the window, switches off the engine.

She maintains a distance behind him and says, "Are you sick, sir? Is there an emergency?"

"I'm fine," he says. "But there is an emergency. I'm trying to get to Memorial Health in Savannah as fast as I can."

"I see," she says. "Family member?"

"No, ma'am," he says. "My coworker. I'm a special agent with the US Army. She's been shot."

The woman bends over a bit. "May I see your license and registration?"

He passes over his California driver's license and rental agreement. "I don't have a registration. This vehicle is a rental."

"Uh-huh," the officer says. She seems to take her time examining his license and the rental agreement.

Minutes seem to drag as traffic roars by, the occasional tractor-trailer truck buffeting the Ford.

What's taking her so long?

"Mr. Sanchez, you say you're a special agent? With the US Army?"

"That's right," he says. "Hold on, I'll show you my identification."

He opens his leather wallet with the badge and identification, and she gives it a quick glance. Her eyes seem to darken, and she bites her lower lip.

"Well, I'll be," she says. "You sure are an agent, then. A special agent."

Sanchez takes back his identification and says, "Yes, ma'am. And please...would you consider giving me an escort to Memorial Health?"

"I clocked you going at one hundred miles an hour, Mr. Sanchez. You think I could do better?"

His hands squeeze the steering wheel. "Ma'am, I—"

"That group in the Army," she says. "Known as CIS or something, right?"

"United States Army Criminal Investigation Division," he says, trying very hard not to lose his temper.

"Ah, that's right," she says, smiling. "I remember now. You see, my boy, Troy, he was an E-4 in the Army, in the 173rd Airborne, stationed over there in Italy. He had a nice Italian girlfriend, but she kept it on the down low, and when her Eye-tie family found out that their blond princess was dating an American black fellow, they freaked. Got the locals to arrest him for rape. And the Army was supposed to protect him...and you know what happened?"

Sanchez grits his teeth. "Ma'am, I'm quite sorry for what happened to your son, but—"

Her voice is louder. "That Army CID over there in Italy and the rest of the Army, they made the rape case go away, by forcing my Troy out of the Army. That's what happened."

"Ma'am, I—"

"You hold your ass right in place till I check you out."

She turns around and goes back to her cruiser, the blue lights on the roof's light bar still flashing. The officer seems to take her time getting back into the cruiser.

Shit, he thinks.

He's done this before, back on the job in LA, showing a suspect or a driver or a pain-in-the-ass civilian who's really in charge.

Now it's this trooper's turn.

Shit, he thinks again.

And...

All right. Suppose she checks through the GCIC system here, looking at his driver's license status. Everything is fine—no out-standing warrants or violations, of course—but suppose Colonel Broderick up at Quantico...could he be so angry at his calls being ignored that he flagged his license?

Meaning that trooper could bring him into custody?

Sanchez looks back at the cruiser, and the traffic.

There's an opening behind him, with two tractor-trailer trucks in the distance, traveling side by side, heading in his direction.

He starts up the Ford's engine, puts the car into drive, and slams the accelerator with his foot, pulling out in front of the approaching trucks.

CHAPTER 77

NINETEEN MINUTES LATER and after screeching the Ford into a space in the parking lot nearest the main entrance, Sanchez barrels his way through the hospital's complex until he finds the facility's Trauma ICU.

The place is pleasant-looking enough, with light wood cabinets and white ceilings and soft overhead lights, but Sanchez is in a hurry, not sure how far that Georgia State Patrol officer will go in tracking him down. Entry into the Trauma ICU looks to be controlled by a big guy at an exterior reception desk. When he buzzes in two hospital personnel, Sanchez follows them inside.

At the nearest nurses' station, he shows his badge, and almost out of breath from running here, he says, "Special Agent Manuel Sanchez, US Army CID. You have a CID agent here, Connie York. Where is she?"

The male nurse is in light-blue scrubs and looks at him with suspicion. After staring at his badge and identification, he says, "She's in trauma room 2, but I don't think visitors—"

"Thanks," Sanchez says, moving on. The place is quiet, but nurses and doctors bustle around him, and down the hallway is a series of sliding-glass doors with handles.

The nurse yells out, "Hey!" but Sanchez ignores him.

There.

Room 2.

He slides the door open, surprising two nurses—one male, the other female—at their work.

The woman says, "Excuse me, who are you?"

He shows his badge and identification. "I'm Special Agent Manuel Sanchez, Army CID. How is she?"

The male nurse slips out, and the woman says, "Have you registered up front?"

"No," he says.

"You need to."

Sanchez snaps, "How is she, damn it?"

"Critical," she says. "Look, you need to—"

"Ma'am, all due respect, you can get the hell out. I'm not going anywhere."

She leaves and Sanchez steps forward, thinking there's been a mistake, a serious mistake, because that's not Connie in that bed, hooked up to IV tubes, wires, and other sensors.

The poor woman there is heavily bandaged about her head, the head mostly shaved, and she's breathing through a tube stuck down her throat. Her eyes are swollen and her cheeks are puffed out.

It can't be Connie.

Can't.

But there's a whiteboard near her bed, and sure enough, in careful block lettering above her vital signs and the names of the doctors and nurses taking care of her, it states, CONSTANCE YORK.

The door slides open. He turns.

A large man is there, dark hair, wearing black trousers, black sneakers, and a black vest over a light-blue shirt, the vest with bright-yellow letters saying SECURITY. Sanchez looks him over, notes the handcuffs, the expandable baton, and another weapon with a bright-yellow handle, denoting a Taser.

"Sir, you need to leave," the man says.

"I want to see this woman's doctor."

He shakes his head. "You can do that outside, once you register up front at the nurses' station."

"I don't—"

The security officer takes two steps forward. "Sir, I know you're upset and you're concerned, but with the way you came in here, the staff and nurses, they're also upset and concerned. Please, be a gentleman. All right? I bet you'll be able to come back in just a few minutes. Please don't make me escalate things, all right?"

Sanchez knows what he means by escalating. Maybe a quick shot from the Taser and then cuffing him on the floor. Then Sanchez will be out of action, and how will that help things?

"All right," he says. "I'll leave."

The security guard smiles, slides the door open. "Thanks so much, sir. You won't regret it."

When the Army guy leaves, Bo Leighton can't believe how much his luck is changing after that disastrous shoot-out at the Waffle House a few hours ago. But God must be riding shotgun, because after getting a good ream-out from his uncle about how he and Ricky screwed up the job, his uncle offered him redemption.

And look here, his second cousin Derek, the son of a bitch actually worked security here at this hospital, and his uniform actually fit, and like most places, if you look as if you belong, you get left alone.

Then his luck really kicked in when he got up to this Trauma ICU unit and found out that this Army agent was making a fuss in the bitch's room, so that gave him the perfect excuse to casually walk down here and kick the guy out.

But no time to press his luck.

There's a chair next to the big bed with the wounded agent—Christ, how the hell was she alive with a .45 jacketed round hitting her head?—and all those wires and tubes, and in the chair is a nice white pillow.

Bo walks over, picks up the pillow.

Just a few seconds and then it'll be right.

And his cousin won't have died in vain.

Bitch.

CHAPTER 78

AS HIS FELLOW squad mate Pierce makes the turn into the crowded parking lot of the Ralston police station and jail, Lieutenant John Huang reaches a decision. Once this horror show of a case is settled, one way or another, he's putting in his papers and resigning from the Army.

Because deep down, he's just a psychiatrist, a head doctor, a shrink. Despite what the Army thinks and especially despite the uncomfortable feeling of the 9mm SIG Sauer digging into his waist, he's not a soldier. He's just a doc, and since he's been here in Georgia, a lousy doc at that, with the bloody suicide of an Army Ranger on his hands and conscience.

His companion, Captain Allen Pierce, whistles and says, "John, I don't see an empty space here. Damn it."

"Then park illegally," Huang replies, "over there by those picnic tables. If we're fortunate, the cops here will be too busy to ticket us."

Pierce smiles, but Huang is not in a joking mood. The lot is filled with cars, news vans, and satellite trucks, all waiting for word from within the jail, where the three surviving Ranger prisoners are being held.

They both get out of the car, and Pierce says, "John, just to give you a heads-up, I intend to sling a lot of legal bullshit in there."

"What kind?" Huang asks.

"The kind I'm currently making up," Pierce says. "All I ask is that you roll with me, give me backup."

Huang wants to argue the point but lets it go. Why get the Army lawyer all spun up now? When this investigation is finished, poor Pierce will probably get disbarred anyway.

"Sure, Allen," he says. "I'll do that."

A few minutes later, they are in the same reception area as before, with an angry Chief Richard Kane staring at them both.

"What?" he says. "You say you're going to do what?"

Huang is impressed at how calm and professional Pierce is, facing down the police chief with nothing to back him up but his lawyer's tongue.

"Like I said, Chief," Pierce says, standing straight and firm, "I intend to spend the night here with Dr. Huang to ensure nothing happens to the three Army personnel before tomorrow's court hearing. We don't have to be in their cells or near their cells, but we will remain here, keeping track of jail staff and any visitors they may receive."

The chief explodes with a series of obscenities and finally says, "What the hell gives you the right? You think I'm running a god-damn Motel 6 here or something? Why should I allow you two to stay here without a warrant?"

Huang admires Pierce for not giving an inch. "At this moment, Chief, a team from the FBI's Civil Rights Unit is en route to investigate you, this facility, and your personnel."

"Civil rights? What the hell are you talking about?"

Pierce gives the angry chief a tight smile. "Specialist Vinnie Tyler. The Ranger who allegedly killed himself in his cell? Have you forgotten him? We certainly haven't. And neither has the Army. Among any other crimes you and your department may have committed, you most definitely violated the specialist's civil rights."

Huang sees exhaustion, anger, and confusion in the chief's eyes.

It's his turn.

Huang says, "In my professional opinion, Chief Kane, you and your personnel offered a hostile environment that adversely affected Specialist Tyler's health. That means you and everyone else here is criminally liable."

"You—"

Pierce jumps right back in. "But with us staying here, keeping watch and recording everyone coming in and out, ensuring nothing untoward happens to the three surviving Rangers, that may help mitigate the situation once the FBI arrives. It will put them in a . . . better frame of mind."

Huang sees the chief's head moving, looking at the JAG lawyer and then at him. Huang imagines what the chief is thinking. An arrest made in a major crime case involving multiple homicides should have been a wonderful publicity coup for a small town like this. Increased media attention, *Well dones* from his fellow cops, even the local mayor and council in a mood to increase the department's budget next year.

Huang knows what the quick glance means from the chief.

He's looking for a way out.

Huang says, "Chief, I know this is an intrusion. And you've got a lot going on with all that news media out there, and with the FBI arriving—"

"Tomorrow," Pierce says. "The FBI will be here tomorrow."

"But we won't disturb you or your staff," Huang goes on. "We'll stay here in the reception area. We won't bother or interact with anyone. We'll just sit in place."

The chief's eyes are still glaring at them with anger, but Huang senses the man is giving up.

"All right," he says, stepping back. "You two...you sit out here. You don't move, 'cept if you've gotta take a piss. And you're on your own. Don't expect food, water, or a blanket. Got it?"

Pierce moves to a nearby orange plastic chair. "Got it, Chief."

The chief opens the door leading to the department's offices, making sure to slam it good and hard.

Huang sits down next to Pierce. "Good job," he says to Pierce.

Pierce just nods, then points to a sign over the doorway leading into the jail.

ALL CONVERSATIONS SUBJECT TO AUDIO AND VIDEO RECORDING.

Huang nods in return, getting the message.

Then Pierce shifts in his chair, pulls out his 9mm SIG Sauer pistol, and slides it between his right leg and the chair.

Huang gets that message as well.

CHAPTER 79

SPECIAL AGENT MANUEL SANCHEZ is walking to the nurses' station at the entrance to the Trauma ICU when he stops and quickly looks back.

The security guard who chased him out of York's room is still in there.

Why?

Bo Leighton spent a summer years back working as a volunteer EMT-firefighter for Sullivan County 'fore he was let go on suspicion of lifting some painkillers—which was true, though nobody could prove it—so he knows to disconnect the bitch's breathing tube before putting the pillow over her to smother out her life.

There.

Pillow down.

The body is so banged up and hooked up it doesn't even move as its airway is cut off.

There's *beeping, booping,* and *bleeping* from various instruments, and then the door slides open with a hard *slam!*

He looks up in surprise, seeing that Army agent standing right in the doorway.

One hand still on the pillow, he goes for the borrowed utility belt . . .

*   *   *

Sanchez steps in and sees the security guard smothering York with a room pillow.

He snaps up his SIG Sauer as the guy reaches for his utility belt and—

Pop! Pop! Pop!

The man falls away and crumples to the floor.

Shouts and yells come from outside.

He steps over to Connie, sees the fake security guard splayed out on the ground like a clumsy starfish, the pillow torn up, and blood starting to pool on the tile. The guard's skin is rapidly graying out.

Sanchez turns as a frightened-looking woman nurse peers in, her face pale in shock.

He holds up his pistol in his right hand, his badge and identification in the other.

"I'm a federal agent!" he calls out. "Special Agent Sanchez, United States Army. This man was trying to murder your patient! Please! I need help in here!"

The nurse ducks back. More yells, shouts out there. He can just imagine the chaos he's caused with the shooting.

Sanchez yells, "Your patient is dying! The man here tried to smother her! Please . . . somebody come in and look at her! Again, I'm a federal agent!"

A strong woman's voice says, "Put your pistol on the floor, then I'll come in."

Sanchez doesn't want to disarm himself but decides there's no other option. He steps forward, puts his SIG Sauer on the tile. "My weapon's on the floor, so you can come in and fix things. Okay?"

A female nurse in light-green scrubs and white sneakers comes in, looks down at the pistol, and then goes right over to York's bed and, in a series of quick, fluid movements, seems to get everything put back in place.

When she's finished, she says, "All right, I've reattached her tube... The man on the floor?"

"Not a security guard, I'm sure."

She starts to walk over. "His condition?"

"Most definitely dead," Sanchez says, and then he scoots over, leans down, and picks up the man's Desert Eagle.

The nurse steps back in shock. "You promised."

"That I did," he says. "So you could come in and fix things. Now you can leave."

The nurse heads to the door. "Mister, you better be what you say you are, and that man better be an imposter. The ICU out there is filling up with every cop and SWAT team member between here and Atlanta."

"I'm sure," Sanchez says. "And if you get a moment, tell them I'm here, and I'm not leaving. The only people who get in and touch that woman will be two medical personnel at the same time, with full identification."

The nurse says, "That must be some woman. Who is she?"

Sanchez looks over to the grievously wounded Connie York.

"She's my boss," he says.

CHAPTER 80

LIEUTENANT JOHN HUANG wakes up in the hard plastic chair, back aching, mouth dry, with Captain Allen Pierce tapping his shoulder and whispering in his ear.

"Somebody's coming," he says. "Wake up."

The tone of voice from Pierce has definitely gotten Huang's attention.

He sits up, rubbing at his eyes. The place is dimly lit. There are three closed doors: one leading to the jail cells, another going into the police department proper, and a glass one leading outside.

Shadows are moving out there.

"What's going on?" Huang asks. "Reporters?"

"I wish," Pierce says, standing up. "It's two in the morning. You ever run into journalists at 2:00 a.m.? Most of the time they're sleeping it off or getting drunk in a motel bar, complaining about their editors."

Huang stands up as well, wiping his face once more. He's hungry and thirsty, and his back is aching something awful.

The shadows are coming closer.

Huang says, "No offense, Allen, but I sure wish Major Cook was here."

"No offense taken," Pierce says. "God knows what kind of reception he's getting in the 'stan."

A moment slips by.

Pierce says, "Get your service weapon out."

"What?"

"You heard me, Lieutenant. Now."

Huang clumsily takes his SIG Sauer out of his side holster, the weight feeling odd and uncomfortable in his hand. Pierce, though, holds his pistol casually, like he's been around weapons all his life.

"They're getting closer," Huang says.

"Yeah."

"Should we tell somebody here?"

"Marcy, the jail attendant? By the time we get real police here it'll be too late."

"At least the door is locked," Huang says.

"Yeah."

Two people come to the door, and Huang feels his heart rate thump right along, and the hand holding his pistol is growing warm and moist.

A *click,* the door is unlocked, and a large man and woman come in, both wearing Sullivan County Sheriff's Department uniforms.

Pierce says, "Help you, Sheriff Williams?"

Huang recognizes the woman, but her whole demeanor and even the look of her face has changed. Earlier she had a hard and confident smile and bearing, like she was in charge of everything around her.

Now?

Her face is pasty and she looks tired, but her eyes are flashing with heat and anger.

The other officer is a deputy with LINDSAY on his name tag.

He is one of the biggest and bulkiest men Huang has ever seen, and Huang can feel violence ready to be released from the man, if the sheriff wills it.

"Holster your weapons," she says. "Now."

Huang waits and follows Pierce's lead. "As a courtesy, Sheriff. No problem."

Pierce returns his SIG Sauer to his holster, and Huang does the same with his own, though it takes two attempts to do so, making the deputy smile.

The sheriff says, "Mind telling me what the hell you two are doing here?"

Pierce says, "Keeping an eye on the place."

"You don't belong here," she says. "Get out."

"I'm afraid that's a nonstarter," Pierce says. "We're staying."

Deputy Lindsay crosses his large arms. "The sheriff told you to leave. Get out."

To Huang's shame, his legs are starting to tremble, but Pierce is still keeping cool. Huang wonders, *Is this a family thing, learning at a very young age as a black man how to stand your ground in front of the police?*

Pierce says, "Gee, thanks for the echo, Deputy. And we're not leaving. An Army Ranger died here a few days ago. Dr. Huang and I are making sure such an event doesn't happen again."

"How?" Williams says. "You're just sittin' on your asses in here."

Pierce says, "Yes, and tired asses they are. But we're also keeping an eye on who's coming in and who's going out."

The deputy looks at the sheriff like he's a Doberman pinscher on a leash, begging to be let loose to attack. Sheriff Williams says, "I could have the two of you arrested."

"For doing our jobs?"

"For trespassing," she says.

"The Ralston police chief said we could stay. Marcy, the

attendant, even came by to tell us some hours ago that she welcomes the vigilance."

"I don't care," Williams says.

Pierce laughs, and Huang notes how he's casually moved his hand back to his holstered SIG Sauer.

"You want to arrest us, is that right, Sheriff?" Pierce asks. "Restart the whole states' rights versus federal rights argument? Drag us out into that parking lot full of reporters from Savannah, Atlanta, DC? Get a whole bit of negative publicity? Is that your game plan?"

Huang wonders if Pierce is pushing the sheriff too hard in front of her subordinate. This may tip her to do something violent, something to save face.

Williams just remains quiet for some long seconds, then says, "The court hearing for Staff Sergeant Jefferson begins in a matter of hours. An hour after it does, you and everyone else from Quantico better be heading up to the Savannah airport. Come along, Clark."

She heads for the door, and Deputy Lindsay shakes his head. "Look at you two. Friggin' Chinaman and colored boy, thinking you can do anything. You boys can't do squat."

Huang wishes he could come back with a good answer, but Pierce does the job.

"You're wrong, Deputy," he says. "We're not a Chinaman or a colored boy. We're officers in the United States Army."

CHAPTER 81

AFGHANISTAN

AFTER THE HOURS TRAVELING on the Gardez Highway to FOB Chadwick—just outside Khost and near the village of Pendahar—the Humvee I'm in finally passes through the barriers, checkpoints, and vehicle traps. I've not slept a wink on this long drive, my body tense and nearly trembling, again thinking of what happened to me at another time, in another Humvee.

This vehicle, however, safely gets into the FOB and stops, and I slowly get out, holding my cane in one hand and my rucksack in the other. There are squat buildings all around us, made of metal shipping containers and concrete, the same dull sandy color. The quiet lieutenant who's in charge of this small convoy comes back to me just as a siren starts wailing, making me feel like I'm in wartime London, 1940.

He swears, says, "Come on, hurry up!" just as a recorded male voice announces over loudspeakers, "Rocket attack, rocket attack, rocket attack."

We move about ten or so meters before there's a far-off *thud* that makes the ground quiver, and I follow the lieutenant and others to a blast shelter. Its walls and roof are made of thick concrete, and the open ends of the roof are protected by a blast barrier that we slip through.

Just as we get inside there's another *thud,* and the six of us, then ten, and then more than a dozen soldiers of different ranks, stand inside.

I say to the lieutenant, "Can you tell me where Major West is, of the Seventy-Fifth Rangers?"

The lieutenant says, "I can, but I won't. Not until the all-clear sounds. Otherwise you might have your head taken off the second you step out."

I know I need to wait, but I look at my watch.

Time is slipping away both here and back in Georgia.

In the shadowy interior of the blast shelter, a soldier says, "Shit, I guess we pissed somebody off, huh?"

Laughter from most of the soldiers in here, but not from me.

Fifteen minutes after the all-clear sounds, I'm in the office of Major Fredericka West, Special Troops Battalion, Seventy-Fifth Ranger Regiment, which is nearly identical to the Ranger office in Bagram: plywood over a wood frame, homemade shelves, no windows, and locked gray metal filing cabinets. Major West is slim, with close-cropped dark-brown hair and brown eyes, wearing a worn ACU. As she moves papers around her gray metal desk, I see her left hand is furrowed with scar tissue. A set of telephones is near her elbow—for both secure and unsecure phone calls—and a military-grade laptop, like the one I'm carrying.

She looks exhausted. "This is where we waste a bunch of time talking about your trip and how you're feeling, and do you need something to eat," she begins, "but we don't have time for that crap. One, I've got, well, a shitload of work to get through, and two, your bosses at Quantico want your ass wrapped up in silver ribbon and sent on the next flight home."

I say, "Then why don't I see a roll of silver ribbon on your desk?"

West grimaces, begins to talk, waits as one helicopter and then another roars overhead, disturbing the dust that's everywhere in this small office. An M4 automatic rifle is in a weapons rack near the corner.

"You're not being rolled in tape because we Rangers owe you one, and because I'm trying to figure out why a fire team from Fourth Battalion is being charged with a crime in Georgia similar to the one they allegedly committed here in-country."

"In a village called Pendahar."

She starts typing on the laptop keyboard. "Aren't you the informed one."

I say, "And aren't you the pissy officer. What's the problem, Major? I'm the one about to be brought up on charges and who's just come in to see you after spending nearly a day in the air."

Quiet, as her fingers work some more.

"No excuse," she says. "Sorry. Been a rotten day in a series of rotten days, not to mention the local *muj* are still sending us 82-millimeter love letters. Can you give me a quick recap of what happened to Staff Sergeant Jefferson and his team in Georgia?"

I say, "A week ago seven residents of a rural house in Georgia, including a two-year-old girl, were murdered in a nighttime attack. The police reports, witnesses, and forensic evidence all led to the staff sergeant's team. They were placed under arrest, and my team was tasked to do an investigation."

"What did you and your team learn?"

I paused, then said, "At first it looked open-and-shut. Then we found discrepancies in the witness testimony, and those witnesses are now missing. And one of the four Rangers committed suicide while in custody."

More typing. "Is your investigation complete?"

"I'm in Afghanistan," I say. "Not yet."

"Yeah, I figured that," she says. "You're wondering about the civilian killings in Pendahar that were linked to those same

Rangers before they were sent home, correct? Seeing what happened here in Afghanistan, if it did something to their psyches that led to them repeating the atrocity in Georgia."

"That's been our thought," I say.

"Then let's take a look," she says. "Here's body-cam footage we managed to secure of that attack."

West turns the computer around so we can both view the screen as it comes to life.

The footage is stamped with running numerals denoting longitude, latitude, and time, and it's in light ghost-green night vision. I hear breathing, murmuring voices. The view comes to a wooden door set against a one-story, small stone house. I see body shapes, and somebody does something to the door. There's a bright flare of light and the *thump* of an explosion.

Yells.

Shots being fired.

The view is shaky as one room is entered, another, and then another.

More gunfire.

Robed women scream, hold up their hands. Rapid fire collapses them. A young boy runs into another room, is cut down.

I see the flash of weapons.

Uniformed men.

More screams.

The video goes black.

My hands and chest feel heavy. "Can I see it again, slower? Muted?"

"Sure."

I look through the video a second time, spotting the mottled look of the uniforms—one bearing the RANGER tab on a left shoulder—and the weapons, from an AK-47 to a pistol, and then I look at Major West's calm yet serious face.

"Well?" she asks. "What say you?"

"It's a fake," I say. "Those aren't Army Rangers."

She nods. "Good job, for a former NYPD detective."

West swivels the computer screen back to her. "I don't know what happened in the States, but those Rangers sure as hell didn't kill a houseful of civilians in Pendahar."

CHAPTER 82

AFGHANISTAN

SHE GIVES ME one more stare and says, "Just out of curiosity, how did you know it was a fake? To most people I'm sure it looks pretty damn real."

I try to swallow, fail. My throat is incredibly dry. A jet takes off outside, the noise silencing me longer in this plywood room.

When the jet engine sound drifts away, I say, "The shootings were real. The casualties look real. But those weren't Army Rangers. The uniforms were wrong. There was a mix of regular ACUs and fatigues of the Afghan National Army. The weapons were wrong, too. I saw an AK-47 and what looked to be a Russian pistol, maybe a Tokarev."

She slightly smiles. "But one of the shooters was wearing a Ranger tab."

"Yes," I say. "But you and I both know that Rangers don't wear any unit patches in the field...and the camera froze there for a second too long, like whoever was doing the taping wanted to make a statement."

"Good job, Major."

"What's the story, then? A setup?"

"That's what we're thinking," she says. "Commit an atrocity, put it up on YouTube or other social media, blame the Rangers and the Crusader unbelievers defiling this holy land, blah, blah, blah. Some unlucky innocents got caught in a cross fire organized by the local Taliban. But we were lucky to have intercepted the video before it was spread around too much. Oh, there were rumblings and the start of an official investigation—which I'm closing out when you go out that door—but the Rangers were innocent. We even showed the video at a local tribal *loya jirga,* and the tribal leaders are on board that the Army didn't do it."

"But...the Rangers are accused of doing the same thing stateside."

"Yeah," she says. "That's a puzzle, isn't it?" She looks down at her notes and says, "Hold on. You said the civilians who were killed in Georgia, some of them were drug dealers. How far up did they go? Big-time players?"

I shake my head. "Some weed, some crystal meth, and fentanyl. Strictly small-time."

"Too bad...well, good, I suppose. But I was thinking if they were players, and they were involved in something to do with opiates, and Afghanistan being the leading cultivator of the same, with a lot of flights going back to the States, there could be some sort of connection."

"Not with that group," I say. "Do you have any additional information on Major Frank Moore, the Fourth Battalion's executive officer?"

West shakes her head. "He was supposed to have been deployed a couple of days back when the Fourth Battalion left Hunter Army Airfield, but he was unable to be located. Then Savannah cops pulled him out of the local river back there, bullet round right to the face. They're running the investigation, but I was able to learn that he was probably killed after meeting with Staff Sergeant Jefferson, who's being held in a local jail, yes?"

"Ralston," I say. "He's in a jail in Ralston."

"And you tell me he's planning to plead guilty to those shootings?"

I check my watch, run the difference in time in my mind and say, "In about eight hours, yeah."

"Hell of a thing to do if he's not guilty, but he's taking the rap anyway."

"He's doing that, but the two surviving members of his team will go free. That's the deal. They don't face a trial, and he pleads guilty, takes whatever sentence comes his way." West ponders this before I add, "You Ranger guys are tough. And loyal."

"Like you wouldn't believe," she says.

"You think Staff Sergeant Jefferson would plead guilty to something he didn't do to see his guys get cut loose?"

"He'd have to have one hell of a good reason," she says.

Something comes to me and I say, "Hold on. This alleged massacre in Pendahar. I heard that was the reason they were sent home ahead of schedule. But you've told me that it was pretty suspicious right from the start."

West carefully says, "It was."

"But why send them home on such flimsy evidence?"

"Good question."

She doesn't say any more, and I quickly realize how to fill in the blanks. "They weren't assigned to a local Ranger company. They were sheep-dipped, borrowed by the CIA."

Her words are even more careful. "That's what I heard."

"What did they do for the CIA?"

"High-value target raids, I'm sure," she says. "Staff Sergeant Jefferson and his fire team were quite experienced in those types of raids. The CIA has a paramilitary unit, the Special Activities Division—I have a Ranger friend who's worked with them—but they don't have as much field experience as some Ranger units."

"The CIA was controlling them," I say. "Why did the CIA send them home ahead of their deployment schedule? This house raid, the killing of civilians, it was just an excuse. A cover story."

"Maybe," she says. "You'll have to talk to the CIA about that."

"All right, where are they?" I ask. "I'll go ahead and do just that."

West says, "It'll be a waste of time. You'd want to talk to the field officer handling those raids, and he's been transferred."

"Who's the officer?"

"Fellow named Kurtz, though God knows if that's his real name. He's at Observation Post Conrad."

"Where's that?"

West points to her door. "About ten klicks that way, up in the mountains between here and Pakistan. Only way up there is by helicopter."

"Can you get me there?"

Her phone rings and she holds up a finger. She takes the call—"West"—and seems to listen for a minute, then says, "Thanks for the heads-up, Sergeant Major."

West hangs up the phone, shakes her head. "You know better than that, Major Cook. We don't have any air assets. We get assigned them for a planned and specific mission, and I'm not in a position to do that. Sorry."

"Major West," I say, "the answer to whatever the hell is going on with those Rangers is up there with that CIA officer. One Ranger is dead. Another is facing life imprisonment for murders he might not have committed. Are you going to let that staff sergeant go to prison for life, probably face execution? Is that what you're saying?"

Her brown eyes flash at me with anger. "What I'm saying is that I can't make up a manifest and put your name on it, Major Cook, because I've just been told that there's an MP unit about twenty minutes out, coming here, looking for you."

Shit, I think. *Shit, shit.*

"Sorry," I say.

Her face calms down. "You're former NYPD, right?"

"That's right," I say. "Nineteen years in."

She nods and says, "Go up two compounds. That's where the Night Stalkers hang out. There's a warrant officer there named Cellucci. You might have some luck with him...but no guarantees. I'll walk you over, see that you get in."

I stand up, grab my rucksack. "Thanks, Major."

"Good luck, Major Cook," she says as she, too, stands, "because you're certainly going to need it."

The sirens start up again, and the steady, calm male voice of the recording comes back.

"Rocket attack, rocket attack, rocket attack."

CHAPTER 83

AFGHANISTAN

THE NIGHT STALKERS is the nickname of the Army's 160th Special Operations Aviation Regiment, probably pound for pound the bravest and craziest helicopter pilots in the world. Responsible for operations in Panama, Yemen, Iraq, and Afghanistan, along with the raid that took out Osama bin Laden, they're the Army aviators called upon to perform the most hazardous and nearly impossible missions.

Their compound is just a short walk from Major West's, and while some of the soldiers and civilian personnel seem a bit jumpy after the two recent mortar attacks, the same isn't true for the Night Stalkers, some of whom I find outdoors after Major West escorts me there. I come upon a rest area for these aviators, set outside three one-story metal-and-wood shacks. Beyond a concrete-block wall and coils of razor wire, their modified and exceptional helicopters of choice are lined up: two rotor transport MH-47s with extended fuel booms up front, Black Hawks for a variety of missions, and the much smaller two-crew Little Birds, used for reconnaissance and close combat and support.

Nearby is a gravel-covered area with weight-lifting equipment, punching bags, and half a dozen wooden picnic tables, where laughing and confident men are having late morning coffee and sausage, eggs, and pancakes on Styrofoam plates. They're dressed in jeans, cut-off sweatshirts, hoodies, and vests, most wearing ball caps. The wind is steady, meaning they have to hold on tight to their food and drink.

As I approach the nearest table, I'm given a quick look by the men, and then they go back to their stories and breakfasts. I can see why I got the quick look: I might be an Army officer, but I'm not one of them, so I don't count.

About then I'm ready to believe them.

I say, "I'm looking for a guy named Cellucci. Is he around?"

One of the aviators, with a close-cropped black beard and wearing sunglasses, a tattered Red Sox baseball cap on his head, says, "What's up, Major?"

"I just need to talk to him," I say. "Can you point him out?"

The aviator says, "Over there on the left. The laughing asshole wearing the Yankees cap."

"Thanks."

I go over to the table where he's sitting, laughing indeed, wearing the offending black-and-white Yankees cap and a black fleece jacket. Cellucci looks to be in his early thirties, muscular, with a happy-looking, red face that can probably go from joy to deadly anger in seconds.

"Excuse me," I ask. "Cellucci?"

The other three guys laugh, and Cellucci says, "The same, Major. Chief Warrant Officer Carmine Cellucci. What can I do for you?"

"I was hoping I could talk to you," I say. "In private."

His grin doesn't waver. "Mind if I ask why? Sir?"

I take out my identification, display it for him. "I'm with the CID. Does that answer your question?"

As one, his three breakfast mates go, "Ooooh, the Looch is in trouble, the Looch is in trouble," and he says something profane to them. They pick up their coffee and plates and leave us alone as I sit down across from him.

"Do I need representation?" he asks. "You looking to jam me up?"

"No, not at all," I say, smelling the sausages and pancakes still before him, my stomach grumbling from not quite remembering the last time I ate.

"Then what's this about?" he asks. His smile is still there, but there's wariness behind those sharp brown eyes.

"I need transport," I say.

He says, "This is a hell of a way to make a request. You got the paperwork, push it through channels."

"I don't have any paperwork."

That takes him aback, and he laughs. "What, you think me and the guys here are flying a taxi service, Major? Where are you looking to go?"

"Observation Post Conrad," I say. "It's up in the nearest mountain range. That's all I know."

He stares at me and starts laughing again. "OP Conrad? For real? Why not Mars while you're at it?"

"Remote, then?"

He shakes his head, takes off his Yankees cap, scratches at his nearly bald head. "Yeah, remote as hell, and the place is legendary. And not in a good way. There's one American up there, a guy named—"

"Kurtz," I interrupt.

The cap goes back on. "That's right, Kurtz. Like Brando in that Vietnam movie. Far away from whatever passes for civilization, he's up there with a group of Pashtun tribesmen who are loyal to him and their tribe, and nothing else."

"What do they do up there?"

"Whatever the hell they want," he says. "Why do you need to see him?"

"I need to talk to him about an investigation I'm conducting."

"Go through channels, get the paperwork. Hell, I wouldn't mind taking a trip up there. That's some ass-puckering flying."

"I don't have time," I say. "I need to talk to him today."

Another shake of his head. "You think you can get Kurtz to answer your questions? You know he's Agency, right? Won't talk to anyone...unless you have a fistful of Hershey bars." Cellucci notices my confused expression and repeats himself. "Yeah. Hershey bars. And not the ones with the almonds. One guy who went up there six months ago for a supply run— even a scheduled one—told me he couldn't even drop his load until Kurtz got his Hershey bars. Tell me, Major, you got some Hershey bars in your ruck?"

"No."

"Then we're just wasting each other's time. Sorry, Major. Wish I could help."

He starts to get up from the picnic table, and I say, "Brooklyn?"

Cellucci says, "Nope. Queens, through and through."

"My bad," I say. "I'm from Staten Island."

He gathers up his trash. "No kidding. How did you end up in CID?"

"NYPD," I say. "Detective second class, Midtown South. I was in the Reserves and decided to stick around after I got injured from an IED."

"Well, good for you. Bet some days you wish you stayed home." I nod. "Some days."

"Sorry, gotta run, Major."

One last chance. "Get out of jail free card."

He pauses as he puts a crumpled brown paper napkin on his plate. "What?"

I say, "You get me up there to see Kurtz, I'll make it so that you don't get another speeding ticket, parking ticket, or any other motor vehicle violation. For a year, starting when you get back home."

That gets his attention. "You got that kind of pull?"

Probably not, I think. "I'm serious."

"I can tell," he says. "Man, you must really want to go up there bad."

"I do."

He crumples everything up in his two strong hands. "Major... sorry. No can do. That's way out-of-bounds, and you know it."

Cellucci goes to a rusty fifty-five-gallon metal drum near a set of weights, drops in his trash, and I rub at my face and turn, just as two soldiers come in from the other side, wearing Military Police brassards on their left arms.

Looking for me, I'm sure.

CHAPTER 84

AFGHANISTAN

AS CASUALLY AS I can, I get up from the picnic table, leaving my cane behind—too blatant a sign of who I am—and I follow Cellucci and two other warrant officers as they walk back into the nearest building. The three of them are laughing and joking, and don't notice me following them, and I hope the two MPs on the other side of the compound are doing the same thing.

They pass through a swinging plywood door, and I'm in a ready room, with couches, chairs, large-scale maps pinned up on the wall, flags from various states, and pennants from every type of sports team imaginable. Some Night Stalkers are seated, thumbing through magazines or playing with handheld video games.

Where to go?

Anywhere, I think, anywhere away from that door the MPs will eventually come through.

Once they get to me, check my ID, it's done. Over.

And what's going on back in Georgia?

Five times since I left Bagram I called Connie on my Iridium, and five times there was no answer. Once or twice I could believe it was due to some satellite problem or solar flare interference, but not five times.

I don't like it, knowing she's back there, riding herd on my crew, with a hostile and criminal county sheriff keeping an eye on everything, and her going to a meeting with a guy who says he knows the truth about the massacre.

I go down a narrow corridor with a concrete floor, more plywood doors and cubicles on it, and the smell is of aviation fuel, sweat, and ill-washed clothes. This smell is also called FAN, for feet, ass, and nuts.

The corridor opens into an operations center with computer screens, communications equipment—radios, secure telephones—and more maps and photographs up on the walls.

Boy, I really don't belong here.

An officer with a colonel's rank starts to get up and say something, and I turn around and take three quick steps, nearly knocking down Chief Warrant Officer Carmine Cellucci, who's carrying a tan plastic bag in his right hand.

He laughs. "Hey, Major, there're two MPs out there looking for a Major Cook who's using a cane. What a coincidence, huh?"

I say, "You see me with a cane?"

"Ah, no, but the MPs will probably go beyond just that," he says. "By the way, two years."

"What?"

He takes my upper arm, starts leading me away from the inquisitive colonel back in the operations center. "You give me what you promised back there, except it's for two years, not one."

"Deal."

"And it includes my girlfriend."

"You're pushing it, Cellucci."

He stops, opens the plastic bag, and lets me look inside. A pile of Hershey's chocolate bars, in their familiar dark-brown packages with gray lettering. "You need to pay to get in."

I don't hesitate. "Your girlfriend, too."

He closes up the bag. "Good," he says. "Just don't tell the wife. C'mon."

"But orders," I say. "Paperwork. What changed?"

"Oh, a sweet coincidence," he says. "One of the Little Birds in my company just finished a maintenance cycle. Somebody needs to take it up for a test flight, make sure the oil doesn't leak or a screw doesn't fall off. How does that sound?"

"Sounds great," I say.

He takes me through a door to the outside and says, "We'll be heading out in about an hour after I do a preflight check and get our gear together. By the way, what kind of investigation you doing, you need to talk to Kurtz about it?"

"A Ranger staff sergeant," I say. "He's up on murder charges, intends to plead guilty later today. I don't think he did it. I hope Kurtz will back me up on this."

"Where's the Ranger being held?"

"Georgia," I say. "And I think he's in danger."

Cellucci whistles. "Once spent six months in Georgia, training some of their pilots. Young and scared, and I'd be scared, too, with Russia and its shit-ass military right next door."

"Not that Georgia," I say as we approach a set of tents. "The one back in the States."

"Oh," he says. "That Georgia. Man, that could be worse."

I say, "It certainly could."

Another glance at my watch.

Time is still slipping away, and I'm so far from being where I need to be.

CHAPTER 85

FOR THE PAST few minutes, dogs have been barking as Sheriff Emma Williams maneuvers her cruiser down the narrow, bumpy dirt road a few hours before sunrise on this day she has to control from start to finish.

The dirt road widens and ends in a wide spot of dirt and gravel, where half a dozen ATVs, four battered pickup trucks with large muddy tires, and one bright-blue and highly polished Mercedes-Benz A-Class sedan are parked.

There are also three trailers set in a semicircle, and another one is farther away. Even at this time of the morning, there are lights on in every trailer, because the chained hound dogs back there make for an effective early warning system. There's also a heavy scent of nail polish remover, and as Williams gets out of her cruiser, then puts on her hat, she knows that not a single ounce of nail polish exists in these four trailers.

She leaves the cruiser's engine running, as well as keeps the headlights on.

The wind comes up and the smell doesn't lessen, because that farther trailer is a meth lab, and in one random spasm of intelligence, the family that operates the lab made sure it was far enough away so that if it exploded, the rest of this isolated compound wouldn't go up as well. Two large barns are visible in the distance, through a stand of trees, which they use to dry their marijuana harvests.

"Hiram Tolliver," she yells. "You up in there?"

Dogs bark inside, and then the door to the closest trailer opens up, and a tall, heavyset man stumbles out, tying tight the string around his dirty gray sweatpants. He also has on an Atlanta Braves tank top. His upper arms are hairy and flabby, and quiver as he comes toward the cruiser.

"You're not Hiram," she says.

"Nope," he says, yawning, rubbing at the back of his head. "I'm his nephew Boyd."

"Boyd," she says. "I don't think we've met."

"No, ma'am," he says, shielding his eyes with a beefy hand. "Look, can you switch off those headlights?"

"No," Williams says. "What did your uncle tell you to do?"

He coughs, scratches at his stomach. "He told me to do whatever you wanted, no questions, no talk back."

"That's a hell of an open ticket, you know."

"Uncle Hiram, he says he'd make it good for me. 'Scuse me." Boyd turns and clears his lungs, spits twice on the dirt. Turning back, he wipes a hand across his mouth and says, "Whaddya need, Sheriff?"

She says, "You're coming with me to the county jail. You're going to be placed in a cell. Later this morning, maybe just before noon or somewhere close to that, a prisoner is going to be put in that cell."

From her left pants pocket she takes out a slim knife. "After he's placed in there with you, you're going to slit his throat with this."

She holds out the knife, and he takes it. "Gosh, ma'am, that's pretty cold, you know? Killin' a man I don't know, I don't have a grudge against."

"He's an uppity nigger that thinks he's better than you."

"Oh," he says, taking the blade, sliding it into the pocket of his sweatpants. "That's okay, then."

"Good."

"But . . . ma'am?"

"Yes?"

"How do I get there? I mean, there's no warrants or anything out there on me. Ma'am?"

Williams smiles. This is going to be all right.

"Boyd, come over here and knock off my hat. Okay?"

"Um, okay."

Boyd comes over, knocks off her hat.

"Now," she says. "Pick it up."

"Yes, ma'am."

He picks up her hat and hands it over, and she puts it back on. She grabs his wrist, turns him around, and quickly and efficiently puts on the handcuffs.

"Boyd Tolliver, I'm placing you under arrest for assaulting a law enforcement officer," she says.

"Ma'am."

"Yes?"

"My wrists are sore from chopping wood yesterday. Mind not putting on the cuffs too tight?"

Williams leads him back to her cruiser.

"Not at all," she says.

CHAPTER 86

CAPTAIN ALLEN PIERCE gets up from his chair and kicks at Lieutenant John Huang's legs. For the past couple of hours Huang has tried to sleep with three chairs pushed together, and that hasn't gone well, with Huang falling twice onto the floor.

Huang jerks awake. "What's up?"

"Circus is about to start," Pierce says, looking at the crowds suddenly moving toward the door of the jailhouse. "A sheriff's van just pulled in."

Huang yawns, stretches, winces. "What's our job?"

Pierce checks his service weapon. "Make sure the staff sergeant gets to the courthouse without a Jack Ruby getting in the way."

The door flings open, and Deputy Sheriff Clark Lindsay comes in, looking the same as he did a few hours ago, except now he's wearing a bullet-resistant vest over his uniform, with yellow letters denoting SULLIVAN COUNTY SHERIFF and a stylized badge underneath.

Two other deputies follow him, carrying shotguns.

Pierce says, "Good morning, Deputy Clark. Taking time away from ironing your white sheets to play bus driver?"

Clark comes up close to Pierce, and Pierce doesn't budge an inch. Clark grins. "Boy, one of these days, you're gonna leave. And I'm gonna stay right here, and Sullivan County will get right back to where it belongs."

Pierce says, "In 1950?"

"No," he says, "where people mind their business. Now get out of my way. Me and my boys got work to do."

"No problem," Pierce says, just as the Ralston police chief, Richard Kane, comes in, carrying a clipboard.

"Clark," the chief says, looking worn down, his thick moustache drooping. "Glad to see you here. Let's get this taken care of so we can get back to normal."

The chief takes out a key set, unlocks the door leading into the cell area, and the three deputies walk in. Pierce follows as well, with Huang right behind him. Deputy Lindsay sees this and says, "Hey, Chief, those Army guys shouldn't be here! Keep 'em out!"

Pierce won't let the chief answer and says, "Let us in, Chief. You don't want an accident or anything untoward to happen to the staff sergeant right now, do you? Dr. Huang and I will just be witnesses, representing the US Army."

Deputy Lindsay says, "Dick, I'm telling you, keep those soldier boys out!"

"Well..." Chief Kane starts.

Pierce is pleased when Huang jumps in. "Chief Kane, this is your facility, correct? Not the county sheriff's, am I right? That means only you have the authority here, not Deputy Lindsay."

The chief has a sly smile on his face, like after months of losing at poker with the deputy, he's about to win this hand. "That's right. C'mon, Clark. It'll only take a few minutes."

The deputy says, "I won't forget this, Dick. And neither will the sheriff."

Pierce says, "Fine, none of us will forget it. We'll all be Mensa candidates later today. After you, Chief."

The small procession goes down the concrete hallway, past two interview rooms, and then to the cells.

The three Army Rangers are standing straight and tall, hands right beside their legs. Staff Sergeant Caleb Jefferson steps close to the bars. "Nice group of visitors," he says. "What a lucky guy I must be."

Deputy Lindsay steps forward and says, "Caleb Jefferson, my deputies and I are here to transport you to the Sullivan County Superior Courthouse. Put your hands through the cell door, we'll get you cuffed and on your way."

Pierce sees Jefferson's dark eyes narrow. "What about my guys? Corporal Barnes and Specialist Ruiz? That was part of the deal. They go free."

Chief Kane speaks up. "Not a problem, Staff Sergeant. I got a phone call a few minutes ago from the district attorney, Mr. Slate. He says your men will be released by the end of the day today. Seems there's so much going on at the courthouse, he just can't get away at the moment."

Jefferson doesn't say a word but quickly looks over at the other two Rangers. "All right," he says. "Chief, I'm holding you responsible for my guys' safety and freedom. Just make sure it happens."

Deputy Lindsay says, "Boy, you threatenin' the police chief?"

"No," he says, thrusting his hands through the cell door opening. "Not making a threat, just making sure there's no misunderstanding down the road."

Lindsay takes handcuffs from his duty belt, snaps them shut around Jefferson's wrists. "Step back now."

Jefferson takes three steps back, and Chief Kane unlocks the cell door, swings it open. Jefferson steps forward, and the other two Rangers snap to attention.

"You take care, Sergeant," Barnes says.

"We got your back, Sergeant," Ruiz says.

As the procession makes its way out of the cell area, Chief Kane says to no one in particular, "That was weird. I thought those two other fellas, I thought they were going to give him a salute."

Pierce says, "That's Hollywood bullshit. Nobody gives a salute indoors, and nobody gives a salute as a prisoner."

"Oh," the chief says.

"Yeah," Pierce says. "This is reality, as real as it gets."

CHAPTER 87

SPECIAL AGENT MANUEL SANCHEZ is sitting in a corner of trauma room 2 with a grievously injured Special Agent Connie York in a hospital bed and one dead assailant sprawled out on the floor. Nothing you really see in cop TV shows or movies, but after just a few minutes a freshly shot body starts to smell, when certain muscles relax and let loose body waste, and now it's been hours, and long hours at that.

Sanchez is on the floor, with a chair and a small cabinet dragged in front to offer some mode of protection. He's impressed that he's managed to stay awake during the night. A few hours ago it looked like a small black snake was about to come into the room, but Sanchez knew it was a flexible optic surveillance device, checking out the situation.

He resisted an urge to give it a cheery wave.

Now suddenly a strong male voice comes from the outside corridor. "Hello, the room!"

Sanchez says, "Hello right back!"

The man says, "I'm Lieutenant Harry Lightner, Savannah Police Department. Who am I talking to?"

"Special Agent Manuel Sanchez, US Army CID," he says. "Nice to make your acquaintance."

"Same here," the Savannah officer replies. "We've got quite the situation here, don't we?"

"That's true, amigo," Sanchez says.

"You seem pretty concerned about Agent York's safety."

"Yep."

"You said earlier that you'd only allow two medical personnel at a time into the room to check on Agent York," Lightner says.

"Roger that," Sanchez says.

"You know we can't allow that, not with you holding a weapon and having discharged it."

Sanchez doesn't know much about emergency medicine, but in looking up at the equipment stationed near York, nothing seems to be in the red or sounding off an alarm.

"Ah, gee, Lieutenant," Sanchez says, "just when I was beginning to establish a bond of trust with you, you have to go ahead and spoil it by insulting me. I didn't discharge my service weapon. I shot a guy trying to murder my boss. And you know and I know he doesn't work for the hospital. I bet you've done a head count of the hospital's security staff and there isn't one missing."

Sanchez waits for a reply, and then the lieutenant says, "You know, this yelling back and forth, it sure is cumbersome. How about I slide in a portable phone, we can talk easier?"

Sanchez laughs. "Sure. A portable phone with a hidden microphone and camera or a flash-bang grenade or a tear-gas canister. Not going to happen, Lieutenant."

He takes out his iPhone, sends off a quick text message. He doesn't think he's going to have much more time in here and wants to make things clear to Pierce and Huang as this day proceeds.

"All right," the lieutenant says. "Can we get you anything in the meantime, Agent Sanchez? Water? Juice? Something to eat?"

He takes another sniff. Damn, is it getting foul in here.

"I want two cops," he says.

"What?"

"Two cops," Sanchez says. "Dressed in nothing except their underwear. No shoes, no socks, nothing. They come in with hands out, and they slowly turn around and lower their shorts, so I know they're not concealing anything. Got it?"

The Savannah lieutenant says, "Are you joking, Agent Sanchez? You can't be serious."

"Oh, serious indeed," he says. "Those two cops come in, just as I say, and they take out the dead guy. That gives you a chance to fingerprint him, do an ID, find out why he tried to kill my boss. How does that sound?"

Sanchez looks at his iPhone. In the upper left-hand portion of the screen, small letters now announce, where they didn't before: No service.

The cops are blocking his cell phone.

No matter.

Sanchez settles in for a long wait, and looks up to York and says, "Hang in there, boss. We need to know what you know."

Captain Allen Pierce is driving their rental Ford sedan right behind the dark-brown van of the Sullivan County Sheriff's Department when his phone chimes, and so does Huang's.

He says, "What's up, John? Who's trying to talk to us? The *Atlanta Journal-Constitution*?"

Huang holds his phone close to his face. "It's from Sanchez."

"What does it say?"

"It says, Still guarding York. Pierce in charge. Protect the Rangers."

"Text him back."

"And tell him what?"

Pierce takes a look in the rearview mirror, sees the line of rented cars and vans belonging to the news media streaming behind them like some ghoulish parade.

"Tell him message received," Pierce says. "Nothing else. Poor guy's got his hands full."

Huang's fingers start working on the handheld's screen. "So do we. Shit, why haven't we heard from Major Cook?"

Pierce says, "Maybe he's gotten held up in some carpet bazaar. Forget Cook for the moment, John. We're on our own."

Gus Millner is a maintenance worker and transport assistant at the Memorial Health University Medical Center, and he's having a busy day. When the ER is busy, he's busy, and right now he's carrying a heavy plastic bag that holds the belongings of a female gunshot victim who was admitted yesterday. There was some sort of foul-up yesterday in delivering this bag, so he needs to bring the bag up to the ICU's nurses' station. Afterward, there's a restroom on the third floor that needs attention.

He's alone in an elevator, going up, when something starts ringing in the bag.

It keeps ringing.

He opens the bag, looks inside. Black slacks, shoes, and—

A heavy phone with a big keypad and a thick, stubby antenna. Not a type of cell phone he's ever seen.

What to do?

Answer it?

He closes the bag, and when he gets to the right floor for the ICU, it stops ringing.

Good.

Last month one of his buds got shit-canned for answering some patient's phone in a bag of possessions like this, and Gus isn't about to lose his job over something so simple and silly.

CHAPTER 88

AFGHANISTAN

I SWITCH OFF my Iridium phone and put it back in my rucksack. Chief Warrant Officer Cellucci is standing to the right of the Little Bird helicopter and waves me forward. It's windy out on the airstrip, hitting us with dust and gravel.

"No answer, Major?"

"None," I say, walking to him as best as I can without my cane, rucksack in my right hand. I'm dressed in a dark-green flight suit, carrying an oversized crash helmet in my left hand.

He shrugs. "Happens sometimes, the signals don't go through. Cosmic rays, sunspots—the atmospherics around here are pretty strange. Here, I'll take your bag."

Cellucci grabs it with little effort, tosses it into the rear, which is used for storage. I go to climb in and hesitate, my left leg screaming at me how stupid this is, and then Cellucci says, "Here you go."

He grabs two fistfuls of my flight-suit fabric and pushes me in, the fabric from the one-piece suit jamming into a very sensitive area, and I sit down in the small, tight canvas seat. Cellucci helps strap me in and then walks around the bubble-glass front, eases himself into the pilot's seat.

"Put your helmet on. Let's get the comm set up so we can chat with each other."

He helps me put the borrowed helmet on, adjusts the mic in front, hooks up the communications cable. I feel like I'm being put into a carnival ride by some smug traveling carnie who secretly hopes I piss myself when the ride ends.

After he buckles himself in, Cellucci starts working the switches, and I try to take it all in. There's a control stick in front of me, with an identical one in front of Cellucci. Large pedals are on the floor, and I keep my feet away from them. Between us is a large console with a square screen and round dials, and I think I recognize a compass, and that's about it.

Cellucci adjusts something, and his voice crackles through the helmet's earphones. "Hear me, Major?"

I adjust the mic in front of my mouth and say, "Just fine, Chief."

"Good," he says. Overhead the engine starts to whine, and he says, "Okay, quick safety demo before we get airborne. If we're up there and I get hit or disabled, so you're the only one conscious, this is what you're going to do. Okay? Pay attention."

Earlier I was warm in my borrowed flight suit, but now I'm near shivering with apprehension. "Paying attention, Chief."

"Good," he says. "If I'm slumped over and you can't revive me, and we're heading to the ground, you unsnap your harness, here, here, and here"—he slaps at my torso—"and slip off your helmet quick as you can, and do your best to kiss your ass good-bye before we hit."

He laughs and maneuvers the control stick in front of him, the collective control by his seat, and working the pedals, he lifts us off from FOB Chadwick.

I've flown other times in helicopters—military and NYPD—and they are Cadillacs compared to the Little Bird, which feels like a Volkswagen Beetle with helicopter blades overhead. Cellucci turns another dial, and I can hear him broadcast. "Tower, this is November Sierra Four," he says. "Clear for departure to the south?"

"Roger that, November Sierra Four," comes the female voice of the airstrip's flight controller. "You are clear."

He takes us up, and my stomach does a few loop-de-loops, for in front of us is a huge Plexiglas bubble, which gives me the feeling that at any moment I could slide out of my seat and break through the window. The fading afternoon sunlight flickers overhead, from the spinning blades casting shadows over the curved bubble. The control stick in front of me moves whenever Cellucci moves his stick.

I swallow twice and look at Cellucci, who smiles at my discomfort and gives me a thumbs-up.

"Doing all right, Major?" he asks, voice strong and confident through the earphones.

I swallow again. "Chief, I know you're an elite flier. The Army knows you're an elite flier, and so does everyone else in the Night Stalkers. Just a favor, all right?"

"What's that, Major?"

I say, "Please don't feel like you have to prove anything to me. Let's just skip that step."

A laugh comes through. "Roger that, Major."

It doesn't take long for us to leave the flat plain that holds the city of Khost and FOB Chadwick. The southern part of the Hindu Kush range, separating Afghanistan from Pakistan, rises straight up before us, left to right, huge stony peaks riven with valleys and ravines containing trees and small forests. Twice I spot a small village, stone and brick homes built on the steep slopes of the lower range.

"Pretty remote down there, ain't it?" Cellucci says.

"It looks like the ends of the earth."

He says, "Maybe so, but there are eyes on us down there, tracking us. Right now cell phones and handheld radios are ringing in every direction for about fifteen or twenty klicks, saying the Americans are coming."

"You ever get shot at?"

"All the time, Major, all the time," he says. "But usually we're moving too fast. The T-men love to track the Chinooks and hit them when they're landing or taking off. That's one of the good things about the Little Birds."

Higher and higher we go, my ears popping, and Cellucci says, "This is the God's honest truth, Major, but last year I inserted a team into a real remote and deep valley, the kind of place where it looks like you have to pipe in the sunshine, and the villagers there, they thought we were the Russians. Can you believe that?"

I say, "Must be true if you say it. Could have been worse, though."

"How?"

"They could have thought you were British."

That earns me a laugh from my pilot as we continue to climb into the ragged mountains.

In less than fifteen minutes Cellucci tilts us as he turns to the left, and he says, "Okay, Major, there it is. OP Conrad, straight ahead."

I look and see just a flat peak with tumbled rocks, stunted trees, and brush.

"Where?"

"You'll see, soon enough," he says, and then he starts transmitting, and I hear his voice. "Oscar Papa Charlie, this is November Sierra Four, November Sierra Four. Do you copy?"

The helicopter starts to descend.

"Oscar Papa Charlie, this is November Sierra Four, inbound. Do you copy?"

I think I see shapes appear.

Then a satellite dish. Another one. A set of antennas.

A cleared, rocky space, about half the size of a basketball court.

"Oscar Papa Charlie, November Sierra Four calling. We are inbound. Do you copy?"

I say, "Doesn't look like anyone's home."

"Oh, they're home all right," Cellucci says. "But maybe they're too busy to chat. Okay, Major, unsnap your straps, drop your crash helmet, get ready to hop out. I'll be back in twenty."

It feels like a cold fist has just punched my gut. "You're not staying with me?"

He curses. "Are you nuts? How long do you think me and my Little Bird will last if I stay up there, like a goddamn fly on a tabletop? The *muj* will start dropping in mortar rounds in about ninety seconds."

The rocky surface rushes up.

"Nope," he goes on. "I'll be back in twenty minutes to pick you up, head back to the FOB. Hope you can get your business done in that amount of time. You got a gold pass for one round trip, and that's it."

I tense up because at our rate of descent, my mind is screaming at me that we're going to crash, but being the expert he is, Chief Cellucci works the controls and flares us up, the twin landing skids barely touching the ground.

He slaps me on the shoulder. "Go! Get the hell moving before I get a mortar round in my lap!"

I get the straps and buckles undone, reach behind me, get my rucksack, open the side door, and toss the rucksack out. I take off the borrowed crash helmet and shift and drop to the ground—making sure I land on my good leg—and I close my eyes and hold my breath as I'm engulfed in a whirling cloud of dust and kicked-up small rocks.

With a humming roar, the Little Bird lifts off and then dips into a ravine, until all I hear is the dimming noise of the engine. Then it pops back into view, and I spot Cellucci as he hugs the contours of the nearest ridge, waggling back and forth, like he finally wants to show off.

Fair enough.

I grab my rucksack and start toward the hidden bunkers of OP Conrad. I notice faded white PVC tubes stuck in the dirt—homemade urinals—and there is netting hanging up, and dirt berms, and HESCO barriers, made of metal webbing and about the size of large freezers, filled with rocks and dirt. There are antennas and satellite dishes, and one, then two, then four men emerge from a dirt entrance, like spelunkers coming up after being lost for a month.

"Hey," I say.

The four men come closer, and now I understand why Cellucci couldn't raise the outpost's radio.

The four men are wiry, tall, bearded, and wearing the traditional sandals, cotton pants, sheepskin vests, and flat wool hats of Afghan villagers.

And fighters. All are carrying AK-47s, with belts and pouches around their skinny waists.

With horror, I realize that at some recent point the Taliban must have overrun this place. I drop my rucksack on the ground, hold out my hands—I have my service weapon holstered at my side, but going for it would be an instant death sentence—and I say, "Hey, does anyone—"

The closest one yells something I don't understand and then hits me in the stomach with the butt of his AK-47.

CHAPTER 89

THE HEARING ROOM in the Sullivan County Superior Courthouse is packed, with not a single seat available along the two sets of four long wooden benches. Before the benches is a wooden bar with a swinging gate, and to the left is the juror's box, which is empty. Captain Allen Pierce and Dr. John Huang are standing against a wall near the doors leading into the outer hall. Only by showing their CID badges and appealing to the patriotism of the courthouse attendants were they able to get in.

Huang says, "What a circus."

Pierce doesn't say a word, just takes it all in. Across from the empty jury box are two tables and sets of chairs. One table is occupied by District Attorney Cornelius Slate, sitting slumped in his chair. The other table and chairs are empty, and that's where Pierce expects Staff Sergeant Caleb Jefferson to show up in a few minutes. At the other side of the enclosure is a witness booth, the raised bench for the judge—also empty—and another booth that looks to be occupied by an older African American woman, probably the court clerk. Two male uniformed court attendants stand by the judge's bench.

Huang nudges him with an elbow. "Look. Over there. Do you see who has a prime seat?"

Pierce spots Sheriff Emma Williams sitting in the first row, with her campaign hat in her lap, and she's laughing and whispering to everyone near her.

Huang says, "She looks happier than hell. Why is that?"

Sheriff Emma Williams checks her watch. In a few minutes that old fool Judge Howell Rollins will come in—hopefully not stumbling after his usual breakfast of two Bloody Marys—and get this show on the road.

She smiles as she takes in all of her people in the courtroom and doesn't even break her smile at seeing those two sad-looking Army folks standing over there against the wall, like theatergoers who were promised orchestra seats and now are forced to stand throughout the show.

And what a show today promises to be. Behind this court-house is the Sullivan County Jail, and that place is *hers*. Boyd Tolliver is in a two-person holding cell, and when that double-crossing piece of shit Staff Sergeant Jefferson pleads guilty and is sent back there, in preparation for being transferred to a state prison, well, the official story will be that he attacked this poor citizen out of rage, and said citizen had to defend himself.

The other two will be taken care of later, tonight or early tomorrow morning.

Of that she has no doubt.

And the woman CID agent who nearly got her head blown off, Williams heard late last night from a nurse at the hospital that she's in a coma and probably won't make it. She rubs at a healing scratch on her hand. Hell, even those two redneck clowns she put down a couple of days back near Hunter Army Airfield haven't yet been reported missing.

Then . . . Tuesday, Election Day, and the day after, she'll start packing her bags.

Williams scans the room, seeing her people. Will Fletcher, who took out a loan from her four years back when his dump trucks needed repair and will be paying off the loan for another three years. Moss Gray, who refused to give her a cut of his 'shine business, and whose two sons are now doing time over in Georgia State Prison. Ray Cass, who illegally dumps waste oil and gasoline from his three service stations in the local state forest, and who is going to do a favor for the sheriff late tonight, by disabling the bay doors for the Ralston Volunteer Fire Department so they can't respond when an electrical fire breaks out at the Ralston jail, incinerating the poor prisoners incarcerated there.

Just the two, of course, but that will be enough.

Williams catches the eye of the tired-looking Chinaman standing back there and gives him a little wave and a smile.

Huang nudges the JAG lawyer with his elbow. "Did you see that? Did you? She waved at us. A big smile and she waved at us."

Pierce says. "Confident little witch, isn't she?"

Huang whispers again, "You don't understand."

"Then clarify it, Doc. The games are about to begin."

"The sheriff is more than just confident," he says, recalling the look on her face. "She's taunting us. She's telling us that no matter what happens today, it's all going to come out in her favor."

Pierce says, "That's news? Staff Sergeant Jefferson is pleading guilty."

"No, it's more than that," Huang says, desperately trying to keep his voice low. "Remember our stay at the jail last night, when the jail attendant told us that she heard the DA had pissed off the sheriff by getting that guilty plea? That humiliated her. She's not a woman to be humiliated."

A door at the far end of the courtroom opens, and an

older man with snow-white hair and wearing black robes slowly comes in.

The woman clerk calls, "All rise!"

Huang whispers, "Allen, I think she means to kill the staff sergeant."

CHAPTER 90

AFGHANISTAN

ONCE MY EYES adjust to the gloom of the bunker's interior, I see five men of various ages and beard lengths staring at me, four of them sitting against a rough rock wall with AK-47s leaning against their knees. The one without an automatic rifle is minding a little gas stove that is heating up a kettle of water. A sixth one, who disarmed me earlier, is about to go through my rucksack.

Electric lamps illuminate the rough interior, and dirty gray blankets are hung in two places, probably leading into other portions of the observation post. Fly strips dangle from the ceiling, dead flies attached.

My breathing is starting to ease, my left leg actually doesn't hurt as much as it should, and I'm leaning against a folded-up gray blanket.

The man with my rucksack opens the top, takes out a plastic bag, grunts, and holds up a fistful of Hershey chocolate bars.

The men laugh.

I say, "Go ahead, laugh. Bet you clowns have never tasted chocolate in your life."

The man with the kettle pours the hot water into a teapot, gently stirs it. In perfect English he says, "Oh, you might be surprised."

I stare at him.

"Care for a cup of tea, Major?"

I say, "Are you Kurtz?"

He carefully sets out small metal cups for the brewed tea. "Apparently so," he says, smiling.

The chocolate bars were passed over to Kurtz, and my weapon and rucksack were returned to me. I now hold a filled cup in my hand but don't take a sip.

"Hell of a welcoming committee," I say. "What's your problem?"

He shrugs. "No problem. I didn't feel like having visitors today. That's why I didn't answer. In two weeks there's a scheduled re-supply drop . . . and your pilot wasn't sending along the necessary code groups to let me know about an unscheduled visit." He pours tea in other cups, and the men reach forward. "I figure, you get a bit roughed up, you'll bring the message back to wher-ever you came from not to come up for some tourist visit."

I say, "This isn't a tourist visit."

"Oh, my apologies," he says. "Who are you, then, and why are you here?"

"Major Jeremiah Cook," I say. "I'm with the Army CID."

"Criminal investigations? Really? I'm afraid you have zero jurisdiction over me and my men."

"It's not involving your actions," I say. "I'm investigating the arrest stateside of a Ranger squad that was under your tempo-rary command. Headed by Staff Sergeant Caleb Jefferson, Alpha Company, Fourth Battalion."

A slight smile through the beard. "Ah, yes, the famed Ninjas. Damn, they were good. I'd give them a house to raid, and I don't know how they did it so well—concealment, taking their time, using distractions—but they could raid the house before the dogs even started barking. What happened to them stateside?"

I say, "Four of them were arrested for multiple homicides, killing seven civilians in a house."

The cup is in midair. "That's pretty screwed up. Do you think they did it?"

"All the forensic evidence and the witnesses say so," I say. "But now the witnesses and most of the evidence are gone. One of the Rangers committed suicide in his cell. And I learned they were set up for an attack committed in a village here in Afghanistan. Pendahar."

He takes a long sip of his tea. "Yeah. Poor Taliban bastards were getting pretty chewed up in that district. They wanted to set up a war-crime incident, blame the Ninjas, get world opinion once again set against the Great Satan. Happily for everyone, they suck at making home movies."

"But they were still sent home early, weren't they? With that potential war crime being used as an excuse. When they were under your command."

"Ah, that's right."

"What happened when they were working for you?"

He puts his cup down on the stone-and-dirt floor. The five Afghan tribesmen have been watching our conversation with intent, their heads moving back and forth like they're watching a tennis match.

"Sorry, Major Cook, that is way above your pay grade, your position, your station in life."

I say, "Mr. Kurtz, please. Staff Sergeant Jefferson is pleading guilty today and is about to be sentenced for those murders."

"And the other two Rangers?"

"Apparently they will be set free, in exchange for Jefferson pleading guilty."

"Sounds like the staff sergeant."

I say, "Sounds like he's protecting his fire team. But why? I don't think he did what he's charged with in Georgia. But their arrests in Georgia came after they were sent home early. Why? What happened here?"

Kurtz stares at me, and I say, "Mr. Kurtz, I'm here under no authority or orders. I've been on aircraft and in convoys for the last forty hours. However my mission wraps up here, I'm heading straight to a court-martial. When that happens, I'd like to think this wasn't all a waste, that I found out what really happened to Staff Sergeant Jefferson and his Rangers."

Kurtz picks up his cup, takes another sip. Mine is getting cold and I don't really give a shit.

I say, "You say you worked with them, admired them. Why won't you help them?"

He says, "Doubt it will help at this point in time."

"Please."

He pours himself more tea. "One night they went on a raid."

"Where?"

"Doesn't matter. They hit the right house, but it was empty. Nobody home. It happens—sometimes the best intelligence gets fouled up. They were then heading back to their pickup point, when they heard screams. Not their business, not their problem, but Staff Sergeant Jefferson...he's not made like that. Someone was in pain, being tortured, and he and his crew were going to stop it."

"Did they?"

"They did," he says. "But there were...complications."

"What kind of complications?"

"The ones that sent them home early to Georgia and sent me up to this remote slice of paradise."

CHAPTER 91

AFTER THE WORDS "the Honorable Judge Howell Rollins presiding" fade away, Lieutenant John Huang leans closer to Pierce and says, "We've got to do something."

"Like what?" Pierce says, feeling on the spot, remembering the urgent words from Agent Sanchez, up there in Savannah, keeping guard over a wounded Agent Cook: Protect the Rangers.

He says to Huang, "I don't have standing here, Doc. You know that."

"But you know something's going on with the sheriff," he urgently says. "We both know it!"

Pierce says, "What the hell do you want me to do? Interrupt the proceedings? Yell out that the Army is here, and we know your sheriff is a crook and is planning to kill this Army Ranger? Hell, considering what he's charged with, most of the people in this town would be fine with it."

Pierce sees one of the courtroom officers—an older male with a paunch who looks like ex-military—staring at him and Huang, and he shuts up.

District Attorney Cornelius Slate is at the judge's bench, talking to the judge, and overhead, huge fans are slowly moving, trying to stir up the dead air.

Abruptly the district attorney goes back to his table, and the judge says, "All right, Gene. Bring in the sergeant, will you?"

The court officer who earlier had been staring at them goes through the door near the clerk's station and comes back with Staff Sergeant Caleb Jefferson. He's dressed in the same orange prison jumpsuit, with RALSTON PD JAIL in black letters on the back. His hands are cuffed, and he moves with grace and confidence, like whatever is going to happen today is a minor annoyance, nothing else.

There are whispers and a few comments after Jefferson comes in, including one woman's harsh voice—"Baby killer!"—but the Ranger goes to the front of the table directly next to the district attorney's and patiently stands there.

The old judge at the bench makes a soft *rap* with his gavel and says, "Okay, folks, simmer down. We're about to begin."

Pierce is reminded of those dreams he has when he's under some heavy stress, the dreams of going to class and realizing that today is exam day, or the dreams of ending a semester and finding an old class schedule, realizing that he's forgotten to attend an important class all these past months.

These dreams are nothing compared to what's happening now, as the Ranger just a few feet away from him—a fellow service member!—is being railroaded and, based on the sheriff's record for removing evidence, will be dead in a day or two.

Protect the Rangers.

But how?

CHAPTER 92

AFGHANISTAN

THE CIA MAN SIGHS. "But don't feel sorry for me, Major Cook. Working back there near Khost, I had forms to fill out, superiors to satisfy, and Company lawyers on my back, making sure I didn't cross any magic lines that had been drawn the previous week in DC. Here, it's like something out of *Lawrence of Arabia*. Just me and these fine fellows. I find it . . . liberating. Clean. Precise."

As much as I want to press him, he seems to be in a mood, and I don't want to disturb it. "What do you do here? And how can you—"

"Trust them?" Kurtz asks. "Is that what you're asking? Well, a few things work in my favor. Deep back there in the rock is my quarters, with a safe that automatically changes its combination every twenty-four hours. In there is a million or so dollars that I dole out at appropriate times. And these tribesmen love to fight. They've been fighting one another for centuries and will continue to do so even when we have colonies on Mars. And two tours ago I converted to Islam. I'm now part of the tribe. Not an infidel."

He says something in Pashto to the men, and they all laugh with pleasure.

Kurtz says to Cook, "Up here, we keep an eye on local ratlines in the deep valleys and ravines, bringing in men from Pakistan. We've got observers in all the local villages. Don't care what tribe they're from or if they're crossing borders. But if they're Al-Qaeda, ISIS, any foreign fighters...they come to a nasty and bloody end."

"But...you're so isolated. Remote."

He smiles through his thick beard. "I've got the finest communication gear the Company can provide. And there are air packages overhead at my disposal. Whenever my guys run into something bigger than they can handle, or if the Taliban try to assault my little fort here, I send a call up to the Air Force. You know, the fellas you use when you want to send the very best."

Now, I think. *Now.*

"Good for you, Mr. Kurtz," I say. "Whatever happened back then, whatever complications ensued, it sent you to your dream job. And it sent those Rangers to jail."

His happy mood is gone.

I push him. "What happened? Are you going to sit up here like some new T. E. Lawrence while men you worked with, men you trusted, men who served this country, are being treated with disgrace? Imprisoned? Ruined?"

Kurtz says, "Probably too late."

"I'm the investigator here. Let me decide."

His fellow tribesmen sense a change in their leader's mood, and they look at me with hate. From friend to enemy in a matter of seconds.

Kurtz sighs. "They went to a house when they heard screaming from inside. They should have ignored it. We're not here to give the Afghan people the Bill of Rights or copies of the Federalist Papers or anything similar. We can't change thousands of years of history—"

"What was going on?"

Kurtz rubs at his beard. "It was...an arrangement. A welcoming gift to a foreign visitor, who was promising lots of millions of dollars of additional aid. An American, who was taking advantage of the local world, with no bloggers or journalists nearby, fulfilling his...needs. A man with a twelve-year-old." He pauses. "A twelve-year-old boy."

"The Rangers broke in and stopped him?"

"Yes."

God.

Then it comes to me, like a series of lightning flashes in the distant sky, remembering a man, with a woman, at a campaign rally, expressing his support of the troops and how he had visited them on the battleground.

CHAPTER 93

STAFF SERGEANT CALEB JEFFERSON is in a familiar place, standing at attention in front of a supposed superior. Even with his hands cuffed in front of him, he's still maintaining his military bearing. The judge is an old man who looks like he keeps photos of his grandpappy in Klan robes in a secret drawer in his desk, but he starts off the process by reading some official paperwork, and the droning goes on and on.

Jefferson looks around the courtroom, crowded with reporters, locals, law enforcement, and, standing up against the wall, the Army doc and lawyer back there, looking tired and discouraged. Poor guys. They thought they could help him and his men. Nope. Wasn't going to happen.

He—Staff Sergeant Caleb Jefferson, Second Platoon, Alpha Company, Fourth Battalion—is going to take care of his men.

Jefferson spots Sheriff Emma Williams sitting in the front row, arms folded, looking pretty damn pleased with herself.

Same look as a week ago.

CHAPTER 94

AFGHANISTAN

THE MEMORY FROM that time at the campaign rally back in Sullivan is fresh in my mind, and I say, "The American was a congressman, from Georgia."

Kurtz grins. "He was."

"And he was being escorted by a woman public affairs officer. From the Georgia National Guard."

A happy nod. "Damn, you are a good investigator, Major Cook."

"What happened?"

"What do you think happened? The Rangers weren't officially there, nothing officially happened, and to make sure I kept quiet, that woman made some calls, pulled a few strings, and here I am."

A *thump* shakes the little bunker, and dust falls from the overhead rocks.

"Ah, shit," Kurtz says. "Looks like the *muj* want to let us know they're around."

Another, closer *thump.*

I turn. "Mortars?"

"The same," he says. "Excuse me. I've got to get to work."

"But—"

"Sorry, pal, you're our guest for the foreseeable future."

He snaps out a series of orders in Pashto, the men grab their AK-47s, and Kurtz stands up, pulling aside a nearby blanket. "Come along, Major. We're going to wait this one out."

The men rush past me as I look at Kurtz, then grab my rucksack and head outside.

Kurtz yells but doesn't follow me as I go after his men, who are moving under the netting, taking up binoculars and grid maps, looking out, two of them talking quickly on handheld radios, probably trying to reach their observers out there among the rocky peaks.

The sun is setting.

I check my watch.

I've been here nineteen minutes.

Where is Chief Cellucci? Where's his Little Bird helicopter?

Twenty minutes.

Twenty-one minutes.

The Night Stalkers pride themselves in arriving on time at a mission, give or take thirty seconds. I have the information to free the Rangers back in Georgia—Kurtz's statement combined with my eventual recovery of travel records and manifests to show Representative Conover and Sheriff Williams were here in Pendahar—and I'm stuck here on a rock in a mountain wilderness, with men out there trying to kill me.

Twenty-two minutes.

Is Cellucci still out there? Was he called to another mission? Is my watch wrong?

A louder, closer mortar explosion tosses up dust and rock fragments, and knocks me down.

CHAPTER 95

ALMOST A WEEK AGO, Staff Sergeant Caleb Jefferson's chest hurt, his arms hurt, and his eyes were sore from the pepper spray used during his arrest at the roadhouse. He and his guys had been unwinding there two nights after tuning up that drug-dealing creep who nearly killed his stepdaughter.

Even his wrists bled from where the metal cuffs dug in.

Across from his cell in the Ralston jail, seated before him, was the county sheriff, whom he immediately recognized. The last time she had been in an Army uniform, outside Pendahar in Afghanistan, screaming and slapping a naked congressman in a ratty hovel with two Afghan businessmen in Western suits looking on in amusement.

"Well," she said, "here's the situation, Staff Sergeant."

"Go on," he said.

"You and your boys saw something you shouldn't have seen, back in Afghanistan. You saw a good man falling to temptation. A man who will do great things for this nation. And a man who will become senator in under two weeks."

"Some man," he said.

She said, "All great men have their faults. FDR, JFK, Martin

Luther King Jr....yet they did great things for their nation. As the congressman will do when he gets back to Washington, as a senator this time."

Jefferson stayed silent. He knew where this was going.

"But here's the situation," Williams said. "How do I keep you and your three boys quiet about what you thought you heard and saw back in Afghanistan?"

"I'm certain about what I saw and heard," he said. "As are my men."

A slight toss of the shoulders. "Not going to debate that. Which goes back to my original problem: keeping you quiet. Which is why you're here. You see, we know what you and the other Rangers did at The Summer House, you beating up Stuart Pike. Maybe that could have been enough to keep you quiet, me holding that over your heads. But I doubted it. So later...well, bad things happen to bad people."

Jefferson clenched his fists. "What the hell are you talking about?"

"Bad things," she said. "Gunmen later went in there and killed everybody in that home. There's forensic evidence and witnesses placing you four Rangers at the scene. You're all under arrest. You're here until I say otherwise. And you'll stay here until the Wednesday after the election, and then...oops! You'll get released. Faulty evidence and all that. Then you'll keep your mouths shut...forever. Because, Staff Sergeant, there's no statute of limitations for murder. And it's amazing what new evidence can pop up at the right time."

Jefferson gave her one good hard stare, and she returned the favor. He said, "I get a phone call. I get a lawyer. I tell him or her everything you just told me here. How's that for evidence?"

Then, like a sniper shot coming from nowhere, hitting him

right in the center of his ballistic plating, taking his breath away, the sheriff said, "And how's your lovely stepdaughter doing. Carol, right? Carol Crosby?"

Jefferson couldn't talk.

"She's at the Damon Harbor Rehabilitation Facility, isn't she? Over in Hilton Head. Second floor. Her day nurse is Sonny Law, her night nurse is Kim Christo. Damn close thing it was, her nearly getting killed."

The sheriff scooted her metal chair up closer to the bars. "You damn idiot, how do you think that Pike fella got that fentanyl to your stepdaughter? Huh? By accident?"

He closed his eyes. He wanted to break down this cell door and kill this smug sheriff sitting in front of him.

But that wasn't possible.

"All right," he said. "My mouth is shut. The same for my guys."

"Then you get free that Wednesday morning, and your mouths stay shut."

Jefferson said, "All right. Me and my three guys...that's what we'll do."

The sheriff grinned, slapped her hands together in satisfaction, stood up. "Wonderful. Hey, no hard feelings, all right, Staff Sergeant? You and your Rangers were just in the wrong place at the wrong time."

He said, "Sheriff, that's our damn job description."

Jefferson snaps to, keeping an eye on the judge, feeling the eyes of the sheriff nearly bore a hole into his unprotected back. So what? With Vinny Tyler dead, the deal has changed. It's on him, and only him. His guys go free, and he'll keep his mouth shut. And right now, he's sure Major Frank Moore has kept his promise of working with his aunt Sophie to move his stepdaughter, Carol, to another, safer facility.

Jefferson will do anything and everything to protect his remaining guys and Carol.

A dark, deep memory, of his dying wife, Melissa, her whispering, *You protect my girl, Caleb Jefferson. You do that.*

"Staff Sergeant Jefferson?"

"Sir?" he asks.

The judge says, "Before we proceed, I just want to ensure that you are here of your own free will, that you have decided to waive counsel, and that you plan to represent yourself. Is that correct, Staff Sergeant Jefferson?"

He says the words with force and certainty. "Yes, Your Honor."

"All right," the judge says. "We will proceed."

CHAPTER 96

AFGHANISTAN

I GET UP, coughing, touch my forehead, pull away my hand, and see bloody fingers. My ears are ringing. The men are shouting. Smoke and clouds of dust are drifting away. Two more explosions—*thump, thump*—hit the other side of this peak, the ground shaking from the impacts.

I scramble up, cough some more, find my rucksack.

A heavy, thrumming noise bursts out, like a high-speed M134 Minigun, its rotating barrel shooting out thousands of rounds every minute, and I duck and scramble across the rocky surface, thinking, *When in the hell did the Taliban get that weapon?* as a black Little Bird helicopter roars up into view from a deep ravine, circles, and then flares down to a landing, its engine sounding just like a weapon.

I grab my rucksack, lower my bleeding head, and run as fast and as best as I can to the churning little aircraft that represents my way out of here, my way to get the Rangers free. Dust and gravel roar around me, and the passenger door opens up. Chief Cellucci is leaning across the empty seat. I can't hear what he's yelling, but I'm sure it's *Move, move, move!*

Unlike before, I have no difficulty getting into the Little Bird. I toss my rucksack into the rear, get into the seat, grab the crash helmet. The next few seconds are a crazed blur as Cellucci lifts the helicopter before I can even get the seat belt and harness fastened. The Little Bird seems to fly up just a score of meters or so, Cellucci wrestling with the controls, before it dives fast and to the right, dipping into the ravine.

I clench my teeth, trying hard not to vomit. The helicopter bounces up and down as we skim over another wide peak, and I get my seat belt and harness fastened, cinching it as tight as possible.

It takes two good tries to get the helmet on, and I fumble with the communications gear before Cellucci's voice comes through loud and clear.

"Did you get what you needed?" he asks.

"Yes."

Cellucci swears, hops us up over another rocky ridge. "Good. Because they're about to get hammered. Saw lots of movement heading their way."

I say, "How long before we get back to the FOB?"

"Ten, fifteen minutes if I push it," Cellucci says.

"Push it," I say. "Can you raise the Ranger detachment there? Major West?"

"I'll see—"

A flare of light just ahead of us.

Tracer rounds come from a heavy machine gun set in the rocks before us, reaching up and up, wanting to touch us and—

Cellucci swears.

Powers us to the left.

We dive, desperately trying to get ahead of the tracer rounds.

The ground is so close it looks like it can reach up and slap us hard.

Instead the bullets get to us first.

It sounds like a sledgehammer is pounding the metal.

Alarms start sounding from the instrument panel.
Flashing red lights.
Cellucci says, "Brace for—"
We hit, bounce.
Upside down.
Hit again.
Go dark.

CHAPTER 97

SITTING COMFORTABLY ON the crowded bench in the Sullivan County courtroom, Sheriff Emma Williams doesn't mind being closed in. She feels like she's in some sort of religious ceremony, where the powers of right—meaning her, of course—are about to get their due.

The courtroom is as it should be, even with that bitch Peggy Reese of the *Sullivan County Times* sitting on the other set of benches, quickly scribbling in her reporter's notebook, as if she'll be the one to scoop all the media rivals on this. For years Williams has ignored the woman, being just a little irritant in her day-to-day business, but once she gets to DC, she'll send word to her deputy, Clark Lindsay, that this situation needs to be resolved.

Earlier today she received a text from a detective at the Savannah Police Department, saying that her poor deputy Dwight Dix had been shot yesterday in an apparent robbery at a Waffle House near Savannah, and could she give him a call when she's free?

Yeah, she thinks. *Tomorrow,* considering how her day is going.

Before her, Judge Howell Rollins continues his droning, pausing every now and then for a heavy cough.

"... in the name of and on behalf of the citizens of the State of Georgia, charge and accuse Caleb Jefferson with the offense of malice murder, for that the said Caleb Jefferson, in the County of Sullivan and the State of Georgia, on or about the twenty-first of October, did unlawfully, with malice aforethought, cause the death of Stuart Pike, a human being, by shooting Stuart Pike with a handgun, contrary to the laws of the State of Georgia, the good order, peace and dignity thereof." The judge coughs. "Mr. Jefferson, how do you plead to this charge?"

Williams takes another look around at the quiet spectators, and then she hears the staff sergeant say in that strong voice, "Guilty."

How confident.

Time to shake that arrogant man's confidence.

"...on or about the twenty-first of October, did unlawfully, with malice aforethought, cause the death of Lillian Zachary, a human being..."

More blah, blah, blah from that alcoholic judge, and then again, Jefferson's voice: "Guilty."

From her pants pocket, she takes out a newspaper clipping from yesterday's *Atlanta Journal-Constitution*.

Waits.

"...on or about the twenty-first of October, did unlawfully, with malice aforethought, cause the death of Polly Zachary, a human being..."

At the mention of the little girl, more sighs and muttered voices from the courtroom attendees, and when the noise settles down, Jefferson doesn't hesitate at all.

"Guilty," he says.

The last name.

She waits for Judge Howell Rollins to make the final arrangements, gavel everything to a conclusion, so that Jefferson will be taken into her county jail, when he shakes his head, wipes at his lips, and says, "Fifteen-minute recess."

He slaps the gavel down and stands up from the bench, and the courtroom attendant calls out, "All rise!"

Williams can't help herself—she turns to the woman standing next to her and whispers loudly, "Looks like the judge needs a rise, too," and there's laughter.

The judge's face flushes in embarrassment. He probably heard what Williams just said, but so what? This is her county, yesterday, today, tomorrow, and next week—forever.

When the judge leaves and everyone sits down, she catches the attention of Cornelius Slate, the district attorney, and beckons him over.

He walks to her, puzzled, and she leans over the court railing, hands him the newspaper clipping.

"Here," she says. "Take this to Staff Sergeant Jefferson."

Slate looks at the newspaper clipping. "Why?"

"Because I said so," she says. "Get a move on, Corny, before the judge comes back."

Like a good boy, Slate walks over to the Army Ranger, puts the newspaper clipping on the table, and walks back to his chair.

Staff Sergeant Caleb Jefferson glances at the newsprint, and it's like he's just been transported from this safe Georgia courtroom to an FOB in the 'stan, guys yelling, *They're coming through the wire!*

The same feeling of danger, of impending death, a dizzying feeling that the safety of one minute ago is gone forever.

The headline reads:

Body of Murdered Ranger Officer Recovered

There's a small photo of Major Frank Moore, and he doesn't bother reading the story.

Moore is dead.

The man who was going to protect his stepdaughter, Carol.

He turns in his seat and sees the happy, smiling face of Sheriff Williams looking at him, and if it weren't for the armed men in this room, he would leap over the railing and strangle her with his handcuffed hands.

CHAPTER 98

AFGHANISTAN

I COME TO, resting on my side on a bunch of sharp rocks. What a goddamn mess. I turn and grind my teeth at the pain. The crumpled metal and broken glass and torn cables from what was once a multimillion-dollar and gorgeous flying machine lay all around me. All I see is the destroyed Little Bird and lots of rocks.

My legs are stuck.

I gingerly move them.

Both hurt like hell, as well as my left hip.

I cough. Blood in my mouth.

"Hey, Chief," I call out. "You there, Chief?"

I hear the sound of the wind and the snap-crackle of electric circuitry shorting out somewhere.

Nothing else.

I smell spilled aviation fuel, and the memory of being trapped in that shattered Humvee and seeing the flames approach my trapped legs makes me start shaking.

"Not again," I whisper. "Please, God, not again."

There's a glow of something still working in the shattered instrument panel, and as my eyes adjust, I see the slumped form of Chief Cellucci, still fastened in his seat, dangling upside down, his arms free.

"Chief!" I call out. "Hey, Chief! Are you okay?"

My eyes adjust better to the deepening darkness. A piece of metal broken from the helicopter's frame has gone right through his neck and out the back.

Guilt hits me like a cold wave. The man is dead because of me, because I bribed him to take me on an unauthorized trip to see a CIA guy . . . and for nothing.

I tug again at my legs, grit my teeth in pain.

I roll to the left, see my rucksack. I strain and strain with my left arm, grab a strap, drag it over to me.

It takes a lot out of me.

I close my eyes, catch my breath.

At least the crackling of the circuitry is gone.

Maybe the damn thing won't catch fire after all.

Something is digging into my right hip. I move around, take out my SIG Sauer.

Worthless for the moment.

I wonder what's going on in Georgia. How the Rangers are doing. How that meeting with Connie and someone involved with the shooting went. Has she found out what I now know, that this whole mess began here in Afghanistan, when the Rangers stumbled across something they shouldn't have witnessed?

I open my eyes, yank the top of my rucksack, manage to get it open.

I push my right hand in, dig around, a few items falling out.

There.

Got the Iridium satellite phone.

I breathe hard, bring it up, push the power button.

Nothing.

The small screen remains dark.

I push the button again and again.

The satellite phone is dead. I drop it, take up the SIG Sauer, put it into the open rucksack.

It's almost completely dark, and a few stars appear overhead.

I think I hear voices.

I stop moving.

Damn, I'm not thinking anymore.

I *am* hearing voices.

Fear is digging right into my gut.

A memory comes to me, of the research I did before my first deployment to Afghanistan, and the books I read, including the poetry of Rudyard Kipling and his tales of British soldiers serving in India and Afghanistan.

A stanza comes right to my mind, about what a young British soldier should do if wounded on Afghanistan's plains, and when the Afghan women came down at you with knives:

> *Jest roll to your rifle and blow out your brains*
> *An' go to your Gawd like a soldier.*

I whisper, "But I'm no soldier. I'm just a goddamn cop."

A wounded, trapped, and alone cop at that.

I try again to free my legs, but the pain digs in deep, like hidden knives are carving me up.

The voices grow louder.

I hear the approaching men, but I can't understand what they're saying.

Yet I *know* what they're saying.

Here's a shot-down American helicopter. Let's see who's alive.

A light comes on, illuminating the wreckage, the dead body of the chief, and then me.

That's when I go to the rucksack, for one final, desperate gamble.

CHAPTER 99

CAPTAIN ALLEN PIERCE is waiting for the judge to come back from his unexpected break, wondering what he's going to do next. A minute after the judge left—which was nearly a half hour ago, and definitely not fifteen minutes—there was a look exchanged between Sheriff Williams and Staff Sergeant Jefferson.

A look of hate from the Ranger; a look of satisfaction from the sheriff.

The Ranger is about to be sentenced for the seven homicides committed here just over a week ago—or as it's called in this state, malice murder—and yet he's staring at the sheriff. Not the judge, not the district attorney who's representing the state.

What is going on here?

Huang whispers, "Allen, you've got to do something."

Pierce whispers back, "Like what? Raise my hand? Throw myself on the mercy of the judge? Does he look like somebody who's flexible enough to bend the rules and let an outsider lawyer interrupt?"

Pierce wants to say something else, but what's the point? Seeing Staff Sergeant Jefferson sitting by himself, an African American defendant in this courtroom, at this time, with so many of the court audience being white. How many of Jefferson's brothers and sisters—hell, Pierce's own brothers and sisters—have been in a similar position? Facing alleged justice with a white judge and a nearly all-white group of residents?

He's no bomb thrower and knows a lot of progress has been made, but seeing Jefferson up there just stirs old history and old memories in him. Seeing the relaxed nature of the attendees in the courtroom, enjoying the break to talk and gossip with their neighbors, Sheriff Williams even holding court with four locals who've come up to talk to her, strengthens those old memories. So many cases of black defendants being railroaded.

The staff sergeant looks back again to the smiling sheriff, sitting in all her glory.

Why is this Ranger allowing himself to be railroaded? Why is he doing this?

Huang's voice comes back to him: *You've got to do something.*

A door opens up, and the court attendant calls out, "All rise!" as the judge slowly walks in and back up to the bench. The attendees stand up, and the judge gavels the session back into order.

How many times has Pierce heard those words, from scared defendants he's represented over the years, facing minor offenses that would ruin a career, or after a drunken brawl that got out of hand or a mistaken case of auto theft. All those defendants, looking to him to find some obscure phrase or reference in a law book to set them free.

You've got to do something.

The judge says, "Staff Sergeant Jefferson, I'm going to take a few minutes to repeat myself here, just so there's no misunderstanding. Now. Before I pass sentence, I need to confirm once more, for my own peace of mind, that you are here of your own free will."

"I am, Your Honor."

"That you're not under the influence of alcohol or drugs."

"I am not, Your Honor."

"That no threats or pressure have been made upon you to enter this guilty plea, correct?"

Just the slightest bit of a hesitation that Pierce notices from Jefferson, a slight tensing of the Ranger's shoulders.

"Not a single threat or mention of pressure, Your Honor," he says.

Something is not right.

Something is wrong.

You've got to do something.

He steps forward, trying to formulate something he'll say after yelling, *Your Honor, please!* when his iPhone suddenly chimes.

Incoming text.

The judge stares at him, the district attorney turns to look at him, almost everyone in the courtroom is now looking at him.

He brings up the iPhone, slides his fingers across, sees the text, and shakes his head in amazement.

By God, he *is* going to do something.

CHAPTER 100

AFGHANISTAN

I FIND MYSELF awake again, my left hip and legs still twisting and burning and crawling with pain. I look up, see chiseled rock and stone. I'm in a place, somewhere.

I spit, blood still in my mouth.

What the hell has happened?

The foreign voices continue talking out there, and I wish I had spent some time learning Pashto back in the day.

It might have been useful.

Might have been.

The voices grow louder. I now remember what's happened in the last long minutes, and as I hear the footsteps of the men coming toward me, I close my eyes and it goes dark again.

CHAPTER 101

SHERIFF EMMA WILLIAMS of Sullivan County thinks it's about time Judge Howell Rollins steps down, because that brief recess stretched to nearly an hour, and it's a wonder the old drunk can keep his eyes open, but her thoughts and mood are abruptly interrupted by the sound of someone's handheld device sounding off.

Hoo boy, she thinks, someone is about to get their ass in a sling, because the judge hates cell phones and hates being interrupted, but before the judge can say a word, that smart-alecky Army lawyer steps forward and starts talking in a loud voice.

"Your Honor, if I may please approach the bench, sir, my name is Allen Pierce, and I'm an Army captain, serving in the Judge Advocate General's Corps."

Loud murmurs and talk from the spectators, and Rollins hammers down his gavel twice. "Are you here to represent Staff Sergeant Jefferson? I'm sorry to tell you, that opportunity is gone. That ship has sailed, Captain Pierce."

"I understand, Your Honor," the lawyer says. "I'm here as part of the Army investigation into those homicides and the alleged participation of the Rangers who were arrested."

At last Corny Slate stands up and says, "Your Honor, this

is unacceptable. There is no alleged participation...There is evidence from the county sheriff's investigation, overwhelming evidence that's led to this Army sergeant pleading guilty."

The Army lawyer steps up to the bar and says, "Your Honor, please, I beg for a few minutes' indulgence. That's all. I've just received an urgent text from Afghanistan saying there is evidence in that country that will be key to determining whether your sentencing should go forward."

Judge Rollins's already red face gets more crimson. "Are you telling me, son, that some judge over there in that Third World country is tryin' to tell me how to run my courtroom?"

The JAG lawyer, leather bag in his right hand, shakes his head. "Not at all, Your Honor. Not at all. In the interest of seeing that the very best outcome is made today, sir, please, will you allow me to approach the bench for a few moments? Please?"

Williams stares at the judge in cold disbelief. What in the hell is going on here? Afghanistan? For real?

It was settled. It was buried. There should be no mention of Afghanistan at all in this sunny courtroom in Georgia. Not a word.

Rollins says, "I'll allow it. No guarantees, you understand. But I'll allow it."

"Thank you, Your Honor," the JAG lawyer says. "You won't regret it."

Rollins barks out a laugh. "You better hope you're right."

The Army lawyer steps through the bar's open gate, and as he approaches the bench, Williams stands up and violently gestures to get the district attorney's attention. Slate spots her and slinks over like a student about to be disciplined in public by a teacher, which is pretty accurate.

She grabs a lapel of his suit jacket and gives it a good twist. "Corny, you go up there and stop this shit, right now. Got it?

Shut it down, or I swear to God, I'll make it hurt for you so bad you'll still be crying ten years from now. Go!"

Williams pushes him away and returns to her seat, breathing hard, realizing that the courtroom has gone quiet, and that most people are staring at her.

Not the judge or the district attorney or that black Army lawyer. Her.

She sits down, watches the huddle up there, the Army lawyer speaking, waving an arm around, and Corny doing the same thing, and the old fool Rollins listening to them both, rubbing at his face, nodding, and speaking loudly: "All right, I've heard enough. Mr. Slate, you may return to your spot. Captain Pierce...all right, then."

Murmurs from the people around her, and even that big, tough staff sergeant over there, in handcuffs and wearing a Ralston jail jumpsuit, looks confused.

"Sheriff Williams," the judge says.

She stands up, now confused as well. "Your Honor?"

He crooks a finger at her, and she nods, stumbles for a moment, and walks through the open gate of the bar and then up to the bench. The judge of course is sitting higher than her, and she feels out of sorts and exposed. She doesn't like the feeling.

Rollins covers the bench's microphone with his hand and in a low voice says, "Emma, just a bit closer. There. You know what?"

She shakes her head. "What's that, Judge?"

He smiles, his teeth yellow and stained. "I heard what you said a while back, when I adjourned for a recess, and you said I needed a rise, too. Right?"

With horror she realizes she's gone too far and says, "Judge Rollins, please, I apologize, I meant—"

He shakes his head, his greasy-looking smile wide and

confident, close enough that she's able to smell his peppermint-scented breath. "This may be your county, Emma, but this is my goddamn courtroom. I'll run it the way I see fit . . . especially if it pisses you off. Now go sit your fat ass down so we can see what the hell Afghanistan has to say."

CHAPTER 102

ALL RIGHT, CAPTAIN Allen Pierce thinks, standing nervously in front of the judge, *let's make sure this happens.* From his leather briefcase he takes out the Army-issue laptop, places it on top of the judge's bench, powers it up. The screen pops into view.

He starts checking the icons, goes through the Applications folder, finds the one for Skype, double-clicks. The icon rotates, rotates, rotates.

"Counselor..." the judge says.

He feels himself warm with embarrassment, remembering the first time he argued a case before a military tribunal and realized ten minutes in that he had forgotten a key folder of paperwork back in his apartment.

"Just a moment, Your Honor," he says, clicking on the keyboard, hearing the titters and giggles from the spectators, knowing the sheriff is probably enjoying his every painful moment.

Someone stands next to him. "If I may, Your Honor, I believe I can fix this," comes Huang's voice.

"And who the hell are you?"

"Dr. John Huang," he says, gently pushing Pierce aside and going to the computer. "I'm an Army lieutenant."

"Well," the judge says, "I guess if anyone can fix a computer, it's

414

someone like you, huh? And this thing...Skip. You can actually talk to someone in Afghanistan?"

Huang says, "Yes, sir. Skype."

Pierce feels sweet relief pour through him as the familiar log-on page pops up. He goes to his iPhone, copies the address onto the Skype page, and the tone of its ringing sounds. He taps a key and boosts the volume, and—

A screen pops up, dark but visible.

Sweet God, it's the major.

And he looks horrible.

A tired-looking Major Jeremiah Cook peers at him, his face lined, worn, and with a growth of beard. Pierce maneuvers the laptop so his own face pops up within the screen.

"Captain Pierce," Cook says, "is the hearing for Staff Sergeant Jefferson concluded?"

"Almost, sir."

"Is the judge nearby?"

"Right here, sir," he says, rotating the screen so Judge Rollins can see Major Cook. "This is Judge Howell Rollins."

The judge leans in and says, "I'll be damned...Who is this?"

The major coughs, grimaces. "I'm Major Jeremiah Cook, with the US Army Criminal Investigation Division, operating out of Quantico. I'm leading the team investigating the alleged involvement of the Rangers in the murders that happened last week in your county. Your Honor...thank you for allowing me to speak to you."

The judge says, "And where the hell are you, anyway?"

Pierce looks back at the spectators, and those who can see the screen are leaning forward. It's so quiet that besides the hiss of the computer's speakers, the only thing he can hear is the gentle *whir-whir* of the large fans overhead.

The screen fades in and out. Cook says, "I'm at an observation post on a mountaintop somewhere in southern Afghanistan... pretty damn close to the Pakistan border. I've just interviewed a key witness who has vital information about this case."

The video screen vibrates and then settles down, as a muffled *boom* is heard.

Cook looks up. "Sorry," he says. "There's a squad of Taliban coming up the north side of the ridge, and they're laying down some mortar rounds. I've got to make this quick..."

Pierce sees that the arrogant and angry face of the judge has changed to something else entirely. "Go on, Major, go on," the judge says. "Why are you in Afghanistan? What does anything over there have to do with Sullivan County and my court?"

Another *boom,* another shake of the screen, and Cook continues, voice tired and strained. "During the course of our investigation, we learned that the Ranger fire team that was arrested in Sullivan County had been accused of committing a similar crime in a small village in Afghanistan. It seemed to be too much of a coincidence. I flew here and found out that this charge was false, that it was a setup by the local Taliban to accuse the Rangers of war crimes."

Rollins says, "Major, you're not telling me that the Taliban came over here and tried to do the same thing again, are you?"

"No, sir, not at all. But I believe that false accusation served as a...template, or an inspiration for someone down the line. I know the staff sergeant is pleading guilty, in exchange for letting his two surviving squad members go free. I believe he's doing this out of dedication and loyalty to his men. But please, Your Honor, please don't accept his plea. I've gathered information over here that I believe is vital to what's going on in Sullivan County."

Pierce hears other voices coming out of the speakers, and Cook turns, nods, and says, "They're approaching the outer wire now, Your Honor."

"Hurry up, Major, tell us what you found out," the judge says, leaning farther over his bench.

"A couple of months ago, the Rangers were sent home early from a regularly scheduled deployment. That happened days after the Rangers discovered a US citizen raping an Afghan civilian in a private home in a small village. A young boy."

Moans and sounds of disgust come from the spectators, and with three sharp blows from his gavel, the judge quiets down the conversations.

"People!" he yells. "I got a goddamn American soldier under fire, trying to tell us the truth here, and the next person who opens his or her damn mouth is gonna regret it!"

Pierce is staring at the screen, willing the video to remain in view, for the signal not to cut out, and the judge says, "Go on, Major, please."

Cook says, "It's my belief, sir, that the Rangers were sent home early, and that they were falsely accused of killing these civilians, to keep their mouths shut about what they witnessed. And what they witnessed was your congressman, Mason Conover, committing this crime, while under the escort of a Georgia National Guard captain, Emma Williams, your county sheriff."

Another *boom* from the computer, the screen goes blank, and the courtroom erupts in shouts and yells.

CHAPTER 103

AFGHANISTAN

IN FRONT OF ME, Kurtz closes down his laptop and says, "Think it'll work?"

"I sure as hell hope so," I say, trying to remain very, very still on a padded bunk bed in Kurtz's communications room. From where I can stretch out my arms, I'm in the Stone Age. But a meter farther away is the twenty-first century, probably edging into the twenty-second, with computer terminals, display screens, surveillance equipment offering up views of the ridges and valleys around this observation post, as well as live feeds from two drones endlessly circling overhead.

One of Kurtz's men steps in, speaks quickly in Pashto, laughs, and then heads out.

I say, "What do you think the Taliban are going to say about all those hand grenades your guys tossed over the side?"

Kurtz steps back and puts the laptop down among a collection of black boxes with blinking white and red lights that mean absolutely nothing to me. "Oh, that crazy American up there, losing his mind over something. As long as it helped you sell your story to that judge in Georgia, who cares? How's the pain?"

"Manageable," I say.

"Good."

He comes back to me, sits on a campstool. "I won't be able to get you out of here until light."

"I'll manage," I say. "What about Chief Cellucci?"

"I've got two of my guys with radios standing guard so the locals don't steal his remains or screw with the Little Bird wreckage," he says. "Either the Night Stalkers or a Ranger unit will come in sometime tonight and retrieve his body, destroy the wreckage. That's how they roll."

A little stab of pain makes itself known among my numbed limbs. "I got him killed."

Kurtz reaches into a deep pocket, pulls out a Hershey bar, which he unwraps. "Nope. A two-man Taliban gun crew using a Soviet-made DShK 1938 heavy machine gun brought him down. The chief was on a mission, even if an unauthorized one." He takes a bite and says, "Good thinking back there, pointing a Hershey bar at my guys when they found you."

"I thought it'd work better than a pistol," I say.

He chews for a moment and says, "Got some stateside news for you that I dug out while you were talking to the judge. I'm sorry, it's not great news."

"Tell me," I say. "I think I'm about to pass out in a minute or two."

He swallows. "There were a couple of news stories about a shooting in Savannah."

I know exactly what's happened. "Is she dead?"

"Nope," he says. "Critically wounded, in an ICU at some hospital in Savannah. Funny thing is, she's not alone. Looks like one of your guys is holding her room hostage."

. My tongue is fuzzy. *Alive,* I think. *Connie's alive.*

"How do you hold a room hostage?" I ask.

He wraps up the Hershey bar, like he's saving it for later. "She was shot while two gunmen killed a sheriff's deputy in her presence. Your CID guy is protecting her, won't let anybody into her room except doctors and nurses. You've got one hell of a team there, Major."

"We do our best," I say, and then I just close my eyes and let things slip away.

CHAPTER 104

A NUMBER OF years ago Sheriff Emma Williams saw a great crime movie in which Robert De Niro played one cool fellow robbing banks and armored cars, and there was one piece of dialogue his character stated that stuck with her:

Don't let yourself get attached to anything you are not willing to walk out on in thirty seconds flat if you feel the heat around the corner.

Good survival advice, and she's taking it, right at this moment.

The heat isn't around the corner. It's coming at her like a burst of fire from a flamethrower.

With the voices and shouts, and the judge hammering his gavel, Williams calmly gets up and walks through the gate of the bar, to the court side of the room, and starts walking deliberately to a door she knows will lead right outside.

Everything is gone.

No time to mourn.

Get the hell out, dump the cruiser somewhere on one of the unmarked dirt roads out there in her county, and pick up one of the three plain-looking pickup trucks she's secured in different locations for just this purpose. Leave Sullivan County, lie low, and at some point, with a new driver's license and passport and access to funds electronically hidden in the Cayman Islands, get the hell out to one of the lovely islands of Micronesia in the Pacific, which doesn't have an extradition treaty with the United States.

She gets to the exit door, ignoring the courtroom noise, including the shouts calling out her name.

Captain Allen Pierce is standing next to Staff Sergeant Caleb Jefferson, intent on keeping the Ranger in one place, and he sees Sheriff Williams start to slip out the door.

No, he thinks, *not on your life.*

"John!" he yells, pointing to the sheriff as she goes through a door marked EXIT. "Don't let her get away!"

Huang looks both frightened and confused, and Pierce yells, "Lieutenant, haul ass!"

The doctor starts running.

Outside now, in the blessed free air. Her cruiser is right in the RESERVED parking spot. There are some people out there, milling about, but it seems like the horrible news from Afghanistan that just dropped in the courtroom hasn't reached outside yet.

When she's a few feet away from the cruiser, a man starts yelling at her.

Huang pushes his way through a small cluster of courtroom officers and attendants, gets through the exit door and to a short hallway.

Left or right? he thinks, heart pounding.

Right.

Where a door leading outside is closing.

He runs down the hallway, bursts outside, and there's the

sheriff, just a few feet away from her cruiser. "Hey!" he yells. "Sheriff Williams, stop!"

The woman turns around and, spotting him, just laughs.

Huang is humiliated.

What the hell can he do?

"Don't you dare leave!" he yells again.

The woman yells something obscene and opens her cruiser door.

Huang gets to the parking lot and, knowing she's about to slip away in the next few seconds, does the only thing he can do.

Like she's part of some dark comedy film, Williams hears that Chinaman yell out, "Stop or I'll shoot!"

For real?

She looks back, and whaddya know, that Army doc is running at her, holding a pistol in both hands.

"Doc," she yells at him, "put that away before you hurt yourself."

He yells back, "I mean it! Stop right there or I'll shoot!"

Williams pulls out her service weapon and yells, "I mean it, too, Doc," and she fires at him, and there's return fire and—

A heavy blow to her chest.

Huang stops, panting.

He shot her.

He can't believe it.

He just shot her.

Huang saw her pull out her pistol and a bit of training came forth. He swerved and ducked and, for all that's holy, heard the round *whee!* overhead as he fired back.

The sheriff is on the ground, writhing back and forth, clutching at her chest.

He steps forward, his medical training kicking in, but before the doctor part of him can get to work, the Army lieutenant works first.

Huang kicks away her weapon.

As an Army officer would.

CHAPTER 105

A WEEK AFTER my return from Afghanistan, I'm in the hospital room of Special Agent Connie York of the US Army CID. With me is Special Agent Manuel Sanchez, also of the CID, and Staff Sergeant Caleb Jefferson, Second Platoon, Alpha Company, Fourth Battalion, Seventy-Fifth Ranger Regiment. The other two members of my squad are at their respective home commands, being debriefed, criticized, and probably disciplined. Captain Allen Pierce is at JAG headquarters in Washington, DC, and Lieutenant John Huang is at the US Army Medical Corps in Fort Sam Houston in San Antonio, Texas.

As for me, I got a late-night phone call yesterday from Colonel Ross Phillips, who chewed me out between bouts of coughing.

When there was a pause, I asked him, "Are you still in the hospital, sir?"

"Shut up," he said. "That's the mess you've made, Major. A pretty deep, muddy hole, pissing off a whole lot of folks in CID, the Medical Corps, and JAG. But…"

I waited, daring not to say a word.

"But on the upside, you and your folks took out a pervert congressman before he became a pervert senator, which is nice, and you also saved three Rangers and the reputation of the

Rangers, which means a big deposit in your depleted karma bank."

I asked him, "What about my group?" knowing full well how experimental it was, but at that point he hung up on me.

In the room, Connie is in a standard hospital bed, still bandaged about her head, her face horribly bruised and her eyes swollen, still hooked up to IVs and sensors, but breathing on her own. The doctors who've talked to me say that part of her skull is missing from where she was shot, and that she might have suffered some brain damage.

Too soon to tell, although what is known is that she hasn't woken up yet.

I'm sitting in a fancy padded wheelchair, both legs stretched out and in casts, and I also have a few stitches here and there. Sanchez is in jeans and a red polo shirt, sitting in one of the visitor's chairs, while Jefferson stands, wearing a plain black T-shirt and khaki slacks. The Ranger looks uncomfortable, like he will never, ever allow his body to relax in civilian clothes.

The mood is quiet, and Sanchez says, "I know I'm not going to be charged with anything, but damn it, I'm tired of having the hospital's security force trail me every time I go down to the cafeteria."

I smile, but Jefferson stands like a polished statue of black granite. I catch his attention and say, "I'm sorry about Specialist Tyler. I wish... I wish it could have ended differently."

For a moment I think he doesn't hear me, but in a low voice he says, "Not your fault, Major. Not his fault, either. Everybody's got a breaking point, especially when you belong to a system that keeps on rotating these boys in and out, in and out, until they've done four, five, six deployments. They get trained to be the best wolves in the world, and then they're expected to come home and put that all away and become nice little sheep again, be quiet, peaceful, and not raise a fuss."

He shakes his head. "Until they're called up to be wolves again. The tour before our last one, there was a marketplace. A kid was coming up to us, showing some DVDs he wanted to sell. Vinny was on point. There was something else in that bag, heavy, not a DVD. The kid wouldn't stop. The kid wouldn't stop . . . and after Vinny shot him, they found a fragmentation grenade in the bag with a trigger cord. Would have taken out our fire team. But Vinny . . . to him, he hadn't saved us. He had killed a kid."

Then Jefferson clears his throat. "And Major Moore, our XO, he was trying to do right by me, by protecting my stepdaughter, Carol. Look what that got him." He shifts and looks directly at me. "Tell me there'll be justice for Major Moore."

I say, "With Sheriff Williams's arrest, her deputies are turning on one another like a Mafia crew after their godfather's been nailed. From what I've heard, she's being kept in the Sullivan County jail, in the general population. Considering everything she's done, I don't think she's going to get a warm reception from her cellmates. Yes, Staff Sergeant, I'm sure there'll be justice for Major Moore."

"Good," he says.

We remain quiet for a while. On the small table next to Connie's hospital bed is my Bruce Catton book about the Civil War, *Glory Road*. The cover's torn, some pages are damaged, and most of all, it smells of smoke and Afghanistan. It's battered but still here, like me.

But what now?

I think about that Kipling poem. And again I think, no, I'm not a soldier. I'm a cop. Just a cop, playing make-believe Army.

Maybe it's time to put in for retirement, heal my legs and hip, and maybe heal my broken family. I tried calling my daughter, Kelli, and son, Kevin, but neither of them returned my messages.

Connie moves a bit in her bed. I reach over, take her hand.

The Ranger says, "There's something else, Major."

"What's that?" I ask.

"An apology," he says, his voice still firm and low. "My guys...and other frontline grunts, you know how it is. We don't trust, don't respect, and don't much like you guys in the rear echelons. The paper pushers. The support staff. The pampered officers. The Fobbits. But you and your crew...you worked for my fire team and me. Even when I was a thickheaded idiot and turned you away. You suffered. You put yourselves out there. You sacrificed for us, when you really didn't have to. Excuse me for what I'm about to say, sir, but that's a fucking big deal. On behalf of my Rangers and me, thank you, sir. We'll never forget."

My eyes seem to get moist and puffy. I squeeze Connie's hand. Sanchez, on the other side of the room, is looking down at his sneakers.

I say, "It was our job, Staff Sergeant. And it was our honor as well."

Quiet returns to the room, until I hear a cough, and a weak voice says, "How the hell do you expect me to sleep with all you guys yapping? Shut up, will you?"

Snap-quick, I turn, and there's Connie, eyes open, her mouth working, stretching some in her bed.

Sanchez gets up and says, "I'll go grab a nurse."

Connie lightly squeezes my hand—and, like the tough cop she is, immediately asks, "Did we get her?"

"Yes," I say.

"The Rangers okay?"

Staff Sergeant Jefferson is at the foot of her bed. "Yes, ma'am. Thanks to you and your folks, we're all okay."

Connie smiles, closes her bruised eyes. "That's good."

Sanchez comes back, saying, "Two nurses are right behind me, Major."

"Thanks," I say.

Sanchez says, "It's going to get pretty crowded in here. It's almost 1:00 p.m. You want to step out, get some lunch?"

I squeeze Connie's hand once more and look at her, and then at the staff sergeant, who's looking at me with something I've rarely seen from a combat soldier.

Respect.

"No," I say, thinking of Connie and the Army. "I'm not going anywhere."

ACKNOWLEDGMENTS

Coauthor Brendan DuBois would like to thank the following for their assistance: US Army Lieutenant Colonel Brian Thiem (Ret.), former deputy commander, Third MP Group (Criminal Investigation Command); former captain Vincent O'Neil, company commander, First Battalion (Airborne), 508th Infantry Regiment; Colonel Keith Landry (Ret.), Airborne Ranger; First Sergeant Matt Eversmann (Ret.), Seventy-Fifth Army Ranger Regiment; Michael Davidson, former officer, Central Intelligence Agency; Laura Gray, director of public relations and communications, Memorial Health University Medical Center, Savannah; Kristin Fulford, public information officer, District Attorney's Office of Chatham County, Georgia; and District Attorney Meg Daly Heap, Chatham County, Georgia.

ABOUT THE AUTHORS

James Patterson is the world's bestselling author and most trusted storyteller. He has created many enduring fictional characters and series, including Alex Cross, the Women's Murder Club, Michael Bennett, Maximum Ride, Middle School, and I Funny. Among his notable literary collaborations are *The President Is Missing*, with President Bill Clinton, and the Max Einstein series, produced in partnership with the Albert Einstein Estate. Patterson's writing career is characterized by a single mission: to prove that there is no such thing as a person who "doesn't like to read," only people who haven't found the right book. He's given over three million books to schoolkids and the military, donated more than seventy million dollars to support education, and endowed over five thousand college scholarships for teachers. For his prodigious imagination and championship of literacy in America, Patterson was awarded the 2019 National Humanities Medal. The National Book Foundation presented him with the Literarian Award for Outstanding Service to the American Literary Community, and he is also the recipient of an Edgar Award and nine Emmy Awards. He lives in Florida with his family.

Brendan DuBois is the award-winning author of 22 novels and more than 180 short stories, garnering him three Shamus Awards from the Private Eye Writers of America. He is also a *Jeopardy!* game show champion.

For a complete list of books by
JAMES PATTERSON

VISIT
JamesPatterson.com

 Follow James Patterson on Facebook
@JamesPatterson

 Follow James Patterson on Twitter
@JP_Books

Follow James Patterson on Instagram
@jamespattersonbooks

COMING SOON